PILGRIM

Also by Timothy Findley

Timothy Findley

PILGRIM

Harper*Perennial*Canada
HarperCollins*Publishers*Ltd

In memory of
Michael Tippett
Not only a child of our time,
but of all time.

And for
Meirion Bowen
who made the journey with him.

Here is no final grieving, but an abiding hope.
Michael Tippett
A Child of Our Time, 1944

PILGRIM

Copyright © 1999 by Timothy Findley.
All rights reserved. No part of this book may be
used or reproduced in any manner whatsoever
without prior written permission except in the case
of brief quotations embodied in reviews. For
information address HarperCollins Publishers Ltd.,
55 Avenue Road, Suite 2900, Toronto, Ontario,
Canada M5R 3L2.

www.harpercanada.com

HarperCollins books may be purchased for educa-
tional, business, or sales promotional use. For
information please write: Special Markets Depart-
ment, HarperCollins Canada, 55 Avenue Road,
Suite 2900, Toronto, Ontario, Canada M5R 3L2.

First HarperCollins hardcover ed.
ISBN 0-00-224258-3
First HarperPerennialCanada edition

Canadian Cataloguing in Publication Data

Findley, Timothy, 1930–
Pilgrim

1st HarperPerennial Canada ed.
ISBN 0-00-648527-8

I. Title.

PS8511.I38P55 2000   C813'.54   C00-930496-7
PR9199.3.F45P55 2000

00 01 02 03 04 RRD 9 8 7 6 5 4 3 2 1

Printed and bound in the United States
Set in Janson Text

Our story ... is much older than its years, its datedness is not to be measured in days, nor the burden of age weighing upon it to be counted by orbits around the sun; in a word, it does not actually owe its pastness to *time*.

Thomas Mann, foreword to *The Magic Mountain*, 1924

There is no light at the end of the tunnel,
only a pack of matches handed down
from one generation to the next.
Humanity does not have a long fuse
and this generation holds the last match.

JonArno Lawson, *Bad News*, in *The Noon Whistle*, 1996

PROLOGUE

In the early morning hours of Wednesday, the 17th of April, 1912, a man called Pilgrim walked bare-footed into the garden of his home in London at number 18 Cheyne Walk. He was dressed much the same as any man of his station might have been at this hour: white pyjamas and a blue silk robe. Royal blue, deep pockets, rolled collar. His unslippered feet were cold. Not that it mattered. In minutes, nothing would matter.

The grass was thick with dew, and seeing it—even in the meagre spill of light from the house—Pilgrim muttered *green* as if the word had only just occurred to him.

A dog barked, possibly far away as the King's Road. From the south, beyond the river, there was the sound of farm carts making their way to Covent Garden. Beside him, a dovecote hummed and fluttered in the dark.

A leaf fell.

Pilgrim made his way across the grass to a maple tree three storeys high, though its height could not be told in the dark. In one hand he carried the silken cord from his dressing-gown—in the other, a Sheraton chair of carefully measured dimensions. Just so tall—just so deep and just so wide.

In spite of his age, Pilgrim got up on the chair and climbed with the energy of someone who had spent his life in trees. He did not look down. There was nothing there he wanted to see.

He correctly knotted the cord and threw it over a substantial branch.

An owl passed. Its wings creaked. Otherwise, there was silence.

Pilgrim looked up at the stars and leapt.

It was 4:00 a.m.

The chair fell sideways.

* * *

The body was not discovered till dawn, more than three hours later. It was Pilgrim's valet-butler—a man called Forster—who came into the garden and found him, cut him down and laid him out on the grass—the grass still cold and wet—after which he covered the body with a blanket brought from his own bed.

Only Doctor Greene was telephoned. The police were not informed. At all costs, dignity must be preserved.

While he waited for the physician's arrival, Forster put on his overcoat, and bringing with him a coal-oil lamp, he returned the Sheraton chair to an upright position and, sitting on it, smoked a cigarette. He thought of nothing. The sun would rise. The doves and pigeons would be fed. The world would turn yet again towards the light. Any minute, Mrs Matheson would start the kitchen fires.

Forster waited and watched. The body did not stir. Nothing. Not a murmur. Not a breath.

Pilgrim, at long last, had succeeded. Or so it seemed.

BOOK ONE

1

Inside the front doors of the Burghölzli Psychiatric Clinic in Zürich, a nurse named Dora Henkel and an orderly whose name was Kessler were waiting to greet a new patient and his companion. Their arrival had been delayed by a heavy fall of snow.

To Kessler it seemed that two wind-blown angels had tumbled down from heaven and were moving towards the steps. The figures of these angels now stood in momentary disorientation, reaching out with helpless arms towards one another through windy clouds of snow, veils, shawls and scarves that altogether gave the appearance of large unfolded wings.

At last they caught hold of one another's hands and the female angel led the male, whose height was quite alarming, beneath the portico and up the steps. Dora Henkel and Kessler moved to open the doors to the vestibule, only to be greeted by a gale of what seemed to be perfumed snow. It was nothing of the kind, of course, but it seemed so. The female angel—Sybil, Lady Quartermaine—had a well-known passion for scent. She would not have dreamt of calling it *perfume. Flowers and spices are perfumed,* she would say. *Persons are scented.*

For a moment, it seemed that her male companion might be blind. He stood in the vestibule staring blankly, still maintaining his angel image—six-foot-six of drooping shoulders, lifeless arms and wings that at last had folded. His scarves and high-necked overcoat, pleated and damp, were hanging draped on his attenuated body as if at any moment they might sigh and slip to the marble floor.

Lady Quartermaine was younger than expected—not by any means the dowager Marchioness she had seemed in her rigid demands and almost military orders, issued by cablegrams five and six times a day, to be delivered by Consulate lackeys. In the flesh, she could not have been more than forty—if that—and was possessed of a presence that radiated charm and beauty with every word and gesture. Dora Henkel instantly fell in love with her and, in some confusion, had to turn away because Lady Quartermaine's beauty had made her blush. Turning back, she bobbed in the German fashion before she spoke.

"Most anxious we have been for your journey, Lady Quartermaine," she said, and smiled—perhaps with too much ingratiation.

Kessler moved towards the inner doors and pulled them open, stepping aside to let the new arrivals pass. He would call this day forevermore *the day the angels fell.* He, too, had been smitten by Lady Quartermaine and her romantic entry with a giant in her wake.

In the entrance hall, an efficient figure in a white coat came forward.

"I am Doctor Furtwängler, Lady Quartermaine. How do you do?"

She offered her hand, over which he bowed. Josef Furtwängler prided himself on his "bedside manner"—in all its connotations. His well-practised smile, while popular with his patients, was suspect amongst his colleagues.

Turning to the figure beside her, Lady Quartermaine said: *"Herr Doktor, ich will Ihnen meinen Freund Herrn Pilgrim vorstellen."*

Furtwängler saw the apprehension in his new patient's eyes. "Perhaps, Lady Quartermaine," he said, "for the sake of your friend, we should continue in English. You will find that most of us in the Burghölzli speak it fluently—including many of the patients." He moved forward, smiling, with his hand extended. "Mister Pilgrim. Welcome."

Pilgrim stared at the proffered hand and rejected it. He said nothing.

Lady Quartermaine explained.

"He is silent, Herr Doktor. Mute. This has been so ever since ... he was found."

"Indeed. It is not unusual." The Doctor gave Pilgrim an even friendlier smile and said: "will you come into the reception room. There's a fire, and we will have some coffee."

Pilgrim glanced at Lady Quartermaine. She nodded and took his hand. "We would be delighted," she said to Furtwängler. "A cup of good Swiss coffee is just what the doctor ordered." She gave an amused shrug. "Which way do we go?"

"Please, come with me."

Furtwängler flicked his fingers at Dora Henkel, who scurried off to the dining-room across the entrance hall to arrange the refreshments while Kessler stood by, trying his best not to look like a bodyguard.

Lady Quartermaine led Pilgrim forward. "All is well," she told him. "All is well. We have safely arrived at our destination and soon you will rest." She slipped her arm through his. "How very glad I am to be with you, my dear. How very glad I am I came."

2

Pilgrim's physician had been discreet. Greene had arrived roughly five hours after the event, reaching Cheyne Walk by cab at 8:45 a.m. Forster had led him directly to the garden where Greene had established that Pilgrim had stopped breathing and his heart was no longer beating.

He took more than usual care in this examination, having experienced a previous attempt at suicide which Pilgrim had failed. On that occasion, his patient had apparently managed to drown himself in the Serpentine. In spite, however, of its being midwinter and ice having formed on the surface of the water, Pilgrim had survived—even though, when he was found, all signs of life had disappeared. It had taken more than two hours of treatment and all of Greene's expertise to bring him around. The physician could hardly credit his success, since Pilgrim had remained seemingly dead for so long.

Over time, Greene had come to acknowledge not only the suicidal tendencies of his patient, but equally to be aware of his extraordinary resilience—as if there were a force inside him that refused to die, no matter what opportunities Pilgrim offered.

Once another hour had passed since his arrival at Cheyne Walk, Doctor Greene pronounced Pilgrim technically dead and began the process of making out the certificate of death which his profession demanded of him. Nonetheless, he called in the services of a second physician to verify his findings. The second physician, whose name was Hammond, happened to be one of London's foremost neurologists. The two men were well known to one another, having taken part together in a good number of autopsies performed on the corpses of suicides and murder victims.

When Doctor Hammond arrived, it was Mrs Matheson, the cook, who admitted him. She had been forced to assume "door duty" since Forster was otherwise engaged. By this time, Pilgrim's body had been brought into the house and laid out on his bed.

Greene explained the circumstances and described his previous experience with Pilgrim, saying that he was nervous of declaring death without the confirmation of a colleague. After a brief examination of the body, Hammond agreed that Pilgrim was indeed dead. *Dead*, as he said to Greene, *as any man can be*.

Having said so, he added his signature to the death certificate.

One half-hour later, Pilgrim's heart began to beat—and shortly thereafter, he started to breathe again.

This, then, was the man Sybil Quartermaine had brought to the Burghölzli Clinic—a determined suicide who, by all appearances, was unable to die.

Having travelled by train via Paris and Strasbourg, Pilgrim and his escorts had arrived in Zürich on a clouded, windy day with squalls of snow in the air. A silver Daimler and driver had been hired to meet them. Phoebe Peebles, who was Lady Quartermaine's personal maid, and Forster, Pilgrim's valet-butler, had ridden with their employers as far as the Clinic, and were then driven on to the Hôtel Baur au Lac—at that time, Zürich's most prestigious haven for foreigners.

Forster and Phoebe Peebles were at a loss, riding alone in the silver Daimler, to know quite how to behave—beyond maintaining their personal dignity.

There they were, seated in the rear of Her Ladyship's motor car without the benefit of protocol. Had the hired chauffeur become *their* chauffeur? Or were they all servants together on a single level?

Forster assumed, as the senior employee, that he had precedence. A valet-butler is, after all, the head of whatever household he belongs to, so long as the master has not deliberately established someone above him. On the other hand, now deprived of Mister Pilgrim's presence, Forster had to acknowledge that he was riding in Lady Quartermaine's motor car, not Mister Pilgrim's—and then what?

The chauffeur, being a hireling, was duty-bound only to the person who happened to be employing him at the moment—in this case, Lady Quartermaine. It was all very difficult. Forster wondered if money should be offered—in the way it would be offered to servants in a house one had been visiting with one's master.

No, he decided. It was not his business. He would leave it all to Lady Quartermaine.

"Do you expect to end up along with Mister Pilgrim in the Clinic—taking care of him there?" Phoebe asked.

"I should think," said Forster.

"I shouldn't want a life in a place where people have mental disturbances," said Phoebe. "Heaven knows what happens there. All them crazies ..."

"They are not crazies," said Forster. "They are ill. And their consignment to the Clinic is to make them well—same as if they had the consumption and went to Davos."

Forster said this with overriding authority and Phoebe, never having heard of Davos, was suitably intimidated.

"I suppose so," she said. "But, still ..."

"You have journeyed thus far with Mister Pilgrim without complaint, Miss Peebles," Forster said, rather pompously. "On the train, did you feel for one moment endangered by his behaviour?"

"No."

"Then please consider that as your answer. I would happily follow him anywhere in order to continue my service to him."

"Yes, Mister Forster."

"Here we are, then. The Hôtel Baur au Lac."

The Daimler, enshrouded in snow, had pulled to a stop

beneath a wide and impressive portico. The chauffeur got out and opened the rear door nearest Phoebe.

"What do I do?" she said to Forster.

"Get down," he told her. "Swing your legs to the right and get down."

Phoebe meekly swung her feet to the ground and stood to one side. Forster followed and greeted the concierge who had come to meet them—along with two young men in uniform who offered the protection of umbrellas—which provided no protection at all, since the snow was blowing up from the ground on every side.

Forster said: "we are of Lady Quartermaine's party. I believe you are expecting us."

"But of course, Mister Forster," said the concierge, beaming. "If you will please follow me."

As they turned towards the steps, Phoebe Peebles leaned closer to Forster and whispered: "crikey! He even knows who you are. I mean, he even knows your *name*!"

Forster removed his bowler hat and banged it against his thigh. "Of course he does," he said. "It's his job."

3

Shortly after their coffee had been consumed—Pilgrim having been taken to his quarters—Lady Quartermaine joined Doctor Furtwängler in his office.

"How long had you thought of staying?" he asked, once his guest was seated.

"Until you feel it is safe for me to leave," she told him. "I don't care how long it takes. I am his closest friend. He has no family. I wish to stay with him until he makes the turn towards recovery."

"It may be some time, Lady Quartermaine. We can guarantee nothing here."

"That's not what matters. What matters is that he's in the best of hands."

Doctor Furtwängler was standing by one of three tall windows, and beyond him, Lady Quartermaine could see that what had seemed an everyday alpine fall of snow had in fact become a blizzard.

"Will your motor car return for you? If not, we can ..."

"No, no. But thank you, it will come when I have called."

Furtwängler sat down opposite Lady Quartermaine, the wide expanse of his desk between them. It was a pleasant, dark-beamed room with recessed windows and shelves of medical books and journals, leather chairs and sofa, brass lamps with green glass shades and flowered drapes with a Chinese motif—flowers intertwined with bamboo fronds, and distant vistas of smoky hills and misted trees.

Lady Quartermaine had shed her overcoat and could now be seen in a lamplit blue, high-waisted gown with a violet-coloured overlay of lace. Her eyes were a mixture of both these colours, though now, her pupils were so enlarged her eyes seemed almost entirely black. She was toying with her gloves, laid out in her lap like pets she might have brought to soothe her. The veils of her wide-brimmed hat had been drawn aside and rested against her hair, giving the appearance of smoke.

"Aren't you going to ask me some questions? It's getting late. I want my tub and dinner."

"Yes. Yes. Of course. Forgive me."

Doctor Furtwängler took up his pen and drew a large pad of paper towards him. "To begin," he said, "can you tell a little something of yourself. It would be helpful."

"My husband is the fifteenth Marquis of Quartermaine. His first name is Harry. There's an *e* at the end of Quartermaine. Too many ignorant people drop the *e*. They don't understand the French connection. Nine centuries ago, we came to England from that quarter of France known as Maine. I say *we*—but of course, I mean my husband's ancestors."

"Of course."

"I was born Sybil Copland. My father was Cyril Copland— Lord Copland, who sat in the Lords longer than any of his contemporaries. He died at the age of ninety-nine when I was twelve. He fathered me in his eighty-sixth year—something of a record, I believe."

"More than a record—phenomenal!"

Watching him write all this down, Sybil said: "your English is very good, Doctor Furtwängler. Are you Swiss or German? Which?"

"Austrian, as a matter of fact, but I took my medical degrees in Edinburgh."

Sybil smiled. "That explains the very slight burr I detect. How charming."

"I was very fond of Scotland. And of England. I am a hiking enthusiast, Lady Quartermaine. During my holidays between semesters, I walked in the Lake District, Wiltshire and Cambridgeshire. Wonderful. You are familiar with these areas?"

"Very much so, yes. All my brothers and my husband attended

King's College at Cambridge. The countryside is a very heaven."

"And Mister Pilgrim?"

"He took his education at Oxford. Magdalen College. I pity him." She smiled.

"Pity him?"

"Yes. In England we call such a comment *ironic*, Doctor. I meant it only as a joke. In an amused way, the students at one university tend to think of the students at any other as being under-privileged."

"I see." Furtwängler looked down at his notes. "And Mister Pilgrim—he is an art historian."

"Yes. Which is one of the bonds between us. My brother Symes was also an art historian."

"Was?"

"Yes. He ..." Her gaze drifted.

Furtwängler watched her.

"You need not tell me."

"No, no. I will. It's just ..." She closed her eyes and fumbled with one of her gloves until it lay against her cheek, in the way that a sympathetic friend might have done with her hand. "He committed suicide and now, with Mister Pilgrim's attempt, it seems that Symes has come back to haunt me."

She opened her eyes and laid the glove beside its mate, fishing afterwards for a handkerchief in her handbag. Doing this, she regained her composure and spoke efficiently.

"Symes Copland was my younger brother. He had only just turned thirty when he died. That was in 1901. September. He had been involved with creating the Tate Gallery, you see. It had only just opened its doors. The strain of his efforts ... he loved it so. He was almost too devoted. Enslaved, you might say. But who could tell? He was too damned good at hiding his emotions." She paused. "Forgive me, but his death still makes me angry. Such a sad, unnecessary waste."

"Clearly, he meant a great deal to you."

"Yes. As children, we were inseparable. The proximity of our ages, I suppose. I felt like his guardian. And then, somehow, I failed him."

"No one's suicide is anyone else's fault, Lady Quartermaine."

"I find that very hard to believe."

"Nonetheless, you must try to be reconciled to it. It was his life to take. You did not kill him. He killed himself."

"Yes." Sybil looked away.

"Were Mister Pilgrim and your brother colleagues?"

"No. Symes was an expert in the field of late sixteenth- and early seventeenth-century art exclusively. Pilgrim ... Mister Pilgrim's range is wider."

"I see. And his name, Lady Quartermaine? Why have we been given no first name?"

"He maintains he hasn't got one."

"Oh?"

"Yes. And however strange that might be, it is something I have learned to accept without question. There is much I know about him. There is also much I do not know."

"Did you meet him through your brother?"

"No. We were friends already, from earlier, younger times."

"Have you children, Lady Quartermaine?"

"Yes. I have five. Two young men, two young women and a girl."

There was a pause. Sybil Quartermaine looked up.

"You are staring at me, Herr Doktor."

"Yes. Forgive me."

"Why? For what reason?"

Furtwängler glanced down at the page before him.

"In my eyes," he said, "you do not appear to be old enough to have young men as sons—young women as daughters."

"Is that all!" She laughed. "I don't mind telling you in the least. I'm forty-four years old. My eldest child is twenty. Surely that's not too amazing. His name is David and—I must be frank—I don't really care for him." She blinked. "My goodness—why did I tell you that?"

"You are under a good deal of strain, Lady Quartermaine. Things slip out, unintended, under such conditions."

"Yes. I suppose."

"Has Mister Pilgrim other friends besides yourself?"

"Some. Yes. A few. And many, many acquaintances—one or two of them relatively close. Most of them men."

"I see."

There was another pause.

"Well? What else?"

"Did he specifically ask for you, after the suicide attempt?"

"No. I had been there the night before and was concerned. He had seemed distracted—lost in some way. Vague. And more than vague—he was unable to converse coherently. Not like one who is drunk—not like that at all—but someone who had lost the thread of his own words even as he spoke them. It occurred to me that he might have suffered a mild stroke. It was like that. And then, instead of saying good night in the usual fashion, with kisses on either cheek—he took my hand and held it very tight and said *goodbye*. Not like him at all. So I went round early. As you will see in the physicians' reports I've provided, before I arrived he had been declared dead. But—also before I arrived—he had begun to show signs of life and the physicians involved were called back. They were still there with him, so I simply waited."

"And ...?"

"And stayed with him all that week. In fact, I went home only to pack my things and collect my maid in order to make this journey."

Silence. Furtwängler made a careful adjustment to the pattern of objects on his desk.

"Lady Quartermaine ..." He leaned forward above his notes. "There is something I must make clear at the outset."

Sybil watched him, impassive.

"After our initial telephone conversation, I did indeed speak with ..." He glanced down at the papers before him. "Doctor Greene, I believe?"

Sybil nodded.

"And so I am aware of the apparently extraordinary nature of Mister Pilgrim's recovery from the trauma of his attempted suicide. My mandate, however, is not to investigate the circumstances of that attempt nor of the physical recovery from it. The sole purposes of any work to be done by me or by any of my colleagues shall be to determine, first, *why* he has wished to end his life—and second, *how* to reawaken his willingness to live. No." He raised his hand, as if to forestall any comment. "How to reawaken his *will* to live."

Sybil waited only a moment before speaking. "Have no fear, Doctor Furtwängler. That is precisely why I have chosen to bring Mister Pilgrim to the Burghölzli. To reawaken his will to live."

"Excellent." He leaned back. "Now. You say you were concerned about his erratic behaviour the night before. Does this mean you had experienced such behaviour before?"

"To some degree, I suppose. He goes through periods when he ..." She considered the next word carefully and then said: "when he drifts."

"Drifts?"

"Yes. Goes off. Away."

"Have such periods in the past preceded his other suicide attempts?"

Sybil said: "really, Doctor, you surprise me. I am shocked. What other suicide attempts?"

"You mean that you are unaware he has done this before?"

"Absolutely."

"You know nothing?"

There was the briefest hesitation before she spoke again. "No," she said. "Nothing."

Doctor Furtwängler made an unobtrusive note beside her name. *Sie lügt* is what he had written. *She is lying.* Then: *warum? Why?*

4

Pilgrim's quarters, it turned out, were on the third floor. He rode up with Kessler in an ornate glass elevator with openwork brass fittings. Beyond the glass, he could see the curving marble staircase that surrounded them not unlike a corkscrew. Its banisters were made of some dark wood he could not identify.

In the elevator there was an operator of indeterminate age. He wore a green uniform without a cap and he sat on a fold-down wooden seat, running the lift with a handle projecting from a wheel. His shoes were so highly polished they gave off light, and his hands were encased in white cotton gloves. There was absolutely no expression on his face the whole way up. He did not speak to Kessler. Nor did Kessler speak to him.

On arrival at the third floor, Pilgrim hung back.

The brass accordion gate stood open. Kessler moved forward and, turning, said from the marble landing: "you may come. All is well."

He held out his hand.

The operator still had not risen from his seat. He sat there, leaning slightly forward in order to hold the gate in place, his other hand folded in his lap.

"Mister Pilgrim?" Kessler smiled.

Pilgrim glanced at the orderly's extended hand and seemed to regard it not as a signal to proceed, but a warning—or perhaps a barrier.

"You have nothing to fear," Kessler said. "You are home."

No sooner was Pilgrim standing on the landing than the metal gate snapped shut behind him. When he turned to look, the operator's still-expressionless face was disappearing below the marbled edge at Pilgrim's feet.

Kessler guided him towards the corridor, where a seamless carpet rolled away into the distance between an avenue of doors.

The carpet, with gold-threaded edges, was a deep maroon in colour. No pattern. All the doors along the way were shut, though light was filtered into the hallway through open transoms.

A long way off—or so it seemed—an old woman wrapped in a sheet stood watching them. Beyond her, a pale white light made an aureole about her figure.

"You are fortunate, Mister Pilgrim," Kessler said. "You will be in Suite number 306. It has a superior view."

He started off—came back—collected Pilgrim and, guiding him once again by the elbow, led him along the silencing carpet.

The woman did not move. Whether she was watching them was not quite clear. Her eyes could not be seen.

Suite number 306 had a tall white door, transom closed.

Kessler led the way—through the vestibule to a second door and thus into a sitting-room that was more in the nature of what a hotel might offer. Nothing visible of a clinic. Between the windows there was an alcove fitted with an ornate desk and there were tables, chairs and carpets—the chairs wicker, with cushions. The carpets were ersatz Turkish—not expensive, but effective. Blue and red and yellow—the final threads undone, unfinished— ersatz dreams included free of charge.

Kessler ushered his patient through to the bedroom.

Pilgrim's steamer trunk stood in the middle of the floor. His suitcases—two of them—sat unopened on the bed. They had all been delivered from the station during the time that coffee was being served.

Both the windows were shuttered on the inside. "Against the wind," Kessler explained. "There is a storm just now, but you will be safe in here and warm." He was moving about the room, turning on lamps. "Here, as you see, is your bathroom. Everything just the same as if you were at home ..."

Pilgrim was paying no attention. He was standing beside the

steamer trunk, using it—so it seemed—as a means of remaining upright. He gripped its edge with his left hand and stared about him.

"Why not sit down, Mister Pilgrim?" said Kessler. "Here, I will bring you this chair."

He carried it to where his patient wavered beside the trunk. "There you are then."

Kessler lowered Pilgrim into the chair, but even so, Pilgrim would not let go of the trunk.

"You cannot want to hold it so, Mister Pilgrim. Please, you must let it go."

Pilgrim held fast.

Kessler reached out and gently, finger by finger, pried the hand free and laid it with the other in Pilgrim's lap.

At the door to the bedroom, a voice said: "have you come for me?"

It was the woman wrapped in the sheet. She walked straight in and up to Pilgrim, staring at him. "You must have come for me," she said, "or you would not be in my room."

Her voice was barely audible. Her tone was not accusatory. In fact, there was little inflection at all.

For the briefest moment, the woman and Pilgrim remained face to face, but it seemed he did not see her. She was not so old as she had appeared in the distance down the corridor. Thirty or thirty-five at the most. Her face was quite unlined, though its colouring was sallow. Under her eyes she might have fingered some kohl, the shadows were so profound. Her hair was completely undone and wet as if it had just been washed.

Kessler said to her: "please, Countess, you do not belong in here."

"But this is my suite," the woman said. Her English was perfect—her accent, Russian. "I have been waiting all these years for him, and now—you see? He knew exactly where to find me."

"No, Madame. No. I will take you home. Come with me."

"But ..."

"Come with me."

Kessler led the woman to the door and beyond it through the sitting-room and vestibule into the corridor. All the while she protested that number 306 was where she belonged and that Pilgrim had arrived expressly and only in her behalf. "We have met before," she said, "in a blizzard on the Moon."

Kessler did not protest. He knew the Countess Blavinskeya. She had been a famous ballerina and was sometimes his responsibility—a source of consternation to others, though not to him. She believed that she lived on the Moon and was the subject of many arguments amongst the doctors. Some, including Doctor Furtwängler, wanted her "returned to earth," claiming Blavinskeya would never recover her mental stability unless she was forced to confront reality. Countering this was the argument that Blavinskeya suffered from "an excess of reality" and could barely function in what most people understood to be the real world. "If her survival depends on her belief that she belongs on the Moon, then we must reconcile ourselves to *her* reality, not she to *ours*." This latter argument was so astonishing that those who propounded it—and there were few enough of them—were considered to be renegade and contra-science. Privately, Furtwängler called them *mad* and complained that if they had their way in her behalf, it would be tantamount to handing the Countess over to the madness that drove her.

Kessler did not care, either way. The "Moon" and Suite 319, where Blavinskeya was housed, were synonymous. He himself would say: *I am going to the Moon* when it was his responsibility to get her through the day. She was exquisite—childlike—eternally innocent. To be with her even briefly was to be returned to those moments in childhood when every blade of grass is a revelation. The Moon need only be reached for to be achieved.

Pilgrim sat transfixed.

He could see his hands. They lay where Kessler had left them, twisted, staring up at him, palms as pale as plates.

He might as well have closed his eyes. He could not see outwards, only inwards. The room he sat in was nothing more nor less than a box—a floor, a ceiling, walls. The windows, shuttered, had no function. They were merely oblong shapes. The lamps and the light they shed were like portholes. Perhaps the sea lay beyond them, moonlit and wavering. Portholes. Moonlight. Water.

In his mind the troubling news was given that the ship he was on was sinking. At any moment, the walls might tilt and spill the contents of the room towards him. The bed was a lifeboat—the table an upturned raft—the carpet, matted seaweed. The chairs were his fellow passengers—bulging with life preservers—floating upside down.

All of this had happened on the night of April 15th, two days before he had hanged himself. He knew that. He had read it and he remembered. The ocean liner *Titanic* had struck an iceberg and sunk. Fifteen hundred persons had died. And he had lived. It wasn't just—that so many had been granted his most fervent wish. It wasn't just—that death was so generous to others.

He sat and waited—listening.

I am a voyager, he thought. *I was going somewhere, but I have been denied my destination.*

The wind rose beyond the windows.

Pilgrim's eyes shifted.

Someone stood beside him.

"Mister Pilgrim?"

It was Kessler.

Pilgrim did not move.

"Are you hungry?"

Hungry?

Kessler waved his hand before the staring eyes.

Nothing. Not a flicker.

Kessler retreated to the bed. He would unpack the suitcases. Then he would attempt the trunk. At any moment Doctor Furtwängler must arrive. And Lady Quartermaine would come to say goodbye. Instructions would be given. Perhaps some medication.

Shirts. Underclothing. Socks ...

Handkerchiefs. Monograms. *P* for *Pilgrim.*

Kessler eyed the seated figure, its uncombed hair a wind-blown halo. The wings were folded now—the shoulders drooping forward, the neck engulfed in tartan scarves.

It was a bony face. Wide-browed. Heavy-lidded eyes. The nose, a beak—nothing less. It hooked out over the upper lip and the upper lip was parted from the lower. Kessler thought he saw it move.

"Would you speak? Do you want to speak?"

Speak? No.

Nothing.

Kessler snapped the first suitcase shut and moved to the second. Before depositing the clothing in drawers, he would lay it out on the bed in order to assess what sort of space would be required for each category.

Pyjamas. Slippers. A dressing-gown; no cord. Expensive. Silk. And blue.

All else was blue. Or white. The handkerchiefs were white. Some shirts. Some underclothes. In the steamer trunk he would find one white suit. But most was blue.

Kessler moved to the bureau, where he set out brushes and combs.

Doctor Furtwängler came to the bedroom door. Lady Quartermaine stood in the sitting-room. Her veils were lowered. She wore her overcoat. She said nothing.

Furtwängler spoke a few words in German and Kessler retreated into the bathroom, where he closed the door and laid out Pilgrim's toiletries. *An angel toothbrush, an angel nailbrush, an angel bar of soap ...* He smiled.

Furtwängler beckoned and Lady Quartermaine joined him.

Pilgrim still sat frozen in his place.

Sybil looked at Doctor Furtwängler.

"Go to him," he said.

As she crossed the carpet, the skirts of her travelling coat made a swishing noise against its surface. *The sea—the sea*, it whispered. *The sea ...*

It was difficult for her to look into Pilgrim's face. His seemingly blinded eyes were more than troubling. They made her want to weep. But no—she must not.

Should she kneel? A supplicant? *Be well. The Lord be with thee.* No. It would make her departure seem too final.

"Pilgrim," she whispered, and took his hands. "I've come to say good night. And in the morning ..."

She looked at Doctor Furtwängler, who nodded.

"... in the morning, I will come again and we ..."

His hands were cold and unresponsive. A dead man's hands.

She lifted her veils. "In the morning we can walk along the terrace," she told him. "In the morning we can look at all the snow. In the morning ... Do you remember, Pilgrim, how you always loved the snow when we were young? The sun will shine again—I'm sure of it. In the morning ..." She closed her eyes. "Good night, dear friend. Good night."

She released his hands and leaned above his face to kiss him on the forehead.

"All is well," she told him. "All is well."

Still he did not move.

"Good night, Doctor Furtwängler. Thank you."

She moved towards the door.

Doctor Furtwängler called to Kessler in German, asking him to accompany Lady Quartermaine to her motor car, which had arrived despite the blizzard and was parked beneath the portico.

Kessler emerged from the bathroom. Holding up a razor, he slipped it into his pocket.

Doctor Furtwängler nodded. *Good.* Lady Quartermaine had told him that, in the intervening days between Pilgrim's bid for suicide and their arrival at the Burghölzli, there had been no further attempts. Still, for the first few days—a week, perhaps—

Kessler could act as barber, shaving the patient or—who knows—it could be Mister Pilgrim would decide, as some men did in his circumstances, to grow a beard.

When the others had departed, Furtwängler closed the door and went to stand where he could get a better view of his patient. Pushing aside the emptied suitcases, he sat on the bed. Something must be said.

He waited.

Pilgrim had shifted the focus of his blind gaze to some interior field of vision Furtwängler could only guess at.

In time, he thought. *In time there will be words. I can wait. But not too long. He must not be allowed to sink any deeper. People have died down there and—even though it is what he wants, it must not be allowed to happen. I cannot—I will not allow it.*

Still, there was no way in and no way out of Pilgrim's mind. It was besieged and all the gates were sealed.

5

The skies beyond the windows of Doctor Furtwängler's office the next morning were bright with sunshine—almost white.

"Tell me your name."

I have no name.

"Can you not—will you not speak to me?"

Speak? It is useless.

"I am told that you want to die, Mister Pilgrim. If this is truly what you wish, I need to know why."

You have no need. How can it possibly matter to you?

"Mister Pilgrim?"

Why do you assume that because I do not answer I cannot hear you?

"Doctor Greene informs me that you have attempted to kill yourself before. Is this true?"

Everything is true. Everything—and nothing.

"Well, at least that's something. You looked the other way. I will accept that, for now, as some kind of answer. And—until you agree to speak and are willing to contradict me—I will assume the answer is *yes: you have tried before.*"

Pilgrim sat in the leather chair that Sybil, only last evening, had occupied. He rubbed the palms of his hands against its arms. Her scent was somewhere in there and he wanted to evoke it. *Moss ... lemons ... ferns ...*

"Are you comfortable?"

Yes.

"I want to know why you refuse to speak. Have you lost your voice? If you have, there is treatment we can provide."

Snow. Mountains. Sky.

"It is perfectly understandable, of course, given the manner in which you attempted to kill yourself ..."

Doctor Furtwängler made no bones about the way in which he phrased this. No point pretending they did not both know exactly why Pilgrim was there. To pass it off in some pale, euphemistic way: *the manner in which you came to grief*, perhaps, or *the condition in which you were found* would be an insult. A hanging is a hanging. Suicide is suicide. It is not a synonym for *accident*. Certainly not a synonym for *unfortunate happenstance*.

"Given the manner in which you attempted to kill yourself," he said, "damage may well have been done to your vocal cords. This afternoon, I will have you escorted to the laboratory of Doctor Felix Hövermeyer, an expert in these matters. He will examine you. If there is cause for concern, I trust you will allow him to treat you."

Avalanche.

"On the other hand, if we have no evidence of trauma in the larynx, I shall persist in asking my questions until, one day, you answer."

Doctors always love it when you smile. They call it enigmatic. Is that enigmatic enough?

"You clearly understand me."

Yes.

"I am not your enemy, Mister Pilgrim. You need not resist me. I am here to help."

Will you help me to your scalpel? Your linden tree with bough of steel? Your hunting knife? Your axe? Your gun?

"You must, I am certain, be aware the circumstances of your recovery were miraculous."

There are no miracles.

"Do you believe in God?"

I have no gods. There is no God.

"Your man—his name is Forster, I believe—is said to have cut you down, and when he did so, you were already dead."

Not dead. I cannot die.

"Doctor Greene and Doctor Hammond. I have here copies of their reports. I have spoken more than once to Greene on the telephone. Every effort they extended failed to produce a heart-beat. And in spite of every method of resuscitation, you also failed to breathe. Three hours—four, Mister Pilgrim, without a heartbeat. Five without breathing. Yet here you are and ..."

It is not a miracle, Doctor. Death would be the miracle. Not life.

"Would you care to see your friend?"

I have no friends.

"Lady Quartermaine ..."

Sybil.

"She is here, and would very much like to talk with you—speak with you. Would you be willing?"

Pilgrim stood up.

He reached across the desk and drew the doctor's notes towards him, tearing off the top grey page. Then, page in hand, he went to the window.

Furtwängler waited and watched him, motionless.

Pilgrim held the paper up to the light. Spreading it against the glass, he smoothed it with his fingers.

Still, Furtwängler did not move.

Pilgrim pressed his forehead against the page. He pressed so hard, the frosting on the windowpane was melted.

Then he turned and handed the page to Furtwängler.

On it, above the Doctor's notes, was a pattern—a design.

For a moment, it looked almost like a word—and the word was *NO*.

Its letters were not formed in ink, but in ice. Even as Furtwängler stared at them, they melted and faded away, leaving only the wet blankness of the page.

6

That evening, Sybil Quartermaine stood staring at a large rectangular parcel that sat on a table beside the bay windows of her sitting-room at the Hôtel Baur au Lac.

Its outer wrapping consisted of thick oiled canvas tied with tough red cords. Now, the cords were cut—thanks to a hotel footman who had bowed out of the room just moments before. Sybil knew that inside, the parcel's contents were further shrouded in layers of linen and paper. This she had discovered when she had first opened the package shortly after it had been presented to her just a week before.

Forster had placed it on a table in her temporary rooms at number 18 Cheyne Walk, where she had taken up residence following Pilgrim's suicide attempt. *Say nothing, m'lady*, he had cautioned her. These had been Pilgrim's instructions to him— in a note deliberately placed on the floor outside Pilgrim's bedroom, on the morning Forster had found his employer hanging from the maple tree in the garden. He had been further instructed to give the package to Lady Quartermaine and to destroy the note once he had read and understood its contents— and this he had done.

The parcel had accompanied the rest of Sybil's luggage to Zürich. Phoebe Peebles, her maid, had seemed puzzled by its presence—but had not dared to ask any questions.

Nor had anyone else. And therefore Sybil Quartermaine was alone in her knowledge that she now possessed a complete set of Pilgrim's journals. And was unsure what to do about them.

Should she read them? They were his. They were private. But why else would Pilgrim have had them sent to her? Still, what if they revealed more than anyone should know? What if they revealed even more than Sybil herself already knew? Or wanted to know.

She sighed.

Then she closed her eyes, opened them—and suddenly sat down at the table. She reached for the canvas and began to pull aside its folds. Then the linen. And finally, the paper.

There they sat, bound in leather. *Pilgrim's writings*, she thought. *Pilgrim's secrets ...*

She lifted the top journal and set it on the table before her. Opening it, she began to leaf through the closely written pages, noting how meticulous Pilgrim had been about the margins—all the paragraphs squared on either side. Suddenly, a particular date caught her eye.

By firelight: 2:00 a.m. Sunday, 1st December, 1901. Hartford Pryde.

Henry James is given to lists. He told me this evening in the drawing-room that his journal entries almost inevitably end with columns of names.

"People you've met?" I ask him. "Places you've been?"

"No, no. Nothing of the kind. People and places I'm waiting to invent. Names, I find, can be so provocative. Take the name *Bleat*, for instance. It occurred to me while riding on a train. What does one think of first?"

"Sheep."

"Precisely. But it's someone's name. Can you see him?"

"None too kindly, I'm afraid. Face like a sheep, I suppose. Head too close to his shoulders. Small, worried eyes. Hands at his sides. Wearing gloves ..."

"Black gloves." James nodded.

"Black gloves, yes."

"Black shoes?"

"Yes. With spats."

"Grey spats, of course. Bleat wears nothing but black and grey, I should think. Never white. Sheep are never truly white."

"That's right. Never white."

I waited. James's eyes shifted to one side. I wondered if we had done with Bleat, but—no.

"What sort of shape do you see?" he asked me.

"Round," I said. "Not fat, but round."

"Not a tall man."

"No. Not tall at all."

"But not a dwarf."

"No. Not a dwarf."

"And you say he's *round?*"

"Yes. Round. Looks as if he has to lie on the floor in order to put on his overcoat. Rolls himself into it. Can't do up the buttons."

"His man must do that for him."

"That and get him to his feet. Yes."

"Wears a homburg," James added.

"Carries it. Never quite sure what to do with it."

"Black wool collar."

"Absolutely. Lamb."

"I suspect he complains a lot."

"Endlessly, I should think."

"Wet-eyed ..."

"And worried. Yes."

"Ever met him?"

"Well, no," I said. "He doesn't exist."

"He does now." James slid his eyes in my direction and gave a childlike smile. Almost smug.

I laughed.

"You see, then, the value of my lists," he said.

"Indeed I do. I've often wondered where writers get their characters' names."

"Most come with them," he said. "Isabel Archer, for instance. I shall never forget the day she walked into my mind and said: *I'm here, now. You may begin.* It was very much as though I were a painter and she had come to sit for me in my studio."

"*The Portrait of a Lady.*"

"Yes. I knew her instantly by name. She might have left her calling card the day before—a week before. A month. I seemed to have been expecting her arrival. Not that I knew her entirely all at once, but knew that she was fascinating to me. Had drawn me towards her after various sightings—teasing glimpses—anecdotes and rumours of her existence. It seemed, in my head, as though others had spoken of her. As if, you know, she were real and I were the last to hear of her. *Her name is Isabel Archer*, inner voices informed me. *Are you interested?* Yes, I said. Yes. *She comes with a great deal of money*, the voices went on—money—tragedy—intrigue—desolation ... I had to stop them while I rushed for paper. And there you have it. Do you understand? A face is seen—a figure—then you hear a name and the gossip in you wants to know it all. The whole sordid tale. Or sad. Or wonderful. Whatever. Isabel Archer—monied and beautiful—or penniless and plain. Which? An American, of course, caught up in the social coils of sophisticated European treachery and home-grown American greed. And what is to become of her? There she sits before you—smiling and seemingly poised—and that is all you know. And then—you begin to write."

"You make it sound almost too easy," I said. I had not enjoyed the story of Isabel Archer, though of course I could not say so. The ending was too painful, however true to life, and I had closed the book with a deep sense of moral frustration. Not that I live a moral life, but I do expect it of others. Don't we all?

James said: "you need only look around this drawing-room at all the people gathered here to see how difficult it really is. Reading a face. Reading a gesture. What can you tell me of any one of them? Less than you may imagine, Pilgrim—even though you may think you know them by heart. Everyone is a liar—one way or another—to one degree or another. No one *can* tell the truth about themselves. It is quite impossible. Something must always be justified. *Always*, something must be justified. We do each other dreadful harm because we refuse to justify the foibles of others—only our own. And this is sad. And so ..." there was an eager light in his eye as he concluded "... that is where I come in. Because I am able to see, articulate and justify the lies of others."

"And yours, Mister James?" I said. "Your own lies?"

"I have none," he replied. "None has been left to me. I have betrayed them all on the page."

"I see."

"Don't go away with the wrong impression, Mister Pilgrim. I do not mean there is no deceit in me—only that I no longer lie to myself. I no longer justify. I merely record."

I believe him. And though it may seem presumptuous, I now forgive him for Isabel Archer's fate. If he had made the ending I had thought I wanted, he would have betrayed the lot of us by painting *The Portrait of a Lily*—not *a Lady*.

As we parted, moving on to other conversations, he said to me: "thank you for Mister Bleat. I hope I shall meet him again." He smiled. "In town, perhaps."

"Yes," I told him. "In town. I shall give him a call, and bring him round."

"In his overcoat, I trust."

"In his overcoat, for certain. I shall roll him into it myself."

Harry Quartermaine took James away to the library, to inspect his collection of antique books. I might have been inclined to join them if I hadn't noted Harcourt beetling after them. Harcourt the bore. "Harcourt of the Bodleian," he always says, when introducing himself with, I trust, an inadvertent imitation of Uriah Heep—all tipped over on his toes, bobbing like something dead in the water. And he actually does rub his hands together in the same Heepish manner—as if he were giving himself a dry wash. I cannot bear the man—nor his prating wife, the dreaded Rose. I can't imagine why they are here, having watched Sybil suffer their endless presence at Portman Square. It must be Quartermaine who invites them, since he suffers fools so gladly. Fools and connivers. Thieves. Sadly, Harcourt may well have a bequest for the Bodleian of Harry's antique books before the evening is out.

Eleanor and Stephen Copland were packed off early to the games room with Margot and David. Being cousins and roughly of an age, they have known each other all their lives. The other Quartermaine children—"our Prydes," as Sybil calls them, using their family name—had been with us briefly at teatime, but Margot and David had been allowed to sit at table in the evening with the adults. Watching them depart—herded away with Susan Copland following—still and apparently ever wearing black—I could not but feel sorry for them all, having lost their father and their uncle two months ago and never knowing why. I suspect that Susan's having gone with them had to do with her concern that none of the wrong questions be asked, and none of Margot's irresponsible speculations.

Death is always provocative and the young require so many answers which none of us can provide. Not so much *what is it?* as *why?* And, of course, in the case of Symes Copland, every question offers the dreadful possibility of a betrayed truth.

I knew him, though not well. He did a masterly job at the Tate, so recently opened. Such a tragedy, following such a triumph. The popular notion is that exhaustion killed him, leaving him run down and prone to a dozen diseases. *He had gone off to Venice, where the plague lurks in every sewer and under every stone.* That was one story. Or *he had gone to Biarritz, made so popular by the Prince of Wales and Mrs Keppel—where Symes,* as some would have it, *had died of a poisoned mussel!* These were the sort of penny-novel stories Rose Harcourt delighted in hearing and spreading from salon to salon. *And of course,* she would add maliciously, *he went without his wife. And we all know what that means ...* In the papers it was stated plainly that *Mister Copland, due at any moment to receive a knighthood honouring his brilliant accomplishments in achieving the sixteenth- and seventeenth-century British Collections at the newly opened Tate Gallery, had gone to Paris on business and succumbed there to a particularly virulent pneumonia.* Or some such words.

This is what the children were told. If not a penny-novel version, then at least a tuppeny-novel truth.

The real truth is, he hanged himself in a hotel room near Vauxhall Station, across the river from his beloved gallery. His body had been discovered by his secretary, a man called Exeter Riley, whom Symes had asked to book the room from time to time so he could take an hour or two of rest before returning to the enormous burden of his work. On that particular weekend, he had let it be known that he was going to Paris to acquire a hitherto unknown Hillyard miniature—which, of course, did not exist. All this was explained to Susan by Exeter Riley himself, standing in her drawing-room on a day in September, while the sun was shining and an out-of-season garden party had been planned.

Sybil told me a farewell letter had been found but Exeter Riley had destroyed it. Susan never saw it. *Exeter Riley has sworn himself to secrecy*, according to Sybil, *and there's not a law in the land that can force him to speak.* Which may be just as well. If Symes had been leading—in whatever way, to whatever degree—a double life or had been ill with some appalling disease, what good could ever be done by revealing such news to his wife. Whatever had become of his will to live is still and will remain a mystery. And in my heart of hearts, I think this right. In a tragic moment of his own perception, he wanted to die—and did. But he left behind him a cherished monument to art, a wife and children who will always remember the best of him and a memory of decency worth some honour. And at least the poor fellow was able to fulfil his wish for death. In that alone, he was lucky.

Sybil shoved the journal away from her and poured herself a portion of whisky, her preferred drink. She drank it neat and without grimacing. It went down like water over velvet. Then she lighted a cigarette.

For the briefest moment, the bodies of Symes and Pilgrim hung in her mind's eye—faint at first, then vivid as a photograph emerging in a tray of developer. There was nothing she had read she did not already know in the broadest terms—including Pilgrim's opinion of Symes and his death. But still ... *there is ever and ever,* she thought, *that fascination with what has been and those we have loved that draws us back and back and back again to those moments of crisis when the whole of one's life is relived. Those moments after which the inevitable conclusion can only be that nothing evermore will ever be the same.*

Don't, she thought. *Don't. Do not think about it. Let it all go.* Then she poured a second portion of whisky and drew the journal back beneath the spill of light.

Dream—recorded at 6:00 a.m.

Image of a sheep. One.

Am I to be amused? I'm not sure. It seems, somehow, less connected to my conversation with James about Mister Bleat than to my other dreams of muddied terrain and distant bursts of light. Besides, the sheep is silent. Nothing of bleating. It stands in profile, turning its head in order to see me—staring at me almost accusingly. *Why have you brought me here?* it seems to say—yet its silence is absolute.

As I watch, I become aware of where I am. This time, no people. The land about me is sodden, but mudless. The grass is matted, lying flat in the rain. I am standing at what appears to be the centre of a landscape so vast I can get no indication of its edges. There is no horizon, only earth. Perhaps I am looking down at myself. I have that impression—even though, in the way of dreams, I am also looking at the sheep not from above but straight on.

Around me, so it seems, there are endless miles of ditches. Not like the ditches by the sides of roads. Deeper than that and with the look of having been dug—to whatever end—by human hands with picks and spades. The edges are cut flat as though with some purpose in mind. A trench for sewage pipes? Or would it be filled with stones and cement—the foundation for some gigantic building. Or walls, perhaps, to surround the field I am in. A priory yard. A graveyard somewhere in Europe where they built such walls around the dead.

I have still not stirred. And though I know that I am clothed, I have no notion of what I am wearing. I see no colour on my sleeve. There is no sense of texture or of cut in what I wear— only of its weight, which seems as I stand there, leaden.

Something happens. I don't know what. But something tremendous either falls or is exploded. The rain all at once is scalding hot. I wipe my eyes, but still have not moved from my place, and when I look about me, I see that a river of sheep has begun to crowd the ditches. *River* is quite the right word. They flow in from all sides, their undulating backs rising and falling— rippling, almost, as they move forward. And when the ditches are filled, the sheep stand motionless, waiting as if for some command that I too anticipate.

The silence goes unbroken. Even though there has been all along a distant soughing of wind, it neither rises nor falls. Nor does it alter its tone. It is simply there. A wind has blown through all my dreams of late, yet always far away. And the trees, whose branches give it its distinctive sound, are never seen.

Agnus Dei, qui tollis peccata mundi,
dona eis requiem.

These words appear, as if by magic, under my hand and make their windblown way across the page. In the dream, I am unaware that I know them. I merely record them.

In the ditch, the backs surge forward and are stilled again.

Agnus Dei, qui tollis peccata mundi,
dona eis requiem sempiternam.
Lamb of God, that takest away the sins of the world,
Grant them eternal rest.

The silence now is universal.

What have I dreamt?

What am I dreaming?

Where is this place that is so bleak and unforgiving—

endlessly crowded, yet seemingly emptied and sad, as if the earth itself has gone into mourning? An abattoir, I fear, and we the sheep.

Knowing what I know of the past, my discomfort with the future is now a burden I think I cannot bear. I will be glad of daylight—and of any other voice but my own.

Sybil closed the book. She was weeping. At first, she did not know why—and then she did. It was the words: *grant them eternal rest*. Pilgrim's quest.

Before she retired, she would ask Phoebe Peebles to put the books away in one of the closets. Along with their wrapping.

Until next time.

7

"Are you certain you have told me everything?"

"Everything about what?"

"About your relationship with Mister Pilgrim."

Facing Sybil the next morning, Furtwängler seemed less a friendly physician than a prosecuting attorney, his manner cool and his questions all but impertinent.

"I don't know what you may be thinking, Doctor, but I can tell you this: Mister Pilgrim and I are not—and never have been—lovers."

"I did not say so."

"It was in your mind."

"I admit that. Yes. But I would not have dreamt of asking for details. What you and Mister Pilgrim do ..."

"You needn't explain your attitude, Herr Doktor. I understand it perfectly. Mister Pilgrim and I do nothing. Have you never heard of simple friendships?"

"Simple friendships between men and women are relatively rare, Lady Quartermaine. I am sure that from your own experience you already know that."

"I know nothing of the kind."

"And your husband, the Marquis. He has lady friends?"

"Lady friends and female friends are not the same thing. And from *your* own experience, Herr Doktor, I am sure you know that."

Doctor Furtwängler had been standing. They were in one of the main-floor reception rooms, where a fire had been lit. He now sat down. They faced each other, each of them guarded, each of them wary, seated on green slip-covered chairs. For his part, Furtwängler was certain Lady Quartermaine had already lied to him. For her part, Sybil had begun to lose her confidence in him. She could—and would—tolerate only so many presumptions.

"You say you have not been lovers," the Doctor said. "But I still need to know the nature of your relationship."

Sybil Quartermaine found the question fatuous and irritating. She waved it aside and said nothing.

"Can you tell me, at least, how long you have known each other?"

"Forever."

"Please, Lady Quartermaine. The more you tell me, the more I can help. *Forever* is not an answer."

"Why not? Perhaps I meant it."

"In terms of what I need to know, *forever* is not instructive. It can mean anything."

Sybil sighed. "Very well, then," she said. "I was twelve. He was eighteen."

"Twelve and eighteen. That would have been in ..."

"1880. It was the year my father died."

"And Mister Pilgrim?"

"I found him in the garden."

"I beg your pardon?"

"I found him in the garden. This was at Chiswick."

"Chiswick?"

"Yes. Where I grew up. West London. It's by the river. The Thames."

"And you were born there?"

"No. Though I might have been. I don't know where I was born. No one ever said."

"I see. And you found him in the garden—Mister Pilgrim."

"Yes. It was summertime. August. My father had died the day before and my mother was distraught. She wanted Symes, my brother, beside her. She did not want me. I was just as pleased. I was distraught, myself. It was early morning. I hadn't slept. I was in my nightdress. Barefoot. I remember that distinctly—the feel of the grass and the dew beneath my feet. I wore some sort of shawl—perhaps a woollen blanket. It was blue. Have you got a cigarette? I would like a cigarette."

Doctor Furtwängler rose and offered his silver case. He also took one himself and lighted them both from the end of a taper drawn from the fire.

Sybil lay back against the cushions in her chair. She squinted at the fire. The smoke from her cigarette coiled up around her face. By daylight, her beauty was more pronounced, although she seemed herself to have no awareness of it. About her appearance there was not a trace of artifice. Her cream-pale face, her swept-back hair and her violet eyes were gifts of nature, acknowledged but unadorned. Her only jewellery was a single strand of pearls, her wedding and engagement rings and a small green shard of jade, set in silver and pinned to her dress. Furtwängler noticed, too, a birthmark on the underside of her left wrist—a tracing, not unlike a snake, but very faint. It was red.

"You had gone into the garden, you said. It was early in the morning?"

"Just after dawn. There was light, but the sun had not yet appeared. Our garden there at Chiswick had a wall around it. An old grey wall with ivy growing on it. Ivy and Virginia creeper. In the autumn, the wall was crimson—orange—it flamed. But then, that morning, it was green. The vines were very lush and dense. You could barely see the stones and ... There were trees. It was charming. Beautiful. One of the trees, an oak, had a ladder propped against it. I don't remember why, but I do remember its being there. And ..."

"And?"

"Beside the ladder, lying on the grass beneath the tree, there was a young man."

"Mister Pilgrim?"

"Yes. Mister Pilgrim. Pilgrim. I had never seen anyone so beautiful in all my life. Not even statues—not even paintings had prepared me for him. Certainly, no other human being. His hair was copper-coloured—flaming—and his face—well, you've seen him. Translucent skin—wide lips—an eagle's beak ... He wore a blue blazer. Pale grey trousers. No tie. A white shirt. I ... He was asleep, you see. And I looked at him and I thought a god had been left, somehow, in the garden. Abandoned."

"And when he woke?"

"I woke him myself. I couldn't bear to see him lying there in the dew. I was sure he would catch his death of cold, so I went and touched his foot with my toe. When he saw me, he smiled and said: *I have been dreaming ...*"

"Dreaming."

"Yes. He said he had fallen asleep and had dreamt."

"But what was he doing in your garden? How did he get there?"

"I asked him that, but gently. I was not afraid of him at all. I was merely curious. And of course I didn't want him to go away."

"What was his answer?"

"He said he didn't know how he had got there. He didn't even know where he was. When I told him my name, it meant nothing to him. I asked him who he was and at first he said he didn't know that, either. But then he said his name was Pilgrim."

"And that is how you met."

"That is how we met. In a garden on a summer's day—the year my father died. In 1880."

There was the sound of activity in the entrance hall. People could be heard greeting one another and stamping their feet to be rid of the snow. The smell of cold fresh air was carried over the threshold. The fire guttered. Sybil reached down and touched her ankles.

"The draught," she said, and smiled. "Isn't it wonderful, the way it speaks to one."

"Speaks to one?"

"Just an expression. Does nothing speak to you, Doctor? Out of nature, I mean. The wind? A fall of rain? A passing animal?"

"No. I fear not. My sense of perception must be rather dull."

"Not necessarily. It's a gift, I suppose. Like music. Some people have it—others do not. I doubt it's a serious offence."

She was still smiling. Best to be graceful. Why antagonize him? At that moment, Doctor Furtwängler was all she had.

"What might the draught have said to you, Lady Quartermaine? I'm curious."

"Someone of importance has just arrived. That's what it said. There was an air of decisiveness—of purpose. I don't know quite how to phrase it. Whatever the source, it was quite refreshing."

"Indeed." Doctor Furtwängler fumbled his watch into view and, having seen the time, appeared to despair.

"I have a patient waiting for me, Lady Quartermaine. I must ask you to excuse me."

"Certainly."

He stood up, adjusting his waistcoat and jacket.

"Shall I see you this afternoon?" he asked.

"Is there any point? If, as you explained, Mister Pilgrim is disinclined to see me now, is he apt to see me then?"

"Perhaps if you come in the neighbourhood of tea-time. He might be in a more receptive frame of mind."

"In that case, I shall come at half past four."

"Nonetheless, I suggest you be prepared for more rejection. Mister Pilgrim is in a precarious position at the moment. I believe he feels endangered. Possibly from within, possibly from without. He still has not spoken."

"I see."

Furtwängler nodded and turned towards the door.

"May I tell you something, Doctor, before you go?"

"Of course." He turned again and waited.

"When he speaks, he will tell you of things—of circumstances—that may seem to verge on the impossible. In fact, there will be incidents ..." she looked away "... which *are* impossible. Nonetheless ..." She threw her cigarette into the fire. "I urge you to believe him, if only briefly, for his sake."

"You think he is mad?"

"I think nothing. I am merely urging you not to destroy his beliefs. He has nothing else to fall back on."

"Thank you, Lady Quartermaine. I will take your advice into consideration. Until this afternoon?"

She nodded. "Yes. Until this afternoon."

"Good day to you."

"Good day."

In the entrance hall, Doctor Furtwängler spoke to Old Konstantine, the concierge. Sybil heard him speak her own name, but neither her ears nor her German were up to making a translation of precisely what was said.

She stood up.

She was tired.

She had not slept.

Warming her hands at the fire, she turned her wrists and saw the birthmark.

She gazed at it ruefully.

"Damn you," she whispered. "Damn you. Damn you. Damn."

8

Furtwängler did not, in fact, have an appointment with a patient. Instead, returning to his office, he found Doctor Jung and Doctor Menken waiting for him, as requested.

It had been Jung's arrival in the front hall that had prompted Lady Quartermaine's remarks about impressive draughts. Knowing this, Furtwängler had been somewhat miffed. Jung, it seemed, had a knack for impressing others, even when making an offstage entrance.

Menken was new at the Clinic, having come from America where he had been one of William James's last pupils at Harvard. He was relatively young—thirty-two—and bright but extremely serious. Jung had made it his mission to produce a daily smile on Menken's lips, but so far he had failed. If James had still been alive, Jung would have written him to complain: *can it not be that one may smile and smile and be a pragmatist?*

Carl Gustav Jung was in his late thirties and breathless with enthusiasms that seemed to have no bounds. He had already begun to gain a name for himself with the publication, in 1907, of *The Psychology of Dementia Praecox*. A study of schizophrenia, it had broken new ground and was also instrumental in drawing Jung to Sigmund Freud's attention—which, in time, would prove disastrous.

As a psychiatric clinic, the Burghölzli had no rival—certainly not in Europe. A research centre of psychiatric studies and practice since 1860, it had gained international stature under the directorship of Auguste Forel, who took it over in 1879. On Forel's retirement, the current director, Eugen Bleuler, had been appointed.

Bleuler's expertise was schizophrenia—a word he himself had

coined to describe *dementia praecox*. His theory was simple. Men and women who suffered from *dementia praecox* had been considered incurable. Those who suffered from schizophrenia—literally, split personalities—could at least be helped, if not cured, by bringing them back into contact with the real world and away from the fantasy world in which they tended to hide themselves and live out their lives.

Unmarried, Bleuler made the Clinic his residence and spent every waking hour either with his patients or with his staff—and, for the latter, his constant presence had become something of a burden. "I sometimes think he keeps a daily record of the number of times we use the toilet," Jung had said.

Both Forel and Bleuler were strict teetotallers. *Alcoholism cannot be treated by doctors who are not themselves abstainers*, ran one of Forel's dictums. "And if a patient suffers from priapism—must the doctor who treats him give up sex?" Jung had asked.

Now, in his sunlit office, Furtwängler greeted his two colleagues with a wave of his hand.

"Gentlemen," he said, "be seated." Going to his cabinet, he unlocked it to reveal a bottle of brandy and several tumblers. Such items could not, of course, be openly displayed. All the Burghölzli doctors had recently received a curt directive from the office of the Director: *Rumours are circulating that some members of the Medical Staff consider it appropriate—even necessary—to maintain a stock of alcoholic beverages in their offices. I trust that such rumours have no basis in fact, since I have already expressed my opinion on such deplorable habits.* Signed: *Bleuler.*

Though humourless and rather dull company, Doctor Bleuler was nonetheless respected. On the other hand, he was not respected enough to force one's taste for alcohol out the door. Every doctor's office had its cache.

Menken sat, but Jung remained on his feet.

"You look perplexed, Carl Gustav," said Furtwängler.

"I am," said Jung. "Tatiana Blavinskeya has had a serious setback and I'm torn between anger and disappointment. Something—I don't yet know what—has forced or persuaded her to give up speech. She is now semi-catatonic—a great, great distraction to me because she was making such excellent progress. Is either one of you aware of any possible cause for this?"

Menken said *no* and accepted his brandy—which was, by coincidence, the very colour of the checked suit he had chosen to wear that day.

Furtwängler crossed the room and handed a tumbler to Jung, who stood by the central window. "Yes," he said. "It is possible I am able to offer an explanation. But ..." He returned to his desk and sat.

"But ...?" Jung asked impatiently. "But—but ...?"

"What I will tell you is pure speculation." Furtwängler drank.

Jung busied himself nervously searching his pockets for a cheroot which, found, he lighted—throwing the burnt-out match on the floor.

"Do you mind?" said Furtwängler testily. "Please, no matches on the floor. And use an ashtray. You leave a trail of ashes everywhere you go."

Jung took up an ashtray and, drink in hand, teeth clamped on his cheroot, hissed: "procee-eed."

Furtwängler said: "Blavinskeya believes she has been sent a messenger from the Moon."

"Oh?" Jung leaned forward.

"Yes. But of course she has not."

"If she believes she has, she *has*," said Jung. He was adamant. "Constantly challenging what the Countess believes is no help at all. Who was this messenger? Did anyone else see him? Him—her? Was it a man or a woman? Did she say? What? What? What did she say?"

"It was a man," said Furtwängler. "I saw him myself."

"Ah-hah!"

"Don't go saying *ah-hah* just yet. The fellow is a new patient. Suite 306—down the corridor from Blavinskeya. Apparently they had an encounter."

"This is wonderful. Wonderful. Are you telling me they recognized one another?"

"Only that she claimed to recognize him."

"And ...? Is he from the Moon?"

"Carl Gustav, please."

"You know what I mean—does he claim to have descended from the Moon?"

"No. He makes no claim whatsoever. He is mute."

"Moon-mutes! Two of them!" said Jung. "Perhaps there will be a convention!"

Menken almost smiled, but did not.

"When did he arrive, this messenger?" Jung asked.

"Yesterday afternoon. And he is not a messenger. He has come—he was brought from England."

"Some people claim that England might as well be the Moon," said Jung—and winked at Menken.

Menken sat stony-faced and silent. He felt like a referee at a tennis game. During such meetings this seemed to be his enduring role: a little less than participant, a little more than spectator. His, however, would be the most impeccable notes of their present encounter, taking no side and giving none.

"What's his name, this man?" Jung asked.

"Pilgrim."

"Pilgrim ... Interesting. I wonder ..."

"You wonder?"

"What do you know about him? Besides the fact that Tatiana Blavinskeya thinks he's a lunar citizen like herself? Is there any chance he comes from the world of art and artists?"

"Good heavens. Yes," said Furtwängler. "You've heard of him?"

"What's his first name?"

"Doesn't have one. Known only as *Pilgrim*."

"That's how he signs himself. I've read him. Art historian. Brilliant. Wrote the definitive work on Leonardo da Vinci. Dazzling fellow. So—what's his problem? What's his condition?"

"He's a potential suicide?"

"Oh, me. How sad. Has he tried it yet?"

"Yes. Several times. This last attempt, by hanging. The circumstances are—believe me—quite extraordinary. The man should be dead."

Furtwängler outlined the medical reports from Greene and Hammond which Sybil Quartermaine had left for him to peruse.

"I'd like to see him," said Jung. "I'd like very much to see him. May I do that?"

"Of course. That's why I've asked you both here."

"And you say he should have died but did not on account of some extraordinary circumstance?" Menken asked.

"Well, it certainly seems so," said Furtwängler. "Both the examining physicians had already signed his death certificate and departed when—all at once, five, six, seven hours after the hanging—he came back to life."

"Could be he really didn't want to die ..." said Menken.

"But you say he'd tried it before. Other suicide attempts?" Jung asked.

"Yes."

"By hanging?"

"No. Other ways. Drowning. Poison. The usual."

"Well. Extraordinary. Unless, of course, Menken is right and he really never tried hard enough."

"I would have said that being apparently dead for seven hours was trying hard enough," said Furtwängler.

"And now Blavinskeya thinks he's come to her from the Moon."

"Yes. Alas ..." Blavinskeya was not Furtwängler's favourite patient.

Jung sat back and slapped his knee decisively. "Well!" he said, "when can we see him?"

"Now, if you like."

"I like it very much. Come along. Drink up. We shall all go

together. To the Moon, gentlemen!" Jung raised his glass and emptied it. "To the Moon—posthaste!"

Furtwängler's hand closed tighter on his tumbler as he drank. Mister Pilgrim was his patient, by prior arrangement with Lady Quartermaine—and with Bleuler's implicit approval. And yet, as he set his glass aside and rose to join the others, he felt a momentary sense of foreboding. He had lost other patients to Jung in the past—most notably the Countess Blavinskeya— which was why he now resented the lack of progress in her recovery. Jung's sometimes overwhelming enthusiasm could pull down the entire structure of another analyst's treatment if he was not carefully monitored.

As they left, Furtwängler turned the key in the door and thought: *one day, I might find a way to have him out of the Clinic altogether.*

9

Pilgrim was standing childlike in the middle of the floor while Kessler attached a collar to his shirt. Kessler himself was sweating rather profusely.

Furtwängler was the first to speak. "Is he not able to do that himself?"

Kessler had only just managed to insert a recalcitrant stud and was somewhat breathless with frustration. "He fights it, sir," he said. "I think he would prefer to dress himself, but there's three other studs down there on the floor somewhere, the result of his having dropped them. I'll just do his tie, if you don't mind."

The orderly had already selected a splendid blue silk cravat, which was draped across his shoulder. He nodded at the two other doctors who stood, white-coated and silent, near the door. "Good morning, gentlemen," he said. And then, referring with a glance to Pilgrim, he went on. "We have been for our walk and are waiting for our lunch." He put the tie around Pilgrim's neck and began to form a knot. "We did not sleep well, but stood a long while over there by the windows staring out at the sky. At six o'clock, an hour before sunrise, we sat down and turned our back on the room with our knees pressed tight against the wall. At seven-fifteen we acknowledged the need to use the toilet, did so and returned to the window. When the sun appeared yonder, we raised our hand in greeting. Most extraordinary. Makes no other gestures. Hands to the sides most times, and clumsy in the use, as witness the three lost studs."

Kessler drew the knot as if to tighten it, but Pilgrim threw up his hands to prevent him.

Kessler stepped back.

"Well now," he said. "Another first."

Pilgrim finished the knot and twisted it to one side.

Furtwängler moved across the carpet.

"Mister Pilgrim," he said—his smile as perfect as practice could make it. "I have brought my colleagues to meet you: Doctor Jung and Doctor Menken."

Pilgrim, who was pulling down the wings of his collar, turned away towards the mirror above the bureau.

"Mister Pilgrim ..." Furtwängler put out his hand as if to take the patient's arm.

"No. Don't," said Jung, stepping forward. "Let him be."

Pilgrim's arms fell to his sides.

Kessler moved towards him, holding a Harris tweed jacket.

Jung put his finger to his lips and took the garment in hand. Kessler moved away and waited with the others.

Jung said: "here is your jacket, Mister Pilgrim."

Pilgrim turned only slightly—not enough to look into Jung's eyes—and slipped his arms into the satin-lined sleeves.

"I know who you are," said Jung.

Pilgrim attempted to do up his buttons.

"My name is Carl Jung and I have read your book about Leonardo da Vinci. Splendid, I thought it was. Splendid. And ..."

Pilgrim suddenly turned and, passing the others, walked into the bathroom, where he shut the door.

"Is there a key?" Jung asked.

"No, sir," said Kessler. "All the keys are in my pocket."

"Is there a razor?"

"No. I've removed it. Shaved him myself this morning."

"What was his reaction to that? To being shaved."

"He knocked the razor out of my hand at one point. Same as he did with the tie, just now."

"Did he try to pick it up?"

"No. He let me do that. Then I finished the shave and there was no more fuss."

"What's his opinion of you?" said Jung. "Does he resent you?"

"He doesn't speak. I've caught him staring at me once or twice, but without expression. He seems to know who I am and that I'm here to help him, but aside from that, I hardly get a flicker."

"Has he done this before—close himself in the bathroom?"

"Only when he's used the toilet. I was in there with him when he bathed. I never leave a patient alone when he bathes. Not ever."

"Good. It's just as well. Even when there's no intention to harm himself, there can still be accidents. And he hasn't said a word?"

"No, sir. Not one."

"Did he eat his breakfast?"

"Yes. Half a grapefruit. A piece of buttered toast and a cup of coffee."

"That was all?"

"That was all."

Jung regarded the bathroom door and turned to Furtwängler, who—after all—was Pilgrim's physician.

"Do you mind?" he asked.

Furtwängler tried not to sound curt. "What are you thinking of doing?" he asked.

"Joining him. And if it seems to be appropriate, I shall close the door behind me. With your permission?"

Furtwängler raised an eyebrow at Menken. "I appear to be losing another patient," he muttered. And then to Jung: "just remember he is mine, Carl Gustav."

"Of course," said Jung. "I merely want to make contact."

"Very well, then. If you must—go ahead," Furtwängler looked again at Menken, who turned away towards the windows. "We shall wait here."

"Thank you." Jung gave a diffident bow and went over to the bathroom door. Slowly and gently, he knocked three times and went in.

10

There was no light. The room was in darkness.

Not knowing its geography, Jung hung back by the door, his left hand still on its handle.

"Would you prefer it if I did not turn on the light, Mister Pilgrim?" he asked.

There was no reply.

Jung waited, motionless.

He listened for Pilgrim's breathing, but there was none.

"The dark has always been of interest to me," he said. "When I was a child, I was afraid of it, of course—the way most children are. My father was a minister—a pastor of the Swiss Reform church. I often saw him in the local graveyard performing the service for the dead—and, being impressionable, I dreamt quite often of the image of him standing there, but in my dreams there was never light. It was always gloomy, murky—dark. I suppose it was the graves that frightened me as much as anything else about the service for the dead. *They put you in the dark and then they leave you there.* That sort of thing. Perhaps you might have had such dreams yourself when you were a child. Or very like. Most children do have them."

Jung waited.

"Mister Pilgrim?"

There was still no reply, and still no sound except for the faintest echo of water running somewhere else in the building.

Jung let go of the doorknob and took a step forward.

Nothing.

He then took another step and waited again.

And again, nothing.

"Later in my life, perhaps around the advent of puberty, the dark took on new meaning for me. I no longer feared it, but welcomed it. No more graves. In fact, I rarely dream of graves any more. I may well in future, of course—growing older. But for the time being, the grave has been replaced by the cradle—you might say: *the life force*. After all, the dark most often is where we procreate ..."

At a distance, someone flushed a toilet. The water pipes began to sing.

"I have never conducted an interview in the dark before," Jung said. "It amuses me. Perhaps it amuses you."

Nothing.

"Mister Pilgrim?"

Jung took a third step forward.

"Why do you insist on silence?" he said. "Is there really nothing you would say?"

Apparently not.

"If I thought it was really of interest to you, I would continue my dissertation on the subject of darkness, but I suspect ..."

There was a knock at the door.

"Go away," Jung said.

"But ..."

"Go away. Be patient. Wait."

Jung could hear conversation beyond the door but made out no words.

How long had he been in here?

He could not tell.

If only he knew where the light switch was.

He felt along the wall behind him.

They usually put it near the entrance, he thought—but there was nothing there.

"If you could assist me, Mister Pilgrim, I need to know where the light switch is because I require the toilet ..."

This was, of course, a ruse, but he thought it might work. Anything might work. Perhaps he should shout for help. Or give a cry of: *FIRE*!

This thought made him laugh out loud.

"I am thinking the strangest, most ridiculous things, Mister Pilgrim," he said. "I was thinking I might cry *fire* in order to trick you into responding—but, of course, if there was a fire you would see it ..."

Matches.

How damnably slow I am!

As he searched his pockets—finding everything but his matches—he began to have the curious thought that somehow Pilgrim had escaped him and that, all this time, he had been talking to himself.

He stumbled forward—and stopped. Sickened.

His toe had caught at the edge of what might be an arm or a leg.

"Mister Pilgrim?

Jung gave a gentle nudge with his shoe.

"Mister Pilgrim?"

He knelt down.

Even as he did so, he made a mental note that he had blundered in his assessment of Pilgrim's state of mind—that he had lost him as a consequence of pride. His confidence that he knew better, that Pilgrim had no real desire to further harm himself had overridden common sense. *A man who really wants to die will try and try and try again ... as this man already has.*

All this went through his mind as he descended to his knees. And furthermore ...

His knees struck the floor.

Pain.

Tiles.

Bruising hard and freezing cold.

He caught his breath and reached out with both his hands, sliding them palm down across what felt like the wind-blown ice of his childhood—the nightmare ice of Lake Constance.

His fingers caught hold of a sleeve.

Tweed.

Rough.

Empty.

He pulled the jacket towards him.

Then a shirt with its collar torn off.

He raced his fingers over every pocket on his body.

Matches. Matches. Where?

He was wearing a white smock and under it, his jacket, waistcoat and shirt. *Pockets. Pockets. Too many pockets ...*

There, you idiot!

Of course.

Lower left waistcoat pocket, exactly where you left them.

It took three unsuccessful attempts before, at last, the fourth match flared.

By its light Jung saw that he was adrift in a pool of discarded clothing—trousers—necktie—underwear—shoes—socks—jacket—shirt ...

Oh God—where is he?

The match burned down to Jung's fingertips. Throwing it into a corner, he struck another and struggled to his feet.

The light switch was on the light above the sink.

Wonder of wonders! Ingenious! A light switch on a light! Idiot!

He pulled its chain.

In the recording part of his brain, he made a note to have *The Universal Designer of Bathrooms* brought before the *Universal Court of Safety Precautions.* Light switches dangling over water taps in a mental institution. *Insanity!*

Pilgrim.

Jung could see him in the mirror. Or, at least, a part of him. The top of his head. A shoulder.

He was lying naked in the bathtub.

Jung stood frozen.

He knew that he had to call the others but his mouth would not open.

In seconds that felt like hours, he had bruised his knees yet again and was kneeling down by Pilgrim's side.

The bottom of the tub was scarlet.

Oh dear God—he's succeeded.

But he had not.

Even as Jung reached out for Pilgrim's wrists, the body convulsed and almost sat up.

It waved its hands in the air and dropped them back to its sides, where they began a frantic search under sodden thighs and buttocks. At last, the right hand rose exultant.

In it, there was a spoon. A small spoon with serrated edges.

The words *half a grapefruit for breakfast* raced through Jung's mind. Half a grapefruit eaten with a serrated spoon.

With his left hand, Pilgrim grasped Jung's lapels and drew him down towards his face.

His mouth opened.

He held out the spoon.

His eyes were filled with anguish.

"Please," he whispered. "*Please,*" he said and thrust the pathetic spoon in Jung's direction. "Kill me."

Jung undid the fingers on his lapel and stood up.

He collected some towels and draped them over Pilgrim's body, putting still more in the sink, into which he had already begun to run cold water.

Placing the spoon in his pocket, he went over to the door and opened it.

Before turning back towards the bathtub, Jung looked out into the other room, which was ablaze with sunlight, and said to his colleagues: "you may come in, now. He has spoken."

11

It was Menken and Kessler who accompanied Pilgrim to the surgery, where the wounds on his wrists were dealt with. Even though a great deal of blood had flowed, the damage was not as severe as it would have been had Pilgrim used a knife. But knives deployed on the trays that went to patients who ate in their rooms were always of the sort with blunt ends and dull edges—knives with which no harm could be done at all.

After the others had departed, Furtwängler gave a sigh and raised his arms in a helpless gesture. "Well then," he said—sinking onto Pilgrim's bed, "what am I to do with you?"

"With *me?*" Jung asked. "Why me?"

"We might have prevented all this, if you hadn't interfered."

"Nothing would have prevented it," said Jung. "I mean—imagine! A man tries to kill himself with a spoon. Sounds like fair desperation to me. I had nothing to do with it."

"You curried favour with him. The minute you held the jacket for him he knew he had you in the palm of his hand. I despair. You did this with Blavinskeya. You raved about the wonders of the Moon. You did it with the Dog-man. You allowed his minder to walk him on a chain. You told the Man-with-the-imaginary-pen you thought he had created the most beautiful writing you had ever read! I swear you don't want to bring them back. You want to leave them stranded in their dreams!"

Jung turned towards the bureau and fingered a photograph there in a silver frame. It showed a woman who appeared to be in mourning—eyes cast down, chin lowered, black beads and dress.

"It isn't true," he said, "that I want to abandon them to their dreams. But someone has to tell them their dreams are real." Then he added: "and their nightmares."

"They aren't real. They're what they are—the manifestations of madness."

"The Moon is real," Jung said. "A dog's life is real. The imagined word is real. If they believe these things, then so must we ... at least until we have learned to talk their language and hear their voices."

"Oh, yes." Furtwängler sighed again. "I know all that. But you take it too far. When Pilgrim spoke, what did he say to you? *Kill me*. He would not have said that to me. Or to Menken. Or to Bleuler. He would not have said that to any other physician in this institution. Not to one of us—only to you. And only to you because you always pretend to be an ally—a co-conspirator with the patient."

"I am the patient's ally. That's why I'm here. It's why we're all here, Josef."

"No. Not to be allies. Not to be co-conspirators. Friends, yes. And with sympathy—yes. But not with connivance—not accepting that only they can set the rules. *We* set the rules. *Reality* sets the rules. Not them. Not madmen ... crazy people ..."

"I thought we had agreed never to use those words," said Jung. "We never say *mad* and we never say *crazy*. It was agreed."

"Well, I say *mad* and I say *crazy* when *mad* and *crazy* pertain. And right now, I think *you* are *mad*." Furtwängler stood up. "Good God," he said. "We have him here only two days and he tries to kill himself again."

"It's in the nature of his nature," said Jung. "Apparently."

"There you go again! *Apparently!* What does apparently mean in Pilgrim's case. You've barely met him."

"I take what I'm given," said Jung. "I take what they have to offer. He offered slit wrists. So?"

"So leave him alone and leave him to me."

"Then why did you ask me here? And Archie Menken. Why did you ask us here?"

Furtwängler wanted to kick himself and say: *because I'm stupid*—but instead, he said: "I don't know. I suppose for the old-fashioned reason that another physician's opinion might be useful. I should have known better. Especially given my experience over time with you."

"I wish you didn't feel that way."

"I have to, don't I. You've given me no choice, Carl Gustav."

"And so?"

"And so I shall have to ask you not to have contact with Mister Pilgrim until further notice."

Having said this, Furtwängler turned away and went to the door between the two rooms, where he lingered briefly and then said over his shoulder: "good morning to you," after which he left.

"Good morning," Jung replied—but only in a whisper. When he heard the outer doors shut, he turned back towards the windows. Then he sat down and looked at his hands. *I have the hands of a peasant*, he thought. *A peasant's hands—and a peasant's blundering ways.*

Less than a minute later, Kessler returned and told him that Mister Pilgrim would be kept in the infirmary for the rest of the day.

"Any serious damage done?" Jung asked.

"Not of any permanent nature, though it seems he cut fairly deep for a man with nothing but a spoon. It's mostly they want to keep an eye on him. I met Doctor Furtwängler in the hall just now and he said he was going to check on him."

"Yes."

"If you'll excuse me, then," said Kessler, "I'll do a bit of cleaning up in the bathroom."

"Of course."

Jung remained in Pilgrim's bedroom, wandering with apparent aimlessness from bed to bureau to desk—inspecting the surfaces with a careless finger, as if checking for the presence or absence of dust. At the bureau, he paused long enough to open and close the drawers one by one, leafing through the handkerchiefs, the shirts, the underclothes, the neatly folded cravats and foulards.

Clearly, Pilgrim was a man of wealth. He also had discerning standards—quality making up for quantity. As with most who are born to a world where grace and wealth go hand in hand, the concept of having more than one needed was vulgar—if not indecent. Laid out beneath Jung's inquiring fingers were shirts that would last for ten or fifteen years, so long as the owner's girth did not increase. Their collars would be a different story, and handkerchiefs, of course, could not be expected to last so long, nor stockings. Simple and serviceable underclothes such as he found could last perhaps three or four years. Ties are for forever.

Forever. Why had this word occurred and recurred in his mind this day? *Forever. Forever.* Not last week. Not yesterday. But only today: *forever.*

Well ...

He gazed again at the woman's face in the silver frame. She had the look of another age and style—of twenty, even thirty years ago, before the century turned. And who was she in mourning for—a dead child—her husband? Perhaps herself?

In the bathroom, Kessler was collecting Pilgrim's discarded clothing and preparing it for the laundry.

"Funny," he said to Jung as he came out to the bed and began to sort through the pile, "how the clothes thrown off by a suicide seem somehow to be soiled. I dressed him this morning and I know that every bit of this was freshly laundered when he put it on. While my fingers know it is clean, some instinct tells me it is not."

"That's what you call *an atavistic reaction*, Kessler," Jung said. "Same as any child—even a baby—would know a viper is dangerous. But Mister Pilgrim has not committed suicide. He is still alive."

"Yes, well ..." said Kessler. "Them as tries and fails will try again. That's my experience of it, anyway. Yours, too, Doctor—I should think."

"Yes. I admit it. Mister Pilgrim will more than likely try again."

Kessler held Pilgrim's discarded shirt in front of him, stretching its cream-coloured arms to the limit. Wings.

"Not a small man, is he."

"No. He certainly towers over me. Let me see that, would you."

Jung put his hand out and Kessler passed him the shirt. "It is what they call Egyptian cotton," he said. "Soft as a baby's kiss."

Jung held it up to his nose.

Kessler said: "if I might say so, sir, that seems a funny sort of thing to do. To smell another man's shirt."

"Lemons," said Jung. "It smells of lemons. Lemons and something else ..."

He threw the shirt back to Kessler, who tested its scent and said: "lemons. Yes. He wears a sort of toilet water. Pats it on his cheeks when I've shaved him. You'll find it in the bathroom."

Jung went through the door and found the bottle above the sink on a marble shelf. It had a round glass stopper. Its label was grey and written in English.

Penhaligon's of London, he read. *By Appointment to His Majesty, King Edward VII, Perfumers.*

And underneath, in scroll-like print, he deciphered: *Blenheim Bouquet.*

Jung removed the stopper and sniffed. *Lemons. Oranges. Limes and moss. And perhaps a touch of rosemary ...*

"There was a woman here this morning," he said. "In the reception room with Doctor Furtwängler ..." He tipped the bottle and wet his finger end with the contents. "Would you happen to know who she was?"

"That would be Lady Quartermaine," said Kessler. "I recognized her motor car. She brought Mister Pilgrim from London yesterday."

Jung reappeared in the doorway.

Kessler was standing beside the armoire, hanging up the tweed jacket. There was a clothes brush in his hand.

"Quartermaine, you say?"

"Yes, sir."

"Then she must wear it, too—this scent. I could smell it on Doctor Furtwängler when he came into the hall."

Kessler turned from the armoire with a shocked expression on his face. "I don't know what you're saying, sir. The notion is inconceivable." He gave the jacket a final swipe with the brush and closed the door.

"No, no, no," said Jung, and laughed. "I'm not suggesting they embraced. Nothing of the kind. It is just that I have the nose of a bloodhound. Lady Quartermaine must have shaken Furtwängler's hand. I could smell it on his fingers."

"Well. That certainly is a talent, sir. I'm amazed."

"Do you know where Lady Quartermaine might be staying?"

"At the Hôtel Baur au Lac, sir. I heard it being said."

"Thank you."

Jung was making for the corridor.

"Doctor?"

Jung turned.

"Before you go, I think I should draw your attention ..." Kessler seemed embarrassed. "There's another little irregularity regarding Mister Pilgrim, sir. I mean—besides his not speaking and his trying to kill himself ..."

"What is that?"

"There's a mark on him, sir. On his backside ..."

"His buttocks, you mean?"

"No, sir. Right between the shoulder blades."

"What sort of mark?"

"Not unlike a tattoo. You've seen a tattoo, I suppose. I mention it, because the sight of it made me wonder, had Mister Pilgrim been to sea. You know how sailors are—drawings all over, some of them."

"What does it show, this tattoo?"

"A butterfly, sir. And one other thing."

"Yes?"

"It is all one colour, Doctor. Red, you see. Most unusual. It has the look of pin pricks—just like someone had pricked it out on Mister Pilgrim's back with a needle or a pin. *Dot—dot. Dot—dot. Dot—dot—dot.* You see? Very odd. Not your normal everyday naval tattoo. I just thought you should know. He tried to hide it. Tried to hurry into his shirt before I got to him. But I saw it, nevertheless, in the mirror plain as day. It made me wonder ..."

"Yes?"

"Well, it made me wonder if maybe it was some kind of—I don't know—insignia. Like he belonged to some kind of club or secret society. That sort of thing. A sign or a signal for others of his kind."

"Thank you, Kessler. All very interesting."

"Yes, sir. Same as a person might say that Mister Pilgrim himself is all very interesting. Not your average lunatic, so to speak. If you know what I mean."

"Yes. Indeed I do. Good morning."

"Good morning, Doctor."

When Jung had gone and shut the door behind him, Kessler went back to the bed and lifted up Pilgrim's shirt—stretching its arms as he had before and holding it out to the sunlight streaming through the windows.

So, angels smell of lemons, do they. Well, well, well. They smell of lemons—and where their wings are fixed, God marks it with a butter-fly—right between the shoulder blades.

Spreading the arms, he watched the wavering sunlight through their folds. And closed—and opened them. And closed—and opened them again—and then again—in angel flight.

12

Kessler, his mother and his sister Elvire lived in a tall narrow house halfway down the slope between the Clinic and the River Limmat. He was the only son in a family that otherwise boasted six daughters, five of whom had been successfully married. The sixth, Elvire, had been chosen to see her parents through to death—to keep house for them, to run their errands and to act, in his early years, as Johannes Kessler's nursemaid.

They were poor. Both parents had worked outside the home— Johannes, Senior, in the flour mill, Frau Eda as cook for a lawyer who happened to be a bachelor—a certain Herr Munster. His unmarried status posed no threat, however. Frau Eda would not have tolerated the most understated of advances. She had ambitions for her children and not a hint of scandal would touch them. They would achieve a place in the middle class, which her parents had spent their lives achieving before them.

Her children's greatest asset had been her own dowry—the house they lived in, a gift from her dying father. If not for the house, which sat at the centre of a middle-class district, they would have been forced to live at the furthest reaches of the city, where the poor were crowded in hovels and tenements packed in amongst the mills and factories. It was to this place that Johannes, Senior, had to make his way each day, and from which, each day, he returned.

Young Kessler's earliest memories were of his father seated alone of an evening, staring exhausted above a bowl of soup, seeing nothing, saying nothing, only lifting a spoon to his mouth and letting it descend until the bowl was empty. At which point Elvire would remove the spoon from his hand and put a fork in its place. Sausage, cabbage and potatoes followed—eaten blankly between mouthfuls of pale beer and sops of bread.

Meanwhile, the child Johannes sat in his high-chair, moving his fingers over a plate of mash made up of whatever his father was given to eat each evening—whether sausage, cabbage and potato, or potato, sausage and cabbage. It was their only diet— though, to her credit, Elvire tried to vary the modes of cooking—sometimes broiling, sometimes baking, sometimes braising the food.

What Johannes saw of his father was two black eyes, two dark nostrils and the gaping pit of a mouth in the oval of a flour-white face, beneath a fall of hair that was dark where his father's cap had been and white where it had not. Shoulders drooping, elbows on the table, minimal, almost mechanical movements— a man-sized wind-up father-doll sitting amongst his brood—a doll whose springs were winding down even as its children watched—until, each evening, it stopped and simply sat there while the dishes, knives, forks and spoons were removed from around it. Then it rose and went away to its bed. No one spoke. Not ever. It was a house of endless fatigue and silence.

In those days, Frau Eda did not come home until Johannes himself had long been in his own bed. He only ever saw his mother in the mornings—once again from the vantage point of his high-chair—while she drank her last cup of coffee, rolled down her sleeves, pulled on her coat and went beyond his view into the world of someone else's house, where she spent the day in someone else's kitchen.

When Johannes was six, his father's sleeve got caught in one of the mill-wheels and, there being no one by to save him, he was drawn in amongst the cogs and crushed to death. At the time, the boy was told none of this, only that his father had gone away and would not return.

Later, at school, he was told the truth by an older boy whose father had also worked at the flour mill. For a very long while, young Kessler said nothing to his mother or to his sisters about what he knew. When he was eleven—or perhaps when he was twelve—he began to ask questions it had never occurred to him to ask before. *Where, when he left, did Father go?* And: *why did he go away alone when he could have taken us with him?* And: *why has he never written? Why has he never come back?*

The answers to these questions were always the same. *He went away to join his mother and father ... to stay with his brothers in Argentina ... he had no money to take us with him ... there is no post from South America ...*

One lie compounded the last and the one that followed. His mother had already grieved and put her grief behind her. A lie was easiest—and even telling it, she could partially believe it herself. She could daydream her husband's life in Argentina. She could call the brothers back into her mind and in their company recreate the sunny days when she and her husband had been young and there was no foreboding. To call him dead at this late date was to take a step towards her own death she was not prepared to take, and even when young Johannes was as old as sixteen, she had still not declared herself a widow.

As for Elvire, she had been glad of her father's death. The burden of his life had overwhelmed and exhausted her. When he died, she had been only fourteen and had borne his needs since she was nine—all his meals, laundry, bathwater and errands and his lack of any acknowledgement of what she did. Not that she had hated him. That, she knew, would be unjust, given that she was aware of the circumstances of his poverty— how little work there was in the world they inhabited and how little return there was when the work was done. Still, she was glad of his absence. She need only thereafter see to her brother's survival and her own, their mother then being an almost invisible presence, so little was ever seen of her.

Frau Eda had a cage of finches which sang to her in the mornings before she left the house to take up her duties in Herr Munster's kitchen. Every day began with the removal of their night-cloth and every day ended with its replacement.

One day, when young Johannes was not quite sixteen, Frau Eda returned from the lawyer's house to discover the bird cage was empty.

Elvire and Johannes were questioned. Both denied having any knowledge of how the birds might have escaped.

Two days later, Elvire opened a drawer in Johannes's bureau in order to deposit some freshly laundered shirts. The drawer was filled with wings. Finch wings.

Horror-stricken, she sat on her brother's bed. It was noon. He would soon return from school and want his lunch.

Rising, she closed the drawer and went downstairs.

While Johannes was seated at table, his face leaning down towards his plate of soup, she watched him—thinking how like his father he had become: the same silent presence, the same hidden mind and nothing said and nothing indicated but the slow slaking of thirst and stilling of hunger.

"Do you know what became of mother's finches?" she asked him, pulling out a chair and sitting opposite him as he ate.

"No. Do you?"

"Yes. I think so."

"Oh? And what might that be?"

"I think you killed them."

For a moment only, he sat still—the spoon just emptied poised above the dish. Then he narrowed his eyes and squinted at her before he spoke—and when he did, his voice was colourless and his words without inflection.

"Oh, that," he said. "I did that day before yesterday."

He then went back to eating.

Soup sounds.

And then: "do you mean to tell her?"

"No. Of course not."

"Am I to tell her?"

"No. No one is to tell her. All we need to say is: *they went away*. She'll understand."

Elvire stood up and turned her back to him. She said nothing more. She wanted to leave the room, but could not. It was impossible to move, she was so afraid.

"I kept the wings," Johannes said.

"I know you did."

"In all my life, I've never seen anything so pretty. Wouldn't you agree?"

Elvire said nothing.

"I'm starting a collection," Johannes went on—barely pausing to swallow his soup between sentences, all but choking on his words—and the words still monotonic, clocklike in their precision. "I like the feel of the feathers—and the way they lie just so ... you know? One lying down beneath the other ... all in a row ... and when you spread them out they make a perfect fan ... just like those Spanish ladies hold in the magazines ... just like a Spanish dancer holds ..."

"Stop it."

"What?"

"Stop it!"

"Stop what?"

"Speaking—talking—saying those horrible things. Stop it!"

"But it isn't horrible. Why call it horrible? Look. Look, Elvire. Look. Turn around and look. I've got another one right here."

Terrified, she turned.

Johannes, dead-faced, sat there, his plate emptied, his spoon laid aside—and in his hand a freshly killed bird.

Elvire stared at him.

Clearly—all too clearly—he was mad.

She reached out her hand and took the bird—it was a young pigeon—and spoke to Johannes quietly.

"I will keep it for you. Yes? You can't want to take it with you back to school. The other boys would harm it. They wouldn't let you keep it."

He said nothing.

When he had gone, Elvire put the pigeon in the stove and burned it.

By the time Johannes returned at five o'clock, Frau Eda was there and, with her, a doctor from the Burghölzli Clinic. Standing at the curb was the famous Yellow Wagon which would take Johannes away.

By the time three years had passed, Johannes Kessler was pronounced cured. What emerged from the Burghölzli wards was a young man whose obsessive violence had been completely turned around. Over time, his gentleness towards his fellow patients had earned him not only the respect of his minders but also the interest of the staff psychiatrists. It would not be the first time that an ex-patient was seen to have potential as a Clinic employee.

When the offer was made to him—to take the training that would allow him to be hired as an orderly—Johannes accepted calmly and gratefully. He had come to be more at peace in the Clinic than anywhere, and although—on the advice of his doctors—he returned to live with his mother and sister, he continued to feel that his true home was the Burghölzli.

For one thing, there were blanks in his memory of the pre-Clinic times. Whole years had taken flight and winged their way out of his mind—including the days of the killing of the birds. All that remained of his obsession was an abiding sense of wonder at the beauty of flying creatures.

Wings. Anything with wings. The very image of wings. Kessler's world was made magical by the flight of birds, of butterflies ... and—most marvellous of all—of angels.

13

Two days after Pilgrim had been taken to the Infirmary, Jung was seated opposite Lady Quartermaine in the dining-room of the Hôtel Baur au Lac.

There was an orchestra. There were palm trees. There was a vaulted roof and windows twelve feet high, which gave a view of lake and mountains.

Jung had often eaten here before. It was the purview, almost exclusively, of the wealthy and titled families who came to Zürich to be with their relatives or friends who were patients at the Clinic.

In the early years of their friendship, before the current schism had begun to do its work, Freud had often sat with him here in one of the private corners, discussing his views on the subject of schizophrenia and praising Jung to the heavens for his exploration of *this treacherous disease*.

This treacherous disease had become a verbal talisman to Jung— almost a mantra. He never heard the words in his mind without the sound of Freud's voice in his ear. Nothing so apt or succinct could be imagined as defining schizophrenia—the mind betrayed by images beyond its control and forced to obey the instructions of strangers who refused to identify themselves.

"It is your supposition, I assume, Doctor Jung, that my friend Mister Pilgrim suffers from this malady. Am I correct?"

Sybil Quartermaine was seated opposite Jung at a table he would later describe in his notes as *occupying centre stage*, quite the opposite of where he used to sit with Freud. Lady Quartermaine was dressed entirely in violet and shades of blue. Her hat was modest in size and had no veil. She did, however, wear dark glasses, a mark of interest to the other diners.

"Physically, my eyes have never been able to tolerate winter light," she told him, "even though I am in love with it. Winter light is a special joy and I have no words to describe its effect on me, Doctor Jung. Perhaps the word *revivifying* comes close. Perhaps *restorative*—perhaps *recuperative* ... But none of these quite tells the tale. I believe that something in a person dies, come winter—almost as though we were meant to hibernate in the fashion of certain animal species. But here, with all these windows and all that snow, the light—for all that I love it—is somewhat overpowering. By mid-afternoon, I shall be sick with its effect on my eyes and retire to a darkened room. Nonetheless, I worship it. The light."

"Indeed, I have a passion for it myself," said Jung.

"Mister Pilgrim, on the other hand, is a child of darkness."

Jung sat back. What Lady Quartermaine had said was mystifying. It could be construed too many ways. Satan himself—or Satan's progeny? It seemed unlikely that either was intended. But Jung, being the child of a stark-minded pastor of the Church, could not shake the image. Yet, surely Pilgrim's dilemma had nothing to do with Satan. With darkness, yes—but evil, never. He was too poignant for evil—too much in need.

"Perhaps you had best explain what you mean, madam, by a child of darkness," he said, attempting to smile.

"I will, if I'm able," Sybil replied. Then she said: "you have been told how we met? And when—Mister Pilgrim and I?"

"Yes. Beneath a tree when you were twelve and he was eighteen."

"Exactly so. Well, the darkness I refer to is the time before that meeting. Eighteen years unaccounted for, in which he claims to have lived—if at all—in a fog; in a mist; in what he once described himself as a permanent twilight. In other words, a kind of darkness."

"What about his family?"

"He has spoken of parents—a mother, a father—and of some

kind of shadowy childhood. But no details. Somehow, to Pilgrim, that was all 'the past.'"

"The past?"

"Yes. To my knowledge, since the day I found him lying there, he has never seen or heard from any of his family. And yet, he lives by means of an inheritance of some weight. He lacks for nothing—though he labours little. Writing, of course, is labour. But his writing, however notable, could hardly afford him the life he leads and the style in which he leads it."

"And no explanation of this unknown family?"

"None whatsoever. Except for one thing. He did once mention that before he woke beneath that tree in my garden, there had been a significant dream. But he has never told me what it was he dreamt. Only that the dream preceded his *arrival at consciousness*. Those are his very words. One day, he arrived at consciousness."

"I see."

"And so ... You believe my friend is—I want to be correct—is the word *schizophrenic*? Have I got the notion of it? Is that what you believe?"

"When I know nothing, Lady Quartermaine, I believe nothing," Jung said, and smiled.

"A clever answer, Doctor—but you avoid me."

"It is not intentional. You must remember, madam, I have barely had time to acquaint myself with your friend's condition."

"It is not a condition," Sybil said, placing her knife on the left-hand side of her service plate. "It is not a disease that has captured him." She moved her fork to the right and slapped it down as a kind of punctuation mark. She was not prepared as yet to explain her vehemence.

An entrée of oysters arrived.

They were displayed on a platter of ice, with cuts of lemon in their midst. There was also a vinaigrette and squares of Melba toast.

"You care for oysters, Doctor Jung? I could live on them."

Sybil moved the platter into a more advantageous position. "If you don't begin, I shall have them all."

"I hope not. I am quite partial."

Each of them took up a shell and, having filled its basin with lemon juice and vinaigrette, loosened its contents and drank.

"Divine!"

"Indeed."

For a moment they ate in silence, wielding protective napkins, digging with their forks at the roots of the oysters—drinking down each one as if it was the last.

"A dozen is not enough," Sybil said. "But it will have to do. I have ordered us *riz de veau*. My spies have told me they are excellent here."

"They are—and happen to be a particular favourite of mine."

"Yes, yes. I knew that."

For the first time since being seated, Jung felt distinctly uncomfortable. *Is there nothing this woman has not exposed to research?*

"I've been reading your book, Doctor Jung. *The Psychology of Dementia Praecox*. I have it with me, in fact, but will not embarrass you by displaying it. Someone anonymous had it left for me only yesterday morning—supposing, I suspect, that it would interest me—which it does. People can be so kind, can't they—leaving little gifts of significance for one to peruse."

"I trust you understand, Lady Quartermaine, my book is not for amateurs," Jung told her. "It was written by one psychologist for others—not for the layman."

"Nonetheless, I seem to be getting on with it quite well."

Here, Sybil reached into her bag and produced a notebook bound in soft Venetian leather. It was green, embossed with gold. Its binding contained a pencil with a thin gold chain.

As the platter of emptied shells was being removed, Lady Quartermaine adjusted her dark glasses, sipped at her wine and consulted her notebook. Jung watched her every move, entranced by her precision and the grace with which she wielded it.

"You write at some length on the subject of *disintegration*," she said, "as observed in your patients here at the Clinic."

"Yes. It is my belief that people suffering from schizophrenia are in fact suffering a disintegration of personality."

"*Fragmentation*, you call it."

"Yes."

"*Fragments like pieces of glass* is one of your phrases."

"Yes."

"*Fragments ... Fragmentary ... fragmentation. A disintegration of personality*, as you say. This is what you believe has happened to Mister Pilgrim?"

"I believe it is a possibility."

"A strong possibility?"

"I would say so, yes."

"What in Mister Pilgrim's behaviour makes you think so? I'm interested."

"His aloofness from reality. His refusal to make contact."

"His silence?"

"Yes."

Jung had thought it best not to tell Lady Quartermaine about the second suicide attempt. Nor the fact that Pilgrim had spoken. Once he did so, she would ask him what had been said and he was not prepared to divulge that yet. In time, yes—but not now. Nor, of course, had he told her of Furtwängler's decree that Pilgrim was *off limits*. In fact, neither had he informed Furtwängler that he was taking his luncheon with Sybil Quartermaine. It had come about at her instigation, not his own. On hearing that Jung was in practice at the Clinic, and knowing of him by reputation, she had taken it upon herself to issue the invitation only that morning.

The *riz de veau* arrived and were served by two young waiters under supervision of the Maître d'.

As the vegetable dishes were uncovered and displayed, Sybil said: "did I order spinach?"

"Yes, my Lady. Expressly. Spinach and parsnips."

"Good. I'd forgotten the spinach. And the wine? The white was excellent. And the red?"

"It is here, my Lady. The claret, just as you requested."

"So." Sybil turned to Jung. "I hope you don't mind. I always prefer a dry wine with sweetbreads."

"It sounds just right."

Sybil nodded at the attendants.

The waiters departed and, having decanted and poured the red wine, the Maître d' followed them. When they had gone, Sybil said: "I'm always relieved when a restaurant has no wine steward. It saves having to argue about one's choices."

She watched as Jung took the first forkful of *riz de veau*.

"They are good?"

"Excellent."

"I'm so pleased. When one has guests in a foreign restaurant, one is never sure ..."

"You need have no fear. Eat and be happy."

She did—and she was.

"Delicious. Delicious. Utterly superb."

She has so many childlike qualities, Jung was thinking. Conniving one minute, innocent the next. Charming, manipulative, endearing and dangerous. Just like a clever child who has learned the ways of the adult world and performs them with consummate skill without giving up an iota of its nursery privileges.

"You said, Lady Quartermaine, that it is not a condition, not a disease that has captured him. Mister Pilgrim."

"Yes. I said that—and I believe it."

"On what basis?"

"I have known him so well for so long. I am familiar, I believe, as anyone can be with his nature. The nature of his passions—the nature of his fears. His foibles, talents, humours—good and bad—and his dearness ... the sadness in him, if you like. His longing to be delivered from the necessity of self. Do you follow me?"

"Possibly."

Sybil looked away from Jung towards the mountains beyond

the window. Her knife and fork were still in hand, though clearly, for the moment, she had forgotten them. "There is no condition that can claim him, Doctor—no mere condition, no mere disease. It's not permissible. I will not allow it."

The statement was, of course, preposterous—but Lady Quartermaine had made it with such simplicity that Jung was moved by her belief in it. It had been confided, he imagined, in the same tone and manner as Saints confide their visions to their confessors—when to walk with God is one thing, but to say one does is another.

The spell was broken when Jung gave a cough and was forced to reach for his water glass.

"Is everyone mad, do you think?" Sybil asked, recovering her poise. "One way or another, do you think it could be so?"

Jung gave one of his shrugs and said: "there are degrees of madness, of course. I have found some traces of it in myself, I do confess." He waved his hand. "But madness is a crafty beast and cannot be caught with theories. Over time, I have learned not only to be distrusting of theories, but to actively oppose them. Facts are what matter. And the facts regarding each individual's madness are all we have. General theories regarding madness merely get in the way of discovering its true nature in each patient, one by one by one. My own madness is quantified by parentheses—just as all madness is. And because of that, I have learned not only to deal with it, but to live with it. And most importantly, as any person must, to function in its presence. It is mine—my own and only mine. What has happened, in Mister Pilgrim's case, is that he can no longer function—and whether this is because he is mad or for some other reason is still to be revealed."

"I am frightened for him."

"That is perfectly understandable."

"I don't want him harmed."

"He will not be harmed." Jung laughed. "How could he be?

"There is harm and there is harm, Doctor Jung. You know

that. I will tell you—and I tell you with regret—that I do not like Doctor Furtwängler. I do not trust his judgement, and to be frank, I did not appreciate his manner."

Jung gave another wave of his hand. There was nothing he could say that would not sound treacherous.

"I did not like the feeling I had from him that he did not believe what I told him."

"There, I think you are wrong, Lady Quartermaine. Doctor Furtwängler does believe what you have told him."

"Be that as it may, I do not trust him. I do not trust his judgement. He was given the highest possible recommendation—but still, I do not trust him. He smiles too much. He smiles at the wrong moments. He smiles without pleasure. He smiles without feeling. He smiles without consideration. I hate ingratiation. It unnerves me and I lose all sense of trust. And not to trust one's doctor—or the doctor in charge of your dearest friend—is intolerable."

Sybil set down her knife and fork and sat back in her chair.

"I am tired," she said. "Tired and not a little lost in most of this. Psychiatry, Doctor Jung, is a complete mystery to me. But if it holds the answer to Mister Pilgrim's survival, then I must abide with it until he is safely delivered."

A silence fell between them which Jung dared not break.

Then Sybil spoke again.

"I realize it would not be proper to have Doctor Furtwängler removed from this case. Perhaps I have overreacted to his manner. Too much smiling—if you get my drift—becomes almost villainous."

Jung was forced to repress his own smile. He knew Josef Furtwängler's curried charms only too well.

"But I must ask—I am determined to ask—would you agree to take Mister Pilgrim on as your patient, Doctor Jung? I like what you have said, though some of it does not beguile me. Nonetheless, I sense a creative attitude in your response to Mister Pilgrim, and in my opinion, that is what he requires above all else. Someone who will take him as he is without assigning a label and pushing him into a corner."

Jung looked down at his plate. He had not finished its contents, but wanted no more. He laid his utensils aside and pressed his napkin to his lips, spreading it afterwards in his lap. Then he said: "I would like to accept your offer, Lady Quartermaine, but I fear I must decline."

"Decline? But you can't decline. I forbid it."

"Nonetheless, Lady Quartermaine, against my own wishes, I must say no."

He then explained—without too much emphasis on Josef Furtwängler's often misguided judgement—that it was Furtwängler's choice to work alone on *the Pilgrim case* and that *he has a particular quarrel with my methods* ...

He said more. He talked, without using names, about the Countess Blavinskeya—about the Dog-man, about the others—but he stressed the fact that *one can always be wrong*—that *one can misread a case*—that *one is fallible*. He told of the profound interest he had in *Mister Pilgrim's dilemma*—et cetera—et cetera—et cetera, until Sybil was utterly charmed and convinced that only Doctor Jung could help her friend and that, if he would not speak to Doctor Bleuler in his own behalf, she would. And she would speak severely to Doctor Furtwängler.

"In that case," said Jung, "I thank you—and I will do—in every way—the very best I can."

"We are well met," said Sybil. She raised her glass. "And on the strength of our meeting, let us drink to our absent friend."

"Our absent friend."

As if on cue, the orchestra broke into *Tales From the Vienna Woods*.

"Oh, perfect, perfect day!" Sybil cried. "Your acceptance! This wine! A waltz! And next, profiteroles!"

Watching her wave a hand in the direction of the Maître d', Jung thought: *and so—the child returns triumphant from her*

mission amongst the Doctors, and will now be offered the crowning
glory of her victory feast. A chocolate sweet.

As for himself, he drank a private toast to the concierge of the
Hôtel Baur au Lac, who yesterday morning had received from
Jung's own hands a slim volume in a plain brown envelope for
delivery to the Marchioness of Quartermaine, "with the compli-
ments of a stranger." His anonymity had cost him three francs.

14

Dora Henkel was leading the Countess Tatiana Blavinskeya along the corridor towards the elevator. She did this every other day. They were on their way to the lower reaches of the building where the Countess would be treated to a course of hydrotherapeutic treatments which were intended to soothe her nerves and relieve her tension.

Dora Henkel enjoyed Tatiana Blavinskeya's company. She had been in love with her from the moment of her arrival and wanted never to leave her, always to be by her side.

The Countess had said: "if you want to come to the Moon, you must have a visa. A diplomatic passport."

Dora was forced to admit she had neither.

"Well, then," the Countess informed her, "that's the end of it. No one is allowed to visit the Moon who has not a diplomatic passport or at least one parent who was born there."

Dora's parents had both been born—as she had been, herself—in the village of Kirschenblumen, on the shores of the Zürichsee. Any clear night, Kirschenblumen was visible—just as the Moon was visible—its lights like frozen crystals in the distance.

The Moon had always fascinated Dora. Even as a child she had worshipped it, sensing in its feminine glow the portents of a possible love affair. That her passion for the Moon was destined to be thwarted did not occur to her at the age of six. She had grown up trusting that anything was possible so long as you believed. Time, of course, was to prove that most beliefs are thwarted by reality. A forced diet of it, in Dora's case.

Her mother, for instance, had informed her at the age of eight that *a person cannot expect to have a successful love affair with a cat.*

Nor, at fourteen, with a horse—nor, at eighteen, with Queen Alexandra. These imagined affairs were like a plague and a constant torment—cats, horses, Queens, Greek goddesses, the Lorelei, the Moon ...

And now, there was the Countess Tatiana Blavinskeya, a genuine expatriate from the Moon. Dora knew it was not the truth, but it gave her pleasure even to pretend that she believed.

This morning, the Countess was wearing a flowing, moon-blue robe and moon-blue slippers. In her hair, there was a moon-blue ribbon ... Beneath the robe, her body was clothed in creamy lingerie, made especially for her in Paris. Every piece of it bore her monogram: *T.S.B.*

As the elevator descended, Tatiana Sergeyevna Blavinskeya drew her robe about her, preparing to make her exit. It was as though the little cage of the elevator was a miniature stage—and its operator a stage manager. She had still not spoken. Perhaps the hydrotherapy would help. At least it could help her unclench her toes and fingers, and perhaps she would even at last be able to close her eyes.

There were crystal chandeliers in the hallway to which she had descended with Dora Henkel, and stepping out onto the carpeted marble floor, the Countess raised her arm as if to protect herself from attack. The chandeliers might be stars—and the stars were her enemies.

Knowing this, Dora hurried her forward towards the glass doors whose glistening surfaces were hatched with wrought-iron arabesques. "Come," she said. "We must hurry."

Beyond the doors, the sound and smell of water was universal. Cubicles lined a dimly lit corridor, each of the cubicles a dressing-room with mirrors and hooks, hairbrushes and combs and ribbons for repairing any damage done to one's coiffure in the baths. Also, in each cubicle, a chaise longue for the patient and a straight-backed chair for the attendant orderly or nurse.

Number ten was free and Dora stood back to let Blavinskeya enter. Once inside, with the door closed, Dora proceeded to remove the lingerie, item by item. Each was neatly folded or suspended from a hook and the Countess was then returned to her robe.

In other psychiatric establishments and spas, a bathing costume was normally provided for those who entered the waters. But here, the patients took their treatments naked. Large white winding sheets and an abundance of bath towels were provided for modesty's sake as well as to keep the bathers from catching a chill.

Not that a chill was likely.

The world which Dora and Blavinskeya were about to enter at the far end of the corridor was a misted world of humid tubs and pools, of steam rooms, sauna baths and fountains of warm water.

Dora loved it here and wished on every occasion when she brought her patients for their treatments that she too could enter the waters wearing only her skin. She had never understood how, in other hydrotherapy centres, the use of bathing costumes was tolerated. They were so confining—so brutally binding and so itchy that they added to, rather than subtracted from the patients' nervous disorders. *They might as well force them to bathe in strait-jackets*, was Dora's opinion.

Beyond the next set of doors, they entered a vast and almost cavernous area, populated by ghostly sheeted figures moving through misted cones of light with nothing heard but the gentle whispers of slippered feet and the plash of falling water. Nothing, that is, except the sound of one ghost singing.

The singer sang at some distance, though the song was carried crystal clear by the moistened air and its lack of echoes. There were no words—simply a lilting, liquid line of melody.

Countess Blavinskeya held out her hand to Dora Henkel as though she were accepting an offer to dance, but otherwise, she remained stock still. *I am lost*, she seemed to say. *Is this a ball-room? Am I being courted? I don't know who you are.*

It was a woman singing.

Mezzo—mezzo—mezzo-soprano!

Did you know the Moon is a mezzo-soprano?

As the silver stream of sound poured through the cellars, others in the steam paused to listen.

Dora turned to look at Blavinskeya.

How beautiful she is, she thought, *with her pale pink hair and her childlike eyes. If only—oh, if only ...*

The song was drawing to its close, the strains of it fading into the mist—until one final note hung in the air, and was gone, as if dissolved.

Tatiana let go of Dora's hand.

Beside them and before them, others were turning away.

If only there was music always, Dora thought, *there would be no need to speak.*

Tatiana blinked. She stood as if waiting for permission to move.

Dora led her forward. She was looking for an empty tub, but everywhere she looked the tubs were occupied. Orderlies and nurses stood or sat beside their patients, turning on taps and wielding hoses as though they stood and sat in gardens, watering wilted flowers in the hopes of bringing them back to life.

At last, they came to an empty tub and Dora planted herself behind the Countess, knowing there would be a moment of panic before her patient could be persuaded to disrobe and climb down into the depths.

The tubs were four feet deep and lined with Connemara from Ireland, its marbled streaks and curlicues green as any seaweed flowing in a tidal pool. The waters here were salted and softened, giving off Atlantic vapours and shining with phosphorescence. The whole effect was of standing on a rocky shore on a warm and misted day.

There are no waters on the Moon, the Countess had said. *No waters—no tides—nor anything but dust and ashes. We bathe in ashes!* she had cried triumphantly. *We bathe in ashes and powder our bodies with dust!*

Dora had wondered how they slaked their thirst.

There is no thirst, the Countess had told her. *No thirst, no hunger, nothing human. No wants. No desires. No yearning. Nothing. We are free.*

How sad that must be, to have no yearning, Dora had replied. You must want *something*.

Never. Nothing. Only to dance. To float beyond the pull of gravity.

There must be a great deal of happiness there if you want so much to go back.

The Countess had turned away at that, but only for the briefest moment.

Dora placed her hands on Blavinskeya's shoulders. It was time to remove the robe and lead her to the steps which descended into the water.

"Undo," Dora said.

Obedient and uncomplaining as a child, the Countess undid the cord and buttons of her robe and moved away from Dora. Dora folded the robe on her arm and watched the Moon Lady climb down the steps.

Dora moved forward, one hand ready to steady the Countess should she fall. The feet were tiny, arched and supple—the legs and arms were plump and round—a dancer's arms and legs— and the buttocks were firm as porcelain moons. The breasts ... Dora closed her eyes. She could not bear to think of them.

Blavinskeya descended into the water with a sigh.

Watching her, Dora sat on the edge of the tub. Below her, the Countess was seated on a built-in bench with her arms spread wide and her head thrown back, eyes closed, lips parted—almost as though she expected to be embraced.

It was impossible. To love someone and not be able to kiss, to touch, to embrace.

Impossible—and yet, endurable.

15

Pilgrim was seated in a Bath chair with a tartan rug across his knees. He was dressed in blue pyjamas, a grey hospital robe, white stockings and chamois slippers lined with fleece. His wrists were bound with surgical gauze and lay exposed in his lap—a reminder of his brief stay in the Infirmary.

Kessler had taken him, under Doctor Furtwängler's instructions, to the glassed-in sun porch which overlooked the gardens. In the far distance beyond the trees, the mountains on the far side of the Zürichsee could be seen, but not the lake itself. Now he sat in perfect silence, expressionless and seemingly without emotion. The mountains meant nothing. The sky meant nothing. The sun, beyond its zenith and deep in its decline, was a stranger to him. He had understood it, once, and even considered it his friend, but now it lacked a name and could not be identified.

My wrists hurt.

Ached.

He did not know why.

He remembered nothing.

Bandages.

White.

Snow ...?

He knew the word for *snow* and recognized its presence beyond the windows.

He also knew the words for *mountain* and for *window*. But not the words for *city—buildings—houses—people*.

Men and women?

Perhaps.

There were other patients—one or two in tall-backed

wheelchairs, others leaning against the wall or by the windows. They seemed to Pilgrim not unlike the figures on a chessboard.

Chessboard.

Has the game commenced?

Game.

This is a game. Someone will move me. A hand will descend.

Fingers.

I will be brooded over.

Someone will cough.

The fingers will touch me. Almost lift me. But not.

They will decide I am safer where I am.

Pilgrim looked about him at the others.

Three pawns, one Bishop, two Knights, a King and Queen.

The King and Queen were separated, the Queen alone and vulnerable, the King protected by his troops, who formed a wall. *White.*

White King, White pawns, White Queen.

Where were all the black pieces? None was visible—all were white. And when would his opponent make the next move?

Doctor Jung came and stood behind him, lifting his finger to his lips so that Kessler would not speak.

Kessler nodded and stepped aside.

Jung came forward on the diagonal, moving to Pilgrim's right, nodding and mouthing words of greeting at various familiar attendants who were standing near their patients.

It was four o'clock.

The sun was moving towards its final position before descending behind the mountains. A low, winter sun, with a curious, almost midsummer redness to it. Orange.

There's an orange out there, Pilgrim thought. *Perhaps it's part of the game. A player. Or a manipulator. God.*

A god.

That was it.

God was a ball of fire in the …

What? What? What? Oh, what is it called?

Jung could now see Pilgrim fully in profile. He said nothing. He watched.

Pilgrim shifted his hands. His wrists had stiffened.

They'd been frozen in the snow.

They will die.

Part of me will die.

How wonderful ...

Jung took note of the fact that Pilgrim's lips had parted, but saw no words being formed.

Twilight. The best of times. The time between.

Jung thought this in Pilgrim's behalf, remembering what Lady Quartermaine had said about the *permanent twilight* of his first eighteen years.

Perhaps there had been no thoughts of suicide then. It seemed, from what Jung had gleaned from his long study of schizophrenia, that its onslaught most often took place at the age of seventeen or eighteen. Nineteen, perhaps, or twenty.

Had Pilgrim lived so long in the shadow of this disease? It seemed impossible—no one could survive that long without detection. He must now be fifty or fifty-one years old. No. The onslaught—if, indeed, there had been one—must have come later—and if so, then it was most unusual, given the norm.

But something certainly had happened when Pilgrim was eighteen. A trauma of some kind—an accident—a sudden death—a disease—the violent breaking of a relationship. Something. And that trauma, whatever it was, had been the progenitor of his present loss of self-possession. And the loss of self-possession, whatever else it was—whether an illness or not—was certainly a *condition*.

There it was again—Lady Quartermaine's *bête noire*—the unacceptable suggestion that Mister Pilgrim was ill.

But he was.

Jung knew that for a certainty.

The man in the Bath chair now under scrutiny could not be anything less than ill. No mere momentary depression or despair had thrown him into this state. His posture alone belied that possibility, given his rigid back and neck, given his motionless feet that might just as well have been shackled—and the stiff, automatonic movements of his hands.

Jung made his way towards the windows, where he stood with his back to the light and was thus unrecognizable. The light, however, was streaming over Pilgrim in his chair. He might have been the stone-carved figure of a king. His hawk's nose, his wide staring eyes, the shock of his hair where it touched his brow and the mouth with its lips so eager to speak and yet, unable.

Jung nodded at Kessler, giving the signal that Pilgrim should be taken to his rooms.

As Kessler kicked the brake and began to move the chair, Pilgrim cried aloud—or thought he did: NO, DON'T! and pointed at the sun. HE HAS NOT DIED YET!

But all was silent; not a sound, excepting the mouselike whispers of the turning wheels as Kessler pushed his patient back towards the dark.

16

The Countess Blavinskeya lay back in her bath. Her feet, gnarled and ruined by dance, were floating way, way off in the mist. Once such tiny, perfect feet. Her mother had always said so. And her father. And her brother.

Alexei.

He put his hands beneath the covers and held my feet in his icy fingers, pressing his thumbs into my soles and whispering: round and round and round we go and where we will stop, no one can know.

A long, long while ago.

Was it?

Yes. A long, long while.

It doesn't seem so. I can still feel the cold of his fingers.

You were just twelve years old.

Twelve? I don't remember. I do remember I was a dancer. That I know.

Yes. And a good one. Even when you were ten, everyone said you would become a great ballerina.

Yes—and I did.

Tatiana could feel the aureole of her hair spreading out around her shoulders, stranding down to her breasts, her nipples rising to its touch. Dora Henkel had told her not to untie the ribbons, but Tatiana had turned away and floated out of reach.

There was salt in the water. *A healing agent,* according to the therapist, and a *relaxant*—a word that Dora had not encountered before. *It simulates weightlessness,* the therapist had said. *This in itself encourages relaxation.*

Certainly, the Countess looked less tense than she had—sleepy and pendent in her Sargasso Sea of hair. Dora sat back and smiled.

According to Doctor Furtwängler, Blavinskeya had been a dancer at first in St. Petersburg, and after with Diaghilev's Ballets Russes. But something had happened—the Doctor would not say what—and her career had been ended some months after her marriage to the Count Blavinsky. That same year, she had been elevated to the rank of ballerina. Choreography for a new ballet had been created for her by Fokine. Music had been composed by Stravinsky. Work had even begun on sets and costume designs, but something ...

Something had happened.

Something had happened and Tatiana Blavinskeya had gone to live on the Moon. She had gone, she said, to seek her mother there. *My mother—Selene, Goddess of the Moon.*

The gods themselves were in love with Selene. All the gods. But she fell in love with a man—a mortal—and was banished from her kingdom. She and her mortal lover were married *in the presence of the Tzar of Russia!* So the Countess said. And in time, they had two children: Alexei Sergeyevitch and Tatiana Sergeyevna.

At first, all was well. To hear the doctors tell it, since both Doctor Jung and Doctor Furtwängler knew her story so well, it seemed that Selene and Sergei Ivanovitch, her husband, had lived in a fairy tale.

But something—something had happened.

Something, but no one knew what.

Doctor Jung insisted that the Countess knew, but would not or could not tell it. Not so, Doctor Furtwängler. Doctor Furtwängler's version of the story was that nothing had happened. She had been ill and could—and would—be cured. *There is nothing wrong with Tatiana Blavinskeya that time and patience cannot put right. No one lives on the Moon. It is impossible.*

On the Moon, Blavinskeya had told Dora Henkel, *we are weightless. That is why I love the water so. It is like going home—as if I could float all the way from here to there.*

As for her husband ...

No.

She would not discuss the subject of her marriage. There were no children. *How could there have been?* she had said enigmatically.

Count Nicolas Blavinsky was dead. Someone had killed him—perhaps, it was rumoured, her father.

Tatiana parted her lips and drew a strand of her hair between them. She stared out vacantly into the steam, but there was no one there she wanted. Everyone she wanted had disappeared. Only those she did not want persisted. Her brother, her father, herself.

Alexei put his hands beneath the covers and held my feet, while someone ...

Who?

While someone watched.

Oh, what? What? What—what—WHAT?

Tatiana began to thrash in the water, biting the strands of her hair clean through.

She made a moaning sound, but no words. She began to choke.

Dora Henkel ran to the far side of the tub.

"Countess! Countess!" she hissed.

She was not allowed to raise her voice, for fear of alarming the other patients.

"Quickly," she called out, *sotto voce*. "Someone help me."

Two attendants came running—an orderly and another nurse.

The orderly climbed down into the tub and pinioned Tatiana's arms. In spite of his strength, she went on thrashing her legs and kicked at him with her heels. Still, he held on while Dora Henkel and the other nurse drew the Countess up and out of the water, where they immobilized her in a makeshift straitjacket of towels.

Tatiana pressed her head back far as her neck would let it go and howled.

"Help me! Help me! Help me! Help!"

But no one came to save her. No one. Only those already present and those already present told her: *you have no need of help. All is well. We are with you. There, there, there—be quiet.*

It was the same old story. No one could see one's enemies but oneself, and all one's enemies could see was you.

17

The next morning, Pilgrim refused to eat.

He could smell the marmalade in the dish beside his plate of toast—toast which Kessler had buttered carefully, just the way he had seen Mister Pilgrim do it: not too much and not too little, with butter all the way to the edges.

There was a teapot filled with a mixture of Lapsang Souchong and English Breakfast—Pilgrim's favourite blend, according to Lady Quartermaine's instruction.

No grapefruit—only tea and marmalade and toast.

Nothing had been touched.

When Doctor Jung arrived a half-hour later, Kessler had carried off the tray and set it on the bed.

"We won't eat," he said. "We've used the toilet with some success—we've bathed and we've brushed our teeth. I thought it best not to shave him. I thought it was not a good idea for him to see the implement just yet."

"Perhaps," said Jung. "But I shouldn't worry too much. Tomorrow, I would shave him."

"Yes, sir."

"Did he sleep?"

"Not a wink. Nor I."

"A pity. Will you be all right?"

"I wouldn't mind a nap when I've carted off these dishes. In fact, I may just eat this breakfast myself. Watching him starve, I'm famished."

"Then take it away and eat. Enjoy yourself. Relax. It's nine o'clock. Come back at noon."

"Thank you, sir."

Kessler collected the tray from the bed and left, passing into the sitting-room.

Pilgrim wore the usual pyjamas—the same grey robe—the same white stockings and chamois slippers. Someone had changed his bandages, even though no good medical reason for them persisted. They were there, in fact, only to keep the scars from falling under Pilgrim's scrutiny.

Jung stood in front of him and smiled.

"You really should sleep, you know," he said. "We all need sleep, even though, I confess, I sleep very little myself. But I couldn't possibly do without it altogether."

Pilgrim shifted his gaze.

There were pigeons on the ...

... battlements.

Pigeons on ...

... the doorstep ...

... the hearth ...

... the place beyond the ...

There. Just there. Beyond just there ...

The ...

"Mister Pilgrim?"

Pigeons.

"Can you see me?"

Yes. You are here.

"Speak, if you are able."

I am not able.

"Are you afraid of me?

What?

"Are—you—afraid—of—me?"

Of course I am. Aren't you?

"Look at me, Mister Pilgrim."

No. Pilgrim turned his attention to the pigeons on the windowsills and balcony, though he could still not identify where they were.

The battlements.

"If you can understand me, nod your head."

Nothing.

"If you can understand me, make some sign. It does not matter what it is—just make some sign."

Nothing.

"I know you can move, Mister Pilgrim. I have seen you do so. Your fingers—your feet—your head. Give me some sign. Can you understand me?"

Nothing.

"Can you hear me?"

One hand reached for the other.

"You can hear me?"

There was a toe-tap. One.

Jung searched his pockets.

"Do you smoke, Mister Pilgrim?"

Nothing.

"I hope you will not object if I indulge in a cheroot. It is a weakness, I fear, against which I have no defence. Cheroots and brandy—I think of them as food."

The box of cheroots was found and one of them extracted.

"My, my, my—oh, my! Delicious!" Jung said this while holding the chosen cheroot beneath his nose. His gaze had not left Pilgrim's face. "I could give you one, if you so desire."

Nothing.

"No? Very well ..." Jung returned the box to its pocket and found his matches.

"Fire," he said—and smiled. "Our gift from the gods," and struck.

Pilgrim moved his eyes. The flame was of interest.

Jung lit up and drew two draughts of smoke before he spoke again.

"You like cigars? Cigarettes? Do you smoke a pipe?"

Still no reply.

"I have noted that your friend Lady Quartermaine is given to cigarettes. I took my luncheon with her yesterday. She extends her regards."

The pigeons squatted in the morning light. The sun itself was still not visible.

No Sun. No God.

The sun rose every morning behind the Clinic and every day, as now, it lingered there as if to tantalize the waiting world. Its slanted rays were fingering the long wooded valley in which the Zürichsee lay out of sight, and farther off than one could calculate, the ghost of *the Jungfrau* was shrouded in sunless clouds where the valley dwindled to oblivion.

"Mister Pilgrim?"

Jung brought a chair and placed it on Pilgrim's right-hand side.

"I should like to hear your opinion of the view. So often, a person's idea of mountains depends on where he grew up. Were there mountains in your boyhood? In mine, there were—but not like these. These mountains here are wider, taller, braver than the mountains of my youth. I trust you follow me."

Pilgrim blinked.

His hands moved—each hand laid palm upward on his knees.

"I have wanted all my life to live beside the sea," Jung went on, "though the sea has never been within my range of choices. I am able, of course, to visit the sea—the ocean. Anyone can do that. But I cannot live in its proximity. The sea is a privilege I must leave to others whose work allows them daily access ..."

Jung slid a glance at Pilgrim's profile.

Pilgrim sat stolid. Still. But listening.

"My work is here. But there is water here, thank heaven—the Zürichsee—the River Limmat—the lakes and rivers all about us. Yes? Still, it is not the sea. It is not the ocean. I must be content."

Pigeons.

"Have you ever considered death by water, Mister Pilgrim? Death by drowning?"

Yes.

"In dreams, I have drowned. But on the other hand, I have died many ways in dreams. As I am sure we all have. Many ways."

Do you ever kill yourself in your dreams, Doctor?

"You have written somewhat of death—of dying. I have read your book on the life and death of Leonardo. Very well done. So full of insights. So enlightening. So full of anger. I was fascinated. Why would one be so angry at Leonardo da Vinci?"

Why not?

"And yet, there is such conviction in what you wrote, that one was almost persuaded."

Almost?

"Where, one wonders, does such conviction come from?"

I knew him.

"Easy enough to be critical—and yes, to have good cause—but the genius of your book—and I speak of its *genius* advisedly—the genius of your book lies in the clarity with which you separate your condemnation of the man from your admiration for his art."

Which is only just.

"I am fascinated. Fascinated."

Pilgrim turned his hands palm down—a gesture duly noted by Jung.

"We shall have an interesting conversation about your book, perhaps—once you decide it is time to speak. Unless, of course, by then you will think the subject of Leonardo has been exhausted—which I doubt somehow. The passion with which you attack him is so vehement, I suspect there is still much to say."

Pilgrim counted the pigeons. *Six.*

The sun rose higher, off to the left of the building—and though an April sun, it had no real promise yet of spring.

Jung had followed Pilgrim's gaze and he remarked: "here in Switzerland you might think that winter will never end. And yet, the snow is already melting. I heard it this morning, making its rivers—running off beneath its surface. And in three weeks' time, I promise you, there will be daffodils and crocuses showing themselves by the lake. It takes no time at all, once it starts, and before you know it, you turn around and it's gone."

Five, now. One's flown away.

Jung stood up.

"What, I wonder, did Leonardo think of snow—down there in Florence, where the mountains are little more than hills? The most he would know of snow, I should think, would be the dreadful floods it causes along the Arno during spring run-off. Mud and sludge and waste—not snow like that out there. He never painted snow, so far as I recall, though of course I am not as familiar with his work as you are, Mister Pilgrim. Nothing in him was drawn to it. It was not there, in his inner eye. His inner eye was filled with other vistas—other imagery. Yes? Not snow—but wind and rain—those stormy clouds of his—all those dramas played out in his landscapes ... And yet, no snow. Perhaps you would agree with me, Mister Pilgrim. We are not free to choose what attracts our attention. It chooses us. This way, I have been chosen by you, Mister Pilgrim. You are my snow."

Jung went away behind Pilgrim's rigid back and moved towards the door.

"I will leave you, now," he said. "I will return when you request my presence. Not before. Good day to you, Mister Pilgrim."

The door opened.

The door closed.

Pilgrim's hands reached up from his lap and gripped the arms of the Bath chair.

He shook.

His lips parted.

He spoke.

"The sky," he said.

And then again: "the sky."
He shaded his eyes and gazed at the sun.
The sun would cure him.
If he was truly snow—he would melt.

18

"Carl Gustav?"

It was Furtwängler.

"Yes, Josef."

Furtwängler had seen Jung's back as he closed the door to Pilgrim's rooms and started away down the corridor.

"Wait for me one moment." Furtwängler hurried forward.

Jung prepared himself for the worst—another of Josef's icy tirades, another of his paranoid accusations.

"So," Furtwängler said, "you have again managed to steal one of my patients."

Here we go, Jung thought. "Yes," he said. "But I wouldn't call it theft."

"What would you call it, then?"

"Acceptance of a professional assignment. As usual, I was asked to say *yes* or *no*. I said *yes*."

"Not the usual. This time you pulled strings. Bleuler had me in his office this morning at 8:30. He said that you were to take over Pilgrim's case—not because he thought it best, but because Lady Quartermaine insisted. But at least he had the decency to apologize."

"Do you want an apology from me, Josef? It's yours and I give it freely."

They came to the stairs and started down.

"I do not accept it," said Furtwängler. "If I thought for one second it was sincere, I would. But I know you too well, Carl Gustav. You have connived in this. You have connived and inveigled and undermined my position. And you did this by going directly to Lady Quartermaine in order to have me removed."

"What makes you think that?"

"You were seen taking lunch with her yesterday. And last evening, so I am told, she paid a personal call on the Director and apparently convinced him in a single sitting that my diagnosis and treatment of Mister Pilgrim were inappropriate and unacceptable. *Inappropriate and unacceptable!* What can I possibly have done to deserve this sort of criticism?"

"You misread your patient."

"*I did not misread him!* How can you say that?"

They had reached the landing and had to fall silent and step aside in order to let two ascending nurses pass. Smiles and nods of pleasure all round. It must not be apparent to staff that an argument was taking place. Not, at least, until it had been settled.

After a moment of silence, Jung spoke without stepping down from the landing. "Yes," he said. "I had lunch with Lady Quartermaine yesterday. At her instigation, not mine. I did nothing to facilitate this transfer," he lied. "Nothing." Then he moved on down the stairs.

Furtwängler, who at all costs could not bear to lose face or to appear at a disadvantage, resisted the temptation to hurry down after him. Instead, he came down as if he expected a welcoming party to greet him at the bottom.

"I must say, Carl Gustav, you do this sort of thing very well," he said icily.

"What sort of thing?"

"Placing knives in people's backs and then behaving as though they had somehow managed to reach round and stab themselves."

"I'm sorry you feel that way, Josef. I was hoping—and I should tell you, Lady Quartermaine herself was rather hoping—that you would continue on with this case as primary consultant."

They were now in the foyer, which was streaming with sunlight. A number of patients, their relatives, orderlies and nurses were going in to an early lunch. It was the first of May and someone had placed several pots of forced bulbs on the reception desk—hyacinths, paperwhites and jonquils—whose colours and whose scent were a welcome foretaste of the season waiting to burgeon beyond the doors.

Furtwängler momentarily was at a loss for words. Then he said: "was that a sincere offer of reconciliation?"

"Of course it was," said Jung—smiling.

"It's only been a week, now, since he was admitted—but I've become quite attached to him. Pilgrim. So much has happened in that time—I'm intrigued by his case and I really would hate to lose contact with it altogether."

"And you needn't. No need at all."

Furtwängler gave a hesitant smile. "Well, then," he said. "In that case, I wish you the best of luck with him."

Jung gave a mock bow. "Thank you," he said.

They stood there, neither one quite certain whether the subject was closed or if there was more to be said. Then Furtwängler—as usual when he needed time to think—took out his handkerchief and began to polish a pair of spectacles which he kept in his pocket, purely to give him a certain cachet—the insignia of an intellectual.

"You were with Mister Pilgrim just now," he finally said. "How did you find him? I must tell you, I spent an hour with him yesterday afternoon and I have never witnessed a man with so much anguish in his gaze."

"Yes. I agree," said Jung. "And, this morning, nothing has changed. He said nothing. Moved his hands thus ..." he demonstrated "... and stared at the mountains. He fixes the distance with something approaching fanaticism, you know— as if he expected someone out there to speak to him. So, I'm trying a ploy. I spoke with him at fairly great length, mostly about the view from the window, the snow—and Leonardo da Vinci. And I sense, having reread his book, that my best chance of persuading him to communicate lies somewhere in the subject of da Vinci. I want to provoke an argument in him. See if I can upset him sufficiently to force him to speak. But I have also told him I will not return until he asks for me."

"Isn't that risky?"

"Perhaps. But I know he wants to speak. What prevents him—God alone knows. He has the motor capacity for speech. There has been no stroke or other impediment. His health is sound, though he rarely eats and never sleeps. He seems to have the constitution of a warhorse."

Furtwängler returned his spectacles to their pocket and began to fold his handkerchief.

"Josef," said Jung. "I am going to ask a favour of you."

"Ah, me. I don't like the sound of this," Furtwängler said. "But go ahead. Ask."

"I want you not to see Mister Pilgrim for a day or two. I want to turn the screws on his need to speak. He will not speak to Kessler. Certainly, he's not about to say to Kessler what he wants to transmit to me or to you. And I insist that it be me. I'm sorry, but I hope you will understand."

Furtwängler gave a pale, unrehearsed smile—a hopeless smile. "One day, Carl Gustav," he said, "you will run this clinic. And when that happens, I am not sure I want to be here."

"Now you are angry again."

"Yes. I want some part of Pilgrim for myself, as you promised. As principal consultant, I must have contact."

"For two days, Josef. Two days only. Then we will share him."

Furtwängler looked away.

"Science comes first," he said. "Science comes first or the patient is lost entirely."

"Nonsense," said Jung. "The patient comes first."

"As you say. But I have to tell you that, in my opinion, you have already failed the agreement we came to on this matter only moments ago. Failed it utterly. Good day to you."

Furtwängler turned on his heel and walked away.

Watching him, Jung thought: *well, that's too bad, but at least it gets him off my back.*

As he began to walk towards his office, he also began to hum the tune of *Tales From the Vienna Woods*—and soon discovered that he was dancing.

19

By eleven o'clock that night, Kessler had persuaded Pilgrim to retire. The Bath chair had been sequestered in a corner and Pilgrim was in his bed.

It had become Kessler's habit to sleep on a small iron cot at the far end of the sitting-room—the cot being a foldaway which he hid behind the armoire by day. He turned out all the lamps but one on a distant table whose glow was quite sufficient, should there be an emergency, but not so strong as to prevent sleep.

"Good night, Mister Pilgrim," he said before climbing fully clothed beneath his blanket. But there was no reply.

Of course there is no reply, Kessler thought bitterly, kicking off his shoes. *His silence is going to last till doomsday.*

At midnight, Kessler heard the clock strike twelve, but he was on the verge of dreams and only counted off the strokes the way some others count sheep.

By two in the morning, Kessler was fully asleep.

"You there?" a voice said.

A dream voice?

"Are you there, man?"

No. Not a dream voice. Wake up.

Kessler struggled to his elbows and listened.

"Speak. Are you there?"

Kessler had never heard Pilgrim's voice. It might as well have belonged to a stranger.

He stood up and fumbled his way to the bedside.

"Mister Pilgrim?"

"Is someone there? A doctor?"

Kessler turned on the bedside lamp.

"Mister Pilgrim?"

Pilgrim was facing away from him.

"Mister Pilgrim?"

There was no reply.

Kessler did not want to chance startling him, and so before he spoke again, he went around to the other side of the bed where he could be seen.

"Are you awake?" he said.

Still there was no answer. Nor was it clear from Pilgrim's posture what state he was in. To Kessler, however, it seemed unlikely that he was awake. There were no motor reactions—except the barely visible fact that he was breathing.

Kessler went to the desk and made a note in German: *speech commenced at roughly 2:05 a.m.* After this, he sat down with his forearm across the page upon which he had written, the pen still uncapped in his other hand. He waited.

"Speak, Mister Pilgrim," he finally said. "Speak again."

Nothing was forthcoming.

Kessler looked at the clock on the desk and turned back to the page. *Speech ceased at roughly 2:14 a.m.*, he wrote. Then he capped the pen, turned out the light and sat in the dark.

While everyone else deserts him, he thought, *I stay. It is me who stays by his side—not Doctor Jung—not Doctor Furtwängler—not his friend Lady Quartermaine. It is me who sits here. I am his watchman. I am his guardian. I am his protector—but they will take the credit. To them, I am nothing more than his keeper. Yet it will be me—I— me that knows him best when he is ready for recovery. Not the others—not his doctors—but me, who stayed with him through the night.*

There was a snore from the bed. Deep sleep.

Kessler rose and returned to his cot.

He was tired. It was impossible to stay awake for one more second. He listened for the sound of wings—and when it commenced, as it always did prior to sleep, he slept.

20

In the morning, when Jung heard that Pilgrim had spoken in his sleep, he asked Kessler to find a cot like his own and set it up at the foot of Pilgrim's bed.

"I shall stay here tonight," he said, "and we shall hope that he speaks again." In the sitting-room, out of Pilgrim's hearing, Jung then asked: "are you certain he asked for me?"

"Not by name," Kessler told him. "No. But he did say *doctor*. He said: *is someone there? A doctor?* But no name."

Jung was just as glad. It allowed him some leeway not to have a name for the moment. Pilgrim, after all, could have meant any doctor—Greene or Hammond or anyone. Though Jung had told him his name, Pilgrim had never uttered it. Therefore there was no proof the name had even registered. And to have the wrong name could bring this chance of communication to a close—whereas, he could stand in for anyone, so long as he remained anonymous.

Throughout the day, Pilgrim was kept distracted by a visit to the baths while two junior interns set up the prescribed cot for Jung and prepared its covers. When Pilgrim returned, still in his robe, he lay down on the cot as if it had been provided for his own use and slept there through the afternoon.

At 7:00 p.m. he awakened, ate a light meal of scrambled eggs and retired to his own bed. He still did not speak. In fact, he had barely seemed to be awake as he had eaten, although he did take up his napkin and return it to its place when he had finished. All this movement was still in the automatic mode.

It was not until the moon had risen, now in its final quarter, that Jung arrived at the door of Suite 306 and knocked lightly for admittance.

"Is he asleep?" he asked.

"Yessir."

"Good."

In the bedroom, Jung unpacked a pair of pyjamas, a robe, a pair of slippers, a notebook and a bottle of brandy.

"That will be all, Kessler," he said. "I shall bed down now and ask you to do the same. If I need you, I will call you."

"Yessir."

Suite 306 had become a military encampment—or so it seemed to Kessler. He felt an irresistible urge to click his heels and bob in Jung's direction. Though he managed not to do so in the doctor's presence, he did click his heels very lightly as he half closed the door between them.

Jung retired to the bathroom, where he removed his clothes and exchanged them for pyjamas and slippers. He brushed his teeth, used the toilet and washed his hands. Then he folded his clothes and carried them into the bedroom, where he laid them on a chair. He set his shoes side by side beneath his cot and turned the covers back. He had not slept alone for so long that the sight of the empty sheets almost unnerved him, until he smiled and thought: *this will be no different than sleeping in the barracks once a year during service—when a hundred empty beds lie in wait for a hundred married men, all dragged away from their homes and their wives. What a dreary time that always is, having to get through the dark with ninety-nine men around you all fingering themselves until they sigh themselves to sleep ...*

Before turning out the lamp on the desk, Jung poured himself a modicum of brandy and stood there watching his patient.

"Speak," he whispered—and threw back the drink. "And pray God I wake to hear you."

Then he pressed the light switch and climbed beneath the covers.

It was 11:30.

Somewhere, a bell rang that told him so.

At 4:00 a.m. Pilgrim spoke.

Jung awoke and waited.

There was a spill of pale light from the sitting-room, where Kessler as always kept one lamp active in case of need.

"Is someone there?"

Jung slid his legs from beneath the covers and fumbled for his slippers.

"Yes," he said. "I am here."

"Who are you?"

"A friend."

Jung went to Pilgrim's bedside and turned on the light.

Pilgrim seemed to be asleep, but he spoke again.

"Give me a pen," he said.

Jung knew better than to question anything the voice asked. It might well be that Pilgrim was a medium. Jung had heard many such voices in the past—dead sounding and distanced from their speakers because they belonged to someone else.

It had been during his researches into spiritualism—a subject abandoned while he pursued his interest in schizophrenia. Men had spoken as women—women had spoken as men—foreign languages had emerged from the mouths of people who could barely speak their own. And this voice had that same disembodied sound to it—the voice of another, rising from another source.

And yet, to date in Jung's observation of Pilgrim, nothing had indicated he was *possessed*, as folklore would have it. Nothing had indicated he was a medium—a seer—a "speaker." He had seemed to be entirely himself, however remote and damaged.

Jung retrieved his own pen and notebook from the desk top and took them back into the light. He placed the pen in Pilgrim's fingers and offered him the paper.

The pen fell onto the coverlet. The fingers seemed unable to hold it.

"Write," said the voice.

Jung returned to the desk and sat.

Pilgrim's back was to him—his own back, of necessity, turned towards the bed. He poured a generous portion of brandy, uncapped the pen and smoothed his notebook, open at an empty page.

"Yes," he said, barely raising his voice, "I am ready. I shall write."

There was a long sigh as Pilgrim rolled onto his back. If Jung had turned to regard him, he would have seen one hand and one bandaged wrist lying in place across the eyes. And he would have seen the other hand palm up on the covers—fisted, its bandaged wrist seeping blood.

"There is a chair," the voice said, "turned towards the windows. The chair has lion's feet, some carving and a cushioned seat. In it, a young man is lying back as though asleep. He is naked—little more than a boy, but nonetheless mature. There is hair beneath his arms and at his groin. One arm has been laid as if to shade his eyes. The other arm hangs down along his leg. Someone ..."

Jung stopped writing and waited.

Pilgrim gave a sigh of frustration.

"Someone I cannot see is ..."

Nothing.

Silence.

Another sigh—and then: "there is a piece of paper. A page turned back in a notebook—the notebook wide and thick, stitched by hand and bound in leather. And ..."

Yes?

"On the paper—on the page—there is a drawing. I can see this drawing even as it is made. The drawing and the hand that makes it—but nothing else, as though the hand were mine—or perhaps I am standing behind the arm and its hand as they draw ..."

Yes?

"Lit—but not by sunlight. Northern light—diffused. Perhaps deliberate diffusion—a masking, a shrouding somehow of light—but good light—ample light—sufficient. And the drawing shows the young man's figure. But he is incomplete. He has no face. And then ..."

Yes?

"And then ..."

Yes?

Jung waited—pen poised.

"The face begins to draw itself. It draws itself. No fingers—hand—no arm to guide the ... what? The crayon ... No hand to guide the crayon and the face begins to draw itself ... Oh, God ..."

Yes?

"Angelo. Angelo ..."

Silence.

Jung waited, but the silence continued. Then he turned and looked at the bed.

Both Pilgrim's wrists were bloodied—though he was still entirely asleep. Clearly, whoever had spoken had now departed.

The bleeding was not serious. That was clear, though it had been profuse enough to stain both bandages. Lifting Pilgrim's hands to verify that he was indeed asleep, Jung stripped away the gauze and carried it into the bathroom. Pulling the light switch, he threw the bandages into the wastebasket and ran the hot-water tap. Then the cold. Wetting one end of a towel, he took it to the bedside where he cleaned Pilgrim's wrists, dried them and laid them on the sleeper's breast. This way, he created the image of a medieval knight at rest in his tomb, surmounted by his iconic self carved in stone.

Jung smiled.

Carved, he thought, *in stone that has finally spoken.*

He was glad the moment was over. To pass through such an experience as watching your patient in the grip of another personality always brought with it a rush of exhilaration followed by emptiness. As if you had been flushed like a toilet, and all your energies drained away in a single stroke.

He poured another two inches of brandy and lighted one last cheroot before he capped his pen and put it aside.

He then pushed himself away from the table, turned out the lamp and stood up. He stretched his arms above his head, and rising to his toes, he gave a great sigh—and sat back down.

Looking towards the windows, he saw that the moon had set. There was only the blue-shadowed snow and the merest hint of starlight.

He glanced into the sitting-room. Kessler had drifted off beneath his covers, curled and cosseted as if his mother had tucked him in and wished him a safe journey through the night.

My mother used to say that sleep is a voyage and one must make it safely to the other side of the Sea of Darkness.

Pilgrim, too, had drifted away as if a weight had been lifted— as if, when his dream had passed, a passenger had disembarked, taking all his luggage with him.

Angelo. Who was he? Who had he been, lying naked in his chair—and when? Surely there was more. And who was making the drawing—Pilgrim himself or another? All very stimulating, intriguing—rife with possibilities.

Jung threw back the last of the brandy in his glass, gathered up his clothes and went into the bathroom, from which he emerged a moment later carrying his pyjamas, his toothbrush and his slippers. All these he placed in his overnight bag—a Gladstone—together with his brandy, his notebook and his pen.

In the sitting-room, anxious not to awaken Kessler, he pulled on his overcoat and scuffled clumsily into his ratty old galoshes.

He debated leaving a note for Kessler, but thought better of it when he caught the image of Pilgrim reading it—either by mistake or by cunning. He wondered, gazing back at the bedroom, if Pilgrim would even remember asking for a doctor, let alone the doctor's presence in the night.

He raised his hand in Kessler's direction and silently bade him *farewell and good day* and left the suite.

Six o'clock. Or nearly.

As he hurried down the corridor he thought: *the air will be welcome. Even the cold will be welcome. Even the snow. Even the troublesome drive in the car.*

There was so much to do.

Lady Quartermaine to see and to consult. Breakfast to be eaten—who cares in what order? And contact to be re-established with the unknown identity with whom he had just spent the night.

And the question—the question. *Who was Angelo?*

21

Kessler struggled to wakefulness through a dream of beating wings.

Beyond the windows, the first of the doves and pigeons had begun to arrive.

There was a smell. What was it?

Cigar smoke. Cheroot smoke. Doctor Jung.

"Doctor Jung?"

There was no answer. Kessler fell back and closed his eyes.

The wings in his mind made a rustling sound. Feminine. The sound of skirts being kicked aside by women walking. His mother. His sister Elvire. He could hear them talking—whispering.

Is he asleep?

No, no—he's just pretending. The way he always does, the lazy-bones!

Somewhere, a door shut. In the corridor, voices. It was morning.

Kessler reopened his eyes and pushed himself all the way to his feet.

Don't go back to sleep.

He went—sock-footed, still disoriented—into the bedroom and stood at the side of Jung's cot and wondered why it was empty.

Where? When? What?

He stared at the figure lying in the bed and said: "do you want some coffee?"

Never, never coffee. Only ever tea.

"Do you want some tea?"

The body rolled onto its stomach, one unbandaged wrist displayed on the pillow.

"Some toast? Marmalade?"

Pilgrim raised his other hand and put two fingers to his lips.

"Is that a *yes* or a *no?*"

There was no response. The fingers remained in place.

Kessler turned away and padded back to the vicinity of his cot. He was awake now and regretted it. *I hate being awake. I'd rather dream,* he thought. *In my dreams, I can fly and escape it all. I can leave them all behind—my mother, Elvire, my absent father, all those sisters I never see anyway ...*

He stared at himself in the mirror on the wall. *There I am,* he thought, *looking like a candidate for the yellow wagon ... But no, I've done all that. All that is over. I'm safe. I'm alive. I'm sane. Or so they tell me.*

He must begin the day.

He returned to the foot of the bed and touched Pilgrim's toes.

"Are you alive?" he said. "Speak and be recognized."

The body did not respond.

It was only then that Kessler remembered hearing Pilgrim's voice adrift in the dark—and the light that had seemed like candlelight beyond the half-open door.

What was it? What had he said? A name. Someone's name.

The birds flew up in a gust of wind beyond the window.

Angels.

Angels.

Angelo.

BOOK TWO

1

When Jung returned home, his wife, Emma, was still in bed. She woke to find him singing in the bathroom, from which there was a sufficient spill of light to show her feet the way to the floor.

Padding to the door, she opened it and peered through the steam. There was Carl Gustav seated in the tub scrubbing his back.

"Do you want me to do that for you?" she asked.

"No, no. Go back to bed. All is well."

"It certainly sounds it," said Emma. "I haven't heard you singing for weeks. Was it Mister Pilgrim? Did he speak in his sleep again?"

"YES!" Jung roared like a triumphant child. "YES! YES! YES!"

Emma folded her arms and smiled. "I'm so happy for you," she said.

"Be happy for the world," said Jung with a laugh. "One of its most interesting citizens is coming back to life."

"Can I get you anything?"

"Yes. You can telephone the Hôtel Baur au Lac and tell them to give Lady Quartermaine a message as soon as she's awake. Don't say a word about Pilgrim. Leave that to me. Just say I'm on my way and want to see her."

"Now, Carl? It's seven o'clock in the morning."

"Yes, now. Of course now. Most emphatically—now!"

Emma departed to make the call. At a quarter past seven Jung was in the downstairs hall pulling on his scarves and overcoat. Pushing his stockinged feet into his galoshes, he bellowed up the stairs: "shoes! Shoes! I've forgotten my shoes!"

Seconds later, Emma appeared on the landing, from which she threw down a pair of brogues.

"Thank you. Thank you. I'm away." Jung blew Emma a kiss, tucked his shoes under his arm, took up his satchel and left the house.

Emma called after him: "hat! It's cold! You'll freeze your ears!" But he was gone.

Emma descended to the hallway, one hand on her belly. "You have a very careless father," she said—and went into the kitchen.

On his arrival at the Hôtel Baur au Lac, Lady Quartermaine was waiting for Jung in the lobby.

"Such an early call," she said. "No matter. Have you had your breakfast? I have not. I normally have it brought to my rooms. But this morning ... Good heavens, Doctor! It's not yet eight o'clock. Have you come with news?"

"I apologize for the hour, Lady Quartermaine. But, yes—I have vital news. He has spoken at length—and I need your help to interpret what has been said. And no, I have not yet had my breakfast. I'm famished."

"We will go in then, and you can bring me up to date."

They made their way to the dining-room, where Jung was relieved of his scarves and overcoat.

"You seem to be wearing galoshes, Doctor. Shouldn't you remove them?"

"I cannot. I am wearing only stockings underneath."

"I see. Well, I won't ask for an explanation—though I assume there must be one."

Jung thought of the shoes still sitting on the front seat of the Fiat—and said nothing.

Sybil Quartermaine allowed the Maître d' to show them to a table "away from too much light."

Grapefruit halves were ordered. Coffee, toast and strawberry preserves. Jung also ordered an omelette and ham.

Sybil wore a violet morning dress with two loops of pale grey opals. She was hatless.

"I think it pretentious to wear a hat just because you're on view in a public place. Would you not agree? Of course, being a man, you never have to think about such things. I noted that you arrived without a hat, Doctor Jung. No shoes. No hat. In the dead of winter. You amaze me."

"It's May."

"So you say. But that's no excuse. It might as well be dead of winter, for all I can tell. I shall be glad of England, where the daffodils had already bloomed and died before we left London."

The coffee arrived. The pot, once their cups had been filled, was left on the table.

"And so? Your news."

"I barely know where to begin."

"You say he spoke. Begin there."

"He spoke in his sleep. This was after midnight. Four o'clock, I believe."

"Spoke in his sleep? But we all do that. Is that your news?"

"No, no, Lady Quartermaine. No. You do not understand. Night before last, Mister Pilgrim asked for me in his sleep. And ..."

"And so ...?"

"Last night I stayed in his room and he spoke again ..." Jung stopped and lifted his hand to his head. "I must look dreadful," he said. "I was so excited, I forgot to brush my hair."

"Oh, do stop going on about it! Tell me what he said."

Jung sat forward.

"Has Mister Pilgrim ever spoken to you about a young man named Angelo?"

Sybil set her cup in its place, dabbed at her lips with her napkin and spread the napkin out on her lap.

"No," she said.

"No?"

"No."

"What a pity. I was hoping you could tell me who he is."

"Angelo, you say. What sort of name is that?"

"I assume it's Italian."

"Italian. Of course, Italian. I'm still not quite awake, I'm afraid."
She withdrew a cigarette case and lighter from her handbag.

To Jung she appeared to be less unawake than nervous and he
wondered why.

"Does it ring a bell of any kind?"

"I'm afraid not. No."

She lighted a cigarette. "And what did Pilgrim say of this
Angelo person, this Italian?"

"He said there was a drawing of him. Naked."

She set aside the case and lighter and said rather tartly: "are
you quite certain the name referred to the subject of the drawing? What about the artist? *Angelo* could very well be *Michelangelo*. I believe he worshipped nude young men ..."

"Michelangelo ..."

"Yes—and why not? It's Pilgrim's period of expertise and you
can imagine the number of such drawings that must have passed
before his eyes. Nudes by the hundreds. Frankly, I prefer the
word *nude* to *naked*—but have it your way. It was your choice."

"You seem angry," Jung said. "Are you?"

"Of course not." Sybil spread her fingers and gave a shrug.
"Why should I be angry?"

"I can't imagine. But you are."

Sybil began to rearrange her cutlery. She pouted and looked
rebellious, not unlike a bad child.

"Lady Quartermaine, I am in the difficult position of having
to deal with a patient about whom I know next to nothing. All I
know is how you met, what he does and how well he does it,
because I have read his book. And I know he has now attempted
suicide twice ..."

"More often than that."

Jung blinked.

Sybil looked off towards the windows. There was a table there
with an attractive young man and woman seated opposite one
another. Clearly, they had recently been married and could
barely keep their eyes from each other.

Sybil turned away and rummaged in her handbag, taking out her dark glasses. "The light ..." she explained. "The snow."

Fitting the glasses in place, she drank more coffee before she spoke again. "Are you married, Doctor Jung?"

"Yes. My wife's name is Emma. At present she is pregnant with our fifth child."

"Congratulations. Emma, you say."

"Yes."

"A gentle name. A lovely name ..."

"Lady Quartermaine—is something wrong?"

"No." She looked at her rings, but still would not look at Jung. "No. Nothing is wrong. You must not persist in asking."

"But you said ..."

Sybil regarded her cigarette. "I said that Pilgrim had attempted suicide more than twice. Which, I am sorry to say, is true. If you want the details, you may have them from Doctor Greene. I cannot bring myself to relive it all." She stubbed her cigarette and then said: "he wants so desperately to die. And I ..."

"And you ...?"

The grapefruit halves were brought by a white-gloved waiter and deposited in place. Each was set in a silver-latticed glass bowl of ice. Each had a sugar-frosted maraschino cherry at its centre. Sybil removed the cherry and put it aside.

All at once, she appeared to be on the verge of tears. "Oh, dear," she said. "Oh, dear. I'm sorry. The truth is, I have been less than honest with you, Doctor Jung ..." She turned her spoon on its back and waved her hand and said: "I ask your forgiveness—but there were and there are reasons."

"Please. It doesn't matter."

"It does matter. It does. It does. If only I knew how to say all this ..."

She drew a handkerchief from her sleeve, and removing her glasses, she dabbed at her eyes. She then replaced the glasses and sat with both hands lightly fisted on the table, one hand still holding the handkerchief. When she spoke again, her voice was misted with what, to Jung, seemed to be grief.

"There is such a great, great mystery about my friend—and I am privy only to some of it. Though I hesitate to tell you this, I must. You should know there are journals. Private journals. Some of which he has allowed me to see. His accountings of various—shall we say—*episodes* in his life. And when you said ..." She pushed her uneaten grapefruit away. "When you asked me if I had ever heard Mister Pilgrim speak of someone whose name was Angelo, I said *no*. Which was true. In the strictest sense, quite true. But ... although he's never spoken the name aloud, I have seen it written. In his journals."

Jung gave a sigh. *There.*

One small glimmer of light had appeared. A brick had been removed from the wall surrounding his patient.

He dug into his grapefruit. "Is he real—this person? Angelo?" he asked.

"Not *is*. *Was*."

"*Was?*"

"Yes. It is a name from the past. The very distant past."

"And it's not a fictional name? Not a fictional person?"

"Not a fiction. No. Very real."

"Who was he, then?"

"A relative of Mister Pilgrim's."

"A relative—and Italian. Interesting."

"Possibly."

Jung by now had finished his grapefruit and Sybil poured them each a second cup of coffee.

"I wonder who invented coffee," she said.

"God, I should think."

"God. Of course. How droll." She drank. "Do you believe in God, Doctor Jung?"

"Whenever I am asked that question, Lady Quartermaine, I have an urge to give a supercilious answer. Just then, for instance, I was tempted to look at my watch and say that I do not believe in God before nine o'clock in the morning."

Sybil gave a smile. "In other words," she said, "it is none of my business."

"No such thing. I meant only ... Ah!"

The white-gloved waiter had arrived with Jung's omelette and ham.

Jung nodded his thanks and continued: "it is simply that I cannot take part in such a weighty discussion before I have finished my breakfast."

"Touché."

"Tell me more about the journals," he said, cutting into his omelette. It was pleasantly runny. "How did you come to gain the privilege of reading them?"

Sybil regarded her grapefruit—pulled it back towards her and began to eat with her handkerchief still in her hand.

"They were delivered to me in a parcel."

"A parcel?"

"Yes. Prepared by Forster. Pilgrim's man."

"And this was ... when?"

"Just after Pilgrim tried to take his life by hanging. That first week, before we brought him here, when he was recuperating and I was making the travel arrangements."

"I see. And now they are ..."

"Now the journals are in my suite here at the hotel."

Jung stared at her, saying nothing.

He carved a piece of ham and ate it. Then he carved another, pushing it around his plate to sop up the juices of his omelette.

Sybil at last was eating her grapefruit, section by section, quite unconsciously counting them off as she ate ... *Twelve ... Thirteen ... Fourteen ...*

Neither one looked at the other. They had fallen unaware into an image of domestic habit—a man and woman seated at the breakfast table, discussing a mutual friend's involvement—

or possible involvement—with someone of mystery. At any moment one of them would ask the other to pass the strawberry conserve—accept it without thanks and spoon it onto a plate.

"About these journals," Jung began again.

"Yes? What?"

"I hesitate to ask ..." Jung put another bit of ham in his mouth and ate.

"But you want to know if there's any possibility of looking into them yourself."

"Exactly."

Jung, still watching her, attempted to place more food in his mouth—and failed.

"You've dropped some ham in your lap."

"I'm sorry."

"Don't apologize to me. Apologize to the ham."

Jung located the wayward slice and placed it on his plate.

"You haven't answered my question," he said.

"Question?"

"Concerning the journals, and the possibility of my seeing them. If I am to cure Mister Pilgrim ..."

"Nobody asked for a cure, Doctor Jung. I asked for your *help*. I asked you to help him—not to cure him. There is a difference. A very great difference."

"My job ..." Jung began.

"Your job is to do the bidding of those who have hired you." Sybil picked up her cigarette case and lighter from the table and lighted another cigarette.

Jung blinked and subsided. The smoke drifted.

"Lady Quartermaine, you disappoint me. You are an extremely intelligent woman, and yet you seem to have no idea—no notion at all of what the practice of medicine requires of its practitioners. We are not free to turn our backs on the quest for cures. We must do everything in our power to achieve them—patient by patient by patient. That is why I am here. It is what my life—my whole life is about."

Sybil fixed him with a stony gaze through her dark glasses. The smoke from her cigarette curled up past her lips and caught a shaft of sunlight above her head. "Mister Pilgrim cannot be cured," she said without emotion. "We none of us can be cured, Doctor Jung. Not of our lives."

Jung sat back and laid aside his utensils. He hardly dared look at her. In what she had said there was too much an echo of what he himself had said of the Countess Blavinskeya: *one cannot be cured of the Moon.*

He looked down at the tablecloth and at his hands, which lay there, newly emptied.

"Help him," said Lady Quartermaine. "That is all I ask. Help him to survive the sickness of his life. No—not the sickness of it—the conditions under which he must live it. A way must be found to help him survive ... survival, Doctor Jung. That is all I ask. One simple ray of hope. A reason—some *reason* to live."

Jung said: "if I could see these journals, Lady Quartermaine ..." He waited and said no more.

Sybil, all at once, stood up. "Very well," she said. She put out her cigarette and gathered her handbag and Kashmir scarf. Drawing the latter about her shoulders, she added: "I shall see what can be done."

Jung got out of his chair and nodded above her extended hand.

"Thank you," he said. "And good morning."

"Yes. Good morning. And good day."

With that, she left.

Jung sat down and pushed his plate away. In the back of his mind was the thought that, in Pilgrim, he had gained not one but two in need of his attention. Pilgrim himself—and his shadow, Lady Quartermaine.

As Jung went back to his coffee and lighted a cheroot, he made note of the fact that, laying down their napkins and rising from their chairs, the handsome young couple had abandoned their table near the window and were hurrying from the dining-room towards the lobby.

Odd.

Or so he thought. It was almost as if, having seen her depart, they were in pursuit of Lady Quartermaine.

Thinking back, he remembered that Sybil, on first seeing the young couple, had turned away and immediately put on her dark glasses. Did she know them? Had she wanted to avoid recognition? Or was it all pure coincidence—meaning nothing.

Jung knew he had a tendency to impose signs and signals on what he observed from time to time, and decided he was reading too much into their sudden departure. It was morning. Everyone was hurrying away to go about their business. That's all it was. They were simply off to the snowfields, and not in pursuit of Lady Quartermaine at all.

He, however, was. That he now knew for certain.

2

Jung could hardly breathe. The sudden advent of summer heat, for May, was quite extraordinary.

Midnight, and the windows open, the undeniable smell of spring in the air. And the acrid smell of all the fires extinguished by his own hand. In the salon, bedroom and his study, stoves that had burned through the day had been doused with a watering can.

Upstairs, Emma was sleeping like a child. Jung had left her in their bed at such an early hour that he could barely believe she was already asleep. But: *I am tired, Carl Gustav, after all this evening's chatter and excitement ...*

There she lay, not quite smiling, in her flannel nightdress with its over-generous sleeves and its high-buttoned collar—hands and neck encircled in a siege of cloth, prisoners of her fear of the cold.

Sunday, May 5th, 1912.

Spring night—spring morning.

Jung did not bother to adjust the dating in his notebook—open before him, propped on the desk in his study, where he sat on a cane-backed chair surrounded by papers, matches, bottles, glasses, half-empty boxes of cheroots and half-full ashtrays.

At the centre of the debris—the scattered, barely civilized salvage of what was usually on his desk—there was an elegant, leatherbound volume of handwritten pages whose frontispiece displayed the squared-off imprimatur of the man whose name was PILGRIM.

The journal was open at the page selected by Lady Quartermaine and marked with a purple ribbon—in keeping with the chosen palette of her wardrobe. The pages before him, in their leather covers, had been delivered late that afternoon. They had arrived in the silver Daimler, driven by Lady Quartermaine's Swiss chauffeur, Otto. That his name was *Otto*, given his occupation, had delighted Sybil. *He and the motor car are thus made one*, she declared.

Otto had nothing to say for himself other than the fact that *Doctor Jung will recognize the contents of this envelope*. No explanation was required.

Inside the envelope, besides the journal, there had been a letter in Lady Quartermaine's hand:

Here is what I have read—and what you may find helpful. I trust you to understand it is both right and necessary that I have not offered volumes other than the one in hand. Access to the remainder may perhaps be discussed later. Under certain conditions. But I warn you here and now, I am unlikely to bend in the direction of generosity.

You will see that I have marked with my card a passage I believe should be your first reading. This journal, like the others, records different aspects of my friend's experience of life—his thoughts and his dreams as well as his day-to-day existence. It is the marked passage, however, that will answer some of your immediate questions. In it, you will find the identity of the young man you seek. I will go so far as to tell you his name: Angelo Gherardini. *I will also tell you he was born in Florence in the late fifteenth century. To be exact, in* 1479. *Here, too, you will meet the artist who made young Angelo the subject of his sketches. This much I will tell you now, and nothing more.*

It is vital, I believe, that you discover the rest for yourself. Only then will you be able to comprehend what is written here at length. As I am sure you must be aware, there is all the difference in the world between comprehension and understanding. Merely to understand my friend would be to fail him entirely. Those who carry the burden of being understood *can too easily be swept away into the corner and condemned to being filed under* CASE COMPLETED.

*You will never have done with Pilgrim unless you begin with the
fact that, at present, I am his only true believer. Unless you comprehend this dilemma at the outset, you will be of no use to him whatsoever.*

*I have put my trust in you. That is all I have to offer. That, and
whatever monies may be required to assure that your efforts in his
behalf may be fulfilled to the utmost.*

I remain yours sincerely,
Sybil Quartermaine

And now the pages were spread before him.
He began to read.

3

Florence, 1497. A year of Plague—a year of Famine.

The great church—Santa Maria Novella—rises above the Piazza. There are fires at every corner and restless straggles of people moving between them. At one of the fires a fight has begun. Weapons—mostly sticks—and voices are raised in counterpoint, one and then the other. Someone has stolen something—food, most likely—and a horde of shabby figures has surrounded the thief—a woman.

Others in the Piazza, also hearing the commotion, have begun to move towards the crowd, by now a mass of dancing arms and swaying clothes whose liquid movement might have been set to music.

The thief breaks free and tries to cross to the middle of the Piazza. Children follow her, tearing at her skirts, but she throws them off and turns towards the open doors of the church. Sanctuary. If she can reach even the steps, she will be safe.

But the woman is thin and weak—already exhausted—and a group of young men and boys quickly overtakes her, racing up the far side of the Piazza, followed by a pack of barking dogs and human cries of encouragement. Nearing the church itself, which still exudes its Mass for the Dead, the mob turns and forms a phalanx, depriving the woman of her destination.

Her skirts by now have been torn and a thin, ragged shawl is her only defence against the cold. She draws this around her and stands irresolute, turning in each direction to gauge the avenues of escape. None is open to her.

The crowd falls silent and the crackling fires all at once can be heard. The sweet boy-singing of the choir that seemed a moment ago to have no earthly connection to the human race rises beyond the doors.

The woman gives a cry and raises her arms towards the sky. But there is no one there to save her—none of God's angels—nothing of God Himself—only the sky beyond the smoke and the stars beyond the sky and the dark beyond the stars. Resigned, she drops to her knees and makes the sign of the cross. She prays and makes the sign again, after which she covers her face with her hands.

At first, the crowd is silent—almost motionless—watching her the way a vigilant fighter watches his felled opponent to see if he will rise again.

Nothing happens. A dog barks. One—and then another.

The mob—still silent—watches the woman praying. Five or six of them, feeling no further need for vengeance, shake their heads and drift back to their fires. For them, the event has concluded.

When it seems she is not to be attacked after all and might be allowed her freedom, the woman at last uncovers her face and reaches into her skirts, from which she draws a piece of bread.

As she begins to eat, she sinks back onto her heels, her vacant gaze on the stones upon which she kneels, and she begins to rock back and forth as if in some kind of ecstasy. Food. To be nourished—to be filled at last—though, of course, what she eats will come nowhere near to filling her. She reaches again into her skirts, where nothing is left but crumbs. Only crumbs—and these she lifts one by one—a final harvest—and places them in her mouth with all the rapture of a woman eating strawberries rolled in sugar and dipped in cream.

One man steps forward. Then another. Neither of them speaks.

More step forward. The woman, her fingers near her lips, looks up.

The choir inside the Church falls silent. There is no amen.

Another—then another and another man steps forward. Now two women. Now a child.

The sparseness of their clothing and their bone-thin bodies places them squarely in the same league of need as the woman they confront. As they increase in numbers, others turn away as before and wander, disconsolate, back to their fires.

Perhaps two hundred people now stand about ten metres from the crouching figure, which stares at them with its mouth open.

Someone raises a cudgel—thick and deadly, encrusted with the stumps of twigs and branches cut away with knives.

There is another shout. And then a cry—the inevitable cry of someone who knows she is going to die.

In the Piazza, the crowd, which up until then has been moving towards the kneeling woman with military precision, all at once breaks ranks. Those who only seconds before have been acting as one, suddenly become a horde of howling individuals. Each in his own or her own way runs forward as though to seize the privilege of striking the first blow. A contest—a race—with a prize to be won.

The woman's shrieks cannot be distinguished from the triumphant wail of her killers. There is just one inhuman shout—and that is all. In minutes, it is over.

The people turn away, staring at the ground before them— some with their arms hanging down and others clasping themselves in what appears to be pain. They make their silent way to the fires, where those who have taken no part in the killing are waiting for their return.

In the centre of the Piazza, all that appears to remain of the woman are tokens of her clothing—severed sleeves, an undergarment, tumbled skirts, a bodice—all of them mangled, all of them bloodied, all of them empty. She has been rendered—so it seems—invisible.

From the fires, which once again are defined by huddles of human shapes, the dogs creep forward, and with ears laid back and tails between their legs, they make their way to the remnants of cloth, inspect them and turn away.

All but one, who lies upon the ground and sets its head on its paws and mourns, as all dogs do, without a sound.

Jung stopped reading.

A stranger had been killed before his eyes—a stranger in another time so distant from his own he could not have conjured it had Pilgrim not written it so vividly in his journal.

Journal. A daily record. What Jung had read was in the present tense, as if ...

As if Pilgrim himself had been there. Yet how could that be? How could that possibly be?

It couldn't. Jung was content with that.

The writing was so cramped and his eyes were so tired, his brain felt as if it might explode.

What was it he was reading?

He flipped the pages of the journal, wondering how much more he was capable of taking in at this hour. Who—including Pilgrim—could have chronicled events in the past with such immediacy? The fires—the woman's clothing—the choirboys singing—the dogs—the children ... Was all this the result of some monumental feat of research? Or was it nothing but a fiction—a novel in progress?

He rubbed his eyes, and was about to light another cheroot when the door to his study slowly opened.

"Carl Gustav, it is three o'clock. Come to bed."

Emma stood in the open doorway, her face apparently disembodied, floating in the darkness out of which she was emerging. The sound of her voice had been so unexpected—sepulchral, almost—that Jung snapped the covers of Pilgrim's journal shut, as if she had caught him looking at his erotic Japanese prints. Behind him, locked beyond glass doors, there were several copies of these which he kept *for technical reasons only, Emmy— only for the sake of one's profession, only in order to verify the actual*

possibilities and separate them from the excessive and dangerous sexual
fantasies of one's most deeply disturbed patients. And I ...

"What are you reading there?"

"Nothing."

"You can't be sitting here reading *nothing* at three o'clock in
the morning."

"It's just ..."

"Yes?"

"It's only ..."

"Only what?" Emma's attitude was brisk. She had come to
return her husband to their bed—not to listen to obfuscations.

Jung smoothed the leather covers under his hand and poured
himself another inch of brandy.

"You want some?" he said, waggling the bottle at his wife.

"Of course not."

"Of course not. Yes. Well ..."

"Well?"

"Emmy, you must not interfere in my work."

"I never have and I never will. Good heavens, I do half your
research for you. I check your manuscript pages and correct
every one of your multiple errors. Do you call that *interference?*"

"I do not make multiple errors."

"You cannot spell, Carl Gustav. You cannot spell—you
know nothing of punctuation and your penmanship is so
appalling that if it weren't for me not a soul on earth could
decipher it. Not even you. Good heavens! I can't begin to
count the number of times you've come to me and said: *can you
tell me what I have written here?* If this constitutes *interference*, I
shall give it up at once and concentrate on learning how to
cook!"

"You needn't be angry. I only meant ..."

"You only meant you don't want to tell me what you're up
to."

"I'm breaking the law."

Emma came all the way into the room and sat in the patient's chair facing her husband.

"Breaking the law?" she said, arranging the folds of her robe in her lap. "Breaking the law? In what way? How?"

"Sometimes it is necessary."

"To break the law? How? Why?"

"Have some brandy. Here." He held out his glass.

"I'm pregnant, Carl Gustav. I don't need to drink and do not want to."

She watched her husband pour another two inches.

"I am waiting," she said. "How have you broken the law? Are you going to be arrested? Are you going to go to jail?"

"I hope not."

"So—what have you done?"

"I have broken a moral law, an ethical law which could—if the wrong people found out about it—place me in jeopardy from a professional point of view. I might be disciplined—I might even lose my position. I simply don't know."

"Carl Gustav, stop this walking around the corner and tell me what you have done."

"This book ..." he tapped it with his index finger— "... is the private journal of one of my patients."

"So?"

"So—I am reading it without his permission."

"Is he in any condition to give you his permission?"

"No."

"So—what is your problem?"

Jung beamed. "Emmy," he said, "I adore you. You have said precisely what I'd hoped you would say."

"I see. So, when you're arrested, it will be my fault."

Now, at last, she laughed, stood up and drew her robe about her.

"I'm going back to bed," she said. "Come when you will—but don't blame me if you're out of sorts in the morning. You have an appointment at nine."

"Who with?"

"I don't know. I'm not your secretary—I'm only your wife. Ask Fräulein Unger. All I know is nine o'clock."

"I'll try not to be too long."

"Do what you must. Good night."

Emma moved to the doorway and turned.

"Carl Gustav," she said, "a wife knows things no other person knows about a man—even the man himself. If I were Josef Furtwängler's wife and found him reading someone else's private papers, I would worry. That I admit. But I am not— thank God in heaven—Heidi Furtwängler. I am Emma Jung, and when I climb back under the covers, I am going to sleep like a baby." She gave him a comical curtsey. "Good night, my dear one. One day, I trust you will tell me what all of this is about."

"I will," he promised. "And soon, because it will require some research from you. Good night."

She turned away from him back into the darkness. Jung sat listening to her climbing the staircase and briefly closed his eyes.

I am a lucky man, he thought, and reopened Pilgrim's journal.

Paddling his fingers amongst the pages, attempting to find his place, he came upon a statement that stopped him cold. In parentheses, Pilgrim had suddenly broken off the narrative and written: *even now, as I write these memoirs, the scene is so well remembered I grip the pen as if to break it in two.*

Memoirs ... So well remembered.

Curious.

As if what Pilgrim had written was truly something he recalled rather than something conjured from a reading of history. Something he must have felt he knew from firsthand experience.

But, of course, that was impossible. Impossible.

Or was it?

Jung reached for his own notebook, shoving Pilgrim's aside. Finding a pen, he wrote: *the life of the psyche requires no space and*

no time ... it works within its own frame—limitless. No constraints.
No confining. None of the demands of reason.

Go on, he decided. *Keep reading.* The question of voice would
solve itself if he gave it a chance to speak unimpeded. Whether
the voice was Pilgrim's or someone else's hardly mattered for
now. The point was—the voice was there and clearly had its
own integrity.

Jung sat forward.

It was four—four-fifteen in the morning.

He would have preferred to pause, reflect and ask more questions, but Pilgrim remained an enigma he could not begin to
clarify until more pages had been turned.

The journal was open.

The reading resumed.

4

Now, a wind has risen—a wind that lifts and shifts the banners hung from every window and balcony in the Piazza Santa Maria Novella—scarlet banners displayed in honour of the Papal Nuncio whose mission to silence Savonarola so recently failed. Some are already ragged, torn by the yearning hands of citizens dying of the cold—and what one sees are merely tatters waving *Goodbye! Go back to Rome!* like windblown men on the decks of a ship that is doomed to sink.

At every distance the bells of all the churches begin to ring. The mighty bell of the Duomo and the tenor bells of Santa Maria Novella—squalls of independent bells, as if the wind itself is shaking them. On all sides of the Piazza, the shrouded figures huddle before their fires, pulling whatever cover they can up over their ears. *Monday, Monday.* Tomorrow, the bells are telling them, is the final day of Carnival, Saint Matthew's Day, when once we all rejoiced and sang together—feasted and drank and danced. But that tomorrow is now forbidden. By Savonarola's edict.

Jung instinctively closed his eyes when they encountered this name. Savonarola had been both a saint and a monster, and in Jung's own view, a good deal more the monster than the saint. That he was a fanatic, there could be no doubt—and fanatics always claim their victims.

He made a note: *Emma research: Savonarola.*

Driven by accelerating updraughts, the fires leap higher against the walls, marking them with jagged shadows. The choir inside the church begins to sing louder, as if afraid.

... Chorus Angelorum te suscipit,
et cum Lazaro, quondam paupere
aeternam habeus requiem.
... May the choir of Angels receive thee,
and with Lazarus, once poor
may thou have eternal rest.

A sudden surge of grey horses clatters on a diagonal across the Piazza, their riders nothing more than silhouettes with streaming hair and lashing arms.

And then ... a man.

Jung tried to turn the page and failed. He wetted his finger and scrabbled it against the paper. At last he succeeded.

And then a man appeared. Bare-headed, so it seemed at first. Cloaked, with the cloak held tight against his waist. Tall. Substantial. Well-made—heavily clothed. A traveller, perhaps. A pilgrim. Who can tell?

He has entered the Piazza from the northeast, where it gives way to the Via Maronni. His shadow falls at first on the tattered banners above him and behind him, but as he moves forward his shadow runs around in front of him and seems to lay a path at his feet, on which he walks like a prince accustomed to ceremony, gazing without apparent concern at the scene around him.

From the periphery of fire, some dogs come forward, curious but unafraid—tentative but sensing their destination and making for it at a steady pace. The pilgrim—for so he still seems—stops and turns to watch the dogs as they approach him.

There are ten or twelve of them at least. They pause for a moment in their advance, but they do not retreat.

One dog slowly begins to wag its tail.

Then it must be that the pilgrim speaks, for the dog comes forward at once and greets him by leaning in against him and gazing up into his firelit face.

The man bends down. He crouches. He puts out both his hands. The dogs push forward. A huntsman and his pack.

Then from beneath his cloak, the pilgrim produces a satchel and the dogs lean further in towards him, some of them scrambling over others, all of them quivering with anticipation.

Whatever he gives them, it is certainly food because they fall upon it ravenously, yelping and baying for more until the satchel is completely emptied.

From their fires, the citizens turn to watch—in silence. The man may be a universal target for their scorn and even their fury—*that any food should be given to dogs!* But no one speaks.

The pilgrim perhaps is known to them. Certainly the dogs know him.

He turns then and walks away into the centre of the Piazza where the one grieving dog remains—having not risen or even moved during the feeding.

It raises its head, though it still does not rise from its prone position. The two gaze at one another. The pilgrim kneels.

What has happened here? Something has happened. What?

The dog does not move. The pilgrim holds out his hand. The dog subsides, but will not give up its place.

The man goes over to the nearest group of scavengers and opens his purse. A boy steps forward and, taking up a firebrand, follows the pilgrim back to the dog.

Because of the light from the torch it is possible now to see the pilgrim's face.

He wears a cap on the back of his head. His hair, quite long, is a dark, rich red—the colour of Tuscan earth—and it shines with streaks of white or grey. He wears his beard in the fashion affected by the kings of France and Spain—shaped and cropped like a conté outline of his jaw and mouth and cheeks. His eyes are large and widely spaced and his nose—as one might have said if he had been a drawing or a painting: *is in the style of Lorenzo the Magnificent.* Indeed, this pilgrim might be a Medici returning to claim his city. A princely authority informs every move and gesture he makes, as if he were born to be obeyed.

While the boy watches, the pilgrim removes his cloak and lays it on the ground beside the dog.

He then sits down on top of the cloak and draws a notebook from a pocket in his long, woven coat. A notebook. And a crayon.

The boy stands closer. The torchlight flares and throws itself down across the page, where it rests on the pilgrim's knees.

And then the pilgrim begins to draw.

I have seen this page, Jung read. *Both to my wonder—and my sorrow—I have seen it. It shows the head and shoulders and the forepaws of a grieving dog. It also shows a brutally severed hand. And in the hand, a piece of bread.*

Beneath this, written at a later time perhaps, in that curious mirror-imaged script for which he was famous, there is this notation:

Hand of a Florentine woman—drawn by torchlight on the night of February 6th, 1497. Dog would not leave her. Died there by morning. The woman's sleeve of dark blue cotton. One button made of wood.

This was my first encounter with Leonardo.

5

Ten minutes later, Jung was still staring blindly at the page.

Leonardo.

Of course. Who else would Pilgrim be writing about in fifteenth-century Florence?

And surely that drawing had been reproduced in his book about da Vinci, the first original Leonardo that Pilgrim had ever seen—to judge from his final notation. And perhaps the first time he had ever laid eyes on the artist's famous backward writing.

Jung reached out and turned off the lamp. Dawn had come and gone. The sun had risen.

He was cold. He could read no more. Young Angelo would have to wait. To have met Leonardo was enough.

He pulled up the collar of his robe and sat there for a moment hugging his sides and grieving for the woman, dead now four hundred and fifteen years.

One button made of wood.

He glanced down at the journal, its page sitting open, waiting to be turned.

No. Not now. Not yet. Enough. Enough.

Taking his half-filled tumbler of brandy, Jung rose and moved to the window.

Had Emma slept through all that turmoil?

What a curious question. What a curious notion. How curious it was to imagine she had witnessed the scene he had just finished reading—that she had heard its gusts of wind, its clatter of horses' hooves, its barking dogs—and seen its leaping shadows.

On the other hand, it seemed to him the scene had played

itself out as if he himself had looked from the windows and seen the figure striding like a pilgrim into the light. Leonardo.

Jung heard the girl passing through the hallway beyond the open door.

Dear heaven—what was her name? Her name? She was new. Frau Emmenthal had hired her only last week. And how could he forget her name? It had been impressed upon him so many times with so much courtesy—repeated eight times a day! Smiling—bobbing—speaking softly: *I am ... I am ... I am ...* the girl had told him.

"Dammit, who are you?"

She was carrying a tray of bread and chocolate to Emma, and stopped in the doorway, mystified. The doctor had spoken, but surely not to her.

She peered into the shadows behind her to see who else might be present.

"Me, sir?"

"Yes. You."

"I am Lotte, Herr Doktor. Charlotte, the new girl. Frau Emmenthal ..."

"Ah, yes." Now what to say? He was making a fool of himself. "Have I seen you before?"

Now, even more of a fool.

"Yes, Herr Doktor. I have been here one whole week."

"Is there any more of that chocolate in the kitchen?"

"Yes, Herr Doktor."

"Good. Then bring that tray in here and fix up another for Frau Doktor Jung."

"Yes, sir."

Lotte, whose honey hair was woven in a plait that hung down her back, came past him with the tray and set it on the library table amongst a horde of books. At once, she scrambled away.

A clock struck.

Seven.

There would be no sleep. Only bread and chocolate—a

pleasant shave—*I will trim my moustache*—take a luxurious bath and move straight on to Pilgrim himself.

Filling his cup, Jung smiled. What an image! *Straight on to Pilgrim without putting on my clothes!* And look—it was snowing again.

Swallowing the first long draught of cocoa, he closed his eyes and conjured the image of his steaming, naked self rising from the bath and moving through a silent fall of snow.

I shall carry my notebook, of course. And my pen. And perhaps a staff.

A staff. That's right.

The perfect image of a naked pilgrim.

6

In the Music Room—so-called because it had been set aside for patients for whom music provided therapy—there were twenty-one windows. Seven and seven and seven. Tall and narrow.

At nine o'clock on the morning Jung had been reading the Pilgrim journal, he stood in this room with his back to the door which led to the corridor. The snow beyond the windows fell as if the clouds were counting out pennies—huge, white ghosts of pennies from the days when pennies were the size of pocket-watches. Or so Jung thought he remembered.

Two clocks were ticking, but not in time—in counterpoint.

A grand piano stood in one corner, its lid raised expectantly. A cello, shrouded, leaned against one wall—despondent, abandoned. Three violins rested invisible inside their cases sitting on three gold chairs.

Will no one come?

A cluster of music stands was gathered in a corner. Gossips. *Have you heard ...? Did you know ...?* Two flutes, an oboe and a clarinet, also encased, had been laid on a shelf—and on the shelf beneath them, neatly piled, scores by Bach and Mozart lying on their sides. Schumann's *Piano Concerto in A Minor* stood upright, turned towards the wall. In another corner, what might have been a giant's boxed ear turned out to be a harp.

Jung had booked the Music Room through Fräulein Unger. Having telephoned the superintendent, she was then dispatched to Suite 306 where Kessler was instructed to bring Mister Pilgrim downstairs at nine o'clock.

It was now twenty minutes past the hour. Had Kessler misunderstood? Had Fräulein Unger misinformed him?

Jung inspected the pictures and pages laid out on a mile-long table—the table set in such a way that when he was seated there, his back would be to the brightest windows.

A mile-long table. Half a mile. Well—it is long, at any rate. To think of its true length was to fail to do it justice. The point was to make an impression—to overwhelm the patient with the dimensions of reality.

As for the light, it was not that he wanted to baffle Pilgrim regarding his identity—but when he spoke, his voice must be disembodied. His intention was to confront Pilgrim directly by indirect means—namely, his word-and-image-association test. Jung delighted in paradoxical phrases such as *direct confrontation by indirect means*. However nonsensical it might sound, it was in fact a precise description of how the test worked. *Here is what is—a word—an object—an image—what do you make of it?*

Furtwängler scoffed at this technique, which Jung had devised—or, more precisely, was in the process of devising by trial and error. In the course of a given session, Jung would speak single words, short phrases, sound images—*bang! bang! bang!*—the patient having been instructed to respond with the first thought that entered his head. On some occasions, saying nothing, Jung would hold up pictures—drawings, photographs, paintings—and wait for a reaction. A patient's silence, Jung was learning, could be just as telling as a verbal response.

Nervous for whatever reason, Jung went over to the piano and sat down.

What?

Something simple. His mother's lullaby, perhaps—if only he could remember the tune. His fingers wandered over the keys, but the tune was fugitive. Perhaps the truth was, Jung did not want to remember it. He played only chords.

All at once he heard Kessler's voice.

"There's no one here," the orderly said. "On the other hand, we're late. Perhaps he's gone."

Jung stood up.

"Good morning," he said in English.

Kessler clicked his heels and nodded.

Pilgrim, seated in his Bath chair, was silent.

Jung came forward, smiling.

"Surely you heard the music," he said. "Perhaps the piano is haunted. Do you believe in ghosts, Mister Pilgrim?"

Pilgrim looked away.

Jung flicked his fingers at Kessler.

Kessler nodded and departed, closing the door behind him.

Jung went behind the mile-long table.

"Why don't you join me?" he said.

Pilgrim did not move.

"I have something here I think you would like to see."

Still silent, Pilgrim closed his eyes. He might have been listening to music.

"I am looking at a human hand," Jung said. "Not my own. Another."

Pilgrim did not stir.

"A woman's hand."

The clocks ticked.

Sunlight made its way across the floor in Pilgrim's direction. Like an animal, it nosed his leather slippers; trousers; knees.

"You've seen this hand, I think," said Jung, the very model of nonchalance. "A woman's hand, curving inward ..."

He waited.

Then he said: "holding ..."

The wind blew. It rattled the windows.

Someone wants in, Pilgrim thought.

Jung deliberately fluttered the piece of paper in his hand.

"It's only a drawing," he said. "Not a real hand." He maintained the easy tone already established. *None of this*, it implied, *is of any real importance. I simply thought it would amuse you.*

Pilgrim's eyes began to open in the fashion of a dozing cat whose slitted eyes feign sleep.

Jung waved the paper to and fro.

"Are you afraid of paper, Mister Pilgrim? Pages? Notebooks?

Sketches?" Jung took up other sheets of paper and shook them all together the way he might have shaken out a piece of cloth to rid it of dust. "Are you frightened? And if so—why?"

He set all the pages aside but one.

Pilgrim lowered his chin and gazed at his hands, resting in his lap.

"In this drawing, Mister Pilgrim," Jung said, "the artist must have had some reason to choose this particular hand as his subject. What do you think that reason might be?"

The hand is beautiful.

"Do you recall that I said the hand was curving inward, holding ...?"

Curving inward. Holding.

Pilgrim opened his mouth, shaping his lips as if to frame a word—but he made no sound.

Jung stood up and closed the distance between himself, the Bath chair and its passenger.

Pilgrim could see the doctor's shoes, the bottoms of his trousers and the white, unbuttoned skirts of his smock. Pressed against these skirts, a piece of paper. Blank. Quite blank.

There is nothing there.

He's lying.

No hand, and therefore nothing in it.

Nothing holds nothing.

Jung began to reverse the page and to hold it out.

The gesture began so slowly, Pilgrim barely realized it was being made. A breeze had entered the room—a draught—and the paper shimmered—blinding him.

He flung his arm across his face.

"Mister Pilgrim?"

Jung stepped further forward and, taking Pilgrim's raised arm in his hand, he lowered it.

All of these gestures might have been choreographed—the Doctor and his patient as dancers moving to numbers.

Jung placed the piece of paper in Pilgrim's hand.

"Look at it," he said, but gently. "Don't be afraid. Just look."

Pilgrim slowly lowered his head. He lifted the page and brought it into focus.

For a moment he stared at the image without expression.

Then he bowed his head entirely and wept.

Jung waited before he spoke and then he said: "you see? You had no need to be afraid, Mister Pilgrim. All is well."

Reaching in, he retrieved the page and returned with it to the far side of the table, where he sat down.

The drawing, taken from Leonardo's notebooks, was titled: *Study of a woman's hands. 1499.*

Pace.

One hand, curving inward, held the other.

7

DREAM: Still the smoke. Still the fires. Fire, it seems, everywhere. Now, it was in the room.

Strazzi crouched beside the fireplace, warming his hands. Gherardini by the window, looking out at the windblown Piazza. The pilgrim gone and the boy gone with him—torch and all. The dog remained, prostrate, its ears laid back against its skull, its paws supporting its long grey jaw, the wind in its ruff and tail. Gherardini closed his eyes but went on seeing. Shadows played across his lids: arms perhaps, waving. Someone is waving—what?—*goodbye?*

Gherardini raised his right hand until his fingers found the panes of glass. They were cold.

Wave back.

Strazzi turned and spoke: "it's all right. It's all right. Say goodbye."

Goodbye.

The dog's head lolled to one side. It died.

Jung had struggled through his long day of work in order to reach this moment—the moment when he could read further into Pilgrim's journal.

But what, by definition, was he reading? What had appeared to be real in the passages preceding this was now called a DREAM.

A DREAM.

A dream in which, so it now appeared, two men had witnessed the murderous scene in the Piazza. And one of them was identified by the name Lady Quartermaine had given to the young man whose figure had been sketched in Pilgrim's sleep-dictation: *Angelo Gherardini.*

Had it all been a dream? All of it? Or was it that Pilgrim—if truly a medium—sometimes recovered his voices in what he called *dreams?* Calling them *dreams*, but meaning something else. Meaning conjurings—gleanings—messages. Disturbances. Other voices, not his own, intruding on his own reality. This was certainly the way of some schizophrenics—to overhear, as from a hiding place, the conversation of intruders. Like a house invaded by marauders, while the owner—helpless, watches and listens.

Now, all at once, what is seen and heard is recalled—no longer in the present tense.

And so—to the dream:

Wood smoke—more than mere lamp oil. More than the incense drifting from the candled mouth of Santa Maria Novella. More than the charcoal winking in the braziers. Wood smoke. Resin. Wax. Gherardini thought of the woods on the Florentine Hills above the city and the rolling forests of umbrella pines behind him to the south. Burning—everything burning ... everything inside his eyes on fire.

A door opened. A draught flooded over him. An air of presence—a perfumed air.

Strazzi said: "welcome. You were not expected."

Gherardini opened his eyes. In the glass, he could see the reflection of the torchlit gallery beyond the doorway—blazing orange with golden tongues. A shadow, not a silhouette, slowly extinguished these lights, moving forward until the open doorway was obliterated.

He wanted to turn, but could not. *Don't.* Had someone come to kill them?

Don't.

He reached for the knife kept hidden in the belted pouch of his doublet.

When Strazzi spoke again, his voice was distant, almost clouded—muffled: "I have made a fire."

The shadow now returned to the door and shut it. The sound said: *I am here now.*

Gherardini felt the swirl of a cloak being removed. The rush of it licked his shoulders.

Wine was poured. Someone drank. The glass was returned to its place and filled again.

"I have not seen you for some time." The voice was thick with barely swallowed wine.

Look at him. You must.

Gherardini turned. In the firelight from the Piazza beyond the windows, a veil had been lifted from the room and a dreadful clarity—*why dreadful?*—gave what had been lost in shadow sudden light and substance.

A man stood before him, wearing a purple *lucco*, the collar standing upright, embroidered and open, revealing a pleated shirt beneath a wine-coloured doublet. Every detail of the stitching was of shining silver.

It was the pilgrim. Leonardo.

Stepping forward, he set his notebook on the window sill—the book lying open, showing the dead woman's hand and her dying dog. It lay in such a way that Gherardini could see the image clearly, drawn in the swift, clean lines of a master draughtsman. Gherardini closed his eyes. One look set all this in place forever.

Now, stepping even closer, Leonardo leaned in, smiling and gazing into Gherardini's eyes. The wine-free hand—enormous, so it seemed—reached out and laid its fingers on Gherardini's cheeks—first one and then the other.

Strazzi stood some way off, watching as one might watch an eagle stooping to its prey—fearful, yet elated by the sight of the eagle's certainty.

Leonardo, his hand still on Gherardini's right cheek, its fingers grazing the boy's damp curls, tilted his head very slightly to one side and kissed him full on the lips.

"I thought I was never going to see you again. How long has it been? A year? A year and a half?"

Gherardini could not answer.

Leonardo's hair and beard were perfumed. Iris root, rose-mary, something ... He placed two fingers on Gherardini's lips. His body pressed in close, then closer—his right thigh breaking free of the *lucco*, on the verge of Gherardini's groin—the way the flank of a grazing animal parts the grasses where it feeds.

Gherardini quivered and tried to slide away but the casement at his back prevented him.

Leonardo parted the boy's lips and inserted his fingers.

To the boy they tasted of conté dust and perfumed gloves.

"Remember how we used to play the game of mother and child and how you used to suck my fingers while I stroked your hair ..."

He shed the *lucco* and moved to the great chest of drawers in which his books and sketches were scattered.

Strazzi looked at Gherardini, shrugged and turned away.

Leonardo rummaged in the drawers, opening and closing them with increasing frustration.

In the fireplace, two new logs of pine had been set ablaze in that way dreams have of shifting through time and motion without reference to how things occur. If Strazzi had fed the fire, then when?

From the Piazza came the sound yet again of horses. Because of Carnival, the Watch was being augmented by a mounted troop of soldiers from the Palazzo Vecchio. Their colours were subdued. *Savonarola.* No more the gold and scarlet of the Medicis, but drab olive tunics and monk's grey cloaks. Their armour was unpolished steel. All it reflected was a hint of the moon.

She, too, had come from nowhere.

The wind must have brought her, blowing off the clouds—the clouds all piled like grey stone castles and ...

"Here. I've found you."

Leonardo swept a tabletop clear of its ornaments and, bring-ing lamps, laid down a notebook long as a yardstick, covered in leather. Turning the heavy pages, he muttered: "these you will know and remember—these, where I taught you the art of seduction ... finger by finger, hair by hair. Eh? Yes? You will remember them."

Strazzi, embarrassed, shifted his stance by the fire.

Gherardini moved closer and watched as Leonardo's hands flashed over the pages. How many boys and youths and men lay buried in his chalks and crayons, his inks, his colours ... And Strazzi amongst them—dozens and dozens of others, all entombed between these covers—every line informed by Leonardo's passionate quest for perfection, his passionate pursuit of detail. *Draw it from nature. Draw the thing itself. Forget all teachers. The only teacher is reality.*

"Here. See here. Here you are. Oh, look. Look. Look. The most beautiful boy I have ever seen."

Gherardini stared. His own head in profile, eyes lowered. His back from shoulder to buttock. Naked. His feet. His arms. His mouth. His fingers.

And seated, one leg extended, one hand resting on his breast—his genitals exposed—his eyes half closed, his head atilt, his hair grazing his shoulder, his lips in the very act of breathing—as though at any moment he might sleep.

Leonardo took a deep breath and gave a long sigh. He had turned another page, over which he waved his open hand as if to lift some veil or shadow from the path of his gaze—his eyes, Gherardini saw, now bright with tears.

Gherardini shifted his own gaze to the page. He reached and with his fingers touched the contours of the figure drawn there—as if they might be warm.

There was a breath of air. The candles flickered. A door was opened—and closed. Strazzi had left them. Gherardini was alone with the image of his brother—and the hand that had conjured it was resting on his shoulder.

*   *   *

Jung closed his eyes.

The image of his brother ...

All right. This was not Angelo, after all—but his brother. Fine. This story, this fantasy, this dream—whatever it might be—was taking yet one more twist.

And I will follow it, wherever it goes.

But what about the mind that had conjured these scenes? How could one enter such a mind—Pilgrim's mind. How could he be helped to deal with all this—with fantasies whose reality was great enough to have taken over true reality. The "real world" of here and now. The world from which Pilgrim had retreated into silence, and the world from which he wished to retreat into death.

In other words, Jung thought as he closed the book, *how am I to proceed from here when* here *is the last place Pilgrim wants to be? As for* now—*to judge from his writing, it seems that* now, *for Pilgrim, lives entirely in the past. Well,* he thought, and stood up, *that's my job. My job, yes. But how do I do it?*

8

Last Christmas, Emma Jung had bought her husband a camera—*a toy*, as she called it. *Every child should have at least one toy for Christmas*, she had written on the card, *and this is for my youngest and most beloved child.*

That was her view of him. Not that he was not possessed of genius—but the same could be said of Mozart at eight. *In fact*, she had told Frau Emmenthal when they were shelling peas one day the previous summer, *it is the child in Carl Gustav that proclaims his genius. He sees and dreams and wonders as only a child will do—without a hint of doubt. What he knows, he knows. What he does not know, he knows he does not know. This is a sure sign of genius: not to be afraid of your own ignorance.*

The camera was a Kodak of the kind that opens like an accordion. *My squeeze-box camera*, Jung called it. *Shall I play you a tune?*

On the 8th of May, 1912, which happened to fall on a Wednesday, Jung looked out the window at breakfast time and saw a daffodil in the garden.

"There's a daffodil in the garden," he told Emma. "As soon as I've finished eating, I'm going to go out and take its picture."

"Don't be fooled by a daffodil, Carl. Put on your galoshes and wear your scarf before you go. You haven't time to be ill and I haven't time to nurse you."

"Yes, ma'am." Jung smiled at his wife and squeezed her hand.

"*Ma'am?*" Emma said. "*Ma-am?* What's that?"

"The English say it. Term of respect for an older and wiser woman. Contraction of *madam*, which the English spell without an *e* to differentiate it from the French, whom they detest. Or pretend they do. The English steal all their words and change them in subtle ways that, in fact—if you want to know the truth—are subtle as a fist shoved under your nose. They keep the spellings and mispronounce the words—or keep the pronunciation and misspell the words. Sometimes both. As in *madam. Maa-dum.* Hah! Sounds like a lost sheep. *Madame* is too, too French! Too, too frightfully foreign! Too, too frightfully pretentious! Then they turn around and use a word like *ambuscade*, which they pronounce in fluting, Frenchified tones—but spell with an *a* instead of an *e.*"

"All very interesting, Carl. And thank you for the lecture." Emma set down her coffee cup and wiped her lips. "Why did you choose *ambuscade?*"

"What do you mean, *why?*"

"Why did you choose *ambuscade* as your example?"

"First word that came into my mind, I suppose. I don't know."

"If I were you, I should give it a little thought. In fact, if I were you, I should worry."

"Worry? Why on earth worry? It's only a word."

"It isn't only a word. It's a minatory statement. A warning. An indication of your state of mind. Or perhaps an indication of your concern for that poor daffodil out there in the snow. Here you sit, plotting your route into the garden, all so you can *shoot* the unsuspecting thing. Isn't that what the Americans call a photograph? A *shot? Carl Gustav shot a daffodil this morning!* My, my, my—what shall we do?"

Emma was smiling and Jung smiled with her. But when she sobered, his smile remained.

"On the other hand," Emma said—and handed him his matches, "it just might be that somewhere in your mind you're afraid that something or someone is hiding in the shadows waiting to get you. Think about it. Now, while I get busy with your Savonarola research—go and shoot your daffodil."

Once in the garden, his open galoshes filling with snow, Jung spoke to the daffodil, telling it he only wanted to take its picture—not that he wanted to cut it for display inside the house. "Be at peace," he said aloud.

Emma, watching from the window, could see his lips moving. *He's doing it again,* she thought. *He's talking to things.* And then—with a smile: *another sure sign of genius.*

At the Clinic, Jung found Lady Quartermaine walking in the garden.

Damn. Mister Pilgrim is with her. Now I can't ask her about the journal.

The couple wandered seemingly at loose ends along the shovelled paths towards the pine grove, past the statue of Psyche and the bust of Auguste Forel on its pedestal. Doctor Forel had brought the Burghölzli Clinic to the world's attention. His reputation was monumental—but, in Jung's opinion, he was a man past his usefulness who nonetheless refused to go away. He paid endless visits—always unannounced—and had, so it seemed, an insatiable appetite for interference. *Do you not realize this-that-or-the-other,* he would pontificate. *Do you not* understand? *Do you not* see *what this-that-or-the-other treatment will lead to? Disaster!* Then you would have to spend hours defending your methods. He was maddening.

Lady Quartermaine was leading Pilgrim across the sloping, buried lawn towards the portico beneath which her motor car waited. She might have been his mother, given her demeanour. Watching them, Jung concluded they could also just as well have been lovers.

Pilgrim was wrapped from neck to toe in his greatcoat, trailing the tails of what appeared to be countless scarves, his long face shadowed by the brim of a tinted trilby pulled to one side and held there by one raised hand. The other hand clung to Lady Quartermaine's arm as if he was afraid of falling.

Jung caught up with them by Psyche.

"Good morning," he said. "Do you mind if I join you?"

Sybil had no smile for him today. "If you wish," she said. She looked as though she had not slept in weeks. Her colour was off. Beneath her careful powdering, blue shadows lingered. Her eyes, like an animal's, were haunted by a fear of daylight.

"Good morning, Mister Pilgrim," Jung persisted. "Out for our constitutional? Isn't that what you English call it?"

"Yes, that's what we call it, Doctor Jung," Sybil said. "And how are you today?"

Jung told Sybil he was well, adding that he had brought along his camera. "I photographed a daffodil at breakfast time," he said. "The first I've seen this season. A sure sign spring is on its way. Any moment, we shall see them everywhere."

"I hope so," Sybil said. "This endless snow is depressing. I don't know how you stand it."

Jung looked up at Psyche.

She was carved in marble, which suited her. Against the snow she was almost insubstantial—wraithlike, where she leaned above her frozen pond in a frame of slender birch trees. Her butterfly wings were sheathed in ice.

"White, white, everything white," Jung muttered.

"Yes," said Sybil. "White." And then: "is there somewhere we could sit for a moment, Doctor? A bench, perhaps? I don't know why, but I'm quite exhausted."

"There's a bench beside Doctor Forel—just over here." Jung led the way. "You know," he said, "one reason you might have tired so easily has to do with the altitude. We're quite high up, you know, which always makes a person lose his breath. Especially if you've come from the lowlands."

"Just so. I hadn't thought of that."

"We're almost fourteen hundred feet above sea level here," Jung told her. "Do be seated."

Sybil stood aside while Jung dusted the snow away from the bench with his handkerchief. He was not wearing gloves. The camera hung around his neck.

It looks like a dead bird, Pilgrim thought.

When all was ready, Sybil sat and Pilgrim sat beside her.

Stepping back, Jung watched them both with a mixture of concern and pleasure. Clearly, Lady Quartermaine was either unwell or deeply troubled—and Pilgrim's pugnacious and insistent silence was beginning to irritate. On the other hand, they made a handsome couple—seated in a snowy garden with Psyche gazing at her frozen pool beyond them. Down below, Jung could see another figure heading towards the Clinic doors.

Archie Menken, his American colleague.

What would Archie make of Pilgrim's journal? he wondered.

Pah! he would more than likely say. *The ramblings of a deranged mind, C.G. Stop trying to make sense of insanity.*

Jung turned his gaze once more to his companions and said: "would you mind if I took your photograph? You look rather splendid there, the two of you. And I'd like to record the memory of it. Purely privately, of course. Such a lovely day. The sun—the snow. Dare I say, a photograph of friends?"

Sybil looked at Pilgrim.

"Would you mind," she asked him, "being photographed?"

Pilgrim glanced aside, in the way of a child being told to behave.

"Yes, please," said Lady Quartermaine. "A photograph would be delightful. A memento for us all."

In his office, Archie Menken stood at the window and looked for a moment at the trio in the garden.

Then he shook his head and crossed the room to his desk. There was plenty to do without worrying about old C.G. and his problems.

Archie Menken was a disciple of William James. His studies with James at Harvard had left him almost powerless with devotion. Everything he thought and did—including everything he thought and did in behalf of his patients—was cast in the image of the Master's precept that *all there is, is what there is. There is nothing more.*

His view of the Countess Blavinskeya was: *there is no human life on the Moon; come home.* His view of Pilgrim was: *you have achieved the silence you seek in death, while standing in a living stream of consciousness. Speak—and be done with it.* Pilgrim's reaction to this had been an enigmatic smile and the silent observation that *the living stream of consciousness is freezing cold.*

As for Archie's view of Jung, whose passion he admired, he nonetheless believed that C.G.'s passion could be put to more practical uses. Archie had no sense, being still so young, that his own "passion" was so entirely geared to his mentor's precepts that he had no vocabulary of his own. His endless references—both in notes and in conversation—to James's *all there is, is what there is* and *the stream of consciousness* showed his own inability to break free of the student he had been and to reach for the analyst he might yet become. James had been dead for two years, but for Menken he was still sitting in the next room, waiting to be consulted.

Jung nearly drove Archie crazy with his endless willingness to accommodate the patient's terms of capitulation.

"It is our job," Archie once shouted at him, "to bring them into our company—not to lend our company to their fantasies! Stop all these lunar journeys, C.G.! Bring Blavinskeya back into the circle of life, where gravity prevails and lives are lived, not dreamt!"

As for Pilgrim: "you enjoy his dilemma. You revel in it. You stole him from Josef, who might have begun to cure him by now, because you couldn't bear the thought that someone else was going to receive the benefit of all that hidden *Sturm und Drang* that have driven Pilgrim to suicide and silence. You're like a child who's jealous of someone else's talking doll. If it's going to speak, it has to speak on your terms—not on its own and never in someone else's purview! In some ways," Archie had shouted, "you're a monster, C.G.! *Mine* is your favourite word—and, Jesus God in Heaven, I swear you'd let a man die before you'd allow him to revive under Josef's aegis—or mine—or *anyone else's!*"

These arguments had all been stated at the top of Archie's voice. To Jung, this shouting was one of Archie's most endearing qualities. *The brash boy aspect, the excitable juvenile who always seems to be on the verge of an intellectual orgasm ...*

By the 8th of May, the day on which Jung took his photographs of Sybil Quartermaine and Pilgrim, there was little left to be said between the two doctors. As for Josef Furtwängler, there was nothing left to be said. He had shut his door on Jung and that was the end of it.

But Jung was deaf to silence. He simply did not admit it was there. For every "silent" hour he spent with Pilgrim, there were—in his view—as many conversations as he might have had with any discursive patient. He and Pilgrim had "discussed" in silence the state of Pilgrim's being, the music he preferred to hear on the Victrola, his favoured views from the windows of the Clinic, his pleasure in wine and his abhorrence of various foods. Also, his preference in ties—his insistence on refusing anything with stripes. In Jung's view, a man's refusals and preferences, though stated only with a gesture, were a perfectly valid substitute for conversation of a verbal nature. As for nuance—a lowered glance, a shrug, a shifted stance were adjectives enough. Comment lay entirely in attitude—not in words. Jung felt it was as much his job to watch as it was to listen. Menken did not understand this.

Jung was now fond of Pilgrim, for all the latter's refusal to speak and his testy attitude to psychiatric inquiries. He would miss him, once he was well and had returned to England. If that should ever happen.

If that should ever happen ...

What had made him think that?

There it was. The ambuscade.

Ambushed by despair.

He won't get well.

There's nothing you can do.

No. Don't say that. You mustn't.

All right. He will get well. He will. And all of us will go to live on the Moon. Bravo!

Jesus.

Jesus.

What did this mean? Who was speaking? An unbidden voice had entered Jung's mind—negative and snide, insinuating failure where he believed there could be none.

Is it possible, this voice now said, *that you might be one of them, not one of us, Carl Gustav? May I remind you of your mother? Think of your mother. All her sleepless nights—all her muttered imprecations—all those threats and warnings laid at every door, including yours. Her dreams—her nightmares—her shouts and whispers in the dark. She was one of them, not one of us, Carl Gustav. You've said so yourself—or you've thought it, haven't you. Haven't you ...*

Yes.

So, why not you? There's nothing to say a doctor can't be ill.

Jung rapped his forehead with an open hand. "Be quiet," he whispered. "Be quiet in there. Go away."

I only want to help, said the voice. *I only want to be helpful.*

You can be most helpful by shutting up.

Very well. I shall be silent.

There was the briefest pause.

For the moment, the voice added. *But I won't go away. I'm here to stay, Carl Gustav. Here to stay.*

This remarkable "conversation"—Jung could call it nothing else—took place around eleven o'clock on the morning of the 8th of May—the same day on which Jung had shot his photographs of Pilgrim and Lady Quartermaine—and of the daffodil to which he had spoken in the garden.

Jung did not return to Küsnacht for his lunch, but stayed alone in his office, where he drank a small amount of brandy and smoked a cheroot and sat in an attitude of contemplation, as though he expected someone to speak.

9

At three o'clock that afternoon, Archie Menken had just returned to his office from a trying hour with a patient who could not and would not be silenced. Over the past weeks, countless sessions had been expended listening—countless others experimenting with ether, chloral hydrate, laudanum, the baths, restraints and other means of bringing the patient's hysteria to a halt. But silence had not yet been forthcoming, only babble—albeit, babble that was intelligent enough. The history of the Danes—the streets of London in alphabetical order—the life of Queen Alexandra—and an explanation of why the guillotine had failed to silence the aristocracy. This latter subject Archie Menken found particularly tempting, given that his patient was the son of a royal duke.

At five past three, while he poured himself an inch of illicit bourbon and lighted a cigarette, there was a knock at the door.

"No," he said, quickly hiding the bottle and glass—just in case the caller was Bleuler. "I can't. I'm busy."

Nonetheless, the door opened.

It was Jung.

"Go away, C.G. I need to be alone," Archie told him.

Jung was ashen—breathless.

In his hand was a clutch of photographs, newly printed.

He came to the patient's side of Archie's desk and fell into the chair as though he had been running.

"What in heaven's name is the matter with you?" Archie asked. "I said I couldn't see you. I need a moment alone."

"Go right ahead." Jung waved his hand. "Take your time. I'll just sit here."

"But you can't just sit there. Dammit—alone means alone."

"Pretend I'm not here."

Archie retrieved his glass and drank.

"What have you been doing—climbing mountains?" he asked. "Why are you so out of breath?"

"I'll explain when you've had your private moment. Just ignore me."

Archie sat back and sighed. He gave up.

"Do you want a drink?" he asked.

"Of course I do."

"Of course you do. Of course. It's you."

Archie turned and took down another glass, poured two fingers of bourbon into it and passed it across the desk. He then topped up his own drink and set the bottle aside.

Archie watched while Jung drank. He still had not let go of the pictures he carried. His lips moved. His knees shifted back and forth, touching and parting like the knees of an overanxious adolescent.

"Well? Speak."

"You through being private?"

"Don't be so childish. Tell me why you came."

Jung fanned the snapshots like a hand of cards. "These," he said. "I'd like you to take a look at them."

Menken leaned forward and took them—eight somewhat sticky photographs.

"I took them this morning," Jung said, "and brought them in to be developed by Vallabreque. I just got them back half an hour ago."

"Jürgen Vallabreque?"

"How many Vallabreques you think we have working here? Eighty? Of course Jürgen, you ..."

"Say it, C.G. Get it out of your system."

"You idiot."

"Thank you. I've long thought you thought so."

"Oh—for God's sake—look at the photographs!"

Jung stood up, polished off his bourbon and went around the desk to pour more from the bottle. This placed him behind Archie Menken's right shoulder.

Archie drew the lamp closer and laid the photographs out on his blotter—four and four. For almost a minute he studied them, one by one.

Three daffodils—three Lady-Quartermaine-Pilgrims—one Psyche—one motor car (a Daimler).

Finally, Jung said: "notice anything?"

"Well," Archie said—and drifted. Then he said: "they're really quite good."

"Not that. Anything unusual?"

Archie looked at each of the images again.

Jung said: "you got a magnifying glass?"

"No." And then: "Lady-What's-her-name looks a bit sad. Is that what you mean? Not well?"

"True—but not what I'm looking for."

Archie scanned each photograph, holding them one by one close under the light.

Jung leaned in above him.

"Well?"

"Nothing in the daffodil pictures, I presume."

"No."

"All the same flower? They really are excellent. You could publish them. The snow—the shadows ..."

"Not the daffodil pictures."

Archie set them aside.

"Psyche?"

"Partly."

"She's in four of them—three with Lady What's-it and Pilgrim—one solo."

"Yes."

"Well—her wings are covered with ice. That's clear. And ..."

"Look at Pilgrim."

Archie laid the three photographs of What's-her-name and

Pilgrim directly beneath the lamp, stood and bent over them.

"Anything?" Jung asked.

"No."

And then: "well ..."

And then: "in this one ..."

Archie picked up the centre photograph and held it closer—crossing to the windows where the light was natural—winter white, less yellow.

"Well ..." he said at last, "in this one, there's something on Pilgrim's shoulder that isn't in the others."

"Thank God," Jung said, and suddenly sat down in Archie's chair.

"Why *thank God?*"

"Because it means I'm not crazy."

Archie laughed. "Not crazy because there's something on Pilgrim's shoulder?"

"Tell me what it is."

"I can't. It's too faint."

"Look again. Look again."

"Really, C.G., this is ridiculous."

"Look again!"

Archie, stunned by Jung's sudden vehemence, said nothing and turned back to the window with the photograph.

Then he said: "it looks ... like a butterfly. Of course, it can't be. Probably snow—but it looks like a butterfly."

Jung closed his eyes and clapped his hands together, locking them in place against his lips.

Archie brought the picture back to the desk and laid it down amongst the others.

"So?" he said. "What is it?"

Jung said nothing.

He stood up, unclasped his hands and gathered the photographs, placed them in his pocket, finished his bourbon, made his way to the door, waved and said: "thank you, Mister Menken."

Then he left.

Archie sat down.

"It can't be a butterfly," he said out loud. "It can't be."

But it was.

The following day, at noon, Jung did return to Küsnacht for his lunch.

"*Psyche:*" Emma read from the textbook beside her soup plate, "*personification of a soul filled with the passion of love, and as such conceived in the form of a small winged maiden, or at other times, a butterfly.*"

Emma looked towards the window, where Jung stood gazing out at his daffodil. "There," she said. "Is that what you wanted?"

"Thank you. Yes."

His voice was barely more than a whisper.

Then he said: "tell me you see it there, as I do."

Emma glanced at the contentious photograph, raising a magnifying glass to bring it more clearly into focus. "Yes," she said. "I see it."

"Archie thinks it's just a bit of snow."

"I thought that myself at first," Emma told him. "After all, it is frigid out there. How could a butterfly survive? Don't they hibernate or something when it's cold. They're immobilized. Where can it possibly have come from?"

"Psyche."

Emma almost smiled. She closed the book and took up her soup spoon. Carl Gustav's back all at once looked rather touching. Sad.

Surely he can't really believe this, she thought. And then: *but he does. He believes—or wants to believe—that Psyche's statue somehow generated the butterfly on Mister Pilgrim's shoulder. Which, of course, is nonsense and quite impossible.*

"Come and eat," she said. "Have you any more patients today?"

"Yes. One."

"I see. Well, eat. It will build you up."

Jung sat down and opened his napkin, tucking it into his collar the way a child might do. Or a peasant.

"Leveritch and his bears," he said.

"Dear me. Mister Leveritch is so energetic. Are you sure you're up to it? You look tired."

"I am tired. But I'm up to it. I have to be. So long as he doesn't sic his dogs on me."

"I thought you said he'd given that up."

"Depends how paranoid he is. For a week, now, yes—there have been no dogs."

Otto Leveritch believed that he lived in a bear pit. It was probable the image came from the fact he was raised in Berne. Legend had it that, when Berne was founded in the twelfth century, the founder had declared it would be named after the first creature killed in the next hunt. Thus, the city's coat of arms displays a bear.

Dancing bears, caged bears, pitted bears and baited bears. These were Leveritch's constant companions—and he, from time to time, was one of them. At the worst of times, he was attacked by dogs—so he believed—and during these incidents he had to be restrained. Jung had once been intrigued by the poor man's predicament, but now, having treated him for three months, he found his sessions with Leveritch exhausting. Too many dogs.

"What time is it now?" he asked.

"Not quite one. Stop fretting. Eat. You must take time to live."

Jung raised his empty spoon and lowered it.

Emma watched him, feigning interest in the garden beyond the windows. *It will be all right*, she thought. *It will be all right. It will pass.*

Bears and dogs and butterflies. Men who should be dead but who wouldn't die. Women who lived on the Moon. This was the life he had chosen and she must keep him alive to live it. The worst of it—moments like this—would pass. He was over-worked and overwrought, and over ... what? He was *overex-tended*—that was the word. His reach had exceeded his grasp. But still, he was there—and watching him proudly, she thought: *he will find his way through. He always has.*

10

Perhaps there was music. It seemed so. Someone singing.

Leonardo went to the windows, his doublet loosened, all its buttons undone and the ties of his shirt hanging free. The ribbon was gone from his hair and his belt thrown aside.

His back was firelit, the wine-coloured velvet of his doublet streaked with orange as if the flames were fingers and had scratched him.

Come here.

Gherardini hesitated.

Come here. I want to show you something.

What?

Come and see. Come along.

Gherardini remained rooted beside the table, staring down at the drawings of the nude young man. *My brother.* Was this how it happened? A seemingly casual invitation—*come here*—and the lamps beginning to gutter, the firelight reaching out across the floor and the smell of iris root, rosemary and oranges on everything.

Gherardini made his way to the window. Leonardo's arm, all at once, was around his shoulder.

There. You see? The Mass is over.

Cloaked and hooded figures were pouring from the open doors of Santa Maria Novella.

Leonardo's arm descended to Gherardini's waist.

I'm tired. You must help me.

I don't know how.

What a feeble thing to say. Of course you know how.

Leonardo leaned forward and kissed the young man's lips. As

he did this, pulling Gherardini closer, his free hand fumbled with the strings of Gherardini's doublet.

Gherardini pulled away.

I have a knife.

Leonardo stood back amazed, but smiling.

A knife?

Yes.

You must be crazy. What have I done? What have I done I haven't done a dozen times before?

You don't understand. I'm afraid.

But you've never been afraid. Never. Never. Not of me.

You don't understand! I'm not ...

Not what? Not in love with me?

Leonardo laughed.

Gherardini glanced at the Piazza. The dog was dead. The mourners had dispersed. The doors of the church were closed. The fires still burned, but all the people sitting in their light were already bending into sleep. Nothing human showed in their collective silhouette, which might as well have been a view of hills and mountains seen from a distance.

Leonardo's hand fell once again on Gherardini's shoulder.

I always began by taking you from behind. Remember? Standing. Just like this.

He pressed himself insistently against Gherardini's back and forced the fingers of his free hand into the boy's mouth, crooning.

There, there, there. You like this, yes?

His lips pressed hard against Gherardini's left ear. With his left hand, he pulled away the boy's doublet, dropping it to one side, reaching at once for the strings that bound Gherardini's hose to his waist.

You smell just the same, the voice said. *Your hair, your neck, your skin.*

Leonardo took Gherardini's hand and laid its palm on his own erect penis.

Don't!

Gherardini spun on Leonardo and struck him in the face.

Leonardo struck back and the force of the blow caused Gherardini to fall.

Leonardo reached down, lifted the boy to his feet and tore his shirt away.

Gherardini's hands flew up in self-defence.

Leonardo struck him twice in the face. Twice—and then again.

The boy's arms were crossed, his elbows pressed against his chest.

Leonardo's voice was barely audible.

No one says don't *to me. No one. Get on your knees and beg my forgiveness.*

The boy sagged.

I'm sorry.

Say it again. And properly.

I am sorry, Master.

Stand up.

Gherardini could not move.

Stand up!

Leonardo seized the boy's hair and dragged him to his feet. Then he took him by the arm and pulled him to the table, where he threw him down and, seizing his hose, stripped it off, boots and all, and flung it into the fire.

Gherardini moved one hand to his groin. He closed his eyes. It was too late.

Leonardo had already seen and turned away.

Gherardini sat up.

"I tried to tell you," she said. "But you wouldn't listen."

11

Jung read this at midnight, sitting in his study wearing pyjamas and robe. Blindly, he reached for his cheroots, freed one from the case and struck a match.

Barely aware of what he was doing, he lifted the lighted match towards his lips and only just managed to stop himself before he put it into his mouth.

"Agh!" he said. "Dammit all!"

Standing, he filled his tumbler with brandy.

You're behaving like a drunkard, Carl Gustav.

Who cares? I need it. Besides, I'm perfectly sober.

Setting oneself on fire is hardly an act of sobriety. My, my ... One whole tumblerful of brandy. You won't be sober for long.

Leave me alone.

You drink too much, Carl Gustav. You oughtn't. Such a fine mind ...

"Oh, for God's sake leave me alone!"

Jung's words rattled the windowpanes.

Who are you talking to, Carl Gustav? There's no one here but thee and me.

Ghosts.

There are no ghosts.

If you say so.

I say so.

Jung sat down and drank. Then he glanced at Pilgrim's infuriating journal with its infuriating story written out in his infuriating hand insinuating infuriating horrors about one of the greatest men who had ever walked the face of the earth and

doing it all in a manner so calm and unreflective that it read like
pornographic dictation taken down in a courtroom.

And now, this. One more twist.

"I tried to tell you," she said.

She said. She said. She said.

All along it's been about some god-damned woman!

Now, now. Nothing wrong with women. Why don't you go on read-
ing and find out who she is?

I don't want to know who she is. She's a god-damned
imposter.

There's that word again, Carl Gustav. You really shouldn't descend
into these tirades. They're unbecoming.

I don't care. I don't *god-damn well* care!

Clearly. But you should. You're slipping. By the way, it hasn't gone
without notice that, while you read, you developed what we used to call
at University a wandering hand. You recall the phrase? Description
of a young man's self-absorption—politely referred to as self-abuse.

I didn't touch myself. I only made an adjustment. It was
uncomfortable.

Are you going to smoke that cheroot?

Yes. Absolutely.

Jung reached out, placed the cheroot in his mouth and lighted
it.

To paraphrase your famous friend—ex-friend—Doctor Freud:
sometimes a cheroot is just a cheroot.

Stop that. This is not phallic.

That's what I said.

You were implying ... Listen. I am not aroused by the seduction of young men. End of insinuation.

But she's not a young man. She's a young woman.

I'm still not aroused.

Then you're not normal.

"Oh, please shut up!"

There you go, talking out loud again.

Very well. Since you won't leave me alone, I shall now

continue reading and I will discover exactly what's going on in this god-damned journal—and why!

Silence.

Except for the riffling of pages.

Then, a sound of satisfaction.

Here.

A gown of sorts—more than likely a costume ...

A gown of sorts—more than likely a costume—was thrown in her direction. She was told to put it on and reminded in a tone that verged on disgust that Leonardo had no interest in her body unless he chose to study it for anatomical reasons.

Wear that.

The girl stood up as best she could and turned her back on him. She had never been exposed in such a fashion to a man's gaze.

The gown perhaps had been worn by one of Leonardo's young men at Carnival before the advent of Savonarola. It was blue and covered with stars—the stars cut from paper, silvered and pasted on the fabric in patterns that echoed the constellations: Orion's belt at the waist, the Pleiades across the breast, Cassiopeia's Chair all down the back and around the hem, the Milky Way. If she had not been so afraid and so tired, she would have admired it—spoken, even, of its apparently joyful nature. But not now.

Instead, once she had draped herself in this unlikely garment, she turned and directed her gaze at the figure who now stood, rigid, staring out of the window.

Finally, she lifted her head.

Will you allow me to speak?

Silence.

Let me tell you who I am. Why I have come here as I have ...

Her voice faltered. Her hands held the gown more tightly.

Leonardo neither moved nor spoke. The only sound came from the fireplace. An angry crackling.

I beg you, let me try, at least, to explain. And to tell about Angelo.
Finally, one word was uttered, tight-lipped.
Speak.
And the story was told.

Angelo was my twin brother.
Our father ...
It doesn't matter why—but I hated him. There's no point trying to disguise the fact or to hide it. There it was—my hatred. It remains. It became a kind of stone in my hand. All my life, I hated men. Hated them—all but one. My Angelo.
My Angelo. My angel.
An angel from Hell! And how I loved him for it. Worshipped his wickedness. His wildness. His delight in mischief.
That was really all it was. A delightful—a delicious sense of mischief. *Let's have some fun!* he would say.
And one of our ways of having fun was dressing up in one another's clothes. He was—oh!—so beautiful. He made a lovely girl.
Not *lovely*. No. That isn't good enough. His beauty was so remarkable, he could sit dead still in a group of other "girls" and command a whole roomful of men. He delighted in this game. He made a far, far better girl than I—and I made a far, far better boy than he.
It is true. It was true.
There was something in the way we played the game that brought the perfect other into focus. Perhaps it was not even conscious. It was just the way we were.
It was not until we started wearing one another's clothes that I understood the liberty men must feel wearing hose and doublet. I could move, at last!
And, oh! To see oneself! Not to be hidden. Not to be masked. To be seen!
There, before me in the glass, were my legs! My feet!
They were beautiful—elegant, shapely—and *visible!*

Whereas, from Angelo's point of view, when he dressed as me it gave him an opportunity to hide, and to move at his own pace—not to feel compelled to run in order to keep up. Not to be forced to adopt *a manly pose*.

At first, it was only a game—and truly a game. No one saw us but the looking-glass. And no one knew but the clothes themselves.

And then, one day when we were dressed as one another, a kind of craziness took possession of us. It was as though the game itself was daring us to play it before an audience. It was springtime—the wild time when anything mad and wonderful can happen. The swallows were returning and the air above Florence was alive with them—thousands—thousands of them, all of them circling above our heads and all of them calling down: *come out! Come out and dance with us in the sky!* All the windows had been opened and all the trees in the gardens were in bloom and Angelo said: *it is time for us to show ourselves in the streets.*

"But people will notice," I said. "They'll know."

"How? How will they know? Most of them will be strangers—and anyone who's met us will assume I'm you and you're me."

He pulled me towards the glass and made me stand beside him.

"Look," he said, "and tell me. If you didn't know—would you know?"

This made me laugh. And it became the motto of our game: *if you didn't know—would you know?*

I confess. It was true. Even I could believe I was seeing myself beside myself.

And when I saw myself that day—whenever that day was—I felt a waking-up—a surge of self-assurance I'd never known before. A surge of *swagger*, if you like, that I'd never felt as Betta. Never. But as *Angelo*, inside myself I felt myself become my *self* as never before. It was here—just here in the solar plexus—and it made a knot and it gave off waves of power that as a girl—a woman—I had never known.

Our palazzo is on one of the steeper hills looking down on the city. It was an easy walk to the Campo di Santa Maria Della Salute, where everyone tended to gather and from which we could see the river. Angelo kept telling me to slow down. I was so excited, I could barely contain myself.

The streets, whether wide or narrow, were always crowded, but now there was such an abundance of people, dogs and horses it seemed the whole of Florence was suffering spring fever.

"You're walking on the wrong side," I told him. "You should be on my left and two paces behind me."

Angelo turned to me and curtsied. "Forgive me, Signor," he said. "It will never happen again."

We made the adjustment just as we entered the Campo.

There were street musicians playing on the porches of Santa Maria Della Salute, but we could barely hear them for the choirs of swallows and the festive crowd. All the dogs had decided to bark and the sound of this was joyous instead of alarming.

I never, never, never wanted to return to womanhood. I could run, if I chose. I could leap on the balustrade and shout out verses. I could clap another man on the back and receive his hand in return. I could show my leg and lift the skirts of my doublet to expose my backside to the world—and none would know I was not a man.

Presently, I became aware of a voice that was near enough behind us to make itself heard above the others.

"There's a back for you," it said. "A Donatello back. A David."

A man was speaking.

"Yes," said another voice—a younger voice. "A good back and decent shoulders. Enticing."

"You know him?" asked the first voice.

"I might, if I could see his face. He does have a certain familiar look about him."

Both voices fell silent.

Who had they been talking about?

Whose back? Whose *Donatello back?*

I glanced to my left, past Angelo's profile—my mirror-self—and I saw that a small knot of men and youths was gathered there.

Amongst them—and seemingly the centrepiece of their group—was a tall, red-headed and bearded man in a velvet hat. He was staring right at me.

I had never felt the impact of such a glance before that moment. Clearly, he was smitten with me—but with a hint of danger, somehow, playing through his gaze, as if one moment he wanted to bed me and the next to strike me—in the way a person might strike an insolent youngster.

I felt a shiver go down my back. My neck froze. I could not look away. It was both astonishing and dreadful—thrilling and frightening. I couldn't tell what I was feeling, because no single feeling except a sense of awe would settle. My mind flew into pieces and I seemed to have no knowledge of how to re-collect them.

The man was surrounded by six or seven youths of extraordinary beauty and arrogance, who glanced at me and forced themselves to look away. It was enough that their master had seen me—for the man was, undoubtedly, somehow their master. They were like graceful Borzoi hounds—long-legged and maned with luxuriant, curling hair. Three or four older men—though younger than the master—stood closest to him and one of these was known to me. Antonio Pelligrini, who was the son of one of the merchants in my father's guild.

Would he recognize us in our reversed roles—or would he simply remark on our similarity to the children of a certain silk merchant?

I took a step away from the iron rails and sought the shadows of the arches. But to no avail. He had seen us both and he knew us.

Yet, it was me he named.

He gestured in my direction and I heard him say to the master: "that is young Angelo Gherardini. He is with his sister, Elisabetta."

I wanted to shout out: *I am his sister! That one there is Angelo!*

And I wanted, too, to shout at the master with the hungry eyes: *stop looking at me like that! I want to be left alone!*

But of course I said nothing. Not a word.

Antonio Pelligrini turned his back on me in order to speak more privately to the master, but this did not prevent the master from continuing his perusal of my whole being—inch, I could see, by inch.

I saw him finger his beard—consider his answer—then shake his head. When this was done, he took Antonio's arm and led him away. They were followed by their clutch of brilliant youths. "Who were they?" I whispered to Angelo. "Who can those men have been? And the man in the hat—who was he?"

I was shaking.

Angelo had paid no attention throughout the whole scene and could not answer.

But a friar who had overheard me, smiled and said: "you may never look on his like again, young man. That was Leonardo—the greatest artist of our time."

Leonardo.

Yes.

You. You had seen me. Your eyes had eaten me alive.

He died, my Angelo. He died of the plague that followed last year's flood.

And when my beloved Angelo was dead, I vowed that I would take his place in the world and become what he might have become—an artist, a great horseman, a musician—even a soldier! I didn't care, so long as I wasn't relegated to the role demanded of my sex. To be less—to be commanded—to be forever degraded and never heard was intolerable to me. You must understand, it was my curse to be born a woman. I always, always wanted to be a man.

In my room, I would put on my brother's clothing. My cat, Cornelia, would lie on my bed and watch me transform myself from Betta to Angelo. I would stuff my hair down my back and put on one of Angelo's caps. I flattened my breasts and wore red hose as a sign of rebellion and put on boots that reached my calf.

I was shameless. I secured a cod piece inside my undergarments to give the impression of total masculinity. It was glorious.

And Cornelia would purr and purr and purr until she was singing. And in the night, while the others were in their beds, I would go out into the streets and walk like a man, unencumbered by the weight of skirts and free to move my arms however I pleased.

And it was in this garb—I refuse to call it a disguise—it was in this garb that I decided to encounter you for a second time. But I needed help. And I remembered hearing that one of Angelo's boyhood friends had become one of your ... young friends. I was still naïve enough not to understand that men could love men. It was simply something I'd never been told. So I dressed in Angelo's clothes and I sought this young man out—Alfredo Strazzi. I did not inform him of Angelo's death and he accepted me as my brother. I think he truly believed. That was my impression. And he also accepted that I did not want to come alone to your studio. I understand now that he must have known about you and Angelo—but he said nothing. He must have assumed that there had been an estrangement of some kind—and that what I wanted from you was reconciliation—if I had been Angelo—but I am not.

I don't really know why I felt compelled to achieve this meeting with you. All I can say is, I had never been able to completely erase the sight of your hungry eyes—and the awe in which others held you as if you were a god.

*   *   *

Jung stared at the page.

It was now one-thirty in the morning.

A bird sang. Once—and then again. A nightingale?

Jung stretched his arms above his head, wiped his eyes, adjusted his glasses and bent again above the book.

Leonardo had fallen into an impersonal, almost clinical mood, cold and devoid of emotion. He spoke without inflection, questioning her almost in the manner of a doctor, or perhaps a lawyer enumerating statistics. *Your name? Your age? How old was your brother Angelo when he died?*

Betta Gherardini.

Eighteen now, and nineteen in June.

Eighteen.

Are you betrothed?

No. But there are suitors.

Are you a virgin?

This was said meanly, with a smile, as if to be a virgin was the lowest one could sink.

Of course.

Of course? What a curious thing to say at your age—given the times we live in.

I'm not a slut.

Did I imply you were a slut?

To my ears, yes.

More and more curious. You not only throw out words as a weapon, you hear them as an assault.

Your description of Angelo—and some of your drawings of him— portray him as a slut. But he was not.

He was, with me, thank God.

I don't believe you. I can't.

He was a liar through and through. It's time you knew.

He never lied to me.

He may not have lied to you, Signorina, but clearly, he withheld a lot of truths.

Did you love him?

Leonardo did not answer this. Instead, he turned his back on her, stood in the windows and pursued another line of questioning.

You call yourself Betta?

Yes.

Another curiosity. Perhaps you have eccentric parents.

It was Angelo's name for me.

I see. Betta ...

It's short for Elisabetta, my given name. Caterina Elisabetta Francesca Gherardini. He called me Betta, I called him 'Gelo.

'Gelo. Charming.

It became him.

'Gelo, yes. Angelo, no. Though I dressed him once in wings ...

Leonardo's voice trailed off.

Watching him, Betta was struck by how young he looked—broad-backed and shouldered, with well-shaped horseman's legs and the torso of someone half his age. His hair, completely loosened now, appeared to be on fire. His shirt was damp with perspiration. It clung to him like a butterfly wing—finely veined and translucent, revealing the pallor of his skin and the sinews in his neck. His hands hung helpless at his sides, the fingers curled to the shape of something absent—another hand, a lock of hair—a word. They closed upon the air, opened and closed again—on nothing.

Some dim part of her—barely accountable—wanted to forgive him. Somewhere inside, a part of her stood up in his defence—as if a vote were in progress and an overwhelming majority had cried out: *shame,* but one lone dissenter begged to differ. *His heart is broken,* she thought. *Mine was—though not for any reason like his. Perhaps in his own way, he did love my brother. Clearly, in his drawings of him, he had worshipped Angelo in the way that only lovers do—without respect to fear. Every line and every nuance portrays him as he was. Or must have been in Leonardo's presence—a slut, perhaps—though I would never say so. And if it was true, then at least Angelo was a glorious slut who revelled in his powers.*

This way, she was reconciled to the brother she had never known, the Angelo who, between the time when Leonardo had spied her wearing his clothes and the time of his death, had become Leonardo's favourite. *Pace. Pace.* At least there had been a life. In those lazy, heat-ridden hours when he lay, being evoked on the page, and the wine-besotted hours when he was tumbled, Angelo's smile in the drawings had said it all. *I am here for you alone—whoever you may be.* Not Leonardo only, but anyone who stumbled on his image. This way, the making of the drawings was an act of bravery on Leonardo's part. With every application of pen and crayon, he had given his beloved away to be shared by anyone who cared to look.

She poured herself a glass of wine, wondering if the sound of it would make Leonardo turn.

At last, he spoke.

Angelo also loved his wine. Trebbiano. Malvasia. Coli Florentini. *I took him once to see the vineyards.*

We have our own.

He never said so. I think he did not want me to know precisely who he was. He never said he had a twin—only brothers and sisters. He claimed his father was a tyrant ...

He is.

... and said that his mother was dead.

She is not.

Leonardo laughed.

Truth and lies! How wonderful he was. Do you have a pet cheetah?

No. I have an alley cat. Cornelia.

He said that one of his sisters had a cheetah called Poppaea, after Nero's wife. This is not true?

Not true at all. Cornelia is two years old and very plain.

No spots?

No spots.

Leonardo laughed again and shook his head.

What a glorious liar he was. The only truth I had from him, apparently, was that his father was a tyrant.

All fathers are tyrants.

Leonardo turned his head and raised an eyebrow.

More than likely that is true.

He turned away again.

Every child must pay for his freedom, he said.

If every child were a boy, I could agree with you. For girls and women, there is no freedom—merely an exchange of tyrants.

Do you hate men?

Yes.

As I hate women. My mother was a barmaid. She deserted me. When I was ten my father took me to meet her. She asked my father for money. She paid no attention to me.

Leaning forward, he began to open the windows one by one. Three of them. Four of them. Five.

Betta sat in a chair that had a cool leather seat. The undersides of her breasts were itchy. Her nipples, angered by the ripple of the stars that rode them side to side with every move, seemed to have caught some disease called *heat*. She wanted to dip her fingers into something icy cold and touch herself there—or apply a kerchief soaked in mountain water.

The fire gave up and died. Betta closed her eyes. The faintest scent of incense drifted through the windows. In spite of the fact that all His acolytes had departed, God was still out there, somewhere in the Piazza—still with His begging bowl, still with His censer swinging in the sleepers' faces: *wake up! Wake up! Pay attention!* Though His church was dark, He was everywhere, the remnants of His Mass still humming in the air. *For I so loved the world that I gave my only begotten Son to nurture you. Eat of his flesh and drink of his blood ...*

Some of the old and some of the children in the Piazza would be dead by morning. Starved, in spite of Carnival. It was a daily occurrence. Betta had seen it so often in the past year she was

numb with impotence. She opened her eyes again, for fear of
seeing the dead in her mind.

A thousand crusts of bread, a thousand litres of milk or wine,
a thousand vats of cheese were insults to the need. Nothing could
be done. In December's riots, when the granaries at last stood
open to be emptied, mothers and children had died beneath each
other's feet. And still, until now, it had rained—and after the
rains, the chilling winds; the mud; the scavenging, terrified dogs;
the terrified, scavenging humans—and the only thing unafraid
was the Plague. Tomorrow, at Carnival's end, another Bonfire of
Vanities, followed by another Lent, another Easter. Christ
would die again and nothing would change—except, perhaps, for
the worse. All of this, Leonardo had carefully avoided during his
sojourn in Milan, where he spent his hours designing masks and
costumes for a ball. Here, in Florence, his focus had closed at
once on a human hand and a dying dog.

Well, Betta decided, he's an artist. What else is he supposed
to do? *Life* is what his life is about, in all its disguises, with all its
surprises.

So, you hate women. Is your mother the only reason?

Reason enough for me.

*But you must have known dozens—hundreds of other women.
How old are you now?*

Forty-five. For what it's worth.

*It must be worth something. Forty-five years old and already
thought to be the greatest artist of your time.*

Pah!

Pah?

*Why not? Of course, pah! Think how many others there are—
Filippino Lippi—Botticelli—Perugino—Michelangelo—every one
of us different from the others. How can you measure greatness in
the face of so much genius? It's ridiculous. I renounce it. For myself,
I am a failure.*

*Who would believe that? The Prince of Milan has spent a fortune
on your work. The Medicis ...*

That is not greatness, Signorina. That is fame—and fame is another story altogether.

And—you will never take a wife?

Take a wife? I think not! Consider what you're saying. Please at least be sensible.

Elisabetta smiled at this, knowing that Leonardo, whose back was still to the room, could not see her. *Please, at least be sensible!* It was wonderful. The outrage. The flaunting of it. Whether he acknowledged it or not, the Master had, at least, something of a sense of humour about himself.

Has any woman ever fallen in love with you?

I do not permit myself to be loved.

I see. It is forbidden.

I should be careful, if I were you, Signorina. You are attempting a dangerous conversation.

And yet, you have been loved.

Being loved by boys and men is different than being loved by women.

So I am told.

Men and boys are fearless lovers. Women are cowards—connivers who go wild in the pursuit of riches. Anything for adornment— anything for rings and chains and pins and shoes—for silver, gold and silk—for servants—palaces, horses and power. Women use their bodies as the Medicis used their banks—as vaults in which to accumulate wealth. Women are usurers dispensing loans for which a man can die of paying interest! No—do not speak! I forbid it! You are one of them—using your feminine wiles to gain ascendancy! You came here disguised as a boy! You even used his name—a dead boy's name—to fulfil your ambition, whatever your ambition is—and now you show yourself to be a woman. What do you want of me? What do you want?

Nothing. Only to know you. Only to understand.

Understand? Understand what? How I seduced your brother?

Perhaps.

He loved being loved! He loved being loved! It was his whole life with me. But I got only his body—not his heart. He loved no one.

Leonardo began to pace the room, picking up books and setting them down—pouring out wine and kicking at tables—moving the chairs from here to there and back again. Beyond the windows, the dogs began to bark. On the upper floor, a group of young men began to sing bawdy songs and threw their boots at the walls. There was the sound three times in a row of breaking glass and raucous laughter.

You hear that?

Leonardo pointed at the ceiling.

They're inviting me to come and join them. And in half an hour, if I don't go up to them, they will come down here to me. They will tumble through that door in their shirts and beg me to take them. Bare-assed and bending! The day a woman does that, without asking to be paid—before ordering up a dozen gowns made of silk, the world will end! Thieving, conniving—never, never to be trusted! And you dare to come here wearing his clothes! You are vile! It is vile! You are vile!

Having stopped her ears and closed her eyes in her attempt to shut out his rage, Elisabetta was unaware of how close Leonardo had come to her. She did not see the colour rising in his face, nor the way in which his hands reached out towards her. She knew only that a storm had blown in through the windows and had flung her back along the table, banging her head against its planks until all the lamps were extinguished and she was barely conscious.

Time passed in and out of her awareness, until she found herself lying on the table, dimly aware of her bloodied thighs—staring at her parted knees and afraid to think what might have become of the rest of her.

Her innards hurt. They had been bruised, it seemed, and were aching, though she could not locate precisely where—only that it was somewhere inside, beyond the known parts of her. She was wet and certain the wet was blood, though she dared not look.

Leonardo was just a shadow now, somewhere on the ceiling. Lamplight must have thrown him there—pitched for some reason from below him. Where?

She rolled as best she could towards one side of the table so that her legs—if only she could manage them—could hang down over the edge. It seemed imperative to gain the floor—stand upright—recover her balance. But this was impossible. She had to use her hands to pull her knees together and then to push her calves until her ankles fell like dead weights away from the rest of her, giving her the impression they had been severed.

Sitting up, she felt the ruckled dress cascade like something liquid over her breasts and belly, until the hem of it made a pool in her lap.

Blue. With silver stars—though bloodied now, like every part of her.

Descending, she turned at once to support herself by clutching the side of the table. Beneath where she had lain, the open notebook still displayed her naked brother, now smeared with blood. The pool of cloth spilled down over her thighs—her knees—her shins—and struck the floor. The sound of it was the very sound Cornelia made descending from a windowsill. If only she could wake and find Cornelia nestled against her back—this then would just have been a dream—a nightmare.

Whatever it had been, it was clearly over.

Leonardo, naked but for his shirt, was crouching by the fire. He must have put more wood in place since there were flames again and it was their light that threw his shadow upward. He did not speak—and did not turn.

I have no shoes, Betta wanted to tell him. *I have no shoes.*

She looked at him the way a beaten dog will look at the next human being who appears. Then she turned and crossed the room to the armoire from which Leonardo had brought the dress she wore. Inside, there were shoes and boots and hats, cloaks, hoods and other costumes. *Garb for the victims of his pen*, she thought.

She pulled on a pair of boots that must have been some boy's. They reached her calves and felt like gloves. She then pulled down a heavy cloak with a hood—a monk's hood, perhaps—and drew it around her shoulders.

I'm going to leave you now, she said in her mind. *I'm going to leave you now, and trust I will never see you again.*

She moved all the way to the door, turned there and took one final look at where she had been and the man with whom she had been so violently coupled. The Master and all his chairs and tables were on the ceiling now—wavering there like seaweed in a tidal pool.

The door was open. Somehow, she had opened it herself. Then it closed and he was gone from her. As she was gone from him.

In the Piazza, Betta paused beside the dead dog, fearful of looking too closely, afraid the woman's hand might still be visible—*the sleeve of dark blue cotton*—*one button, made of wood.* But it was not, though it would remain forever in her mind.

Crossing herself, she stood and turned eastward, walking beyond the huddled backs and all the fires until there was no more sight of her—and not a sound.

With some dismay, Jung saw that he had come to the last page but one of Pilgrim's journal.

Why not look?

Because I don't want to. Yet.

It must be very late. Or early. Wouldn't it be best to go to bed with the last page read?

I will go to bed when I choose. And I will read when and what I choose.

What are you afraid of?

Nothing.

Sounds like pretty well everything, to me.

WHERE DID YOU COME FROM? WHY WON'T YOU LEAVE ME ALONE?

I am such stuff as psychotic dreams are made on ...

Hah!

As for why I won't leave you alone, consider the possibility that one of us, at least, has an ethical sense of responsibility.

I see. Furtwängler sent you to spy on me.

Goodness. What an extraordinary sense of humour.

You sound just like him.

Paranoid schizophrenia, I believe we call it. If an enemy agent, entering your mind, is carrying a gun, he can blow your brains out from the inside. Is that it? Why don't you turn the page, Carl Gustav? Are you so immature that you are afraid of turning a page??

Immature?

It's only a word. A word meaning childishly defenceless *in the face of perfectly ordinary situations. Opening a window. Turning a page ...*

I AM NOT AFRAID OF TURNING PAGES!

Turn it, then.

I WILL TURN IT IN MY OWN TIME!

Very well. Have it your way. Here we sit ...

Jung stood up.

... while the mental stability of our patient Pilgrim hangs in the balance between an unturned page and its predecessor.

It was now four-thirty. Jung looked at the windows. Any minute, the world would turn and let in the sun.

The sun will arrive at precisely six forty-three. You have two hours and thirteen minutes.

Jung came very close to filling his tumbler with brandy—thought better of it and poured only one-third.

Two hours and twelve minutes.

Jung returned to the desk and confronted the journal.

In the Piazza, Betta paused beside the dead dog ...

Who in God's name was she? And why was Pilgrim writing out her story? Why was he maligning da Vinci—why was he doing this? Calling him a rapist, for heaven's sake.

May I remind you? We wrote the following—or something very like it—in 1907: "the patient strikes us at first as being completely normal ..."—I am quoting—"... he may hold office, be in a lucrative position—or even serve as resident physician at a famous psychiatric hospital. We suspect nothing. We converse normally with him, and at some point let fall the word Leonardo. *Suddenly the ordinary face before us changes; a piercing look full of abysmal mistrust and inhuman fanaticism meets us from his eye. He has become a hunted, dangerous animal, surrounded by invisible enemies—some of them with guns. The other ego has risen to the surface ..."* Unquote, more or less. Interesting concept—the other ego.

Jung bent forward over the page, his eyes closed.

I remind you that Pilgrim's most recent task was a treatise on the subject of Leonardo da Vinci. We ourselves admired it, though we found it was sometimes offensively outspoken. In defence of Leonardo's homosexuality, for instance ... Nonetheless, it was a spirited, well-reasoned rebuttal in defence—not so much of homosexuality as of Leonardo's right to be who and what he was. You will recall that in April of 1476, Leonardo was requested to appear before the Signory in Florence and questioned about his all too apparent taste for beautiful young men?

Yes.

You will also recall that many of these young men were first sighted by Leonardo during his weekly visits to the baths—where he went each Saturday specifically in order to see them when they were naked? Mister Pilgrim made a rather strenuous argument defending this decadent habit, to which you strenuously objected. Is that not so?

Of course it's so. I objected because it's a despicable thing for an old man to do.

But he wasn't an old man, Carl Gustav. He was still under twenty-five.

Be that as it may—and I don't care if he was *ten*—it's still a despicable thing to do—sneaking off to the baths to look at naked men. A person is entitled to some privacy.

In the baths?

You know what I mean! I mean privacy from the prying eyes of a pervert.

So now Leonardo is a pervert.

YES!

Dear me. Such a reaction. Calm down.

I'm perfectly calm.

You're nothing of the kind. And by the way, may one point out the presence of an erection. Is it possible the subject of the baths excites you?

How would I know? I've never gone near them.

Carl Gustav ...

All right! I've been twice.

Just so. And for what reason?

Jung said nothing. Thought nothing.

We know why you went. We know precisely why you went. You wanted to see if, by comparison to other men, you were deficient. Isn't that so. It's nothing to be ashamed of. Every man wants to know the answer to that question. It's the most normal thing in the world.

It may be. Yes. All right. But I didn't hide in the shadows, staring. I didn't lurk ...

No. You merely glanced. I was there. I remember. But what makes you think Leonardo hid in the shadows—that he lurked, as you put it so coyly? What you will not accept, Carl Gustav, is the fact that some men want to be seen. Especially young men. It's a way of making a statement. I am here, now, and this is what I have to offer—not in a homosexual sense, but in the sense of potency and progeny. Bring on your daughters and I will give them sons.

I think that's disgusting.

So be it. But if you were a homosexual ...

Don't even begin to say that.

If you were a homosexual, you would find it enlightening. Encouraging. As Leonardo did. But—he paid for it. As you have never had to pay for your own little excursions into lust. He was arrested—taken before the Signory of Florence, humiliated by them and fined. Reviled. All because of who and what he was. Two months after his first encounter with the authorities, they imprisoned him. Not because they caught him in the act—and not because someone had complained of his actions. They did it simply because they knew he was homosexual and they wanted to shame him. What Mister Pilgrim said regarding this matter was that Leonardo's imprisonment was unjust. That it embittered him for life—which it did—and that he never, never forgot it—and never forgave the society which allowed such things to happen. But Mister Pilgrim's researches—however they were achieved—unearthed this other episode with the girl which you have just read. And while, for whatever reason, he could not bring himself to include it in his treatise, he did place it in his journals. May I therefore suggest, in all humility, that perhaps Mister Pilgrim's overall encounter with the Master—with his suffering and genius on the one hand, and his violence and lack of humanity on the other—may have somewhat overwhelmed him, leaving him both distraught and speechless?

But hardly suicidal.

Regard the last paragraph.

Jung opened his eyes and, speaking aloud, ran his finger under the words: "Crossing herself, she stood and turned eastward, walking beyond the huddled backs and all the fires until there was no more sight of her—and not a sound."

Until there was no more sight of her—and not a sound.

So?

Does this not suggest something to you? The possibility that Pilgrim knows something about this woman—something he wishes he did not know and wishes to suppress—that has cast him into the depths?

If she existed at all, for heaven's sake—which I doubt. She's been dead over four hundred years. How can the story of a woman dead over four hundred years cause a man who's alive in 1912 to be cast into the depths? It's absolutely unreasonable.

Is it?

Absolutely.

Turn the page.

Jung sighed and sat back.

Two hours and five minutes, Carl Gustav.

He leaned forward and thumbed the lower right-hand corner of the paper. Then he closed his eyes, opened them, drank—and turned the page and read.

This, from Leonardo's notebooks. The act of procreation and the members employed therein are so repulsive that if it were not for the beauty of the faces and the adornment of the actors and the pent-up impulse, nature would lose the human species.

Underneath this was written what appeared to be the annotation of an afterthought—starred with a modest asterisk, suggesting that the afterthought was Pilgrim's.

* If he had only written these words before that Monday morning, they might have proved my salvation. As it was, come Wednesday, I was in need of ashes—not for my brow alone, but for the whole of my being—and for my mind.

In the margin, Pilgrim had written: *Date was: Friday, 10th February, 1497, two days after Ash Wednesday. Three days following the Bonfire of Vanities, to which I should have consigned myself.*

12

Clearly, something was wrong with Her Ladyship. The door to her bedroom was locked more often than not. Getting the breakfast tray delivered had become a nightmare. Madam would order it the night before, and when the bellboy brought it up in the morning—prompt to the second—she would call out: *no— not now*, and Phoebe Peebles would have to try to keep it warm on the radiator.

This, of course, was never greatly successful. If the eggs were boiled, they would harden. Scrambled, they would congeal. *En cocotte*, the milk and butter would separate and the yolks would crack. The toast dried out and curled at the edges—the tea or coffee or chocolate turned lukewarm and flavourless. The jams and jellies developed a film on top and the grapefruit shrivelled and dried. It was awful.

Every morning, Phoebe would knock as gently as she dared— *a person must be heard, after all*—approaching the door at first in fifteen-minute intervals and then by the half-hour—until at last she gave up and telephoned the kitchen. Up the boy would come and take the tray away, while Phoebe shrugged and said: *there's nothing I can do.*

This routine began every day at eight o'clock, and the tray removed at ten-thirty. At eleven, Phoebe—who by then was starved—would hear the lock being turned and Her Ladyship's voice: *where are you?*

As if a person might not be there.

In the bedroom, the curtains must first be drawn and the radiator activated. Her Ladyship preferred to sleep in frigid air and always then complained that she was cold, as if to say it was Phoebe's fault.

Is there breakfast? This came next, as Madam struggled with the bedclothes, wrenching herself into a sitting position, pushing and striking the pillows much the way she might have pushed and struck at people on a sinking ship.

Phoebe then must inform Her Ladyship that breakfast had *gone back down to the kitchen, seeing as it was ruined.*

Then order more.

Yes, Madam.

Four days running this had happened. Four days running, the second breakfast had been ordered, delivered and ignored. Four days running, only the coffee, tea or chocolate had been touched—and even then, barely finished.

A great many cigarettes were smoked and Phoebe noted a number of empty wine bottles. Three of the four days, Her Ladyship did not wish to dress or to be disturbed. Having *tubbed*, as she put it, she would have Phoebe rub her back and shoulders with mildly scented oil (it smelled of roses) and request a clean nightgown and her mauve-and-lilac wrapper. She would then sit for as long as half an hour or more, staring out the windows at the mountains.

Phoebe Peebles was sufficiently concerned to feel she must consult Mister Forster on the matter. Consequently, she sought him out one afternoon while Her Ladyship was cloistered with her bottles and cigarettes.

"Whatever can be happening?" she said, when she had told her story. "It frightens me to see her so unlike herself this way."

Forster's room was on the top floor, *under the eaves*, as he put it. *Under the eaves, as befits a lifelong servant.*

Phoebe sat in the only chair. Forster sat on his bed. He offered her a glass of beer, which she declined.

"I've seen enough of alcohol, what with Madam, though I do admit I like a bit with my supper in the evenings. But I should never sit with a gentlemen and drink it in his bedroom. I hope you're not offended."

"Not at all."

Phoebe looked away and bit her lip. "Oh, what shall I do?" she said.

"I should sit it out, if I was you," said Forster. "That's what I'm having to do—sit here waiting, while God knows what they're doing to him over there." He gestured to the window.

"You mean Mister Pilgrim?"

"Yes. I mean Mister Pilgrim. I tried now five times to get to see him, but they won't let me near him. They say he's silent and will speak to no one. That and the fact there's doctors round him all the time. Every waking hour, someone's got an eye on him, they tell me. Sort of like they don't trust him not to try again. Poor man. I should want to go home, if I was him."

"I want to go home," said Phoebe. "I don't like it here. I don't like the way they all go on. All of them strangers, except yourself—except Her Ladyship. No one smiles at you. They all speak German. They treat me disdainful, as if I'm less than nothing and I hate it. And notes come from strangers. There must have been three by now—handed in through the door. Just a footman brings them and won't say nothing."

"You know who they're from?"

"Of course not. I can't hardly open them, can I? And they all come in sealed envelopes so, if I tried to look, she'd know."

"Other day, she met someone in the lobby," Forster said. "Nice-looking young couple. Spoke with them for some time. You know that?"

"No. Her Ladyship? When? What other day?"

"Day before yesterday. Day before that. I don't remember. I was passing through on my way in from trying to see Mister Pilgrim one more time and there she was with perfect strangers. Struck me as odd. She saw me, I think, but she made no sign. I went on into the bar and had a glass and when I came back out, she was still there."

"How long? I mean—in the bar?"

"Twenty—maybe twenty-five minutes. Like I said, a nice

young couple. Well-dressed. Her class, I shouldn't doubt. He had a kind of military bearing. Like her own son he might have been. If I didn't know the son, I mean—Earl Hartford. Same age. Could've been a friend of his, come to think of it. Someone from schooldays. You know—Sandhurst sort of thing."

"But they were strangers. You said so."

"Yes. Clear's can be. She didn't begin to know them. A person can tell. But it could be they knew her—through the Earl, you see, her son. It's possible. 'Cept, now that I think of it, they were speaking a foreign language when I passed the first time. Maybe French. I couldn't hear too well."

"Have you seen them since?"

"In the distance, yes. On their way in—on their way out—waiting for the lift. Times like that."

"Did it seem like a serious conversation, or what?"

"With Lady Quartermaine? I should say somewhat serious. Yes. There wasn't much smiling. Young man never sat down, but the young woman—his wife, I take it—sat in a chair next to Her Ladyship."

"It's them that's sending the notes, then. Say it was one of Mister Pilgrim's doctors who was sending them, there'd be an address on the back. But what came through the door was on hotel stationery. So it must be them."

"See if you can nick one of the notes next time she isn't looking. Might as well know. In the meantime, keep your chin up. If she turns worse, come and get me."

Phoebe rose to leave and turned at the door to thank Forster for having listened to her. "I get fair lonely down there with just her—and her in this condition."

"Not to worry," said Forster. "Think what it's like up here—and me with my man in what might be a prison, far as I can tell. But we'll all get through it. Wait and see. Cheerio, then."

"Yes," Phoebe said rather wistfully. "Cheerio, Mister Forster. And good afternoon."

* * *

On the third day, Lady Quartermaine sent down for hotel stationery to augment her own dwindling stock of Portman Place blue-and-grey vellum. *Envelopes too, please.* This day, she ate nothing, but ordered wine and whisky, drinking steadily but soberly through the afternoon till twilight. Telephone calls were placed more than once, but Phoebe could not make out the words—but one: *messenger.* When she went in to see if an evening meal would be required, she found Her Ladyship lying on the floor and a lighted cigarette burning in the ashtray.

On the desk, there were letters addressed to each of her five children, her husband, Mister Pilgrim and to Doctor Jung. The latter epistle appeared to be unfinished and sat half inside its envelope. None was addressed to strangers.

Phoebe attempted to rouse her mistress but could not. She debated telephoning for help in reviving her, but thought better of it. *Think of the scandal,* she said to herself, and covered Madam where she lay with a cashmere blanket—blue and violet woven in a madras tartan that was Her Ladyship's talisman and travelled with her everywhere.

At nine, Phoebe went to see that all was well and found her mistress had retired to her bed. Phoebe left the door ajar and the bathroom light turned on and took the liberty of telephoning to the kitchen for sandwiches and beer. At midnight, she retired to her own small bedroom off the sitting-room and, rising at six, found that Her Ladyship's door was locked again.

On the fourth day, Madam sent down for wrapping paper, string and shears.

A small lunch was taken, consisting of a dozen oysters and a bottle of champagne.

In the afternoon, at four o'clock, Phoebe was called in to help her mistress dress for tea. A guest was expected—but no guest arrived. What did arrive was another envelope.

Was Forster available?

Phoebe went to see, but found he was absent. She had taken

the envelope with her. Now it was in her hand. How might she open it?

Through one of the doorways on Mister Forster's floor she spied a maid who was ironing pillow-slips ...

Phoebe went in, held up the envelope and smiled.

"*Bitte?*" the maid asked.

Phoebe mimed trying to lift the flap. She gestured towards the iron and held out the envelope. Taking it, the maid smiled wisely.

At once, she scattered a bit of water on the back of the envelope and lightly applied the iron. Steam rose. Then, triumphantly, she fingered the flap open and said: "*Sie wollen wissen ...? Ja?*"

Phoebe retrieved the envelope and said: "*danke,*" the one German word she knew, having used it so often on receipt of the multiple breakfasts. Then, not knowing what else to do, she curtsied and went back into the corridor.

At the top of the stairs, she paused and extracted a single folded sheet of paper. On it was written: *Tomorrow*, and then, as signature: *Messager*. That was all. *Tomorrow—Messager*. It was meaningless.

Phoebe folded the page and put it back in its place, licked the flap of the envelope, sealed it and smoothed it out against her skirt—and went her way.

Half an hour later, a messenger was summoned and when he arrived, Her Ladyship presented him with an envelope addressed to *Herr Doktor C.G. Jung* at the Burghölzli Psychiatric Clinic, Zürich. Also six brown paper parcels addressed to Herr Doktor.

When the messenger had gone, his thinly clad legs and muscular backside closely observed by Phoebe Peebles, Madam closed and locked her door, explaining that she would rest until seven. At seven-thirty, a supper of cold roast beef, some Spanish green beans, a chafing-dish of scalloped potatoes, two bottles of wine and a decanter of cognac was ordered. At eight, the meal arrived, to be eaten in the sitting-room at a table near the window. Once it was all in place and the waiter sent away, Phoebe was told she might have the evening to herself, so long as she returned by ten.

Phoebe ate down the street in the dining-room of a *Bierlokal* and lingered there until nine-thirty, half hoping, half dreaming her messenger might turn up for an evening beer. But no such luck. Still, the dreaming of him was pleasant enough. The air outside, as she made her way back to the Hôtel Baur au Lac, held for the very first time the promise of spring.

Madam's supper had been mostly eaten and one bottle emptied. The second bottle and the decanter had been retired with Madam to her bedroom.

On her own bed, Phoebe found an envelope with a note which read: *I have ordered the car for eleven o'clock and will be driving in the mountains. I expect to return by late afternoon. You may have the day off to do as you will. I trust your evening was pleasant.*

Tucked inside the envelope was a five-franc note. Almost a full week's wages.

On the morning of the fifth day, it being the 14th of May, Her Ladyship rose and unlocked her door at eight o'clock. A light breakfast had been ordered and was consumed. Madam tubbed—and Phoebe helped her to dress in her blue tweed suit, black boots and her coat of black lamb.

At eleven, Otto arrived with the silver Daimler. Much to Phoebe's surprise, Her Ladyship kissed her *ever so kindly* on the cheek as she departed.

That was the last they saw of one another, except that Phoebe was asked the next day—a Wednesday—to select a black gown from madam's wardrobe and deliver it to the mortuary. On this occasion, Phoebe said her last farewell.

High in the Albis Pass to the west of the Zürichsee, on a winding road that seemed to make its way directly to the sun, an avalanche had occurred—and Sybil Quartermaine, her chauffeur Otto Mohr and the silver Daimler had been swept away into oblivion.

On the writing desk from which she had dispatched her final message to Doctor Jung were seven envelopes—blue and grey and hotel beige—and a folded note.

The note was addressed to *Miss Phoebe Peebles*, and concluded with *be a good girl and do as Mister Forster advises. All will be well, as you will see. In the meantime, thank you, my dear. Goodbye.*

It was the first warm day of the year. All around the lake, as Jung had promised, the daffodils and crocuses crested what remained of the snow, and doves from the cathedral flew down into the square and walked amongst the people on the ground.

13

Late on the evening of Tuesday, the 14th of May, Jung had not long returned to Küsnacht from his duties at the Clinic when Lotte came to his study and informed him that a messenger had arrived who would not depart until he had spoken to Jung himself.

"How troublesome. Where has he come from?"

"From Lady Quartermaine at the Hôtel Baur au Lac, Herr Doktor. He says that she told him he must deliver what he has brought into your own hands and to none other."

"Very well—show him through."

When the messenger entered, he placed six brown paper parcels on the library table and handed Jung an envelope.

"My instructions were to see that you understood the contents before I could take my leave, Herr Doktor."

"I see." Jung, cutting the envelope with a pair of scissors, removed and read the letter it contained, while the messenger stood to one side and scratched his thigh.

My dear Doctor Jung,

How pleasant and how reassuring it has been to make your acquaintance. Since I must now leave my dear old friend in your hands, I feel that I can do so with confidence. I suspect that no one is better qualified to guide him through this present crisis than yourself.

Be patient. He will respond. I have no doubts of this and trust you to persevere in behalf of his sanity. What a pity I am unable to continue as your confidante in this matter, but circumstances beyond my control compel me to take my leave.

As a consequence, I am having Mister Pilgrim's six remaining

*journals delivered to you by the present messenger, each of them
under separate cover. There is good reason for this, which I must
trust you to take into account. The order in which they are to be read
is of the utmost importance. If it was within my power to command
your obedience in this matter, I should do so, and had indeed
expected to be dealing them to you one by one. Alas, this is not to be.
Please believe me, the order is vital. Without it, there can be no
comprehension of Mister Pilgrim's dilemma. In certain matters
that govern all our lives, there are decisions we must make alone—
and some of these demand complete secrecy. This is the position I find
myself in at the moment. There is nothing I am at liberty to tell you
that would explain my present actions. Time may tell all, as is its
wont. We shall see.*

*I said early on, whether to you or to Doctor Furtwängler, that
aspects of Mister Pilgrim's present condition cannot be clarified by
rational means. I urge you to invest your trust in my friend's
apparent fabrications, if only because of his desperate need to be
believed. In seeming to lie, he struggles to deliver truths. I hope
this explanation will help. He longs to be released from what he
calls the dread necessity of self—an identity whose burden he can
no longer bear. I can tell you nothing more profound than that
about my friend.*

*In one of our early encounters, I asked you if you believed in
God. Your answer, as I think I may have said at the time, was
droll. You remarked that you could not believe in God before nine
o'clock in the morning. Taking that at face value, I can only
assume that the subject of the Almighty is somewhat alarming to
you and that mere chat cannot encompass Him. I would agree
with this, though I remain somewhat sorry that we did not pursue
the subject. I should like to have known your views before I depart.
You will speak of God with Mister Pilgrim, of that I can assure
you. Tell him, when you do, that my final thought on the matter
of belief was this: In the wilderness, I found an altar with this
inscription:* TO THE UNKNOWN GOD ... *And I have made
my sacrifice accordingly.*

I thank you for all you have done and for all you have yet to do in
Mister Pilgrim's behalf.

I remain most sincerely,
Sybil Quartermaine
P.S. The enclosed cheque should cover the expenses for some time to
come.

S.Q.

This cheque was for a great deal of money, made out not to
Jung, but to the Burghölzli Clinic. Still, he was leery of accepting it.

He turned to the messenger, who by now was reading the
titles of the books on Jung's shelves and had reached the works
of Goethe.

"If you will wait one moment, I shall give you a letter to Lady
Quartermaine ..."

It was his intention to return the cheque.

But the messenger said: "I have been instructed by Her Ladyship not to accept a reply."

"How very odd."

"She was ad'mint, sir. That was her word for it: *ad'mint*."

"I see. Well. Thank you."

Jung gave the young man a modest tip for his trouble and sent
him on his way.

There were six packets, each presumably containing a single
volume of Pilgrim's journal. Each was numbered. Jung spread
them out in order on the library table and looked at them in
much the same way one might regard a windfall of Christmas
gifts from strangers. *What could be inside ...?*

"One at a time," he said out loud. "Only one."

Of course, who would know the difference if he were to open
them all at once?

I would know—that's who would know.

Yes. I thought it wouldn't be long before you chimed in.

It's my job.

What—to drive me mad?

Possibly.

Jung made a stack of the journals and carried them over to his desk, where he locked them—all but *Number One*—in the bottom drawer and pocketed the key.

He then went to the window and gazed out at his garden.

The first daffodil—the one he had photographed—was fading now, and turning dry and crisp. A wind in the night might carry it away. But others—a host of others—were pushing into the light.

His mind drifted back to Lady Quartermaine's letter. How sad it was—and odd.

In the wilderness I found an altar with this inscription: TO THE UNKNOWN GOD ... *And I have made my sacrifice accordingly.*

He decided she must be unwell. After all, more than a week ago he had thought how poorly she looked. Distressed. Sleepless, perhaps. Certainly anguished. If only he had kept his appointment with her for tea on the previous afternoon. But fate, in its lunar manifestation, had intervened in the form of an episode with Countess Blavinskeya, and the meeting with Lady Quartermaine had completely slipped his mind.

Well.

He would not think about it now. There was wine to be drunk and dinner to be had and all of Emma's research regarding Savonarola to discuss. And the children—and the dogs—and what to do with the garden furniture now that spring was here.

In the morning, he would read.

In the morning. In the morning.

And then, the sun went down.

BOOK THREE

1

On the morning of Tuesday, the 14th of May, at about the time Otto Mohr was assisting Sybil Quartermaine into the rear of the silver Daimler, Kessler was assisting Pilgrim into the lift on the third floor of the Burghölzli Clinic.

Sybil's blue-and-violet cashmere afghan, received from Otto Mohr's arm, was spread across her knees—while over Kessler's arm hung two large sheets in which to wrap his patient once the baths were achieved. Envelopes.

While Sybil sat back and admired the view of various bridges, cobbled streets and water, Pilgrim sat rigid in front of Kessler and counted the floors as they fell away above him. One. Two. Three. Four.

Otto Mohr turned left and shifted gears.

When they arrived at the basement, the operator—dead-eyed as ever, unfolded the gate.

"You see?" said Kessler. "There's nothing to fear."

Sybil, in the Daimler, reached for the hand-bar, noting it was made of wine-coloured marble. Against it, her grey kid glove had the look of a water-coloured hand, its fingers drawn in black-ink stitches. *I am insubstantial as a blot on someone's page*, she thought. And then: *how curious, to feel so intangible and yet so alive ...*

Pilgrim's chair rolled free of the cage and stopped on the carpet laid along the marble floor. *We are in a mausoleum*, he thought. *Someone has died.* The air was filled with salted mist. He could taste it.

As they began to gain the heights, Sybil turned to see the Zürichsee. *How beautiful it is*, she thought, *with all its trees along the shore and all its flowers on show. Just as Doctor Jung said it would be.*

"This way, please."

Kessler nodded at the Duty Nurse, who sat unsmiling at her desk. With his back, he pushed against the heavy glass door which was hers to defend against invaders. And escapees. Judging from her expression, the latter would be lucky to survive.

Kessler turned the Bath chair and began to push it forward.

Doors, doors and more doors. Cubicles—curtains—lounges—the dead laid out in bathrobes, or so it seemed. Steam and the sound of falling water everywhere.

Blavinskeya's mezzo was singing at a distance.

> *The water is wide,*
> *I cannot cross o'er*
> *And neither have I wings*
> *To fly ...*

Sybil leaned forward. There was a dog on the road.

He has come to greet me, she thought. *Someone somewhere is kind and has unchained him ...*

"Where are we now?" she asked.

"On the other side of the lake, my Lady, you will see the village of Küsnacht. Soon, we will come to the forest."

"Is that dog all right?"

"Yes, Madam."

"Please blow your horn to warn him. He doesn't seem to be going to move."

"He will move, Madam. I assure you," said Otto.

It was perhaps a Saint Bernard. Sybil had never seen a dog so large. And, sure enough, it padded aside as the Daimler passed. Sybil turned to watch it staring after them, its tail a flag, its head atilt as if to catch their departing scent.

Something prompted her to raise her hand in greeting—and farewell—and as she did, the dog raised its head and barked.

How curious and felicitous. How thoughtful of someone, to set him free and in our path.

Looking back again, she saw that the dog had disappeared. And, turning forward, she saw that they were entering a wood of varied trees—of aspen and poplars, of shadow pines with candelabrum arms and the tannenbaum of childhood. There were asphodel in bloom. It had to be impossible—yet there they were. And a nightingale, it seemed, was singing.

> *Build me a boat*
> *That will carry two*
> *And both shall row,*
> *My love and I.*

What on earth could have made her think of that?

I must be drifting again, she thought. And settled back to enjoy the view of slanted light and latticed trees whose branches reached out on either side. Barely stirring, she lifted her hand as if to welcome them.

> *The water is wide,*
> *I cannot cross o'er ...*
> *And I forget the rest.*

She almost slept.

In the baths, Kessler removed Pilgrim's robe and watched him rise and approach the waters.

His attenuated body might have been a cadaver, activated by clockwork. Each step was laid before the last as if some childhood game was being recalled. *Did we play it thus—or did we play it so?*

Thus and so. Thus and so.

Pilgrim raised his arms.

Walking the tightrope, Kessler decided. *That's what he's up to. Up on the high wire miles above us all.*

"You want some help, Mister Pilgrim?"

The arms descended.

His skin was almost blue, it was so pale. The colour of mother of pearl. And where it was stretched across his ribs, it was translucent. He might have pulled on stockings and sleeves and gloves of skin, with seams of violet veins and pure white toe- and fingernails like buttons. And yet his muscles were trim and his buttocks firm, for all their lack of flesh.

Between his shoulder blades, the butterfly had stretched its wings and the rope burns on his neck and throat were turning to scabs that one would soon be able to peel away like a chrysalis.

"You want me to help you, Mister Pilgrim? Mind you don't slip."

Pilgrim was poised now on the marble rim of the bath, his toes curled down to grip the edge.

"Nice hot water. You'll like it. Very relaxing. Soothing, you might say, just like a warm massage."

Sister Dora drifted past with Countess Blavinskeya on her arm. *A proper twosome*, Kessler thought—and smiled. In the steam, they looked as though their feet had left the ground—and the way the Countess danced along, they might have.

Pilgrim, watching them pass, made a gesture of modesty to cover his genitals, even though neither woman had looked in his direction.

At last, he descended into the water. All around him, the ghosts of beings who must have been human once went to and fro, some lost and others merely distracted. All were wrapped in winding sheets.

Pilgrim closed his eyes and spread his arms and legs. Sitting upon the sunken step, he let the water envelop him, exploring every plane and crevice—the prairie of his belly and the foothills of his breasts, the mountains of his shoulders. *I am a continent of possibilities*, he thought, *waisted by the Equator, divided by the Tropics, drawn and quartered by longitudes and latitudes, floating my islands—fingers, penis, toes and testicles—and if I draw myself into a ball, I am the very model of the earth itself ...*

He smiled. *What a pity*, he thought, *that I have sunk so low*. Waisted by the Equator, indeed! Divided by the Tropics. Drawn and quartered by longitudes and latitudes ... *Am I Dante Gabriel Rossetti? I pray not! Have I also lilies in my hand and stars in my hair?*

"Mister Pilgrim?"

Kessler came and stooped beside him, reaching out and holding him more or less upright by placing his hands on Pilgrim's shoulders.

"You mustn't put your head underwater, Mister Pilgrim. That's a rule. You're here to relax, not play at being a fish."

Pilgrim sat again on the submerged step and laid his arms along the rim of the tub.

"That's better," Kessler smiled. "We don't want you drowned."

At the crest of the Albis Pass, there is a brief plateau from which a spectacular view of the world above and below may be had.

Sybil Quartermaine, having asked Otto to stop the motor car, wrapped her afghan around her shoulders and, telling him she wanted to stand outside, waited for him to open the door and offer his hand.

Tilting her head, she took a draught of air.

"Oh," she said, closing her eyes, "what a lovely scented wind. Can you smell the trees? It's perfect heaven!"

"Yes, Madam. Perfect heaven."

"Take me to the edge. I want to look."

Otto proffered his arm and escorted her to the verge. All the Zürichsee was spread out before them—and far below, a river and a road. Otto pointed into the distance at the misted, floating image of the Jungfrau—a majestic grey mirage, unattached, adrift.

Sybil clutched at her afghan.

"The wind," she said. "The wind ..."

"It is called *der Föhn*, Madam. It comes out of Italy and causes troubles."

"Troubles?"

"Rains and storms and sometimes an avalanche."

Sybil adjusted the afghan, took a last look at the view and returned to the Daimler.

"Let us move on," she said.

These were her final words.

* * *

All at once, Pilgrim felt cold.

He stood up.

Unaccountably, he reached for Kessler's hand and held it as he might have held a lifeline thrown into the sea.

Is there a dog? There must be a dog, he was thinking.

Kessler assisted his patient from the bath and drew a sheet around his shoulders. It did not make sense that Pilgrim should be so cold while Kessler sweated in the steam, but plainly the man was shivering.

"You want to go now, sir? Return to your room?"

No, no, no. I want to find the dog.

Pilgrim moved forward into the mist.

"Don't," he whispered. "Don't. Not now. You mustn't. Don't."

Kessler felt a thrill pass over his back.

Pilgrim had spoken.

Words. Not just sounds—but words.

Had spoken—and now had disappeared.

Kessler followed as best he could—checking each steam-shrouded figure he encountered—until at last he found his patient seated on one hip, his right hand against the tiles. Beside him, a bald and naked man, whose minder had him tied at the wrist with a cotton leash, was staring blank-eyed and open-mouthed at the ceiling.

Pilgrim was pale as the mist itself.

"Did this one fall?" Kessler asked the minder, an intern whose name was Fröelich.

"No. I just found him sitting here," Fröelich said. "My patient tripped on him and tried to bite his hand. Is he yours?"

"Yes. His name is Pilgrim."

Kessler hunkered down and said: "come along, sir. Up we get."

He reached for Pilgrim's left hand and found it bloodied.

"He's bleeding," he told Fröelich. "You shouldn't bring that man down here. He's dangerous."

"I won't again," Fröelich said, "but Doctor Furtwängler believed it would be good for him. Frankly," Fröelich grinned and giggled and leaned in close to Kessler's ear, "this man thinks he's a dog and sometimes I have to put his dinner plate on the floor before he'll eat."

"You shouldn't laugh," said Kessler. "It isn't funny. He might have hurt someone very badly. If you want my opinion, Doctor Furtwängler is crazy."

Pulling Pilgrim to his feet, he wrapped him in the second sheet.

"We'll get your robe and go back upstairs to your room," he said. "I'll clean your hand and then we'll have some tea. That's what's needed now—a nice, strong cup of tea. And then we'll have a rest before our dinner."

Kessler turned Pilgrim towards the distant Bath chair, where his robe had been left and where he could be dried and dressed.

Like a child, Kessler thought. *Just like a child—and me his mother. It doesn't do, sometimes, to venture forth. It simply doesn't do when there's a man out here who thinks he's a bear and now another thinking he's a dog. Pray God the lions and tigers don't come next.*

And then he thought: *but he spoke! He spoke! My man has spoken!*

2

*If he had only written these words before that Monday morning,
they might have proved my salvation. As it was, come Wednesday,
I was in need of ashes—not for my brow alone, but for the whole of
my being—and for my mind.*

Jung had now read this dubious marginalia twenty times.
Date was: Friday, 10th February, 1497 ...
What was Pilgrim's source for this pompous assumption? And
the words themselves—on what basis were they formulated?
Who was this *I*, who broke so suddenly into the narrative?
It was maddening.
Out of Pilgrim's dreams, all at once a voice of authority. *I*.
Not only that, but this *I* kept notes and dated them. Record-
ing a dream was one thing, but pinning the dream events in
time, right down to the day, the month and the year was quite
another. Especially when the date given was hundreds of years
before the dreamer's own life.
On again, off again, Jung was beginning to wish he had
resisted the impulse to turn the page. But his damned *Inquisitor*
had tricked him into it.
Don't blame me.
Why not? It was your doing.
*No amount of not turning pages will eradicate what's written on
them. Turning a blind eye solves nothing, Carl Gustav. Turning the
page solves at least something.*
True enough.
There you go then. TURN THE PAGE! should become your motto.
I don't want a motto.
Too bad. You've got one. Turn the page.
I can't before I know what it means. Who was—who is this *I?*

Pilgrim.

Don't be ridiculous. He wasn't there.

He was, in his dreams.

Only as an observer. He did not experience those things—that rape.

You think so.

Of course I think so! For one thing, Pilgrim is a man.

So was Elisabetta.

The doorbell rang.

"I will go!" Jung called, rising from his desk, grateful to escape the debate.

In the hallway, he could see an indistinct figure beyond the frosted light beside the door.

The sun was setting. The sky was orange.

Yesterday's messenger, for whatever reason, had returned. His golden head appeared to have an aureole of fire. His cap was in his hand.

"Come in."

"I must speak with you in private, Herr Doktor, if I may."

"Of course. We'll go along to my study."

"Thank you."

Once the study door was closed and Jung was seated at his desk, he invited the messenger to speak.

"I have come with unhappy news," the young man said.

"I see." Jung removed his glasses and laid them on top of Pilgrim's journal. Best, he believed, not to witness the delivery of bad news—so often an embarrassment for those who must deliver it. Give the impression one is fixed on the messenger, but avoid eye contact. Be blind and seem to focus on the mouth—the lips—the words.

"There has been an avalanche on the Albis Pass road. This morning just before noon. Lady Quartermaine's motor car ..."

Every clock in the house all at once seemed to stop.

"I understand."

"Yes, sir. Thank you, sir."

Jung stood up and went to the window.

Daffodils.

Dusk.

And so ...

"Has she been found?"

"Yes, sir. And her chauffeur. The dogs found them."

"Were there others?"

"No, sir. The Alpine Patrol has issued a statement. Only the English woman and her driver. No other vehicles. No other persons. A charabanc on its way to the Obersee was passing on the road below, but it escaped."

"And who has sent you?"

"Lady Quartermaine's maid-servant, Herr Doktor. She was extremely upset, but said she was certain you would want to know."

"And her name?"

"Fräulein Peebles, sir."

"Is she alone?"

"No, sir. There's an Englishman with her, name of Forster."

"Ah, yes. I know of him."

"Yes, sir."

Jung's mind drifted off towards the fatal Pass beyond the lake.

The messenger coughed.

Jung turned.

"Will that be all, sir?" the young man asked.

"Yes—and thank you."

Jung passed him a franc piece and clapped him on the shoulder.

"I will walk you to the door," he said.

Just as the messenger was leaving, Jung asked if anything had been said about a man called Pilgrim.

"No, sir. Nothing."

"Very well. Good day to you."

Jung went back to his study.

The news could wait, he decided. There was no point telling Emma just yet. Nor Mister Pilgrim. Not until he knew more.

3

Referring to Giorgio Vasari's *Lives of the Most Eminent Painters, Sculptors and Architects*, Walter Pater's *Studies in the History of the Renaissance* and the newly published 1911 edition of *The Encyclopædia Britannica*, Emma had assembled the following notes, which she had laid on Jung's desk for his perusal. In the aftermath of Sybil Quartermaine's death, he reached for them as a welcome distraction.

For most of 1496 and the early weeks of 1497, Leonardo had been living in Milan at the court of its Prince, Lodovico Sforza. While much was accomplished, the larger part of his work was a frivolous waste of the artist's talents. Leonardo himself was apparently the major cause of this waste. He seemed not to care, Emma had written. *He spent his mornings designing scenery for masques, his afternoons copying scientific data into his notebooks, his evenings sketching fantastic notions of futuristic cannons, crossbows, siege-craft and the like— his nights in the arms of his boys.*

On the other hand, she had added, *he had begun the creation of* The Last Supper *in 1495 and would not be satisfied it was complete until 1498. In 1497 he returned to Florence briefly in late February and again in June.*

The Last Supper, *a fresco, is on the walls of the refectory of the Dominicans of Santa Maria delle Grazie in Milan. I have seen it, you have not—though I've told you about it often enough. In Leonardo's own time, rumour had it that he would arrive at the convent helter-skelter, any old time of day or night, and add a single brush stroke of colour or delete a single shadow. If you have read Mister Pilgrim's treatise, you will also know, Leonardo did not himself create the face of Christ—but left it blank.*

*   *   *

Yes. Jung had forgotten that.

Next, there were notes regarding Savonarola:

Girolamo Savonarola was a Dominican friar born in 1452, the same year as da Vinci. He was L.'s absolute opposite in almost every respect. Where L. the artist dared not choose a human model for the Son of God, S. the priest had offered himself as Heaven's emissary—possibly even the second Son of God. L. left the face of his Christ unpainted for fear of offence, whereas S. stood behind Christ's very image and claimed to speak in His voice. S. had risen quickly through the ranks of his order and caught the attention of Rome. By 1497, he had gained a following of thousands, was inducted into the Signory and stood to become the next ruler of Florence.

There was more concerning Savonarola's rise to power; the death of Lorenzo di Medici in April of 1492; the surrender of Florence to Charles VIII of France and the flight of Piero di Medici, Lorenzo's son, in October of 1494. That a mere five years had elapsed between the death of Lorenzo the Magnificent and Savonarola's supremacy was all the proof a reader of history required to assess the potency of the Priest's charisma.

And the Bonfire of Vanities?

Jung turned to the next page.

On the evening of Tuesday, the 7th of February, 1497, Emma had written, *an extraordinary event took place in the Piazza della Signoria in Florence.*

The Priest—or the hated Priest, as he was known to some—had called for a gigantic bonfire on which the citizens of Florence were to throw their most prized and valued possessions. Burn everything you love, *he had said,* for the love of things is evil and obstructs the way to God.

This was not the first such bonfire, but it would be the largest. Its smoke would reach the heavens. *This was Savonarola's decree.*

All through the time of Carnival, the priest's Choirboys had policed the streets, breaking up gambling games, assaulting prostitutes with sticks and tearing lace and jewellery from the clothing even of the merchants' wives. Savonarola had dubbed these boys his little bands of hope *and, ostensibly, they were collecting alms for the Church, though the alms might be anything from a man's whole purse to a woman's silver bracelets and glass earrings—even to a child's toy horse, a painted ball or a doll wearing red.*

(What a dreadful time!) Emma had written.

For two years now, the Priest had overseen the structuring of laws that were designed to control the wanton spread of immoral values and the dominance of sin. *It was the Signory and its Council who must enforce these laws, but it was Savonarola, as a member of that Council, who articulated the laws and persuaded his fellow Councillors to vote for them.*

Horse racing had been forbidden; gambling was punishable with torture; profanity was banned and blasphemers, if caught, had their tongues pierced. Secular song was discouraged—also dancing—also games. (Dear me! It sounds more as if Martin Luther was doing all this! E.J.) Jews, as Lent approached, were paraded through the streets, while the general populace pelted them with manure. Brothels were set on fire and the women driven beyond the gates of the city. Servants were paid to inform on their masters in all these matters, but escaped retribution by making their charges in the confessional.

And yet, for all its Lutheran ideals and notions of how the State should be governed, the Signory and its Council under Savonarola's guidance was popular. Especially with the merchants of the middle and upper classes, whose taxes had been adjusted to favour them—while the taxes of the rich and poor alike had been adjusted—as some would have it—to ruin them.

It was a time of religious zeal and piety on the one hand, and a time of muted rebellion and growing unrest on the other.

All of this came to its climax with the Bonfire of Vanities in 1497.

(I hope all this helps, but the fact is, it more than turns my stomach and makes me glad I did not have to suffer it. On the Bonfire of Vanities, my darling, what would you have sacrificed? I can think of nothing. The smallest beloved object would be too precious. E.)

* * *

Jung had already cut the binding twine—regretting as he did the sight of Sybil Quartermaine's Italianate hand, in blue ink, addressing him as *Herr Doktor C.G. Jung* and reminding him that this was *Parcel Number One*. The latter had been underscored with three thick lines drawn without a ruler. That they wavered was more than likely the result of the wine she had drunk—though Jung did not know this.

On setting aside the brown wrapping paper, Jung discovered that Pilgrim's taste in bindings was as meticulous as his penmanship. This volume, unlike the first he had perused, was covered in a smoky grey broadcloth—giving it the appearance of a ship's log. Could the colour have been a tribute to Leonardo's *sfumato*—the "mists of time" he had layered onto his paintings? Perhaps so.

For a moment, Jung sat with one hand resting on this cover, smoothing it absently, telling himself to *turn the page*.

Oh, why, he thought, *is it all so sad?*

And then he thought: *because the last hand to touch this cloth was Lady Quartermaine's, now swept away by snow.*

Page one was almost barren. Near the bottom, on the right-hand side, Pilgrim had written: *Make prayers against despair.* And underneath this, the letters *S.l.J.*

S.l.J. meant nothing, but Jung would ask.

On page two, another impertinent, infuriating number, sitting there—floating above the words without any reference to its meaning:

7th

And then:

Ye women who glory in your ornaments, your hair, your hands, I tell you—you are ugly. Would you see true beauty? Look at the pious man or woman in whom the spirit dominates matter; watch him that prays and see how the light of divine beauty glows upon him when his prayer is ended. You will see then the beauty of God shining in his face and behold the face of an angel.

Thus were we admonished by the Priest.

Followed by:

A dream:

Antonio Gherardini, his wife, daughters and servants were preparing to attend the Bonfire of Vanities in the Piazza della Signoria. All had been assigned the task of selecting their own contributions to the conflagration. Anything was acceptable, so long as it was not already chosen by another member of the household. They would drive the distance in their carriage, but wear no insignia, as a sign of piety.

At four o'clock in the afternoon, Elisabetta was in her bedchamber completing her selection and laying it onto a large white tablecloth whose corners she would tie in order to carry it. The cloth was spread in the sunlight on her bed and there was only one more thing to add to its contents.

Cornelia, her cat, was sitting in the doorway—the door ajar, the sunlight streaming. Her coat was of dappled red and grey. Her eyes were closed and her tail was curled like a question mark in the dust.

The windows were open. The villa, on its hill, faced south and west and Elisabetta could see the smudge marks on the sky where the Duomo and its campanile rose above the river mists and the smoke of early fires.

She sat down.

One last thing I love.

She shied her glance towards Cornelia.

Never. Never. No. An animal is not a vanity.

Already folded on the tablecloth were Angelo's favoured hose and doublets—his doeskin boots—his ribbon-wristed gloves—his velvet toques—his pleated shirts. Now one last thing.

Elisabetta already knew what it was, because she held it in her hand. Her most beloved object. Her most beloved possession. Her brother Angelo's portrait in its silver locket which, when opened, showed him in his fifteenth year. Opposite, and painted in miniature by the same artist, was a portrait of Elisabetta herself. Each of them wore their favoured grey and blue. Neither of them smiled. It had been forbidden.

Now, she was a woman. She wore a woman's clothes. She had unbound her breasts and bound her hair in modest veiling. She wore no jewellery, no gloves, no scarves and only the plainest shoes.

The bruises on her hips, her thighs and on her wrists were hidden. No one had seen them but herself. Not even Violetta, her nurse.

That morning, after prayers, Elisabetta had told her father she was now prepared to consider suitors. She had quit men's attire forever. Her mourning for Angelo was over. Life must continue. She must do her duty—marry, have children and take her modest place in society.

She had sung this litany of platitudes in a monotone, staring at her father's hands where they rested, folded on the table across from where she sat. She was tired. She was beaten. She had surrendered.

Her father was kind—even conciliatory. He welcomed her back, he kissed her and blessed her. He even smiled.

Now, they would go to the Bonfire of Vanities, make their contributions, pay their tributes and depart. It would be over.

At twilight, the carriage arrived on the drive. Its pale green sides, with her father's painted monograms and guild crests, were draped in black. Elisabetta smiled. They were, after all, on their way to a funeral of sorts—the cremation of her former self, whose life had been so short.

There were so many carriages, so many horsemen, so many people streaming on foot from every direction, Signor Gherardini said the coachman must dismount and lead the horses through the crowd until all forward movement was impossible. Only then would they descend.

A parade of singing priests and acolytes cut in front of them. They were led by four child-angels who carried Donatello's infant Christ on their shoulders—the angels got up in white and paper wings, and the priests robed in grey.

The bells of all the churches within the city walls began to toll. In any other year, this would have been a riotous scene of Carnival—with colours flying from every window and crowds of dancers, musicians, hawkers and costumed men and women wearing masks. All the horses would have pranced and all the dogs set barking. But not on this occasion.

The zealous wept and chanted the holy names; crosses were borne on every side by would-be martyrs; the smell of incense was universal. Each of the citizens carried a token of sacrifice— some with sacks and some with boxes, some with paintings, some with books and some with masks and ribbons, carnival costumes, hats and pretty coloured flags—all denoting the denial of pleasure.

The bonfire itself, when at last it could be seen, was built in the shape of a pyramid sixty feet high or more—and, so it was later claimed, two hundred and forty feet in circumference. There were seven separate stages already laden with vanities, and at the crown, an effigy of Satan, painted red.

Four young men and four young women—*the purest of the pure*—had been chosen from more than a hundred candidates, all put forward by their parents—and these were, two by two, to set the bonfire ablaze at four assigned stations.

As the chanting and the singing rose above the Piazza, Savonarola watched from the campanile of the Palazzo Vecchio— standing in the shadows, his hood in place, his face unseen.

When the signal was given and the chosen ones stepped forward with their torches, a hush descended—and as if they had sensed what was going to happen, the doves on all the surrounding cornices and window ledges suddenly rose with a universal clap of wings and, for a moment before they departed, blackened the twilit sky.

Elisabetta put her hand out, asking Alessandro, her father's stable boy, to assist her. Her nurse Violetta came after and then her parents. Her sister Ginetta did not get down, but handed her vanity—a treasured collar of Belgian lace—to her mother and remained behind with the coachman, who had been told to stay with the horses.

It was all but impossible to get through. The crowd had surged forward as soon as the fires were lit and the assembled vanities on all seven stages had begun to burn.

Elisabetta put one arm around Violetta's waist and together they pushed towards the conflagration, using their shoulders and elbows to force their way through.

Signor Gherardini took his wife Alicia's hand and, followed by young Alessandro bearing their vanities—a doublet of crimson taffeta, a gown of cream-coloured silk encrusted with beads of glass—they waded into the sea of backs.

The heat was so great, Elisabetta thought for a moment she herself was on fire. She and Violetta finally gained the perimeter, which now was ringed with armed soldiers attempting to hold the zealots back, for fear they might attempt to immolate themselves. Beyond them, some of the priests had formed an inner circle and were reaching out to take the newly offered vanities and throw them into the flames. Violetta, who had waited until this moment to show her chosen vanity, drew a rough wooden crucifix from her pocket, held it up for the priests to see and threw it beyond their waiting hands into the fire. "I offer this because the Bonfire itself is a vanity and shows a perverted love of God!" she shouted, though no one heard her but Elisabetta.

Before Elisabetta lifted her bundle over the wall of arms, she snatched the silver locket away from its folds—turned again and, clutching still at Violetta's waist, began to make her way back towards her father's carriage.

Within twenty feet of her goal, she stopped dead in her tracks with Violetta beside her.

"What is it? What?" the nurse asked.

Elisabetta said nothing.

Seated nearby on a sorrel horse, Leonardo was staring at them, his eyes narrowed, his lips parted—his hair pulled away from his face and tucked beneath a wide-brimmed hat.

Elisabetta gazed at him without expression. *Yes—you know me. Yes—it is I. Good day to you, my bastard lord.*

As if he had read her thought, Leonardo turned and rode away.

Elisabetta closed her eyes. Her insides ached. Her knees gave way and she fell against Violetta, catching at her shoulders.

Somehow they achieved the carriage, where Ginetta held out her hands and helped her sister to climb inside.

Nothing was said. They sat and waited.

All around them, the crowd had raised its collective hands as if to catch the moon—but the moon escaped and rode out the rest of the night in a veil of smoke, while the city below it seemed to be cast adrift on a sea of singing fire.

> *Tyrannus impius non habet spem,*
> *et si quidem longae vitae erit,*
> *in nihilum computabitur.*

> *The ungodly ruler has no hope,*
> *and even though he live forever,*
> *he shall be seen as nothing.*

By midnight, all was ashes and by dawn, there was a rising wind.

In the early hours, while the lamps were being extinguished, Leonardo packed his satchel and his saddlebags and, taking Strazzi with him, left the studio and triple-locked its doors.

Last seen by the Watch, they were passing through the Porto Milano and riding northward.

Elisabetta, on her hillside, could feel their presence being lifted from her as she saw the sun's first rays strike the towers and spires below her. Calling to Cornelia, she climbed like a sleepy child onto her bed, lay there with her cat against her belly, closed her eyes and drifted towards what remained of her life as though it was a dream already dreamt and a future already possessed.

I am a circle, she was thinking. *A circle within a circle, bearing yet more circles within me all the way to eternity, for surely, now that he is gone, I shall never die.*

4

There was music—this is true. Dwarfs, there were none—though you promised them. A juggler—yes. And an angel with wings whose every feather had been cut from paper, tinted with blue and gold and pink and fitted one by one into frames you had fashioned with your own hands. Nothing was spared for my entertainment.

My husband had said: *I want her as she is, before she fades.*

You told me that—and thought, I suppose: *it will make her smile.*

And smile I did.

To *fade* when you are still a girl at heart and only twenty-four years old was not a possibility I entertained, although it is true I had borne four of my children by then and something, somewhere in me, had begun to fade.

There was a monkey—do you remember?—and from time to time he sat beside me. Once, he climbed onto my head and several times he climbed onto my shoulder. When he climbed onto my head, we all laughed and his master had to tempt him with fruit before he would descend without tearing my veil. As it was, he pulled the veil aside, revealing my birthmark—and you were angry, wanting the monkey removed. But I demanded it remain. *I will not sit*, I said, *unless the monkey stays.*

Yes. It was all familiar to me: the windows facing north which gave the light in which I sat; the giant chest of drawers, the drawers all crammed with your notebooks, sketches, boxes of crayons and sheets of ragged paper; the fireplace with its rampant lions supporting the mantel; the armoire with its toys and costumes, masks and hats and shoes and one blue dress with silver stars—the remnants of your happy days. And the heavy chairs, each one of them; the lamps, their gryphon sconces; and the table.

And the table.

And the table. Yes?

Someone, I don't remember who it was—a friend of yours perhaps, perhaps a lover—came on certain days and sang. I did not so much dislike his voice as the way in which he presented his songs. He sang to you, not me. One day, I said: *you might as well sing to the monkey.* He never came back.

There were lutes and flutes and oboes and something not unlike a lute that was called a *mandolin.* A choirboy came and sang very sweetly. They brought my babies to me—not that Ernesto, at four, could be called a baby, but was and is and always will be my baby. All my babies—six of them, now. And the two who died.

I will have no more. And have said so. Francesco has his requisite sons and I have done all I can to give his name and his blood to posterity. What remains of my life, I shall devote entirely to the enjoyment of watching my babies grow.

Once a mother, always a mother. The same cannot be said for fathers. Fathers scatter their progeny so far afield from where they live, I think that half the children now alive will never know who their father is—or was. Or might have been. And half the fathers living do not know the names, the shapes, the sexes or the smiles of half their children. Or the touch of a searching hand that asks for safety in the dark.

How sad to be a father.

And how damnable.

Sometimes as I sat and watched you from my place in the filtered light, I thought of telling you. It occurred to me once or twice, as I sat, that you had a right to know. But I was silent. Wisely.

I wanted some kind of revenge. But nothing I could think of was sufficient. Except the child. The child was my secret weapon, like the knife with which I almost stabbed you all those years ago. I would tell you first that you had a child. A boy. A lovely golden boy—your hair, your eyes, your form. I would drive you mad with descriptions of his beauty—his smell—his laughter—his smile and his wondrous openness to everything I showed him; all the doors I opened before his eyes ... his joyous, joyous willingness to live.

And then I would tell you of his death.

His dreadful, wasteful, stupid, godless death.

And then I would think—and I remember thinking this so clearly—*no. I will not share his death with you.*

It was my death, too. More mine than his. At least he had no notion what had happened to him. He slept—that was all. He went to sleep alive, and in the night—he died.

Just died.

That is all I can tell you.

He was one year old.

He could walk the whole distance across a room by himself.

He called me *Mama* and Cornelia *'Nelia* and Violetta *Nanna.* He also had a doll he called *Da.*

I will tell no more.

But how proud I was that I refrained from telling you then. I kept the knowledge of him with me as my weapon against despair—knowing that whatever else happened to me, I had the protection of his existence, no matter how brief, as proof that anything can be survived.

It was his gift to me—that I survived you—and gave him life in spite of your deadly malice.

Why would I tell you his name—our child? He was no concern of yours. Though we "made" him, there was no union— merely violence. *Fusion, copulation, propagation, coupling*—even *mating*—for all that they reflect the labours of the marriage bed when love is absent, these are noble words compared to the getting of our son. We *grappled.* Don't you remember?

I was vandalized. You stole my life.

And gave me his.

And for all that, you hated what you did and got no pleasure from it. At least my husband sighs when he is on me. You had no sighs—no murmurs even of triumph. One great cry is all I hear in memory of that moment—not mine, but yours. A cry of pain, Leonardo. Agony. And it is my belief that in that moment when the cry was given, you had discovered what it is to kill. It was a killer's cry. A beast's in the heat of dragging down its victim—a winning cry—that you had seized your opponent by the throat and disemboweled him, as the panther does and the leopard when he curls upon his prey. In fact, for one whole year I called you *Leopardo* in my mind. *Leopardo da Vinci.*

Yes?

This is true.

All this is true.

You might have cried out: *while I slay, I am slain!* It merely depended on which of us would be the first to die. For while you mortally wounded me, I mortally wounded you. And knew it. Now, unless Heaven falls upon you, I have beaten you to the grave. You are dying, Leonardo—but I am dead. You killed me long ago. Not my body—but my love of life.

My parents knew of the child and to my great surprise, they came in time to cherish him, not knowing he was yours—though I hesitate still to use that word. *Yours* denotes caring—longing—pride—enjoyment. *Yours* denotes devotion to a vanity. Yes? You must recall the Bonfire of Vanities on which we laid what was cherished. I laid my freedom there that night. I shed my brother Angelo's clothes and burned them so that I would never again be tempted by their allure. I also noted that you laid nothing down, but turned away and departed. This way, I knew that you regarded nothing as yours because you honoured nothing to be worthy of a sacrifice. Beyond one thing—your personal vanity. That, I grant you, remained in your possession.

You told me that you loved my brother. I believe you. I loved him, too, though the Angelo I loved and the one you called your lover were not the same young man. If he was wanton, then I rejoice for him because it means that he gained his freedom before he died. I never did and never will. But I do not wish to be misunderstood in this. There is a wantonness in men that is not akin to the wantonness in women. If I were to gain my freedom now, I could no longer be myself. If I had gained it then, I should not now be who I am. As it is, I have a wanton will that my children—those who remain—shall live full lives. And those who are dead shall never be forgotten. One, you know of—the other was my husband's child, the girl Alida, who died six months before I sat to you.

I sat in velvet and satin. You bade me wear some veiling on my hair and draped the upper reaches of the windows in the same pale gauze. It was blue. You wanted always some diffusion of the light—or so you told me. This way, the play of it was constant.

You refused to paint my birthmark, as if its being a butterfly offended you. I wore a silver locket, which you also did not paint. This is true. And a marriage ring which is not seen and a pillow at my back which was made for me by Violetta Cappici, who sat, all the while you worked, near the window with my babies and a book. She carried, you may remember, a painted fan with which she cooled my forehead, time to time. It showed a garden in the south with peacocks and a laurel tree—the laurel all in bloom.

And I removed my shoes and, having sat so long, could not replace them because my feet were swollen. And the angel with the paper wings knelt down and soothed them in a basin filled with scented water. Roses. Do you remember these things? I do. And now you are in France. A great way off, or so it seems. I cannot count the distance. There are rumours of your decline. Surely it will please you to know that at least you are spoken of in Florence—remembered and, yes, in some households, revered. That you will die is certain. But I have no wish to dwell on that beyond the fact that, before you die, I wanted you to know the truth about the child. If Heaven exists, you may see him there. If not, so be it.

I am told you have taken me with you. Some say you will not be parted from me and others say the story of my husband's refusal to have the portrait in his house is false and that you would not let him have me. This story goes that you claim the painting is unfinished. Another goes that you are in love with me.

I think not.

In all the time I sat to you, you never once acknowledged that we had met. Certainly never that we had *grappled* and that you had won. You gave me entertainments instead—the choirboy and the mandolin—the angel and the monkey. The making of my image cost us three whole years of being in one another's company. I was given rocks and rivers to sit amongst and colonnades to sit between and a kitchen chair to sit on. The chair was real, the rest was not. And nothing for my mind to rest on—or my heart. *If posterity looks on me,* I thought, *they will recognize only the man who painted me.*

If I am smiling still, then we alone will know that what is hidden there is the memory of a golden child. Not yours—but mine. And I will take him to my grave.

I do not wish you ill, nor any dread of me. We will pass together silent into time. But I wonder, will you write somewhere of me before you die: *face of a Florentine woman—painted by blue light, 1503–1506. Sleeves of dark green velvet. One button—made of wood.*

This is the last you shall hear of me. The button here enclosed is from his jacket, which I keep beside me always. It is all of him that you shall ever have.

Go then, in whatever peace you can achieve.

Elisabetta Giocondo,

The Florentine Woman.

April 12, 1519.

On the second of May, in the same year, Leonardo da Vinci died at Cloux, in the valley of the Loire. He was sixty-seven.

5

It was not unlike the day of recovery after a long battle with illness. A calm had descended, marked by the presence of sunlight and the opening of windows. A fresh breeze stirred the curtains and turned the pages of open books. In various rooms, the occupants looked up from whatever had preoccupied them and wondered—sometimes aloud—what might have caused the silence that, for a moment only, was universal.

At eight o'clock on the morning of Monday, May 20th—six days after Sybil Quartermaine's death—Jung made his way along the third-floor corridor of the Zürich Clinic to Suite 306. In his hand was a brown leather bag such as those employed by piano students to transport their sheet music. It was, in fact, the property of his six-year-old daughter, Anna—who had relinquished it only on the promise that it would be returned when her father had found a suitable replacement. His own satchel had gone missing.

Inside the bag were the fragments of what Jung had culled and copied from his notebooks concerning Pilgrim—some as loose pages, others as torn remnants of envelopes—others, the backs of calling cards—others, mere scraps of paper, crisp shards of cardboard, magazines, and the Clinic's internal memos and bits that had once been menus in restaurants or the insides of matchboxes. All of these bore scribbles—phrases—single words—whole paragraphs—and, in one or two cases, Fräulein Unger's transcripts of passages from Jung's notebooks, reference books and daybooks.

There was an envelope containing photographs—a replica of the *Mona Lisa* cut from a magazine—a monograph, with tinted illustrations, concerning the genus of butterfly collectively known as *Psyche*—a handwritten copy of Elisabetta Giocondo's letter to Leonardo (as though it had only to be posted) and finally, the envelope addressed to Pilgrim from Sybil Quartermaine.

The copy of Elisabetta's missive was intended for Archie Menken, whose opinion of it Jung was eager to seek—and since he could not show Archie the journal itself, he had thought to provide the letter as an enticement. No version of the name appeared—*Elisabetta del Giocondo, La Gioconda, Madonna Elisabetta* (shortened over time to *Mona Lisa*). It was entirely as Pilgrim had presented it—but unsigned. *Who might have written this?* Jung intended to ask. Just to see ... just to see what sort of reaction it might elicit. Emma had transcribed it for him—weeping as she had done so.

All of these, but for La Gioconda's letter, were weapons, ready to be wielded in the ongoing war between Pilgrim's belligerent silence and Jung's aggressive pursuit of his patient's voice. Kessler, in the meantime, had informed Jung of Pilgrim's brief sentences, whispered on the day of Sybil Quartermaine's death. But still ... To have whispered in the baths was not to speak to one's doctor. *To whisper to the air is not to address a person*—and Jung was prudent. *They might not even have been words, for all Kessler could tell*, he concluded. There was also the fact that on his return from the baths that day, Pilgrim had slowly subsided into a state that was almost comatose, and had not truly wakened except to stumble to the toilet and back to his bed. Kessler had informed Jung of this, as well, and was instructed to record any words that might be spoken, to monitor Mister Pilgrim's breathing and pulse rate and to call at once if any significant change took place. All remained stable, however, and Mister Pilgrim did not utter. He did not even snore, Kessler noted, which meant that his own sleep was undisturbed.

For all the gravity of its contents, the music bag seemed to Jung to be as light as air. What it contained, after all, might make it possible to negotiate an armistice. If these would not provoke whole speech, then nothing would. These, and the dreadful news of Lady Quartermaine's death.

In debating his own attitude to the latter, Jung at first had considered setting the subject aside as a separate encounter—that he would not connect it with any of the weapons in his arsenal ...

Really, Carl Gustav! Weapons! Arsenal! Such a pompous attitude!

I am thinking only of the patient's good.

Hit him on the head with a hammer? Knock him down with a wooden mallet? Kick him in the shins and box his ears?

I must be cruel only to be kind.

Oh, for heaven's sake!

Well, it's true. I've coddled him too long.

Seems to me, it's you who've been coddled. You're more considerate of yourself than you are of Mister Pilgrim—avoiding at every turn the simple courtesy of treating him like a patient. You treat him, instead, like a prize. A trophy. Look what I have here! The oddity of oddities! The man who cannot die! And I'm his keeper! Me!

The shameful truth is, I'm afraid of him.

He's only another human being, Carl Gustav. You deal with them every day.

Do I?

Look down the corridor. What do you see? A dozen doorways beyond which hides the human race in all its complexities and wondrous manifestations. In 308, a bear pit—in 309, the Moon. Back there in 301, a musical genius whose hands will not obey her, insisting they are the hands of Robert Schumann. In 304, a man who writes incessantly in an imaginary notebook. You have opened the door on these people day in, day out for as long almost as a year, and you have never doubted your competence to meet them on their own terms, without a qualm. What, after all, is so different about Mister Pilgrim that you doubt your ability to cope with him? Nothing, Carl Gustav. Nothing. At the beginning of every journey on this floor, you have stepped into the dark with nothing but your intelligence, your interest, your instincts, your understanding of psychiatry and your dedication to medicine. All that's lacking is a willingness to admit the extent of your ignorance.

Just then, Furtwängler appeared at the far end of the corridor, walking beside an intense young woman who wore an intern's smock. At once, Jung was reminded of Emma—a slimmer, slightly younger Emma, to be sure—but Emma nonetheless. Her hair was darker—her stature somewhat less—her manner more effusive. And clearly, she had Furtwängler's ear and was bending it at a furious rate. This was not like Emma. Emma would not have made such excitable gestures. She would not have given Furtwängler the benefit of her enthusiasm to anything like the degree this woman deployed. But she would have been an equally engaging companion. And was, when she was younger. Once ...

Carl Gustav.

Yes, yes—indeed. My appointment with Mister Pilgrim. Though surely, I could wait to be introduced to the young lady. So attractive ... So ...

No, Carl Gustav. Get on with your work. The Pilgrim case, after all, is your job at the moment.

Of course.

Jung saw that Furtwängler was stopping just short of room 308.

"Mister Leveritch lives in a bear pit," he told his young companion. "Be prepared."

As they went through the door, Furtwängler gave Jung a smile which Jung did not return. Instead, he went through into Suite 306.

"I've been waiting for you," Pilgrim said.

The sunlight was overwhelming, and when Jung at last could more or less see, he found his patient seated in the bedroom on a straight-backed chair—the Bath chair having been pushed into a darkened corner.

Kessler stood with one protective hand on Pilgrim's shoulder. "Good morning, Doctor," he said. He was smiling.

"Yes. Good morning," Jung replied, still half-blind. He looked sideways, guardedly, at Pilgrim. Had he indeed spoken—or was Kessler a ventriloquist? Or was it just a trick of Jung's embattled imagination?

Pilgrim was fully dressed, including a pair of elegant boots, the boots—like his trousers, jacket and waistcoat—white. And a bright bow tie which sat like a butterfly below a high collar. The tie was blue, with a touch of violet—a colour in between the two, neither completely one nor the other. It seemed almost to have settled there of its own volition. From Pilgrim's breast pocket, a handkerchief of similar hue made a graceful puff, as of smoke.

The expression on Pilgrim's face was that of a child who, expecting good news, has just divined that the news is bad.

Jung looked away, seeking refuge.

A chair had been placed near the foot of the bed. Plus a table—and on the table, an ashtray. *There.*

Jung sat down and slid the music bag onto the coverlet beside him.

Pilgrim followed this motion with his eyes. He made fists of both hands and pressed his knees together. His great height remained evident, even when he was seated. The curious cut of his hair was almost boylike, causing it to sit up over his brow as if the wind or a careless sweep of his hand had put it there. His cheeks, for all his general pallor, were pink. He might have just returned from a vigorous turn around the garden.

"Have you nothing to say?" he said to Jung. "I was expecting congratulations. My white suit ... the abandoned chair ... the undoubted pleasure of hearing my voice ..." Pilgrim gave a nervous smile. "Of course, I believe you've heard it before ... on a certain occasion. Though I cannot quite recall when that was, time is so ... what? So out of kilter? I think that is what I mean. *Out of joint.* Someone said that. Hamlet, more than likely. Hamlet says everything, doesn't he. Almost anything you can think of—so long as it's in blank verse ..."

He fell quiet.

Kessler shifted in his place and moved his fingers over Pilgrim's shoulder. He eased himself from one foot to the other. His shoes squeaked. He coughed into one cupped hand.

Pilgrim looked down.

Jung looked up.

"Mister Pilgrim ... There has been ..."

"An accident."

Pilgrim's voice was hoarse, as though he had spent the last week shouting. He glanced away sideways towards the window and lifted his head.

"*The water is wide,*" he whispered. "*I can not cross o'er.*"

"I beg your pardon?"

"It's a song. Just a song. Is she dead? My friend?"

"I'm afraid so. Yes."

Pilgrim stood up. Kessler's hand fell aside.

Pilgrim adjusted his tie. "I wore this for her," he said. "I suppose I knew. In fact ... I did know. I was hoping only that you ..." He went to the window. "I thought perhaps you might have come to tell me I was wrong."

"I'm afraid not."

"An accident, you say."

"Yes. In her motor car. She was killed in an instant, I can assure you."

Pilgrim shrugged.

"Why do people always feel they have to say that?" he said. "It's never true. And you know it isn't. If I'm supposed to trust you, you'll have to do better than that, Doctor."

"I'm sorry."

"You can tell me in a word. Just say it."

"Avalanche."

"Avalanche."

"Yes."

"I see." Pilgrim sighed. In his mind, the image of the silver Daimler was turned and tumbled by a child creating a giant snowball. Inside, the occupants were rolled and tossed like laboratory mice in a revolving wheel. He reached out and ran his fingers along the edge of the gauze curtain to his right. "Was Miss Peebles with her?"

"No."

"I thought not."

"Only her chauffeur."

"He must have had a name, Doctor Jung. They usually do."

"Yes. His name was Otto Mohr."

"Another instant death, no doubt."

"One can only hope so."

Pilgrim turned back into the room.

"I see that you have brought a child's music bag with you."

Surprised by the fact that Pilgrim had noticed the bag at all, let alone that he had guessed its true owner, Jung could only mutter: "I borrowed it from my daughter."

Pilgrim indicated the bed, where the bag lay. "Is there anything in it for me?" he asked. He said this not so much coyly as meanly. It seemed almost that he was taunting Jung and Jung was not sure how to respond.

Pilgrim was now standing in the middle of the room, to Jung's left. "A toy, perhaps?" he said. "I'm like a child, myself, you know," he went on. "And a child's bag ought to contain at least one toy. If you give me a toy, I'm yours forever. Isn't that the way of children?"

Jung stood up.

"No toys, I'm afraid," he said. "But there is a letter."

He went to the bag, unbuckled it and drew out an envelope.

"Here," he said—and handed it to Pilgrim.

Pilgrim went away to the farthest window in the sitting-room before he withdrew the letter from its white pocket.

White, white—everything white, Jung thought. *What is that? Japanese? White for mourning—black for rejoicing? Something ...*

All at once, Pilgrim dropped the letter to the floor. He could not have read more than one or two sentences.

Jung waited nervously for Pilgrim to retrieve the fallen pages.

Surely the man must want to know what his friend had to say to him, but Pilgrim remained motionless, the envelope dangling from his fingers. Slowly, Jung turned with mute panic to the music bag. Looking inside, he saw at once what he had done. There sat Lady Quartermaine's letter.

He went to the sitting-room, leaned down and scooped up the scattered pages, afterward taking their envelope from Pilgrim's hand.

Turning back to the bedroom and the music bag, he glanced with a sinking heart at the writing before him.

There was music—this is true. Dwarfs, there were none—though you promised them ...

He had given Pilgrim Elisabetta's letter to Leonardo, which he had not, of course, intended him to see at all. If Pilgrim ever knew of Jung's access to the journals, he would have every right to retrieve them, and Jung would then lose a precious commodity in his pursuit of Pilgrim's sanity. All at once, he found himself praying that Pilgrim had not, in fact, created the letter himself as an act of imagination, but had found it mouldering in some barely known archive from which Jung could then claim to have obtained a copy. *Prie Jesu.*

Ah, yes—the-chance-encounter-with-a-buried-treasure syndrome, to which so many dreamers succumb.

I thought you had agreed not to interfere.

I'm only here as an observer, Carl Gustav. Un témoin, as the French say. A witness. I could leave, of course. But if I depart, then any kind of accurate record of this encounter goes with me. After all, I am your memory as well as your conscience.

I don't want a conscience.

Well, I'm sorry to tell you, but you have one. And why, I might ask, don't you want one?

Because you stand in the way of spontaneity.

Don't make me laugh, Carl Gustav! Don't make me laugh. In your life, conscience never *comes before the fact—only after. That's what*

*makes you a scientist instead of a philosopher—a psychiatrist and not
a surgeon. Everything you do depends on leaping before you have a
chance to think. If you had consulted me earlier, you would never have
accepted the gift of Mister Pilgrim's journals. You would have
returned them instantly to Lady Quartermaine. Your judgement—to
date, at any rate—has always been empirical. I never get my way until
it's too late. But ...*

The Inquisitor sighed and took a deep, internal breath.

*... I am yours and you are mine. In the American parlance of Archie
Menken—sometimes so infuriatingly apt—you and I are stuck with
one another. And I think you ought to know that your patient is looking at you expectantly. Amongst his last words, before you handed him
the fatal letter, were: "if you give me a toy, I'm yours forever."*

Jung folded the treacherous pages back into their envelope
and returned them to the music bag. There, at hand, were the
other two envelopes—one containing photographs—the other,
Sybil Quartermaine's letter. Also, the monograph concerning
Psyche butterflies.

Jung drew the latter out—and the photographs.

Toys?

Well—the next best thing. *Divertissements.* This was what
Pilgrim needed, now. Not a letter from a dead friend, but something entirely other. The shock of being confronted with La
Gioconda's words might, after all, have driven him back to
silence and that, at all costs, must be prevented.

Jung returned to Pilgrim.

"I thought you might want to see these," he said, and pulled
the photographs into the light. Some, of course, would be
meaningless to Pilgrim. The daffodil, the bust of Doctor Forel,
the façade of the Jung house at Küsnacht. Emma looking pregnant, the children—Agathe, the eldest, holding Marianne, the
youngest—Anna and little Franz. And the dogs, Philemon and
Salome.

*No. Don't show him those. Too many happy faces. Some other time,
perhaps. Not now.*

But the pictures of Lady Quartermaine and Pilgrim in the garden—yes. Not the one showing Otto Mohr and the silver Daimler. Had it been nothing more than coincidence that all these latter photographs could be so neatly juxtaposed on the events that followed?

And, of course, the butterfly.

"I have brought these along," Jung said as he crossed the room. "I took them last week, as you may well remember. They show you both together. In the garden. The garden just out there to the left of the ..."

Don't say Clinic.

"... building."

Jung shuffled the photographs. Cards.

Pick a card. Any card. Do not tell me what it is. Put it back in the deck ...

He fanned and offered them, palming the one that showed the butterfly. That must come last.

Pilgrim seized the fan and closed it.

Looking down, he discerned that Sybil indeed was sitting there.

How beautiful she is, he thought. *Is, was and always will be.*

"May I have this?" he asked. "Just the one. I should like to have it by me."

"Certainly. Absolutely."

Jung took back the other photographs.

"There's a silver frame on the bureau," Pilgrim said rather dreamily. "A photograph of the woman who claimed to be my mother, though I know better. I no longer need or want her. I shall destroy her—burn her at last and flush her down the toilet."

He looked up and smiled at Jung like an evil child whose parents will one day be murdered. A shiver passed over Jung's shoulders. Though he tried not to show his shock, he was barely able to nod in response.

"Then I shall set this photograph of Sybil in its place and look at it every day. I thank you for it. You are kind. Very kind. More than kind. You are thoughtful and considerate. You have an understanding heart. You are filled with compassion. What a burden it must be, to love the human race to such a degree. Overwhelming, I should imagine. Overwhelming, overpowering. Soul-consuming—ruinous, almost. Annihilating. To think that you do such thoughtful, kindly, generous things as hand out photographs of the deceased. It is unimaginable. Some kind of miracle—indeed, the very essence of the milk of human kindness. What must your filing system cost you in upkeep! Cellars filled with photographs! The whole human race! And all with one little camera! May I see it? One day, I should like to see it. Truly. Really. Absolutely. Doctor Jung and his *camera compassionata!* Think of it! The whole human race in black and white ..."

All of this had been spoken with a sleepy, offhand drawl delivered from a languid stance—the photograph drooping from Pilgrim's hand the way a handkerchief might dangle from the fingers of a dandified raconteur while he entertains his host with amusing gossip. But Pilgrim's eyes belied any thought of humour or of entertainment. They grew increasingly narrowed until, at the end of his diatribe—for it had been precisely that—they were closed.

Then, all at once, he shouted: "WHY HAVE YOU MADE ME LOOK AT HER? SHE'S DEAD. SHE HAS ACHIEVED WHAT I CANNOT ACHIEVE. WHY HAVE YOU SHOWN ME THIS? WHY?"

Jung put out his hand and guided Pilgrim to a chair, where he seated his patient and asked Kessler to bring a glass of water.

Pilgrim sat, desolate—the photograph upside down in his lap.

Jung stood back and put the other photographs, including the butterfly, in his pocket.

He realized that a window, if not a door, had been opened—prompting Pilgrim's flood of words. But he did not quite know what to do next. Why, for instance, had Pilgrim not mentioned

Elisabetta's letter? Had he truly not known what it was—or was something about it so deeply buried in Pilgrim's psyche that he could not speak of it?

When Kessler returned, he offered a tall glass of water to Pilgrim and a second glass to Jung. In a war, Kessler had reasoned, both sides are thirsty.

6

A walk in the garden would do her a world of good. Carl Gustav would not return for the midday meal, having expected that his encounter with Patient Pilgrim would, in some way, be *traumatic*. That had been his word, although of course he had not intended a clinical reading of it. He had meant only to convey the range of what might take place between himself and his *recalcitrant adversary*.

"Really, Carl Gustav," Emma had said, "you must not refer to your patients as adversaries. They are not your enemies."

"Yes, they are," Jung had replied. "In their way, they are. Each and every patient is like a territory lost in a war—or a tract of the homeland that must be reclaimed. Some aspect of some disease or condition has won them away and convinced them they are now the citizens of another country. That's why they show so much hostility. They've been propagandized by their demons and made to recite some alien catechism. And in the long run, they believe it—this alien catechism. That's what mental disease is about, Emmy. Or any disease. As Pilgrim himself has cited in his journal, though he puts the words in Leonardo da Vinci's mouth: *everything wants to live, including contagion*. The whole struggle is to win the war not only against the disease or the condition, but against the victim who carries it. That's why one must listen and believe. That's why I encourage the Countess to go on living on the Moon. Until I can recognize the Moon's voice—or Blavinskeya's version of it—there's no way I can help her. It's not enough—it's not enough—it's never enough to do what Furtwängler does and simply tell her there can be no life on the Moon. If she believes it—we must find out *why*.

"You must recall your sister Mutti's struggle with tuberculosis," he went on. "*It's going to kill me*, she said. *Wailed*, in fact. Don't you remember? *Oh! Oh! Oh! I'm going to die of this*, she cried, *sure as fate!* Yes? Pure propaganda. Nothing more and nothing less. The contagion itself sets up a Ministry of Culture and sets about distributing handbills and pronouncements. *You are a conquered nation! Do not resist. The outcome of our occupation can only end in your death!* Yes? You remember? But we won. And why? Because we wanted her back and we set up our own Ministry of Culture in order to claim her—reclaim her. We never denied the other Ministry existed. We heard what it told her and we fought back. We told her that cures were being developed. We told her that she need not die. We told her not to surrender. We put her in the best sanitarium in all of Switzerland. We gave her hope—and one year later, she walked away as healthy as a horse."

"And one year after that, she died."

"To be sure," Jung had said. "To be sure. But only because she fell back under the spell of despair. And despair is always fatal."

Emma put on her overcoat, wrapped a scarf around her neck and pulled a green woollen cap down around her ears. *I look like a bear*, she thought when she saw herself in the vestibule mirror. *A big, fat pregnant Mama Bear*.

"Hello, Mama!" she said to her reflection—and waved a mitted hand.

Five months pregnant almost to the day. December 10th of last year. She had made the entry in her private daybook on the morning of the 11th. *A hit! A hit! A palpable hit!* she had written in English. *A woman knows*.

The night of the 10th had been momentous. Christmas was coming. The girls were about to be released from school. Franzie was making a Father Christmas in the nursery with Albertine, the children's nurse. Sunday, a feast day. Snowfall. Tannenbaum. Music. And guests.

In her mind, there was a blur of friendly faces—everyone rosy-cheeked and drunk on wine. Laughter. Dancing. Anna playing a one-fingered version of *Frère Jacques* on the piano. *Oh, oh, oh—and Carl Gustav looking along at me from the head of the table with that unmistakeable look in his eye ...*

And in our bed, not even waiting to put on nightgown or pyjama, we threw back the covers and he played with me as if he had just discovered what I was. And this! And this! And this! A WOMAN! *And he put his head in my lap and peeled me open the way a man will suck a peach—one and then another—then another—and me the orchard—an orchard of peaches. And when he came to me with "himself" in his hand, I was so eager for him I wept. And we rode together, my ankles pressed against his flank—my horse—and we rode and we rode and I bit his neck ...*

Emma laughed out loud at the memory of it.

And when it happened ...

When it happened, I felt it. I could feel him reaching all the way to my core and I felt him spurting—as men say, shooting—*as if a gun had been fired. A hit! A hit! A palpable hit!*

This is all true. It was so. And I knew it in the very instant: this is a child, *I thought.* A child. We have made another child.

Suddenly, Emma stopped in her tracks. How had she got out here—beyond the house and into the garden? She could not remember. But it didn't matter. The memory of their love-making had carried her, lost in the reliving of it, lost in the telling.

I like the part about the peaches.

She smiled and pulled at the branch of a cedar tree and wandered on towards the lake.

We've made such a lovely house and garden here. All our own doing. And all our own design. We've been—we are so happy here. Carl Gustav—me—the children—even the servants. Our lives here are all so good.

And only that once. Only that one bad time. And I, of course, didn't care for it. It made me so unhappy—so unsure. Sabina. *At least the name was apt!*

She laughed again.

At the shore, she stood on the pebbled beach and gazed out over the lake.

Sabina Spielrein.

First, she had been Carl Gustav's patient. Then she had been his pupil. He had treated her for *hysteria.*

Whatever that might be ...

One of Freud's favourite words and taken up by Carl Gustav because it presented such a wide field of interpretation. *Hysteria.* Sexual, of course. Laden with sexual tensions and possible mani-festations. *Why, the poor girl—*this, according to Carl Gustav himself—*the poor girl had the misfortune to fall in love with me!*

Oh, the poor, dear girl! Oh, my poor, dear husband! The poor, dear innocent doctor and the poor, dear innocent Jewess with her big black innocent eyes the size of saucers. Oh, the poor, dear pair of them, sitting there batting their poor, dear lashes at one another! What, oh what—whatever shall we do? Why—copulate, of course. It's the only right and proper hysterical thing to do!

God! And I forgave him!

Why did I forgive him? How?

Sabina wanted his child. Dear Christ—she wanted his child! She told him so herself. Our own Jewish-Aryan love child! *Those were her very words.*

But I ...

I am his wife.

I am the mother of ...

I am his orchard.

I am ...

I.

There will be soup for lunch. Delicious tomato soup—the tomatoes from Spain—out-of-season tomatoes, out-of-season lettuce and onions from Spain. In the merry, merry month of May.

English. Everything in English. Why?

That woman. The Marchioness of Quartermaine. La Duchesse du Baur au Lac. The Countess of Avalanche. Lady Death herself.

He had her, too, I'd bet.

Wanted to. Thought about it. Dreamt of it. Invaded her disguised as her friend's saviour. How many invasions have there been, I wonder? I'm sure I'll never know. Patients—nurses—students—the titled lady friends who bring their charges to be saved. Sets up his Ministry of Culture and launches his campaign. He's even done it with me. The Husband's Invasion of December, 1911! *And the consequent* Occupation by Imperial Forces. *This—his child.* Our child.

And so, what is sauce for the gander can also be sauce for the goose. Why not?

But who shall I choose? A Spanish gardener with thick black hair and muscular arms, who will bring me onions and tomatoes in his naked lap. Rich, ripe tomatoes nesting in black curly hair and spilling all their juices down his thighs and I ...

If Carl Gustav can, so can I.

But no.

I am Emma Jung—his wife. I am Emma Jung—the mother of ... I am his orchard. I am ...

I.

Go back in and sigh and be content. There are no Spanish gardeners here. *Only tomato soup. And this sunlit day. This high, blue, loveless day.*

Emma splayed her feet in their square-toed rubber boots, making watery pits for her heels amongst the pebbles. She placed her hands inside her coat and made a nest for her belly. *I am the bearer of this good news,* she thought. *Of one new life. And the new shall save the old. That is all that matters.*

Out on the lake, there were three white gulls.

Inside her, there was a kick.

Emma smiled.

"Hello," she said. "There are three white gulls on the lake.

Three white gulls on the lake—and all around us—can you smell it? Oh, I hope you can—the garden where we live is coming back to life—and I—and I and you—and we are cloistered here in paradise and nothing—nothing—*nothing* will ever break our happiness again. I will not allow it."

There had been no Jewish-Aryan love-child. Sabina Spielrein had married a Russian doctor and departed. The English woman had died, albeit tragically—and not a death that Emma would have wished on anyone. But she was gone—departed into memory and all was well.

Turning, Emma saw the garden sloping to her feet—its flowers, its lawns, its trees, its paths and destinations—its aspen grove, its summer house, its benches set amidst the arboured shade and the house itself, beyond, and glancing westward to the sun. And she rejoiced that *so much offers hope and so little offers despair in this, my private moment with my child, walking here, sunlit in the garden of my love and poised with my spoon in hand at the lip of a bowl of tomato soup from Spain.*

7

"I have always admired this view," Jung said. "My office windows show much the same—the trees, the distant mountains rising above them. I must admit, I look out at all this whenever I'm tired—or depressed. It's all so peaceful."

"Unless there's a storm," said Pilgrim.

Jung had risen. Pilgrim had not. He still sat somewhat askew in his chair, with the water glass—now emptied—in his hand and the photograph lying in his lap. "I'm not the least bit interested in peace," he went on. "What I want—and all I want—is death. And you won't give it to me."

"It isn't mine to give," said Jung. "A physician, by definition, is devoted to life. You know that."

"Yes. I know that. Which is why you're all so useless."

"I've said this to you already, Mister Pilgrim. If you want to kill yourself, go right ahead. So long as that is your choice, there isn't a great deal I can do to prevent you."

"Then why did you?"

"Why did I what?"

"Prevent me."

"I cannot help you die—and I cannot let you die, Mister Pilgrim. You will have to accomplish your aim somewhere out of my purview. But you have been put in my charge and so long as you remain in my charge, it is my sworn duty to see that you live—even if that means reviving you at death's door."

Pilgrim turned the glass in his hand upside down and glanced at the photograph, whose back was staring up at him.

"Since it was my friend who consigned me to your care," he said, "and now that my friend is mercifully dead—am I free to go?"

"No. You are to stay here for as long as it takes to come to terms with—if not to solve—your dilemma; namely, why you want to die."

"I want to die because I am unable to die."

"Everyone is able when it comes to death, Mister Pilgrim. That is the human condition. But why not wait until nature takes its course and kills you as it kills us all—either with time or with disease or in war or by means of accident? Why do you reject your humanity?"

"I have not rejected my humanity. My humanity has rejected me. I have none—not one of its privileges."

"As a statement, that is incomprehensible. Just to look at you—to see you—all I can see is a living, breathing upright human being. Granted, an unhappy human being—a troubled human being. But to say you lack the privileges of humanity is ridiculous. There's a roof up there above you—food on the table—money in your pocket—clothes on your back ..."

"Those things are all *acquired*, Doctor Jung. Store-bought privileges. The results of my labour. I mean the privilege of running free—of making choices—of not being duty-bound to fail in my quest for death. I want the privilege of never, never, never again having to bow three times and mutter: *thy will be done. Thy* will only. *Never* mine."

"I'm not aware of having issued any decrees, Mister Pilgrim."

"WHAT MAKES YOU THINK I'M TALKING ABOUT YOU, YOU POMPOUS IDIOT!"

Pilgrim rose from his chair and went to the door of the sitting-room.

"There are greater powers than C.G. Jung, Doctor Vanity! Doctor Narcissus, sir! Doctor Pride! There are greater powers than God!"

He walked away out of sight and Jung and Kessler heard the sound of breaking glass.

Kessler stepped forward, but Jung put out his hand.

"No," he said. "I will do this. You stay here."

When he stepped to the door, he was empty-handed. *No*, he decided. *I must take something with me to distract him.*

Pilgrim had opened a window and was standing with his back to Jung. The broken glass was scattered up against the base-board underneath a large shattered mirror.

"Aren't you aware that breaking a mirror is bad luck?" Jung spoke as lightly as he dared, not wanting to startle his patient.

"When all else fails, bring on the old wives' tales—is that it? Fear of black cats—fear of stepping on cracks—fear of killing spiders inside the house?" Pilgrim did not turn, but remained motionless—upright and ramrod stiff. Even his fingers were frozen, laid against the window panes as if he wished to study them one by one. "The only bad luck that can befall me, Doctor, is that I will live."

"You must explain this to me, Mister Pilgrim. As one who loves life, I find your reaction to it baffling. You are not ill. You are not in physical pain. You are not destitute. You are not untalented. You are not unsung. You have friends, so I under-stand, and a decent mode of life. You are barely more than middle-aged and you live in what everyone agrees is a progres-sive, creative and hopeful era. And yet, you want to close the windows, bolt the door and turn on the gas. This leaves me at a loss for understanding, and I need some instruction. Consider that I am your pupil and know nothing."

As Jung spoke, he moved farther into the room, ignoring the shattered mirror and the broken glass. Here, the furniture was all of a very pleasant green-shaded wicker, with seat cushions covered in blue cotton and set off with pillows wrapped in burnt orange ticking. There were three chairs and a small settee, plus tables strategically placed to offer ample space for ashtrays, magazines and books. The curtains, as seemed to be universal throughout the residential floor of the Clinic, were made of white muslin. Pilgrim had pushed these aside where he stood and they framed him now like shrouds awaiting the dead. There was nothing, Jung concluded as he watched his patient's white-suited back, that did not somehow conjure death in Pilgrim's presence.

Jung sat down at the furthest distance, setting aside his intended "distraction"—the monograph on the subject of *Psyche* butterflies.

"If I were to tell you the truth, Doctor Jung, no matter how brilliantly, you would not believe me. As a teacher—as an instructor on the subject of the conditions under which I live— you would fail me instantly and send for the next candidate."

"Try me."

"You will not believe me. Even Sybil Quartermaine, my oldest, dearest and most understanding friend, did not completely comprehend how what I told her could possibly be true."

"Nonetheless, try me," Jung said. "Think of yourself as Darwin in the early days of his ordeal with the scientific community. Or Galileo, perhaps—struggling to make us believe that the sun does not orbit the earth. Or Louis Pasteur, facing the ignorant wrath of the medical profession. No one believed them, either. Not one soul—at first. But now we know that Darwin, Galileo and Pasteur were indisputably correct in their assumptions and the shoe is on the other foot. So, try me. Make it simple. Remember—I am a child in this. A willing child, but an innocent, nonetheless. I bruise rather easily where belief is concerned. But I'm seated here, as you see, so I won't keel over and harm myself, no matter what you say."

Pilgrim said nothing.

Then his fingers moved. The fingers of his right hand spread out wider on the glass while the fingers of his left hand curled into a gentle fist, as if they held some precious insect whose wings he was afraid of damaging.

"It is true," he said—his back still to Jung, "that I cannot die. And that I have been alive forever is also true. Of course, there are truths and there are also *truths*. The sky is blue. There's a truth for you. We all know that. But what is blue, Doctor Jung? What if blue to me is green to you? Have you ever thought of that? *Oh, yes,* we both say, *the sky is blue*—but how will I ever know that what you see as blue is what I see? And so, if I say to you: *I have lived forever*—how am I to make you understand what I mean by that? After all, there are so many valid interpretations of *forever*. Aren't there. For instance, there are some who believe they pass instantly from one existence to another, living and dying first in one form, then another—forever. There are also some who believe in vampires—whose lives are forever perpetuated by imbibing the blood of others. But I have never been a fox, a dragonfly or a tree. I have always been me—sometimes a man, sometimes a woman—but always uniquely me. Myself. And I am not a Gothic monster living in a box. I think the evidence for this is fairly clear. You will never have to drive a stake through my heart, Doctor Jung—and if you did, it would not kill me. Nothing can kill me. Nothing. Not even myself. And I am tired. I am tired of being captive to the human condition. Of being so endlessly a human being."

"Such thoughts occur to all of us, Mister Pilgrim."

"What—that you have lived forever?"

"Sometimes it certainly feels like it." Jung smiled, but Pilgrim failed to see him.

"I am mad, of course. Insane," Pilgrim said. "I keep believing someone will believe me. But they never do, and perhaps this is why I have made so many attempts to take my life—thinking, when the experts recognize I should be dead but am not, that one of them at least—and at last—will say: *this is a man who cannot die.* But no one says it. Ever."

Jung was silent.

"And now, even you, the vaunted patron of the impossible, do not believe me. So what am I to do?"

Jung closed his eyes. Pilgrim was so obviously in pain. He was the proverbial witness who, all alone, had seen a falling star and could not convince the world the sky was falling. Or the child, Bernadette, who had seen the Holy Virgin—but who in their right mind could believe her?

Pilgrim said: "*muero porque no muero.*"

"I beg your pardon."

"*I die because I cannot die.* St. John of the Cross—a crazy Spaniard said it. Wrote it. But no one understood."

"I see."

"I doubt it."

"Scepticism is the hiding place of the fool, Mister Pilgrim."

"Yes. But who is here the sceptic? Me or you?"

Jung thought: *Lady Quartermaine said:* "*I urge you to believe him, if only briefly, for his own sake.*"

"I have not yet said I do not believe you," he offered. "What I need is concrete evidence. More than your mere survival."

Pilgrim turned back into the room and looked about him. There was sunlight, there were shadows, there were streamers of airborne dust. There were shards of sparkling glass and a mirror splintered within its frame. And there were butterflies. Dozens of them. They were everywhere.

And there sat Jung—the enemy.

Above his head, three butterflies danced. Their wings were the colours of mother-of-pearl and each wing dotted with pale blue coins.

Pilgrim smiled.

The world was filled with the unbelievable. With unicorns and færies, mermaids and miracles, flying horses, Moonmen and Charon's Messengers.

And me. The difference being that I can be seen.

Pilgrim went to the mirror and brushed its broken surface with his fingers, cutting them lightly in the process. Staring at his fragmented image, he traced it with his own blood.

"All the thoughts and experiences of the world," he whispered, "have been etched and moulded here ... the animalism of Greece, the lust of Rome, the mysticism of medieval times, the return of pagan ideals, the sins of the Medicis and the Borgias ... I am older than the mountains beyond those windows, and like the vampire I despise, I have lived many times, Doctor Jung.

Who knows, as Leda I might have been the mother of Helen—or, as Anne, the mother of Mary. I was Orion once, who lost his sight and regained it. I was also a crippled shepherd in thrall of Saint Teresa of Avila; an Irish stable boy and a maker of stained glass at Chartres. I stood on the ramparts of Troy and witnessed the death of Hector. I saw the first performance of *Hamlet* and the last performance of Molière, the actor. I was a friend to Oscar Wilde and an enemy to Leonardo ... I am both male and female. I am ageless, and I have no access to death." He turned. "And, by the way, there's a butterfly sitting on your thumb."

Going to the window, he opened it and said: "you must bring it here and set it free."

Jung could barely move. He was both alarmed and thrilled.

"Make a cup with your other hand," Pilgrim said, "and bring the butterfly here."

Jung stood up and lightly folded one hand over the other.

"Come along, now. Quickly."

Jung made his way to the window—aware, but afraid of what he felt or thought he felt beneath his fingers. The fluttering of wings.

At the window, he thrust both his hands outside and drew them apart.

"There it goes," said Pilgrim. "You have set your imagination free at last." Then he closed the window.

8

The silver Daimler that had greeted Sybil Quartermaine's arrival was not there to bid her farewell. It had survived the avalanche, but was in some need of repair and had been returned to its makers in Austria. That departure had taken place on the morning of Wednesday, the 22nd of May.

On the afternoon of that same day, at about the fourteenth hour—which is to say, at two o'clock—the horse-drawn hearse containing Sybil's casket was driven into the forecourt of Zürich's Hauptbahnhof, followed by two open landaus whose horses wore black plumes and whose drivers wore appropriate tall black hats and purple armbands.

In one of these carriages, Phoebe Peebles was accompanied by Pilgrim's valet, Forster. Seated with them was the "nice young couple" by the name of Messager, whom Forster had spotted chatting with Lady Quartermaine in the lobby of the Hôtel Baur au Lac. All were dressed in black.

In the second carriage, Jung rode side by side with Pilgrim—while Kessler sat opposite with his back to the driver. Jung and Kessler wore black suits. Beneath his ulster, Pilgrim still wore white. In his hand was a small bouquet of violets, and on his head a wide, soft trilby the colour of port wine.

A cart had been manœuvred into place on which Sybil's casket would be delivered to the train, which even then was building steam at the Hauptbahnhof's platform number three.

It was a beautiful day—*high, wide and blue*, as Jung would note in his journal. And when the hearse arrived, a host of pigeons rose into the air above it, settling on the glass and ironwork canopy that covered the entrance to the station.

Beyond the forecourt, there were trees and an overview of the

River Limmat down the slope of a gently rolling hill, where strollers turned their backs and went their way, as people should and most often do in the presence of other people's grief. Uniformed nurses with perambulators; soldiers from foreign armies; scholars with books in hand and boys who should have been in school, riding bicycles decorated with coloured ribbons. There were also lovers—*of course*, Jung would write, *how could there not be?* And children with hoops, balloons and barking dogs. Nuns in grey and white and fishermen down by the quays and women selling lemonade and others selling favours from baskets slung from their necks.

Beneath the canopy, the sound of the horses' hooves on the cobblestones was intensified. Pilgrim sat taller, if that was possible, and Phoebe Peebles stood up in the forward carriage while Forster descended and put his hand out to Madame Messager. The latter was extremely young and pretty, but veiled. She alighted from the landau as if a feather had floated to earth. Monsieur Messager followed and then Phoebe Peebles—who had never worn formal mourning dress before and was lost in her veils and crepe the way a child will lose itself in its parent's clothes. Who the Messagers were remained a mystery. Although they had introduced themselves to Phoebe and to Forster as *friends of the deceased*, it was still not clear on what basis the "friendship" had been established or to what extent it gave them the right to go into full mourning. They were French, that was known—but little else, beyond their evident concern.

Not until the forward carriage had been emptied did Kessler get out and stand aside, making room on the stones for Doctor Jung and Mister Pilgrim, who got down last.

Pilgrim removed his trilby and his ulster and laid them back on the seat and closed the door. All in white and carrying violets, he put on a pair of dark glasses and faced the sky.

Jung, taking note of all this, also saw that Pilgrim nodded at the sun, in the way that one will pay respects to a superior figure in a public place—a higher rank in the aristocracy—a Prince of the Church—a minor deity. *Interesting*.

Only now visible as Jung and Pilgrim stepped forward, the Quartermaine family in its entirety was lined up on the far side of the forecourt. All the women were veiled, the men bareheaded, hats in hand, and the youngest child—a girl of perhaps fourteen—with a water spaniel on a lead, the dog with a black crape bow around its collar.

Lord Quartermaine was somewhat older than Sybil had been. Perhaps he was in his early fifties, greying and balding and sad. His eldest daughter, Lady Margot Pryde, stood beside him giving a firm impression that if she did not support him, he might have wavered—even have fallen. On his other side stood David, the eldest son and Earl of Hartford, whose demeanour was absolutely military. All he lacked was a uniform. It was David of whom Sybil had confided to Furtwängler that *I do not really care for him*. But he was there to do his duty, and he did it well. There was not a trace of emotion in his expression—unless it could be said that *control* is an emotion. He was supremely self-contained.

Jung's immediate impression was of a family blessed with universal beauty. Every single one of them was a masterpiece of Aryan Anglo-Saxon breeding—blond and blue-eyed—buffed and shining, with superlative carriage and presence.

Lord Toby, who was just sixteen, stood between the remaining sisters—Lady Catherine and Lady Temple, the child who had brought her dog. The dog's name was Alice—*because she goes down rabbit holes. Or tries to.*

Jung and Pilgrim passed the occupants of the other carriage, who were clustered on the stones and not quite sure how to make their next move. Jung took note that, while Forster was on the alert and clearly prepared to speak to Pilgrim, he did not do so. Nor did Pilgrim speak to him.

Kessler, Jung also noted, gave Forster a look almost of disdain. *I've got him now, and you might not get him back.* Jung had to suppress a smile. *Servants are funny creatures,* he thought. *They're so possessive—like children showing off their toys.*

There were brief introductions. The Messager couple were total strangers to Pilgrim, though Jung had the distinct impression he himself had either met or seen them before. But Madame Messager's veiling was too clouded to allow a proper viewing of her features. Her husband was handsome enough, but not distinguished. He had a face that one sees every day in restaurants, banks and riding on the Küsnacht ferry—pleasant, unmarked and clearly innocent.

Once all the names had been exchanged, Jung took the lead and stepped towards the hearse. As they passed, each member of their party paused to bow before the casket, visible beyond the glass—and, if Catholic, to cross themselves. They then made their way across the open drive from which all public traffic had been diverted for the moment, and passed along the line of principal mourners, introducing themselves as they went.

Forster was keenly observant of the Messagers' introduction to the family. Was the young husband known to Lord David? Were they school chums, as he had surmised? But no. Clearly not. There was no sign of recognition from either young man.

Pilgrim shook hands with Quartermaine and the two sons and was embraced by all the daughters—and with special warmth by Lady Temple. For his part, Pilgrim barely spoke and Jung could see he was on the verge of tears. This perhaps was not just because they had gathered to see Sybil off on her final journey—but because it was Pilgrim's first taste of being in the presence of old friends since his own troubles had placed him in jeopardy.

There was a moment of silence. Then, with no apparent signal being given, Lords David and Toby moved to the rear of the hearse, and together with the driver and his attendants, they drew the casket forward into the light and carried it to the waiting cart.

Lord Quartermaine, foundering on Lady Margot's arm, leaned down and kissed the lid of the mahogany coffin and laid his forehead against the wood, stretched his arms as if to embrace its burden and stayed this way until the Ladies Catherine and Margot drew him away to one side.

The cart was then pulled forward, all the veils on all the women waving like flags and standards and all heads bowed—but Pilgrim's.

Then, at the very last moment Pilgrim, laying his violets on the coffin, said—for all to hear: *ave atque vale* and turned away.

To Lady Temple, he offered a penny, saying to her: *you will know what to do with this*—to which she nodded.

The ceremony was over. Sybil had been drawn into the dark by her attendants and was gone.

9

That evening, after dinner, Jung sat desolate at his desk beneath the lamplight, pondering the events of the day. His journal was open before him, in which he had already recorded the departure of Sybil Quartermaine's remains and the melancholy return to the Clinic.

Phoebe Peebles had followed her mistress to England and would continue in service there as maid to Lady Catherine Pryde—the Quartermaine daughter known as Kate, who would one day acquire a reputation as one of British theatre's brightest stars.

Forster had returned to the Hôtel Baur au Lac in the company of the charming though somewhat mysterious Messager couple, whose connection to Lady Quartermaine remained totally unexplained. On leaving, neither Forster nor Pilgrim had so much as nodded at one another—and thus, another mystery.

As the landau bearing Pilgrim, Kessler and Jung himself had climbed the heights through the woods and gardens below the Clinic, Pilgrim had sat like a deposed king on the far side of the carriage, refusing to acknowledge his fellow passengers and the world at large around him. His gaze was entirely inward, his hands stilled and empty, his dark glasses showing the reflections of passing trees and floating clouds.

Kessler was in mourning, as he would confess that evening to his mother, for the loss of one angel—*perhaps the most beautiful I have ever seen*. At the station, confronted by the casket, he had wondered what might become of angels when they die. His mother, on hearing this, kept her counsel. She feared all references to winged creatures and said only: *like all of us, they are returned to heaven*.

Watching Pilgrim, Jung could not help feeling his own deep sense of depression. That things should work out so badly in some people's lives. That triumph—if, as and when it was achieved—could be won only at the cost of lost dreams, discarded hopes and displaced relationships. Friends fall aside— or are pushed—ejected—refused admittance. Husbands, wives and lovers are separated—children abandoned. Place means nothing. Lost health—fatigue replacing stamina—fear replacing joy—recklessness replacing reason. Then death. This had been the story of his parents' lives—not only one by one, but as a couple. He had spent his whole childhood in the embrace of their sorrows—of his father's failure to connect with God and his mother's ultimate failure to connect with reality. And yet, they had devoted their lives to making those connections. It was more than sad, Jung decided. It was unjust.

Nonetheless, it had to be said that in her final hours and with her final gestures, Sybil Quartermaine had achieved a kind of triumph. Her life had been rounded with a sacrifice—*to the unknown God*—as she had written herself—who perhaps was the god of reason who would also deliver Pilgrim. Certainly, she had made every effort in Pilgrim's behalf to guide him to a safe, good place in which to begin the rest of his life.

In the dark, surrounded by his study lamps and by his sleeping family, Jung had the first of what would prove to be a series of revelations regarding his own immediate journey—an epiphany of sorts—almost religious, but not. He eschewed the religious at every turn. All at once, his journal still open before him, he scribbled that *happiness is not our goal*. And further: *that the achievement of happiness deflects us from our true destiny, which is the utter realization of self.*

The utter realization of self.

Jung sat back and dragged a handkerchief from a pocket, wiped his glasses, wiped his brow and wiped his lips.

When I came here first, he wrote, *to the Burghölzli Clinic at Zürich, it was an entry into a monastery world, a submission to a vow*

*to believe only in what was probable, average, commonplace, barren of
meaning; to renounce everything strange and significant and reduce
anything extraordinary to the banal. Henceforth there were only
surfaces that hid nothing—Furtwängler's cursory "get it done!"
Menken's "all there is, is what there is!" My own "the Moon! The
Moon!" Only beginnings without continuations, knowledge that
shrank to ever smaller circles, oppressively narrow horizons and the
unending desert of routine ...*

He reached for the decanter and refilled his emptied glass—
emptied but once—and relit a cheroot that had died in the
ashtray. But these were mere distractions. The brandy burned
where it should and the smoke reopened his throat and the smell
of the sulphurous match-end made him wipe his eyes yet again.

And once more—the pen.

*For six months I locked myself within these monastic walls in order
to get accustomed to the life and spirit of the asylum—and I read
through the fifty volumes—fifty!—of the* Allgemeine Zeitschrift für
Psychiatrie *from its very beginnings, in order to acquaint myself with
the psychiatric mentality. I wanted to know how the human mind
reacted to the sight of its own destruction, for psychiatry seemed to me
an articulate expression of that biological reaction which seizes upon
the so-called healthy mind in the presence of mental illness.*

And yet ... And yet ...

The pen stuttered.

Jung set it aside, and wrote only in his mind.

*The realization of self is all there is or can be or should be. The I
that is in everyone, struggling to achieve breath.*

*The I in me. The I in Pilgrim. The I in Blavinskeya. The I in
Emma. The I in that child already lying in our bed in Emma's belly.*

*The I in Sybil Quartermaine's avalanche. The I in Pilgrim's
butterfly.*

*Yes! The butterfly had been as real as I am, sitting here—reaching
for its mountains beyond the window. And I—that blind I—did not
see it and yet, thank God, the I in Pilgrim did, and it was he who
opened the window and set it free.*

Jung closed his eyes and removed his glasses and set them down away from the light.

"I do believe him," he whispered. "I do believe. For if I could not, I would perish untried."

10

Pilgrim, too, sat alone late that evening. He had pulled the curtains aside and was watching from his bedroom window as the Moon began her climb. The Moon, however, was not in his thoughts. There, another subject had risen, baffling at first, being unbidden.

... then there was the tale of the industrious rabbit. His name was Peter and his mother was a widow by the name of Josephine. He had three sisters: Mopsy, Flopsy and Cottontail. There was also a cousin whose name was ...

Barnaby?

No. That doesn't seem right—though the B *is correct. I think.*

Bobby?

No. That can't be it. Not Bobby Rabbit. *Bobby Rabbit does not sound right, though* Peter *does and* Mopsy, Flopsy, Josephine *and* Cottontail. *These are true rabbit names and ...*

Barraclough.

*Barraclough Rabbit. That is plausible. There was that boy—that young man at Christ's who lived on lettuce. Lettuce, peas and cabbages—a panacea of greens. Barra-*cloe*—Barra-*cluff. *He was always being teased—and, more than teased, ragged—even made to wear a sign around his neck that read:*

> My name is Barra-
> What-you-choose.
> I know not how
> To say it.
> But if you rag me
> Long enough,
> I will confess to
> Barra-cluff.

And if you let
Your urine flow
Upon my shoes, I'm
Barra-cloe.

Boys were ever so. Thus and so. The makers of schoolyard wars that spilled out into the playing fields and on to Waterloo. Poor old Barraclough. He might have been a Belgian battlefield himself for all the good it did him. Then he went out and died in the Sudan at Omdurman. Wherever that might be.

And all because he ate lettuce.

He wanted to be a playwright. Had wanted to be another Ibsen. Ibsen.

Of all the absurd and wonderful ... As if an Englishman could be an Ibsen. And yet, he was—he had been dedicated to it: to the truth and the plain realities of life as life is lived.

Why, I would slam all the doors from here to kingdom come if I had my chance! he would say. If Ibsen hadn't slammed them all before me. Slam all the doors—not just a doll's house door. And nurture all the wild ducks in the whole wide world! Yes— and I would fire off all the guns, even though they say people never do such things ... But Hedda did—and she was right. Right, because other women had faced such choices and done such things. But now, for every Hedda who fires a gun, there must be a multitude who need not do it—need not die. Yes, Pilgrim! Yes! Do you not believe it? I do. I do. That's why plays are written—or should be written. To break the bonds. To set us free of one another and all the silly, stifling, killing rules we live by. And that's what I would do—and will do, one day—if I'm given half a chance!

And so to Omdurman. And death.

Barraclough.

But that's not it.

Brainerd?

Hardly.

Beverly?

Possibly.

Beverly Rabbit and his cousin Peter. Yes, it could be. Didn't he end up marrying one of Peter's sisters? I think so.

But no. It was still not right.

Pilgrim took *The Tale of Peter Rabbit* from its place in the top drawer of the bureau and glanced inside the cover. *Temple Pryde,* he read. *Her book, with love from Mommy, Christmas, 1905.* He kept it hidden in amongst his handkerchiefs for fear some other erudite reader might find it and steal it away. Just as Peter had ventured into Mister McGregor's garden in the hopes of stealing some lettuce, anyone with half a mind to expand his horizons would spy and abscond with and cherish this book.

There was Peter in his blue jacket and his black slippers.

Possibly the finest novel written in the English language, Pilgrim thought. *Entirely possible.*

All the requisite qualities had been laid out in order. Tension. Jeopardy. A quest. Poverty. Striving. Deceit and Truthfulness. Crime and Punishment. Problem and Resolution. Not to say, a morality tale, and something of a love story—if sad. For hadn't Josephine Rabbit been widowed with four young children to raise and her husband baked in a pie by a veritable Medea?

Well—not quite.

But still, an evil figure—and a force to contend with in the world of rabbits ... the redoubtable, hideous, nightmare figure of Mrs McGregor, with her spoons and pans and knives. And Mister McGregor himself, with everything a man could imagine standing at hand with which to kill a poor fellow.

And all for the love of a cabbage leaf and a hankering for French beans and radishes.

Barraclough. Cabbage. Boy-wars. Waterloo. Omdurman.

You eats what you're given, sonny. Take it or starve.

Pilgrim thumbed the little book in his hand.

Beloved. Or is that stupid—sentimental—mad?

A grown man—a child's treasure. A child's first encounter, perhaps, with harsh reality. Certainly the first such encounter for a child of privilege. A child ensconced and barricaded in a nursery world of cosy fires and cambric tea, of toy soldiers, storytelling, cosseting and the long stairs down to one's parents and the adult world.

I must have had some such book myself, though I don't remember what it was. The Fables of Aesop, *perhaps ...*

He smiled.

Of all the many childhoods I've had access to, none remains clarified in memory. I know that I have lain in darkened cellars and in lighted toy-strewn attics—in castles, cottages and caves—and there are glimmers still in my mind of the view from a mother's arms or a father's shoulders. How many mothers—how many fathers—all of whom I should mourn, if I were a proper human being. But I am not. Am not and never have been. I slept, or so it seems, through all my childhoods—every one—though I remember other children who must have been my siblings or companions—a brother in Florence—a sister in Spain—a boy somewhere in Greece ... But otherwise, it seems I slept. And while asleep, I dreamt.

No one understands. The only childhood I've ever truly known—or at least that I can identify, outside of my dreams—was gleaned by watching the childhood of others. Of Temple, Toby, Kate, Cassandra ... Antigone ... Astyanax ... To say I have been a long time aborning *is not to grasp the half of it. All these childhoods and not a single nursery of one's own to remember.*

I slept. I woke. And was found. Always found. A foundling. As Sybil found me. Lying beneath a tree. A chestnut? An oak? I don't remember.

Eighteen. Eighteen years old. I was always eighteen *at birth. Or so it seemed. Whatever had happened before then was just a dream.*

Perhaps this was funny. Amusing. He smiled, but could not laugh out loud. Not quite.

It might have been interesting to remember, absolutely, *being a child—not just to dream a childhood. To have held this book in my own small hand. To have pierced the meaning of the words with my own child's eyes. To have placed my finger, thus and so, upon the phrases ...*

It was a blue jacket with brass buttons, quite new.

And:

Peter asked her the way to the gate ...

And:

Mister McGregor hung up the little jacket and the shoes for a scarecrow to frighten the blackbirds.

And:

His mother put him to bed, and made some camomile tea; and she gave a dose of it to Peter!

"One table-spoonful to be taken at bed-time."

Pilgrim smoothed the pages and closed the book.

Barnaby? Bobby? Barraclough?

If I had a cousin whose name began with B, what might I want it to be?

Benedict, *perhaps. Or* Benedick.

The traitor, Arnold—or Shakespeare's wonder man of words, the jealous bachelor—like me. All this time—and married only as a woman.

But surely I would not want my cousin to be a traitor—just because his name begins with B?

I'm not so sure. A traitor knows where he stands. The rest of us waffle and put on shows of patriotism. Better to settle once and for all on the other side of the fence. At least it means that a person has a choice—that his conscience is alive and that he's capable of argument. Just to be born an American—an Englishman—a Greek—means nothing, until you make the choice *to be so. Everyone should be given the opportunity of being born in opposition to one's beliefs. Mere patriotism is bondage.*

So much for Benedict Arnold.

So much for Benedict Bunny.

No. *So much for rejecting* Benedict Bunny *out of hand.*

And Cousin Benedick? I might opt for him, but for one flaw. He married.

Pilgrim set the book aside and sat on the bed.

Poor old Barraclough. At Omdurman.

Empire.

He glanced aside at the cover.

Blue coat. Brass buttons. Radishes. Robin. Handle of a spade. Slippered toes.

The robin singing. Peter ecstatic—nibbling. And string beans a-growing. And the earth turned over—hoed and healthy. Resplendent. And the robin, with one foot raised and Peter, with one foot crossed upon the other—the very image of song. The very image of contentment.

And each intruding in another's empire: Mister McGregor's garden.

Why did it all sound so familiar?

"Let me stake this land and set out my cabbages," Pilgrim said to the Moon beyond the window. "These, my cabbages, are flags—my flags—and with these flags I claim this land. My land. And if you enter here, to trifle with my flags and my intentions—my wife will bake you in a pie ..."

He smiled and closed his eyes.

Shut out the Moon—it has no flags, but one day it shall—and Barraclough will die up there, sure as fate. For the love of cabbages and lettuce.

Cousin Benedict, I salute you. I am on the other side of this argument already, having witnessed too many warlords claiming their gardens with a cannon.

What—oh, what, what, what was his name?

Benedict? Benedick? Abou Ben Adhem?

Pilgrim smiled.

Benedictus qui venit in nomine Domine ...?

Blessed is he that comes in the name of the Lord ...

Peter Rabbit.

And now she is gone, who was my last finder—who came to me beneath a tree and said: are you lost—and may I help you find your way?

And in her hand she carried a book—a childhood book like this— the Brothers Grimm.

I am twelve, *she said*. And really too old to be reading fairy tales. But it was on the shelf and I couldn't sleep and so ... Do you know the story of Hansel and Gretel?

And I said: No. My name is Pilgrim.

And she was Sybil—*whose daughter Temple, twenty-five years later, presented me with* The Tale of Peter Rabbit.

Temple Pryde, he read again. *Her book, with love from Mommy, Christmas, 1905.*

Barraclough. Cabbages. Empire. Death.

If only I could remember ...

He turned out the light and lay down, drawing the covers up to his chin.

I will lie here and the name will come to me.

Brahms. Beethoven. Bach. Boccherini. Bellerophon. Baal. Beëlzebub. Bacon. Bleat. Brontosaurus. Barrie. Barnum. Belloc. Blake. Borgia. Bulwer-Lytton. Benjamin ....

Benjamin. Ah, yes. My cousin Benjamin. *I bid you welcome.*

In his mind's eye, Temple stood as she had that afternoon at the train station—black-bowed Alice beside her—and her brothers and sisters towering over her. Her mother, Sybil, had died—been killed. Was gone. Truly gone—into the woods with Hansel and Gretel, where he and Sybil had met all those years ago—and who was to know if he would ever be allowed to follow?

11

The Moon was full that night and Tatiana Blavinskeya could not sleep. She was dressed as she might have been when preparing to go on stage as Queen of the Wilis in the second act of *Giselle*. Her rounded arms were bare, except that streamers of pale chiffon were loosely stretched from shoulder to wrist. Beneath her calf-length skirts she wore her best white stockings and her waist was tightly bound with a pale green taffeta sash whose bow ends looked like wings. Her hair was plaited and wound from ear to ear across the back of her head. She had tied green ribbons to her wrists and she held a pair of pointe shoes in her lap.

She was seated by her window, staring up at the Moon—which had risen over the heights behind the Clinic and was now shining down so brightly that every new leaf on every tree could be counted.

Sister Dora sat on the bed, afraid to leave her patient alone in such a wistful mood. All evening long, the Countess had been playing with her costumes—dragging them one by one from the armoire and the steamer trunk in the corner, holding each one up for inspection in the mirror and laying them aside on the bed, the backs of chairs and even on the floor.

Princess Florine's feathered bodice for the Bluebird pas de deux from *Sleeping Beauty*. The scarlet, high-waisted tutu—*and the fan!*—for the *Don Quixote* variations. The butterfly wings from *Papillons*. The Sugar Plum Fairy's violet and purple costume from *The Nutcracker*, with its faux-amethyst coronet and wand. Three swans—two white, one black—and the Princess Aurora herself: "Imperial Russia in all its glory! Regard the beading here and here and here! And this! My favourite, favourite, favourite! Set in Moonlight—danced by the light of the Moon—Myrthe, Queen of the Wilis! Oh—if we could only find an audience—an orchestra—a corps—I would dance till dawn!"

Blavinskeya regarded herself in the full-length mirror. "You may not understand," she said, "how I had to beg for the role of Myrthe. I have not the body for it, you see. And yet it was my greatest triumph. By tradition, she is tall—and I am not. By tradition, she is slim as a fall of water, which I am not ..." She smiled. "By tradition, she is cold—which I was not. But, oh, I wanted ... I wanted ... I *had* to dance her. And I begged them to give her to me—and I danced her for them and they relented. They had to!" She laughed. "I was magnificent!" She subsided. "Magnificent." She whispered, "because I, too, had died a virgin ..."

Sister Dora always kept a sedative standing by—a vial of ether, another of laudanum. But she was reluctant to apply them except in the gravest emergencies. Tonight, however, she had already sat with the Countess for three hours into the dark and now it was two o'clock and there was no sign of abatement. The Countess was already breathless—in spite of being seated. It was as if she had just returned from a performance.

"We dance as the dead," Blavinskeya said in her Russian-accented German. "And all by Moonlight. All by the light of the Moon. We are the dead young virgins who have perished before their marriage vows. And yet ... it is the living who watch us. The living who watch."

Blavinskeya leaned down and pulled her pointe shoes onto her feet—one and then the other, rising to adjust their "comfort." "Comfort is never the right word for pointe shoes," she explained. "They are agony personified. Invented in hell—by a man, of course. Nonetheless, over time your feet adapt to them. Each moulds the other—the foot the shoe, the shoe the foot—and a certain ease can be achieved. But never comfort."

She adjusted the ribbons, wrapping them more tightly around

her ankles, tying them neatly and giving each a pat of satisfaction with her chubby hand.

"*Bon! Je suis prête.* Let us go—and I will dance in the Moonlight."

Blavinskeya started past Sister Dora, snatching up a cashmere shawl as she went, and made for the door.

"But, madame!"

"No time for *buts*, Schwester dear. We are for the gardens. Follow me."

Saying this, Blavinskeya was already out in the corridor and marching towards the stairs.

Sister Dora, struggling to disentangle herself from a white swan, a black swan and a scarlet tutu, discovered to her dismay as she rose to her feet that her left leg had fallen asleep.

"Damn! Damnation!"

She fell to her knees and scrambled up again, following as best she could Myrthe, Queen of the Wilis, limping along the corridor and down the stairs, across the entrance hall and past the dozing concierge into the foyer and beyond the foyer, through the doors and into the night.

12

At Küsnacht, the moonlight filtered through the curtains, falling across the foot of the bed where Jung lay awake with Emma.

His hand was on her belly, having already felt one kick, to which he had replied by tapping out a message in Morse code with his fingers: *hello in there! Hello!*

"The kicking only started just today," Emma told him. "I love to think of her shouting: *I need more room! I need more room!*"

"She?" Jung said. "With a kick like that, it has to be a boy. Our second son."

"It's a girl. We've spoken—and I know it."

"Spoken? Please be serious."

"Believe me or not, Carl Gustav, a mother and her child converse. Not always in words, but in many other ways as well. I send down thoughts and I know she receives them. She sends back waves as answers—even as questions—and the waves flood all the way through me. It is true. It is true. Believe it. She is my little fish, and I am her ocean. She is my swimmer—I am her sea. You must remember what it feels like, floating in the sea, my darling. At Capri, how we floated hand in hand ... don't you remember? How we drifted out so far they had to come and fetch us back with a rowboat."

"We could have drowned."

"Nonsense. Not together. We had each other—hand in hand and it was all so warm and peaceful—blue and bright and safe. It seems to me that swimming in the sea is just like my little fish in here ... whatever it is they call the waters of the womb—I always forget it ... what?"

"Amniotic fluid," Jung muttered through his moustache,

bending down to kiss Emma's belly. Then he laid his hand out flat against her skin and made the shape of the child inside.

"You ever hear the phrase *ontogeny recapitulates phylogeny?*" he said.

"I'm sure I'd remember if I had," Emma laughed. "I couldn't begin to tell you what it means."

"Man called *Haeckel*. Ernst Haeckel. Biologist. German. Long dead—but controversial in his time. We had to study him at university. He had a lot of theories, some of them useful—some of them not. In some ways, you might say he was a pupil—not a pupil, a disciple—of Darwin's. Disciple and extrapolator. Went a few steps beyond the master, so to speak. Such as: *ontogeny recapitulates phylogeny.*"

"Heavens—what huge words!"

"*Ontogeny—the origin and development of the individual.*" Jung pronounced the words as a teacher might to a classroom—tapping them out on Emma's stomach, the way he might have tapped them out on a desk. "Like your little fish in here," he added. "Then: *phylogeny,*" he pronounced, "*the evolutionary development of groups of organisms.* You understand? And it was Haeckel's notion—Haeckel's *theory* that your little fish in there is passing through some of the same stages of development that, collectively, we all passed through in the evolution of the human race. From *protozoa* to *Homo sapiens.* Do you see?"

"Not entirely, no."

"Let me start again," Jung said, getting up and crossing the room to sit in a chair. "Haeckel said: *ontogeny recapitulates phylogeny*—but what he should have said is ontogeny *repeats* phylogeny. Still, he was a biologist—a scientist—and you have to forgive him a few self-important words. And so ..."

Jung lifted a box of cheroots from the table beside him and struck a match. In the moonlight, he looked like a Chinese Buddha in a cloud of incense.

"What Haeckel suggested was that in the development of any individual, human or otherwise—a frog, for instance—from conception to birth, the embryo's increasing complexity *retells* the evolutionary history of its own particular species. That way, your little fish began as a single cell—as a fertilized egg—which reflects one of the most primitive of life forms, namely the one-celled protozoa. Are you with me?"

"Tell me *protozoa*." Emma pushed herself higher in the bed, leaning in against the pillows. "I think I know it, but I want to hear you say it."

Jung adored the role of mentor and posed for a moment with the cheroot in his hand, his profile moonlit and his Prussian haircut standing at attention.

"*Proto-zoa*," he said. "*First animals*. Or, if you like, *first beings*. Now it gets exciting. As the fertilized egg develops, it divides and multiplies ..."

"Does it also add and subtract?" Emma smiled.

"Don't interrupt. As it divides and multiplies, what it is doing is forming a mass of cells—an *unorganized* mass, not unlike a sponge. Think of the sponge in your bath and all the different shapes and sizes it comes in. So ... it passes on through stages that resemble a jellyfish. Later—after it's started to elongate, its nerve cells migrate to the back and become encased in a sheath of cartilage. This ultimately stiffens into bone—a spine and a spinal cord—and this way, it takes on the characteristics of the earliest marine vertebrates. *Gills* develop, like those of a fish ..."

"My little fish."

"Precisely. And then these gills, over time, are replaced by lungs. Et cetera, et cetera. Do you see? All of these things have already happened to your little fish, and more and more and more until it is ready to climb up ..."

"... out of the sea. Which is, to be born."

"Which is to be born, my dear one. And thus—the whole process of embryonic development reflects the process of evolution. Ontogeny repeating phylogeny. *And here endeth the lesson*, as my father used to say from his pulpit. And yet, there's more to be had from Haeckel's theory than mere biology ..."

"No, Carl Gustav. No. Not more. I'm tired. It's after two o'clock in the morning."

"But this is important. Immensely important. You don't understand. It has to do with my work. It has to do with ..."

Everything.

Oh, no. Don't you start.

I just thought you'd like to know I've been listening. And I agree with you: there is more.

"Emma, please. Just stay awake long enough to hear one last thing."

"Yes, Carl Gustav. But tell it quickly."

Jung sat forward. He had—but why?—an erection.

You get too excited, Carl Gustav. You get too excited about ideas.

I can't—I can't help it. Oh, dear. Pray God she can't see me.

It wouldn't matter if she did. She isn't interested. Not now.

I hadn't thought I wanted to—but there it is. Jesus. Look at it.

I don't need to look at it. I can feel it. What you suffer from—amongst other things—is nothing less than intellectual priapism. It's that simple. Get an idea—get an erection.

Stop.

Why don't you say your piece? Emma has begun to drift—and if you don't begin your dissertation, she will be gone before you can impregnate her mind with your brilliance. An image I think you rather enjoy ... Remember Sabina Spielrein. Think of that luscious new intern you saw in the corridor with Furtwängler. Think of your traumatized pianist, whose lovely hands are longing to be busy. Say your piece, Carl Gustav. Say your piece. All of us are longing to hear it—begging you to undo your mental flies and flood our brains with your theories. Please. Please begin.

You bastard.

Well, I like to tell the truth. You just don't like to hear it. Tell us, oh wondrous doctor of the soul, what it is you want to say.

It was only ...

Say it aloud. Remember, it is Emma you want to impress.

For the moment.

"It was only ... it is only that, given the obvious rightness of Haeckel's theory, I cannot help wondering—pondering the possibility that if ontogeny repeats phylogeny in the biological sense, then might it not also repeat it in the psychological sense. Might not each individual inherit the psyche—or a portion of the collective psyche—of the whole human race? Don't you see? If Haeckel is right—and he is—then doesn't his principle suggest something more than merely one *physical* process reflecting and repeating another *physical* process? Could it not be that the individual's nature—which is unique—also reflects and repeats to whatever degree the nature and the experience of its ancestors? The whole race? Why not? Why not? Isn't that why some of what we *know* we never had to *learn?* Emma? Emma ...?"

Too late. She was asleep.

Jung stubbed the cheroot in the ashtray and hurried across the floor to the bureau, where he rummaged amongst the debris from his pockets for notebook and pen.

In the bathroom, he sat on the closed seat of the toilet and, using his knees as a desk, wrote in his journal:

I am my mother's dreams incarnate. I am my father's atavistic fears. In this cave where I am sitting ...

He looked up and blinked.

The lights above and around the mirror were glaring at him, reflected in every tile and in all the glass and all the metal with which he was surrounded.

What cave?

Why had he written *cave?*

In this cave where I am sitting ...

All at once, he wanted to weep and did not know why.

A notion had taken hold of him.

An intellectual erection.

And its power was as overwhelming and all-pervasive as the power of the erection straining against the thin white cotton of his pyjama trousers.

Out. Out.

Could there be such a thing as an intellectual ejaculation?

Why not?

Stay out of this.

I can't stay out. I'm part of it. Conscience. Remember? Conscience and memory, pressing against the thin white membrane of your brain. This cave you are sitting in, Carl Gustav, is your mind. *Look around you. What has been painted here? What animals are there? What other creatures—other men?*

Jung stared at the ceiling.

Whose handprint is that? Whose gods were these? Whose totems— emblems—signs and symbols ...? Don't be afraid of it. Stand up and look at it.

The notebook fell to the floor. Using the sink to propel him to his feet, Jung dropped the uncapped pen into the cavern of its white enamel bowl.

He stood on the toilet seat and raised his arms.

There were shadows in the corners—cracks in the ceiling. Did they form the shapes of beings he had never seen before? Or were they maps of rivers and mountain ranges—routes for the journeys made by others who had gone before him ...

Jung felt like a suppliant, his arms outstretched, his fingers splayed, his sight overwhelmed with tears.

I have come such a long, long way, he thought in a voice he had never heard before. *We have come such a long, long way. And I can* remember *it ...*

I can remember ...

Ontogeny had just repeated phylogeny in a voice as clear and distinct as if it had spoken aloud.

I can know what I never had to learn. And I can remember what I never, never myself, experienced.

Jung climbed down and wept.

He would never be the same.

13

There are some whose experience of life is so far removed from our own
that we call them mad. *This is mere convenience. We call them so in*
order to relieve ourselves of taking responsibility for their place in the
human community. Thus, we relegate them to asylums, shutting them
out of view and beyond calling distance behind locked doors. But for
them, there is no difference between what we think of as dreams *and*
nightmares *and the world in which they live their daily lives. What*
we call visions *and relegate to mystics—the miracles of Christ—the*
lives of the Saints—the apocalyptic revelations of John—are for them
the stuff of common, everyday experience. In their view, there can be
sanctity in trees and toads—living gods in fire and water—and a voice
in the whirlwind to which, if only we would listen, they would direct
our attention. Such are the conditions under which those who suffer
dementia *exist. They do not live in "other worlds," but in a dimen-*
sion of this world *which we, out of fear, refuse to acknowledge.*

This had been written in 1901 by a man whose existence was
rarely mentioned in 1912—or thereafter. His family had gone
so far as to change its name in the belief that his disgrace was so
great and so universal that even to speak of him amongst themselves was ruinous. The spectacle of his decline and death had
brought catastrophe to everyone with whom he was connected.

Robert Daniel Parsons was an American student of psychology. He had come to Europe in 1898 in order to complete his
studies with the then pre-eminent teacher of psychopathology,
Pierre Janet at the Salpêtrière Hospital in Paris and with Eugen
Bleuler at the Burghölzli Clinic in Zürich.

Both Janet and Bleuler were regarded by their students with
nothing less than awe. Together with the Austrian Krafft-Ebbing,

these two men had broken the restraining skin that had separated psychiatry from the rest of the medical profession. Freud had not yet entered the larger picture with his *Interpretation of Dreams*, leaving the field largely to Janet and Bleuler. There were disagreements between them, but never a major schism. They were not so much the founders of different theories as the self-appointed spokesmen for different schools.

Jung, as a student, had experienced the teachings of both these "giants"—giants, that is to say, in their own time. That Jung would outstrip them both was not even a subject of discussion prior to 1912. By then, however, it was becoming perfectly clear to Jung himself—and somewhat resentfully clear to his masters—that he and Freud were to claim the entire attention of the twentieth century where psychiatry and psychotherapy were concerned. While Janet and Bleuler tended to hang back in the safety of their established reputations, Jung strode forward fearlessly into what he would come to realize was an ever-widening sphere of understanding—sometimes alarming, sometimes even terrifying—but never to be rejected. From the night of May 12th, 1912, when he experienced his "bathroom epiphany," there would be no turning back. Terror, yes—and terror, as we will see, is quite the right word—but no turning back.

As for Robert Daniel Parsons and his place in history, he became an advocate of the "sorry mass of madmen" to whom he dedicated his life and, in time, his agony and his death.

In Paris in 1901, he experienced an epiphany equal to Jung's 1912 revelation, but more profound in that it was more political—and more revolutionary.

By declaring that *the mad are not mad but merely different*, Parsons embraced the psychiatric equivalent of anarchy. If anarchism is the belief that all government should be abolished, Parsons's version of this was that all governance of the mad should be abolished. *Down with Sanitoria, down with psychiatric wards in hospitals, down with Bedlam and down with psychiatric experiments.* Down, too, with all enforced medication, treatments and restraints. Down with laudanum, ether and chloral hydrate. Down with hydrotherapy. Down with straitjackets, locked doors and barred windows.

At first, Robert Daniel Parsons was perceived as a kind of manic entertainment. He was barely twenty-two years old—a tall, lanky, curly-headed Westerner from Wyoming whose handsome figure and *angelic boy-face*, as someone described it, drew an immediate audience amongst his fellow students. They delighted in his antic interruptions of Professor Janet's lectures, and even Janet himself thought him charming. At first.

But Parsons's ideas burned far too hot for them to be contained in a few eccentric outbursts in the lecture hall. They spilled out into the corridors and through the doors of the Salpêtrière into the streets. They took possession of student cafés and bistros. They started appearing in the press. There were soon disciples and fellow advocates—many of them women. *The mad have rights* became a rallying cry and raids were conducted in which groups of *Parsonites* attempted to release the mad from their "prisons and torture chambers."

In the long run, Parsons was effectively expelled from the Salpêtrière Hospital—no longer allowed entrance to its halls and disavowed by both staff and faculty. Professor Janet refused to acknowledge having him as a student, claiming only to be acquainted with Parsons's extra-curricular escapades.

Parsons then "disappeared" for two years, becoming a farm labourer near Rossinière in the high valleys of the Alps northeast of Montreux. His only correspondence was with his younger sister Eunice, who was then a student at a women's college in New Hampshire.

Eunice Parsons was, at this point, probably the only friend her brother had. She was seventeen years old and on her way to becoming a passably good writer of what she called "journalistic fictions." It was the time of Stephen Crane and Jack London, a time when Mark Twain was the American god of gods—a time when, perhaps uniquely, American writers were creating a new form of fiction whose impetus came from the journalistic careers of its practitioners. All this would ultimately peak in the writing of Ernest Hemingway and John Dos Passos.

What Robert Daniel Parsons achieved in his two-year "sabbatical" at Rossinière was a manifesto, written in behalf of the insane. He called it *In Defense of Dementia* and it can still be found in various university libraries, the Smithsonian Institute and in the archives of the Jung Institute at Zürich. Its epigraph was taken from the work of Christopher Smart, some of whose writing had been scratched on the walls of an eighteenth-century asylum. Parsons had been caught by a phrase from Smart's religious testament: *A Song of David:*

> *Where ask is have, where seek is find,*
> *Where knock is open wide.*

Parsons's manifesto was a sensation. To begin with, it took Janet, Bleuler and Freud to task for having commandeered the lives of what he called *a mass already deprived of the rights to their own integrity*. The word *mass* seemed to appeal to Parsons, who used it often in his descriptions of the inhabitants of his chosen constituency, *The Mad.*

Because of her faith in Robert Daniel, whom she called "Rad," Eunice Parsons pursued publication of her brother's manuscript with the zeal of John the Baptist proclaiming the coming of Jesus Christ. She abased herself to the degree that she gave up all hope of achieving her own academic goals, leaving her college to speak out in Rad's behalf and to find a publisher of stature who would risk placing her brother's radical beliefs before the public. This way, *In Defense of Dementia* was published in America by Pitt, Horner and Platt in September of 1904.

It was an immediate and electrifying success. In a moment when Marie Curie produced the first evidence of radioactive elements in uranium ore, when Anton Chekhov's masterpiece *The Cherry Orchard* was first produced in Moscow—and when Claude Monet began his exploration of the water lily—Robert

Daniel Parsons's plea for "the freedom of madness" outbid them all for the attention of the *cognoscenti*.

The doors were opened—and the mad spilled into the streets.

It was, of course, a disaster. No precautions had been taken. No accommodations had been provided. No guides had been appointed. The fashion in which it all happened had nothing to do with Parsons's intentions. His advocacy had been for what were later called *minders* and *halfway houses*, and for financial security provided by government. None of these things had been set in place or motion and the fires that followed were amongst the saddest horrors of their time.

When Eunice Parsons introduced her brother's manifesto to European publishers, none of the effects of its American publication had been sufficiently publicized to deter them from seizing on *In Defense of Dementia* as an "intellectual bauble" to float on the current tide of public interest in *things Freudian—things libidinous—things dangerous*.

The word *dangerous* was everywhere. Literature was intended to be *dangerous*—art was meant to be *dangerous*—ideas were nothing if they were not *dangerous*. André Gide, Pablo Picasso and Isadora Duncan were *dangerous*. On top of all this, the public was presented with *In Defense of Dementia*.

Jung thought it was a *valuable contribution to the literature of our field*. Freud concurred—but they were alone. Janet, Bleuler, Krafft-Ebbing and other leaders in the field turned their backs.

Nonetheless, Robert Daniel "Rad" Parsons came out of exile into Paris, where the doors had been forced, the gates thrown wide and the mad unleashed.

Using the monies accrued through the sale of his book and with Eunice beside him, Parsons opened a *Hospice des aliénés* at number 37, rue de Fleurus, in the shadow of the Luxembourg Palace. Partway down that tiny street, Gertrude Stein had recently been joined in her atelier by Alice B. Toklas. Every day in the autumn of 1904, Miss Stein and Miss Toklas walked with their dog to the Luxembourg Gardens, waving a cheery hand at the residents of number 37, many of them sitting naked in the courtyard beyond its wrought-iron gates and amongst its fading geraniums. In her journal entry of October 14th, 1904, Miss Toklas notes: *they were there again this morning, the* Parsonite Peculiars, *seated on tiny Moroccan carpets, all quite splendid in their unabashed nudity, tatting curtains made of string. G.S. remarked that* if one chooses to sit upon the ground, there can be no finer ground than a Moroccan carpet. The colours, *she said*, are so receptive of human flesh. *I must think about this—and will.*

Gertrude Stein and Alice Toklas aside, little attention was paid to the Parsonites. That is to say, little official attention. The police passed by and looked the other way, so long as the gates remained closed. Citizens of high standing—high, in their own opinion—avoided the rue de Fleurus entirely. Children and dogs were hurried on to the Gardens. No one complained.

And then it happened.

Amongst the patients "rescued" from the Salpêtrière was a man by the name of Jean-Claude Vainqueur, who believed he had come to earth from *another place*—never named—in order to pursue and kill the Antichrist and all who believed in him.

He had first come to official notice thirty-five years before his rescue from the asylum, when—near Marseilles—he had been washed ashore in his dead mother's arms. They had been amongst two hundred passengers on an overcrowded sloop that had foundered at sea between Algiers and the French coast. All had perished. A paper was found in the pocket of the unidentified woman's apron—a paper on which the name Jean-Claude Vainqueur had been pencilled, doubtless the name of a man she had intended to contact after landing on French soil.

The boy had been, at most, four years old—possibly less. He had no language known to anyone who had encountered him—and no identifiable origin. He was placed in one orphanage after another—each time provoking his own rejection by lighting fires and screaming invective at the authorities who came to put them out.

In the final stages of his life as an orphan-ward of the state, a language had been devised by a patient, almost saintlike Jesuit who had decided, quite properly, that one of the child's greatest frustrations was his inability to communicate. What emerged was a mix of basic French, even more basic Latin and an agreed upon lexicon of grunts, murmurs and sighs. God was *Deo-Dieu*, Christ was *Corpus* and the Antichrist was *Diabolo*.

Ultimately, the priest's body was discovered—piece by piece. It had been dismembered and scattered. His head was never found. Jean-Claude Vainqueur was incarcerated, supposedly for life, in a prison for the criminally insane at *L'avoir Paix* on the outskirts of Paris. One month prior to Parsons's return from exile, Vainqueur was brought to Salpêtrière as a study case in the language of the mad.

And then *The Mad* began to be released.

Jean-Claude Vainqueur ended up in the *Hospice des aliénés* on rue de Fleurus. There, acting on some vicious logic of his own, he came to the conclusion that Parsons, himself, was the Devil incarnate—possibly based on something as simple as the fact that Parsons had chosen to sit at the head of the communal table. Vainqueur and his disciples consequently dragged Parsons from his bed, stripped him and nailed him to a cross. The cross was then suspended upside down over a bonfire in the locked courtyard at number 37, rue de Fleurus. Before her expulsion from the *Hospice*, Eunice Parsons was forced to witness the agony of her brother's death.

These events occurred on the night of October 16th/17th, 1904—a Sunday and a Monday. On the Monday, the militia was called in to storm the gates and imprison the fifteen Parsonites who were then in residence, together with Jean-Claude Vainqueur.

Alice Toklas noted in her journal that *fires and human cries of anguish* had occurred in the night. *Many dogs were set to barking and G.S., on being wakened, said to me:* do not light the lamp but only candles. For all we know, since so many Russians now reside in Paris, we may be in the midst of a pogrom and do not want to draw attention to ourselves. *I duly lighted one candle only and set it in the middle of the room, where it could not be seen through any window.*

As for the press, it responded with the usual sensational head-lines: *PARSONITE EXPERIMENT ENDS IN FIRE! PARSON-ISM DIES ON THE CROSS!* Et cetera. The reaction worldwide was immediate. This was when the Parsons family in Wyoming and elsewhere went into hiding, changed their names to various others and disappeared altogether from further noto-riety. For two years, Eunice attempted to publish her own work, failed—and committed suicide. In Toronto, Ernest Jones, a Freudian disciple, delivered a lecture on the dangers of *flirting with Parsonism* in any experimentations in the field of psychopathology. In Paris and Zürich, Janet and Bleuler crowed their triumph over the demise of *The Madmen's Madman* and in Vienna, Freud burned his copy of *In Defense of Dementia*.

Not so in Küsnacht. Jung took the precaution of wrapping his own copy of Parsons's book in butcher's waxed brown paper, tying it with string and locking it inside a cabinet otherwise reserved for private journals, letters and a spare bottle of cognac.

Early in the pre-dawn light following his "bathroom epiphany," Jung put on his robe, shuffled into his slippers and went down-stairs.

In his office, he opened the windows and the shutters, went to the locked cabinet, inserted the key, pulled the door towards his knees, reached inside and drew forth the string-tied brown-paper package containing *In Defense of Dementia*.

Pilgrim, he was thinking. *Blavinskeya. Haeckel.* And *in this cave where I am sitting.*

He undid the string and set it aside on his desk. He unfolded and smoothed the butcher's waxed brown paper—laying it, too, where he could see it from the corner of his eye. The little book itself—no more than fifty pages long—had the look of something newly purchased, its blue-grey covers unsoiled, its black lettering unfaded. Jung laid his right-hand palm down on its face, as if to say: *pace, pace.*

There was a martyr here. He recognized that without question. *Appallingly wrong—yet undeniably right.*

Another Luther. Another Rousseau. Another da Vinci. Another monster hiding inside another saint—another saint inside another monster.

And if you free the saint, you also free the monster.

A voice in the whirlwind, he read, *to which, if only we would listen, they would direct our attention ...*

Pilgrim. Blavinskeya. Emma's little fish—our child.

And he wrote:

Between his exposure to Leonardo's eye and his exposure to mine, there is no time and space in Pilgrim's mind. Nor between her life on the Moon, for Blavinskeya, and her residence here. Nor between the ocean of Emma's womb and the shore on which our little fish shall one day be angled.

All one.

That's right.

All one place and all one time.

That's right.

It is how we see—that's all that matters.

And what we remember.

Yes. And feel.

And tell.

Embrace it all. It is all one.

Jung sat forward.

The pen wavered and then he wrote:

All time—all space—is mine. The collective memory of the whole human race is beside me, sitting in this cave—my brain. And if I join the mad in claiming this, so be it. I am mad.

14

Hôtel Baur au Lac
Zürich
14th May, 1912

And so my dearest friend, I address you for the last time. To my sorrow, I must do so through the medium of this letter, though I would have preferred that we take leave of one another in our usual fashion, with a clasping of human hands and a kiss.

As you will guess, I am—of course—afraid. After so much life—my death. How certain we were that it would never come! And think how often we wished that it could, while knowing that what mortals call "death" was not, for us, even a remote possibility. The gods would not sanction it. They would not permit it. They would not so much as countenance the thought of it—and yet, here it is.

The *Envoys*, two of them, arrived in Zürich even as you and I did. You will remember we arrived in the midst of a blizzard—and it seems that same blizzard was their means of transport. Their name is Messager. *Messenger.* They masquerade at being French, speak that language perfectly, but otherwise have no human dimensions. I recognized them instantly, though I did not at first foresee their portent. I assumed that perhaps there was to be a meeting in the Grove—and of course, my heart leapt up because I assumed such a congress might have to do with your release from present conditions. Such was not the case.

It may amuse Doctor Jung to know—should you ever be inclined to tell him of these events—that he himself took note of my visitors' presence, since both Messagers, posing as man and newly wedded wife, were in the dining-room on the morning of our first extended encounter. He was, I could not fail to see, more than somewhat impressed with their ethereal beauty.

This is quite the right phrase. They were clearly not of this world—though how would any mortal know this? What a great pity, for all our sakes, the gods and their minions do not appear more often.

Though my "life" has not by any means approached the extent of your own, you will recognize, I am sure, the mixture of joy and trepidation with which I allowed them to approach me. As you know too well, this is the accepted protocol: *one does not go to them—they come to you*. I did, however, make myself amply available, taking up a prominent place in the hotel lobby and making sure that I was paged by name.

I cannot tell how soon it was that I realized they had come to "call me home." In the past, as I assume has been the case in your own experience, there was never any doubt one's stay was to be extended. My own stay has not, as you know, been overly long. I have, so it now seems, been granted the average years of one human life—no more. I had a job to do—and it seems that job has come to an end. As I sit here now, I shrug at the thought of this—for how is one to know what it means? I suspect I shall never know—and must accept that.

You spoke to me once in the greatest confidence about these matters—and believe me, my dear, it remains a confidence never breached—saying that your encounters with the Others always took place in what you taught me to call the Grove. This was an honour accorded only once to me—and not, by any means, an honour I expected. But I will confess to you now that it was an honour I had hoped would be repeated many times, so long as you were in the world to be there with me. In your bitterness, however, you explained that honour, once, as being *the honour of being dishonoured*.

That you have suffered, I can bear witness. And to know that your suffering must continue is the greatest cause of my sorrow in being called away. But called I am.

That their name is *Messager* is almost amusing, they have so little tact in this. But they have been courteous otherwise and have treated me with complete respect. I was given a bouquet of freesia by Monsieur and a curtsey by Madame. Think of it! In that moment, I was royalty to them! They have that look, which you would recognize, of pristine champions—of athletes newly crowned with laurels—of youth as youth so rarely is, without the stamp of mortality—all breath and skin and clear-eyed wonder.

Dear one—to live—to die. What do we know? Nothing. Or perhaps, one thing. *To live is worse than to die.*

To be rid—to be shed—to be done with life. Not to *have to*. Never again to *have to* get up at dawning—*be*—take responsibility—see what we see—know sadness—miss the presence of loved ones—touch and minister to dead infants, animals, strangers—never again to have to say *I can't, but I will try. I cannot, but I shall.* To know what is expected of one, because one has eyes, ears and nerve ends—but never again to be placed in a position of having to say *I recognize—I see, I hear, I feel.* All these "human" qualities are about to pass from me, and while I rejoice in being able to shed them, I cannot bear the knowledge that in shedding them I must be also shed of you.

Now, there is nothing I can do for you. Nothing.

Oh, God. Oh, gods. Oh, everyone.

To be thus helpless is already less than to be alive.

Our usefulness to one another has come, for whatever reason, to an end. And in this end, I recognize the need for my own demise.

My demise. Yes. We must learn to practise the words for death. *Extinction. Quietude. Passing. Gone. Over. Final. Nothingness.*

It is all so trite. So meaningless. I hope you are laughing. I am. Don't you think it's funny?

Je suis passée, monsieur. Life itself is passé.

Laugh, Pilgrim, laugh. One of us has made it to the end. I did it all. I loved a mortal—gave birth to mortal children—suffered mortality in all its far-too-many manifestations. I listed myself amongst the most privileged of my time and place. I saw wrongs—and corrected them. I also failed to do so. I have been very—utterly—human. But still ...

We all forgive ourselves, don't we. We all forgive ourselves and blame some other—someone anonymous, but seen with such convenience from the corner of our eye. Always, when we need them, there is someone there to blame. But never self. Never, never self.

As death approaches me, I regret this most, Pilgrim—aside from my loss of you. I regret that I blamed, so often, others— for faults and problems of my own making. And, if not of my own making, certainly of my own tolerance. That men could not love men—or women, women—that poverty was the fault and responsibility of the poverty-stricken (how can I have thought so!)—and that "good" was something that could be decreed by governments, as if by creating laws we could establish the boundaries of someone else's needs and joys and confidence. How dare we decree what is "good" for others when for us it has been a gift!

I learned all this—so little!—in the moment I knew I was to be recalled. I learned that—aside from my experience of you, dear friend—I have barely lived at all. My love of Harry and of all my children—even my darkest love of David, whose predictable future is so ruinous to all my beliefs—was "merely human." I had money, place and station. All the privileges, and took no advantage—except where you were concerned. Isn't it odd—*or is it, one wonders*—that I should have missed so much within such a wide spectrum?

I think of so many—even of my own blessed children—of how often I failed to see them. Did not—could not—would not see them, while claiming to love them.

It is over. All of life. All of my opportunity. Once given, once missed—forever deprived. So wide a sweep. So narrow an experience. To have lived. To have been alive.

I am to be led into some valley, so I understand. A motor car will be involved. There will be snow. I know nothing else. And care not.

This one last thing remains to be said—and I have said it also to Doctor Jung in my final letter to him: *In the wilderness, I found an altar with this inscription:* TO THE UNKNOWN GOD... And I have made my sacrifice accordingly.

I know you will understand this, though Doctor Jung may not.

And now, I must say to you what you can never say to me. *Goodbye.*

My love to you, dare I say *always* ...

Sybil.

Jung, having read, folded the letter back into its envelope and, without remorse at having read it, placed it again in Anna's music bag.

He sighed and sank farther back in his chair. Did all this signify that he was dealing not with one mental patient, but with two? And one of them, now dead.

The moment, of course, would come when he must show the letter to Pilgrim—but before that moment came, Jung knew, he would have to come to terms with the thought—if only the *thought*—that what he had just finished reading had been addressed to an immortal.

BOOK FOUR

1

Word has reached me that Oscar Wilde died shortly after noon today in Paris. I wonder what the papers will make of this, if anything. They have been so meticulous in avoiding his name, they may well persist and print nothing. I thought of him this evening during my walk.

Emma stared at the page in fascination. *Oscar Wilde*. She remembered reading about his life—his trials and his death—when she was still a girl. She looked again at the date. *1900*. Three years before she and Carl Gustav were married.

She wondered what Mister Pilgrim would have to say about this infamous man. And about anyone else. She was still in a state of pleasant amazement that Carl Gustav had given her permission to take a look at the journals. And more than mere permission—it was an *assignment*.

I must find out more about this man, Jung had said that morning at breakfast. *I must find out why he is writing these incredible stories—or whatever they are. Dreams—fables ... I must find out what has happened in his life to prompt him to create these fantasies.*

Emma's assignment, then, was to browse through the journals looking for entries that dealt with Mister Pilgrim, himself—and with his life in London. Before that morning, her only experience of his writing had been to copy out that remarkable letter to Leonardo da Vinci. She remembered the tears falling onto the page as she wrote.

And now, before her for the first time, lay Mister Pilgrim's own memories—of an evening walk in 1900, and of Oscar Wilde.

* * *

I had dined alone, though Agamemnon was at my feet as usual—dear little Aga, with all his snorts and sneezes. He has a cold, which I assume will pass. I think, somehow, he glories in it—barely waiting for the chill of winter before his snuffling begins. He knows it will bring him evenings with his basket by the fire and bowls of warm milk. Forster is very patient with him—constantly in danger of tripping over him because the dog delights in choosing hallway shadows for his daytime naps.

Dinner consisted of consommé heavily laced with sherry—a fillet of sole in a delicious sauce—a roast of beef *au jus*—Brussels sprouts (*al dente*, which I enjoy) and duchess potatoes. This was followed by a rice pudding, which contained the fattest, sweetest raisins I've had in years. And a bottle of *Nuits-St-Georges*. Superb. I must remember to speak with Mrs Matheson and congratulate her. Her way with sweets and sauces is particularly good and the joint was cooked to perfection.

As I reached the front hall and had my walking stick in hand, poor little Aga pretended he would like to come with me—thinking, I suppose, it was his duty to walk me. But he hung back close to Forster and the minute I turned away towards the door, I heard him dash back into the library and his basket.

I never cross the river. Consequently, three directions only are open to me. Will I ever tire of this? I doubt it. Each direction offers its own delights and mysteries. My game of making up the lives beyond the windows I pass is sufficiently intriguing to entertain me, should I have nothing else on my mind. Besides which, there are real lives beyond the windows with which I am all too familiar, and—depending on the moment—I praise or damn them, throwing a mental bouquet or brick at the glass before I go my way. (Later, coming to Whistler's house—even though he no longer lives there—I cursed him out loud for Oscar's sake and threw a ton of bricks. The brute.)

I went up Cheyne Row and over then to Oakley Street and back to Cheyne Walk and up again on Flood—and, turning right, along Saint Leonard's Terrace until I came to Tedworth

Square. I often create a maze this way of ups and downs. I suppose it's a kind of game. To be lost, I sometimes think, would be wonderful. *Where am I, now?* And then the joy of finding home again, as if by chance. To be lost. To be lost. And no one knowing who I am.

London seems, these years, to be impossibly safe and civilized. Nothing visible requires the eye to look away, and the advent of the coming century, with all its predicted wonders lends a kind of security, much as to say: *we are safely harboured here and nothing can harm us now.*

Except ...

This morning, in the dark at 6:00 a.m., I had another of these dreams that have been plaguing me of late and I woke, cold-sweated—fumbling for the lamp. I nearly knocked it over, but managed to catch it in time. In the drawer beside me, I found my notebook with its pen. My fingers were shaking so, I could barely get them to function. Once I had managed to pull myself together, I began the transcript of what had passed in the dream—but still, as with the others, I have no idea what it means. The word, this time, was *Menin.* I now have three of these in a column, each name spoken, as at Delphi, through a wreath of fire and smoke.

Arras.

Saint Quentin.

And, today: Menin.

And the phrase *there are only pine trees, now, because nothing else will grow here any more.*

What can it mean, I wonder. Of all these names I know only one: *Arras*—a place in France. Of the saints, I have too little knowledge, though I presume that *Quentin* is French. And who might *Menin* be? A kind of feeble joke occurs to me: that Menin and Saint Quentin, like Polonius, are in behind the Arras about to be killed. But by whom? Not Hamlet, surely. Hamlet has never played a role in my dreams. Nor anyone theatrical— barring that one occasion when Sarah Bernhardt went beneath the guillotine wrong way round and lost her legs. It was because she insisted on giving one of her speeches from *L'Aiglon* all the way to the end. In the dream, they fed her to the knife in sections. Her lips went on moving, even after her head was severed. Dreadful—though amusing. I recall that I thought, on waking: *well, this is what all great artists have in common—persistence.*

As to the pine trees, I have no explanation. This image, too, is one of a "set," or sequence. Four days ago I dreamt of a landscape over which an unfamiliar river went into flood because its weirs and dams were clogged with dead animals—sheep and horses, cattle and so forth. And a week ago, some figures dressed in ancient armour—iron helmets, masks and breastplates—moved across an unidentified hill, dispensing fire from what appeared to be garden hoses. Everything in their path was laid to waste.

All of these names and pictures I have recorded in the notebook by my bed. If they persist, there is only one conclusion I can draw: namely, that I am being returned to that dreaded condition of which I have prayed so fervently to be relieved. Not on my knees. I never pray on my knees. It is undignified and childish. If God is truly there, I suspect He prefers to meet us face to face and eye to eye. That has always been my way with Him, and I think it has always been His way with me. But if the situation warrants, I shall go to my knees at once.

I turned towards the Chelsea Embankment, seeing the distant lights of Battersea shining beyond the river, and walked along Tite Street.

Number 16 was dark. One presumes that since Wilde was forced to give it up in order to pay his debts, and all its contents sold for a penny—no one has cared to live there. High above the street its graceful balconies are painted white, and in the moonlight and the lamplight, they take on a somewhat sad and lonely desolation. No one now will stand there any more, gazing down, or out towards the river. Gone. And Constance dead as he is dead. God knows what became of their sons. There's not a printed word.

He would stand, as I recall, immensely tall in the open doorway. "There you are—and I've been waiting." Not a rebuke, but a greeting—bespeaking the pleasure with which he anticipated your company. He never failed to make you feel you'd taken on the role of most-honoured-guest, in spite of whomsoever else might dine with you that night. I have sat with artists of the highest rank at Wilde's table—painters, actors, writers. He gave of himself without stint—the best of wines, exquisite food—*and all the pearls I cast with not a swine in sight.* I quote himself.

The last time I saw Oscar Wilde was, in its way, prophetic. This was last summer. I had gone to France, along with half the world, to view the wonders of the Paris Exposition.

Few were given the privilege—and I'm not sure why the honour was accorded to me—of a private visit to Rodin's studio. While the works of sculptors from around the world were exhibited collectively in the *Grand Palais*, the works of Auguste Rodin were put on show in a separate pavilion. It remains a simple truth about this extraordinary man that no other artist since Michelangelo has brought the human form to life with such compassion and vivacity.

But it was not to the Rodin pavilion I was bidden. It was to his private atelier on the rue de l'Université in order to see the unfinished *Gates of Hell*. And there, when I arrived, was Wilde, together with two friends. One of these was his new young companion, a French marine of exquisite beauty and proportions whom Rodin would later use as one of his nude models. I believe his name was Gilbert, though whether this was his first or last name I do not recall. The other was an effusive woman who had apparently attached herself to Wilde only recently.

Her name was Seonaid Eggett, and she was as Irish as Wilde himself. When the Rodin evening's activities were being arranged, she gave me her card, *so that you will know how to spell it. It is not, in Ireland, an unusual name, though I've discovered many*

of you English have a problem with it. It is pronounced Shay-nid.
Only weeks before, so Oscar had said, Mrs Eggett had *accosted*
him on the street, lifted his lapels and planted a kiss on his lips.
And I hope the whole world saw me! she had said. *I worship you.*

Though more than somewhat taken aback by the effulgence of
her greeting, Wilde had become enchanted with her company.
She is, he told me, *a bold adventuress in the wilderness of art.*

"Dear boy," Wilde said, once the introductions were accomplished. *Boy*, in spite of the fact that I was only one year younger
than he. "I hadn't thought to see you ever again."

"I came because of you," I lied. "It seemed appropriate.
Where else could one expect to meet the master of the word but
beside the master of stony silence. No one here to rebuke you,
Oscar. No one to beat you at your own game."

"Whoever could?" he said, and smiled. I noted he had lost
some teeth.

We shook hands.

There were tears in his eyes—and in his hand, a dreadful lack
of presence. All his strength was gone, and he could barely
respond.

It is a dreadful thing to see a giant in the moment of his fall.
Here was Wilde—just weeks away from death, standing at *The
Gates of Hell* as though he had come to take his place in the spec-
tacle of Rodin's imagery. *Shall I pause just here—or there?* he
seemed to say. *Shall I raise one arm or both? Shall I stand this way
or that? Tell me what you would have me do. Perhaps you will notice
there is nothing in my present stance that hints at yesterday's regret.
That is all gone from me, now. All gone.*

"Dear boy," he said, as our fingers parted, "do come and look
at Hell with me. There is nothing here I cannot explain."

We moved away from the others and stood alone before a
gigantic plaster model of *The Gates*. It was over twenty feet high
and over half as wide. Rodin had explained his original commis-
sion was to design the "portals" (his word) for a projected
museum of the decorative arts. The museum was never built. Of

course, it was to have been in Paris. When I saw his abandoned contribution last summer, the sculptor had already spent twenty years devising and creating its various components—some of which had achieved renown on their own.

Rodin had remarked: *these portals are my Noah's Ark. I can people them with whomever I choose, since no one but Dante has ever been to Hell and come back in order to contradict me.* He had said this laughing, though I noted that his affection for this vast and wondrous creation still brought something of a tremble to his voice.

Brooding on the lintel was the figure we have come to know as *The Thinker*. *The Kiss* was also intended for *The Gates of Hell*, but was removed when Rodin was dissatisfied with his inability to place it in the context of the themes he was exploring. Equally famous in its own right is the grouping of *Ugolino and his Sons*, which depicts the horrifying tragedy of the blind and maddened nobleman who, when imprisoned, devoured his children.

But the piece that most intrigued Oscar was the falling figure of Icarus, whose sin was to fly too close to the sun. Staring up at him, he said: "I have myself become a master of the fall, and might have taken my lessons from him."

I spent little time with Rodin, his attentions having been claimed by the gushing Mrs Eggett. Still, I thanked him for his invitation and the chance to pay my respects to his work.

As I was preparing to leave, I could see that Wilde's young marine had brought a wooden chair and there was Oscar seated in it, hat in hand, before *The Gates of Hell*, smoking a gold-tipped Turkish cigarette—a handsome uniformed lad by his side and both of them damned in the eyes of "decent" society.

Wilde mentioned he was expecting his young Canadian friend Robert Ross, who would be taking him and his companions to dine at *Le Jardin des Lilas*, one of the few cafés where the exiled writer was still accepted. Afterwards, they planned an excursion into Parisian night life. Would I care to join them?

Indeed.

Ross, who was small, had once been described by Wilde as having *the face of Puck and the heart of an angel*. When I first met him, I was surprised to find that he was also trim and had something of the athlete in his appearance. It was said that at the age of seventeen in 1886, when Wilde was thirty-two, Ross had "seduced" the older man and introduced him to the physical mysteries of homosexuality. Latterly, Ross had proved to be a good deal more than a merely seductive young man of the world and was one of the very few friends who stood by Wilde's side to the very end, offering him both practical and emotional support.

It had been suggested that it would be appropriate—*in order to complete Mrs Eggett's worldly education*—that the "night life" following dinner would entail a visit to the famous brothel *La Vieille Reine*—the Old Queen.

"There," Wilde had told them, "everything is done with style and panache, but also with grace. There will not be a moment's embarrassment. The ladies of *La Vieille Reine* are beyond reproach—chosen not only for their beauty, but their manner. There is nothing crude nor unsightly. I have been many times, just to watch the way it is all achieved. Everything is enthralling and enticing."

Robert Ross had agreed. "It has the feel of a blue-stocking salon," he had said.

And as I would discover, indeed it had—with one rather significant difference. The stockings would be black.

The hostess was known as *Madame la Madame*. She otherwise had no name known to anyone but her parents, who were dead.

Madame la Madame greeted Wilde with kisses on the hand and affectionate pats on the arm. She greeted Ross with a more formal *bisou* on either cheek. Mrs Eggett was offered a nod and I the same. Gilbert, on the other hand, was taken by both elbows and drawn to Madame's bosom as though he were a long-lost child—a prodigal son returning. *Oh!* she kept saying,

how perfectly enchanting! How utterly beautiful! What a find!
Monsieur Wilde—how can you have kept him hidden for so long?
Why, any minute, he will be fourteen and we should have lost all the
joy of introducing him to the arts of pleasure. Have you brought him
here to make a present of him? Is he a gift?

Even Wilde was somewhat thrown off balance by this effu-
siveness. Gilbert shrank away from Madame's embrace and took
refuge behind Mrs Eggett. But Madame la Madame had other
ambitions.

"I will pay you for him," she said to Wilde.

"No, Madame. No," Wilde told her—smiling. "He is neither
mine to sell nor yours to buy. He is his own man and I have
brought him here only to show him a side of life he has not yet
imagined. We are not here as customers, Madame, nor as
custom. We are here as spectators at your delightful court."

"What a pity," Madame said. "Nonetheless, you are all
welcome. I shall send Roselle to see to your needs."

With that, she led them to a table in the corner of the room
and hurried off.

The salon was large, crowded and elegantly furnished. The
most striking element of the decor was a large wisteria vine—
cunningly fashioned in painted plaster. It twisted and curved all
across the ceiling and partway down the walls. Hanging from its
green-leafed arms were its "blossoms," an endless series of tiny
chandeliers made of Venetian glass—each one a cluster of glow-
ing mauve flowers that cast their soft light through the haze of
cigar and cigarette smoke that hovered above the assemblage.
There were also Chinese lanterns, as in a garden.

"Charming!" Mrs Eggett exclaimed. "Utterly charming!"

Mrs Eggett had not been in Paris since her childhood, when
on three or four occasions she had been brought there by her
parents. She then, of course, had no experience of men like
Wilde and the circle of fame in which he walked. And yet, that
very day she had stood with Wilde, just as I had done, in the
presence of Auguste Rodin.

"It was simply too thrilling," she said. "Do you know what he said to me? He said *in classical sculpture, artists sought the* logic *of the human body, whereas in my work I seek its* psychology. Isn't that too wonderful? Isn't it just too perfect for words? The *logic* and the *psychology* of the human body! I shall always remember it and just the way he said it. Too, too perfect. And absolutely right, of course. Absolutely right. I do like an artist who can explain himself. So much more satisfying than those at a loss for words."

I was beginning to wish that Mrs Eggett might find herself at a loss for words.

Roselle duly arrived—tall and expertly lacquered. She wore a bodice of pink satin and Turkish trousers of an almost chocolate colour. Her dyed bronze hair was piled on her head and decorated with silver stars and red sequins. Giving a discreet salaam, she asked if anything was required.

Wilde ordered champagne.

I noted that other women were dressed in the same fashion as Roselle—but in different combinations of colours—blues and greens—purples and oranges—yellows and greens—reds and blues. They were all of a similar height, between five and a half and six feet. They wore, besides the Turkish trousers, curl-toed shoes and long fringed sashes. Clearly, they were there exclusively to see to the mundane comforts of the clientele—to bring drinks, cigars, ashtrays, pillows and to distribute fans, each one decorated with a female nude.

Once Roselle had departed, Ross turned to me and said, *sotto voce*, "you realize, of course, that our waitress is a man."

"Good heavens, no!"

"They all are," said Ross with an easy smile, "so as to discourage the customers from engaging them in place of the girls whose job it is to provide the necessary pleasures of such an establishment."

I looked about and realized with some amusement that each of the pantalooned "waitresses" had extremely large hands and feet and an excess of theatrical make-up. Still, it made an interesting spectacle and would make an equally interesting entry in my journal.

At one point, holding up his glass of champagne and gazing through it at the wisteria chandeliers, Wilde remarked that *a Channel crossing is something more than a mere sea-change, you realize. Once landed in France, you are in the very heart of wine-heaven. The English, on the other hand*, he said, *have an unfailing ability to change wine into water.*

Everyone laughed and Wilde gave a toast *to this glorious vacation from the process of dying.*

I found myself reflecting: here we are, gathered together in a Parisian brothel on a warm summer's night, while all about us, the ending of one age and the beginning of another have no more significance than the changing of the guard at Buckingham Palace. Guard? Guardian of what? Eternity? Why do I doubt it?

As I continued my walk through Chelsea, thoughts of Wilde and of Rodin inevitably led me to memories of another artist.

James McNeill Whistler had lived some twenty years ago at number 13 Tite Street and prior to that, but briefly, in the ill-fated *White House* at number 35. He now lives, to my sorrow, on Cheyne Walk at number 21. I say *to my sorrow* because this makes him my neighbour.

For all his undoubted talent—some would say genius—and for all his famous wit and dash, Whistler is a bigot—a man of mean spirit and something akin to treacherous when it comes to friendship. He took Wilde up and made a pet of him, slowly becoming paranoid because of Wilde's increasing forays in the direction of fame. That anyone—especially a protégé—should shine more brightly, be more lionized, cut a more recognizable figure than Whistler, was unforgivable.

The press became involved by way of Whistler's copious letters and Wilde's equally copious and enthusiastic responses. Noting that a *contretemps of dandies* was under way, the papers

encouraged it—flaunting Wilde in Whistler's face and vice
versa. It was the usual flourish of red flags and bulls—much
raised dust and a lot of *hooey*. Wilde enjoyed it; Whistler did not.
Whistler, after all, had gone to court in order to defend his
reputation, which he claimed had been ruined when Ruskin
pilloried his painting style. Ruskin was then, of course, at the
height of his critical powers and reputation. I believe all this
occurred in 1877 or 1878. I don't remember precisely. What I
do remember is Ruskin's famous claim that James McNeill
Whistler had *flung a pot of paint in the public's face!*

This was not then, nor is it now, my opinion of Whistler's
paintings. I deeply admire them and even though I loathe the
man, Ruskin had clearly gone too far.

The Judge's charge to the jury, as I recall it, stated that *certain
words* being used by John Ruskin, *beyond a doubt, amounted to
libel.* Or some such thing. What remained for the jury was to
decide whether the injury caused by these words to Whistler's
reputation was worthy of the thousand guineas he was claiming
in damages—or merely worth a farthing.

Whistler won the farthing.

And financial ruin. It was in that time that he had built and
lost his beloved *White House*, which ended up being occupied
by—of all people—an art critic!

For this, I offer Whistler my sympathy. But when it comes to
Wilde, who suffered far greater ignominy as the result of public
insults, Whistler was nowhere in sight. Merely within earshot.
He delighted, time and again, in what I have already described
as mean-spirited, bigoted remarks at Wilde's expense. Yes—the
man can be amusing. Perhaps his most famous remark, delivered during the early stages of Whistler's paranoia regarding
Wilde, was his response to Oscar's having complimented him
on some witticism by saying: "by God, Jimmy—I wish I'd said
that." To which Whistler had replied: "you will, Oscar. You
will."

In Paris, I happened to be present in a restaurant—though I

forget which—when Whistler and his cronies were dining at a nearby table. Clearly, Oscar Wilde was the subject of some part of their conversation. The name alone produced rude sounds and loud guffaws. Fun was made of Wilde, the dandy in velvet, being made to wear prison garb.

"And where in his cell do you think he kept his lilies?"

"In the po! In the po! In the beautiful po!" someone sang, to the tune of *By the Beautiful Sea*.

"And how do you mince in shackles?" asked someone else.

"Can't imagine. Tell."

"*Very* carefully."

Roars of laughter.

More wine was ordered. Cigarettes were lighted. Nearby diners joined in the amusements, since Whistler and his friends were clearly making an effort to be overheard.

All I could think was: *Oscar himself would never have behaved this way*. Certainly never to someone who was down and out, as Whistler had once been.

Wilde's public jibes at well-known friends and enemies were never vicious. They never cut to the bone—unless it was the bone of an attitude—and they certainly never addressed the subject of his victims' private lives.

I thought: *well, something must be done in Oscar's behalf—and I must do it.*

I paid my bill, collected my hat and walking-stick, and taking a pitcher of rosé wine from a passing tray, I went to Whistler's table and flung the contents in his face.

"This, for Oscar Wilde," I said. "A genius. A gentleman. And a friend."

Whistler, of course, recognized me. A tight, rather frightened smile appeared beneath his moustache.

"Good day," I said. And left.

As I did so, every eye was on me. And behind my back, as I departed, I heard Whistler's nasal voice, with its unmistakeable American drawl: "well! And still a friend of Oscar's! My, my, my! Off now, no doubt, to visit with the great man in his flea-bag hotel, where—guess what?"

"What? What? What?" cawed the cronies.

"Oscar is writing *The Bugger's Opera!*"

This produced a cascade of laughter. I paid the *Maître d'* for the rosé wine and went my way. Oscar might even have done the same, if he had been there. He never did like rosé.

"A mere reflection, dear boy, of wine's divine potential. A pale reflection in a tinted glass."

Which is not a bad description of Oscar's current reputation.

May he rest in peace.

At last.

I will close these pages tonight with a final salute to Oscar, dead now these ten hours. (Only ten? It seems a decade. Perhaps he really "passed away" in Reading Gaol.)

At some point in the past year, he said to his brother's widow: *I am dying beyond my means.*

This was bravado.

He also wrote that *one should live as if there were no death.*

This was brave. And remarkably apt, in my own case.

Emma stopped reading. The words had completely blurred. As she reached for her handkerchief, she found herself smiling. Was she destined always to be so deeply moved by the writing of her husband's most enigmatic patient?

2

Pilgrim was debating the difference between the doves and the pigeons on his balcony and windowsills, and for the last week, having begun to eat his breakfast in the dining-room, he had been stealing bread and toast in order to feed them. At least, he thought of it as stealing. If the food was not for oneself, it should not be taken. The serving girls were somewhat puzzled by his seemingly infinite capacity for toast and bread, which Pilgrim ordered as many as three times during a single sitting. His habit was to slip the excess of these items into a wide red handkerchief kept in his pocket. This he then transported to his rooms, breaking the pieces into crumbs which he scattered where the birds were certain to find them.

Watching his doves and pigeons (Pilgrim thought of them as his own) he would sometimes leave the windows open so that he could hear as well as see the birds as they ate.

He studied the markings on their wings and bodies and the moulding of their heads. The doves, of which there were two kinds, were obviously the prettier, though not by any means the most colourful. The pigeons, Pilgrim had always thought, were clearly the more resplendent. Their plumage ranged from various greens and blues and purples to all the shades of grey a person could imagine.

At home in Chelsea, in his garden at number 18 Cheyne Walk, he had spent endless mornings feeding his own and Forster's birds with expensive seed. Down they had descended from the dovecote, almost as if they had been called by number—one and then the next—each with its own coloration—each with its own distinct personality—*pouting and strutting like so many Regency courtiers*, he had noted in his journal, *pushing one another aside in order to be seen to the best advantage at the ball.* Ah! Lady Pearl-and-Burgundy! Baroness Violet! Duchess Rose! *And all the males spreading their wings to show their epaulettes and decorations! Wonderful!*

With all their nodding to and fro and all their whispering of one another's names, it was indeed a kind of pigeon court—with all that such a place entailed of gossip, display and hierarchy.

The doves were entirely different. To begin with, they were slimmer, sometimes smaller and always more elegant. Also sedate. They remained, for the most part, chastely paired and did not congregate in such a crowd as the pigeons—choosing instead to *sit out the dances* on the railings, while the pigeons formed quadrilles and eights and never left the ballroom floor.

The doves, too, were more subtly coloured, shading through brown to tan and pink, sometimes with ruby eyes, sometimes not—but always blue-toed, red-footed, their feet more finely shaped than the pigeons'. The larger doves wore rings around their necks—like pets that had been collared. They were Jane Austen birds, he had decided, the Elliot and Bennet sisters at a gathering where none of the suitors was suitable and ...

They're only birds, you raging idiot.

Pilgrim froze at the open window with broken pieces of toast in his hand.

Someone had spoken.

Who had spoken?

Whispered.

Don't, Pilgrim wanted to say. *Don't do this.* But he was silent.

There must be someone in the room with him, but he knew it could not be Kessler or Doctor Jung. Jung was not due for another hour and Kessler had gone to his mother's house to collect a pair of springtime boots.

Pilgrim glanced at the windowsill.

Only birds.

Did it matter that they were only birds?

"Why does it matter?" he said out loud.

There was no reply.

Slowly, he turned.

"Is someone there?" he asked.

Certainly no one visible.

Sometimes, voices pretended to be God. Pilgrim was well aware of this. Also, they could pretend to be the Devil. Or the Dead.

The sitting-room where Pilgrim stood and the bedroom beyond it were clearly empty of anything but furniture.

Had the furniture spoken? A chair? A table? Perhaps a lamp or a lampshade. A mirror. A picture frame. A carpet, jealous that Pilgrim had created a Regency pigeon court and a chaste society of Jane Austen doves while ignoring the needs and feelings—the emotions and desires—of their concrete selves. Their loneliness for one another, scattered and spread and separated as they were in a fixed and never-ending pattern—while life, being alive, demands variation, focus, something other than the same old place on the wall and the same old four-square space on the floor and the same dry rain of dust on all one's surfaces, cutting off one's view and clouding one's countenance. To spend whole weeks unsat in. To be a drawer that is never opened or a lamp that is never lit. To be an unused cushion, never turned or plumped or held. To be a fallen pin that is never found. To be a broken pencil that is never sharpened—or a spotted piece of glass that is never polished. To be set forever with your back to the wall and your face to the light. To be an unstruck match or an unread book. To be grime. To be dust itself or the unswept dirt from someone's boots. To spend one's whole existence unsaluted and unthanked. To be ...

Only furniture, you maniac!

Beyond the windows, the doves and pigeons fluttered and fussed because their feeding had been interrupted.

Pilgrim sat down.

The chair sighed: *at last.*

Pilgrim raised his hands to cover his face before he realized they were full of crumbs. There was toast in his eyes and toast in his hair.

Leaning forward, he fell to his knees in the middle of the floor.

"I implore you," he whispered. "Someone save me from this moment."

But there was only silence. All the doves and pigeons had flown away to forage or to be fed elsewhere.

When Kessler returned in his squeaky new boots, he found Pilgrim still kneeling in what appeared to be prayer.

"Mister Pilgrim? Sir?" the orderly said. "Can I help you?"

Pilgrim said nothing.

"You can't just kneel there," Kessler went on. "We have to get you up for Doctor Jung."

Nothing. Wordless and still.

Twenty minutes later, Jung arrived with Anna's music bag in hand, his smock still undone and his hair in disarray.

When Kessler had taken him aside into the bedroom to explain the situation, Jung returned alone and said to Pilgrim: "Mister Pilgrim—shall I pray with you?"

Pilgrim nodded.

Always prepared to go to whatever lengths were required to decipher a patient's mood or quandary, Jung got down on his knees directly opposite Pilgrim.

"What are we praying for?" he asked, speaking gently and without condescension.

"Trees," said Pilgrim.

"Trees?" Jung responded. "You mean we should pray for the trees?"

Pilgrim shook his head.

"Take me to them," he whispered. "I must go to the trees."

"To the trees," Jung said. "Very well, then. Let me help you up."

Ten minutes later, Jung and Pilgrim, loosely dressed in their spring coats, went into the garden to the east of the Clinic.

Kessler followed at a discreet distance, though discretion in squeaky boots was difficult to achieve.

Pilgrim was noticeably shaky on his feet. He clung to Jung's arm like an invalid and seemed barely able to make his way along the path.

All at once, he looked up—and doing so, fell again to his knees.

"Mister Pilgrim—Mister Pilgrim," Jung said, bending forward to lift his patient.

But Pilgrim brushed him aside and said: "no, no—look! Don't you see her?"

Jung could see nothing unusual.

"Her, Mister Pilgrim? Who?"

"There," Pilgrim whispered. "There."

And he pointed.

Jung turned and looked. Seated high above them, in the crown of a giant pine, was a kingfisher—blue and green and shining—with a fish in its beak. For a moment it gazed down at the humans on the path below, seeming to mark them one by one. Then, having gulped its catch, it gave a cry and flew away.

Jung stepped aside and sat down on a bench. From there, he watched his patient, who was kneeling still on the gravel with an expression of almost religious ecstasy on his face.

So, Jung was thinking, *we have come at last to the visionary. We have come at last to the visions.*

They waited there half an hour, just so, with Jung on the bench, Pilgrim kneeling and Kessler leaning against a tree.

At last, Pilgrim rose and dusted his knees. There were toast crumbs still in his hair and he brushed these aside, collecting them in the palm of one hand. He turned then for one last look at the tree—the deserted pine with its empty crown shining in the sun.

I will come back, he decided. *I shall return and mark it.*

He then led the way, no longer limping, no longer frail but striding forward down the path towards the Clinic, spreading crumbs as he went.

Jung rose and shrugged. What would it mean, this mystical response of Pilgrim's? Man—tree—and bird. *Kingfisher*. There were few enough of these about the Zürichsee. At Küsnacht, Jung had seen only one—and that had been three or four years before. And yet, clearly Pilgrim had some affinity with this rare and beautiful bird. But why—and how?

Perhaps in England they were plentiful and Pilgrim was merely homesick for them. He lived, after all, beside a river— though of course it was a river devoted to commerce where Pilgrim had his home. Farther inland ... where did it rise, this river, the Thames? Oxfordshire—somewhere—Jung could not remember the other counties northwest of London. Not that it mattered. It rose for certain in pastoral splendour away from all that cities implied of dead waters and a dying countryside. Somewhere there a man could boat upon the rivers and spy upon whatever nature still had to offer.

The image of Pilgrim—garbed in white, seated, even reclin- ing in a punt on the upper reaches of the Thames—was all too easily conjured. A parasol, perhaps—a woven hat—a notebook open on the knee—and a kingfisher diving to its prey in some undisturbed backwater. Very English. Very true to England. Very Edwardian. Very secure. Totally unthreatened.

And there was more. On the outskirts of this manorial vision, country lads and lasses lolled against the farmland fences, suit- ably *déshabillé* so as to suggest availability should one desire a roll in the hay with a dairymaid or a knelt encounter with a stable boy. *England, this England.* All of it a lie, which nonetheless is dreamt upon and mourned before its imminent death.

> *With rue my heart is laden*
> *For golden friends I had,*
> *For many a rose-lipt maiden*
> *And many a lightfoot lad ...*

That Jung was familiar with A.E. Housman's poetry was not unusual, given the clientele at the Burghölzli. The English upper classes always brought such poetry with them. It was, for

them, a sentimental crutch—a way of dealing with the realities
their privileged lives had denied them. Ladies fell back, fainting,
into the arms of Elizabeth Barrett Browning and Christina
Rossetti. Gentlemen wept into the pages of Wordsworth,
Tennyson and Keats—and positively sobbed into the pages of
Housman. Many times, Jung had had to look away, he was so
embarrassed. *The English! The English! God help the snob-ridden,
long-nosed, God-chosen English!*

All this from having sighted a kingfisher.

*In this, you yourself, Carl Gustav, are showing signs of a certain
Germanic Aryan superiority to which you have no birthright*, the
Inquisitor said. *You are—and please remember it—*Swiss!

They had finally reached the portico. Jung watched Pilgrim
climb the steps and enter the building, followed by the squeak-
ing orderly.

As Jung himself achieved the upper level, he turned back to
look out over the serried tops of the trees towards the mountains. The Zürichsee was not visible. In fact, its absence in the
viewable landscape was quite deliberate. In planting the trees
that rose between the Clinic and the lake, the founders of the
Burghölzli had determined that none of their patients should
have access to the sight of water, since too many of them were
potential suicides and death by drowning is so easily achieved.
But the mountains were there—the heights and the sky and the
distant other ranges, grey and purple and misted.

Kingfisher, Jung was thinking.

Kingfisher. Visions. Visionary.

Well, he decided, *we shall see.*

3

It did not take long for the next encounter with the visionary aspect of Pilgrim's troubled mind.

Two days later, Jung was walking with Archie Menken on the same path where Pilgrim had knelt in the gravel. They were debating the rift between Freud and Jung, which had begun in the early months of 1912 and was now beginning to widen. In time, it would culminate in a complete schism, but this had not yet occurred. Still, the relationship was greatly strained and it wavered back and forth between tentative attempts at reconciliation and outbursts on Freud's part of outrage that his *appointed deputy—his adopted heir—the crown prince of psychoanalysis* should dare to contravene Freud's universal law that all psychoses rise from a well of sexual repression, sexual frustration and sexual abuse. Jung was deeply troubled. His admiration of Freud was basically unshakable. Nonetheless, he more and more disagreed with him. The more Jung learned—the more he explored—the more he believed that Freud had stumbled.

"It is the very same as having a life and death struggle with your father," he told Archie Menken. "There are moments when I cannot bear it. Worst of all, there are moments when—dare I say it?—I resent him to the point of hatred. In some matters, he is simply a tyrant—and that I will not tolerate."

Archie Menken shrugged and smiled. "You're something of a tyrant yourself, C.G.," he said.

"Maybe," Jung granted. "Maybe." He knew it was true. But genius itself was the tyrant. That was the problem in both his own case and Freud's.

They had reached the bench where Jung had sat watching

Pilgrim two days earlier and Jung, all at once, pulled Archie Menken by the arm.

"Look at that," he said.

"At what?"

"That pine tree. There. Do you see what I see?"

Archie squinted.

"Possibly," he said. But he saw nothing unusual.

Jung approached the tree and bent towards its trunk, supporting himself with one hand.

"Here," he said. "This."

Archie stepped forward and examined the place at which Jung had gestured.

Someone had carved the letter *T* into the bark, and the wound was bleeding resin.

"Maybe there should be a heart carved round it," Archie joked.

"I think not," said Jung.

The tone of Jung's response was so completely serious that Archie Menken gave him a sideways glance.

"Does it mean something to you?" he asked.

Jung said: "yes," though he did not yet know what it really meant. He knew only that Pilgrim had put it there—and knowing that, for the moment, was enough.

It would be some time before Jung discovered more about Pilgrim's mark on the tree—and why it had been put there. The explanation lay in yet another volume of Pilgrim's journals—a story still unread by any eye other than its writer's.

4

I began these journals in part with the notion that I might recapture some of what I have experienced deep in the past, as well as recording what I have experienced day by day in my present life. Sometimes, it has been appropriate to record the past as dreams, since dreams form such an important part of my consciousness. Other times, there is nothing for it but to set things down in the same way I would formulate an academic statement—never a theory (I detest theories!) but a statement of those certainties which I hold to be the centre of all my beliefs—truths and yet more truths. Never anything more and never anything less.

The story I must attempt to articulate now, however—in spite of its many truths and multiple certainties—is one more suitably told in the fashion of a tale. Indeed, almost in the fashion of a fairy tale. There is something so magical, mysterious and mystical about this story that it might have been conjured by Hans Christian Andersen, the Brothers Grimm or Charles Perrault.

Where their tales may be metaphorically true, this one is literally true, drawing as it does on my memories of life as a poor shepherd, and on the scholarship of later times.

Thus, though akin to what has been spun by greater imaginations than mine, this tale is itself entirely.

In the hills of the Sierra de Gredos to the northwest of Avila in Castile, there is a river called *la Mujer, the Woman*. The countryside is dusty and olive green—not drab, but always in need of washing down, of rain. The dust itself has a golden hue, and it lends a patina to everything on which it rests. A man's hair, a woman's skirts, the roofs of all the houses and the leaves of all the trees are gilded. The sheep who graze in these hills and the cattle who graze in their valleys are stained with this hue to such a degree that their hides and wool are prized for the making of boots and the weaving of carpets.

Deep in the Sierra there is a place known as *Las Aguas—The Waters*. Here, a certain landowner, Pedro de Cepeda, had created a small lake by damming la Mujer with a daub-and-wattle weir so that his sheep, his cattle and his shepherds would have a universal meeting place for the twice-yearly gathering of the flocks and herds, during which the twin ritual of shearing and of slaughter could be organized.

Those cattle and sheep who were destined for slaughter—mostly steers and ewes—were separated here and driven southward over the mountains to the abattoirs at Riodiaz, from which their meats would go on to grace the tables of Madrid. Both shepherds and cowherds were always somewhat saddened by this gathering of doomed animals, the births of which they had overseen, and the care of which they had assumed over the years. In order to accommodate the sad emotions engendered by these moments, Don Pedro de Cepeda always provided a quantity of wine and music and rode out himself to be with his people.

Amongst his shepherds, in the year 1533, there was an eighteen-year-old simpleton whose name was Manolo. That he was simple-minded did not in any way prevent him from fulfilling his duties. He was both devoted to the sheep in his care and to the terrain in which they grazed. These hills and valleys were all he had ever known and his experience of life and of the world was limited to the ten-mile radius of the land he inhabited—*la tierra dorada*—its golden hue and its green shade. He had no memory of his mother. The man who claimed to be his father, having taught the boy everything a simple mind could grasp, had moved on to a neighbouring area—still in the employ of Don Pedro de Cepeda, but entirely separated from his son.

In the high summer months of July and August, Manolo's greatest pleasure during the hours of siesta was to swim in the tiny lake at Las Aguas. He would leave his sheep in the shade of a grove of scrub oak and his clothes on the shore, where his dog, Perro, could oversee the care of both. Sometimes Perro would plunge into the waters and swim with Manolo, but he always returned to the bank and to the shade. The heat was so oppressive there was very little motivation to do more than doze.

Manolo was lanky, long-legged and sinewy. If El Greco, still unborn, had wandered into viewing distance of Manolo at that time, his eye would have fallen on the perfect prize—the very model of his attenuated version of the male physique. Even to the colour of its flesh and the dance-like attitudes it assumed.

If beauty is a quality unto itself and not dependent on artifice, then it would be fair to say that Manolo was beautiful. So long as he was seen in the context of water or of sleep. In sleep, his busy arms and legs were stilled—while swimming, floating or paddling with Perro and—once ashore—streaming with the long, shining lines of water falling from his frame, he was a masterpiece of elongated proportions that were nothing less than perfect. But once in search of his shirt, his ragged trousers and his sandals, he lost all cohesion—every muscle fighting every other for control of his movements. To say that he was *spastic* was to understate the case—though he could control his spasms while leaning on his sticks.

These sticks had been made for him by Don Pedro himself, who saw in the boy such a willingness to stand upright that his appeal was irresistible.

As for Manolo's speech, he had a stammer. It began in his brain, where words would flood his need to speak. He sometimes did not have the wit to realize the words were in the wrong order, and this way he would say: *want sleep do I.* Smiling at Perro, he would add: *sleep thou too thou? Now thou thee and I lie down. Yes?*

And so:

On an afternoon in late July in 1533, Manolo was floating face upwards in the lake when Perro, who had been dozing on the shore, all at once stood up and turned to face the trees in whose shade the sheep were sleeping.

There had not been a drop of rain for more than two weeks and the golden dust was particularly heavy on the leaves and over the ground. Perro's coat, as well, was thick with it.

Was there a wolf?

A wild dog?

A thief?

High above him in the sky, Manolo could see the outstretched wings of a pair of eagles. Or were they buzzards? Had there already been a death—or were the birds merely following the hunting track of whatever was out there, certain that in time it would lead them to a kill? Manolo had known this to happen—that the birds had divined the consequences of a certain pattern in the behaviour of wolves, wild dogs and foxes and followed it through to its inevitable conclusion.

Amongst the scrub oak there were also fir and pine, plus a modicum of cork and plane trees—these latter, together with some of the pines, rising above the general growth. Their upper branches often played host to flocks of magpies and crows or starlings. Manolo called these trees the *Talking Place* because of the chattering birds.

Manolo began to tread water, fixing his gaze—as Perro had done—on the highest branches of the Talking Place, which stood on the rising slopes above the lake.

A bird—or what appeared to be a bird of gigantic size—was seated there, its wings outstretched as if to grasp the branches for support. Or perhaps to dry them in the sun as a pelican will do, or a buzzard after feeding on offal.

What could it be?

No bird on earth was so large or so white or so wide.

Staring, Manolo stopped treading water and sank.

Spluttering back to the surface, his eyes streaming and the sun so bright it almost blinded him, he could see now that what he beheld was an angel. For only angels have wings so wide and only angels sit so still.

Manolo swam to shore, clambered onto the bank and took up his sticks.

The hair on the ridge of Perro's back was raised and his tail drooped.

"Come thee with me," Manolo whispered, touching the dog's ears and leading the way upward, beneath the trees.

In the dappled shade as he hobbled amongst the dozing sheep, Manolo had the look of a creature half-seen, as if the particles of his being were only then forming to become coherent. He stumbled—he flailed—and the sparkling light and the golden shade divided his limbs, his sticks and his torso into segments that were so disjointed he was barely recognizable as human. And beside him, the shadow of his dog seemed to be a part of Manolo that had been shed and was waiting to be redefined. That it moved was a certainty, but what it was could not be told.

At last—and out of breath—they came to the foot of the tree in which the angel sat. In fact, she gave the appearance more of being entangled in the branches than of sitting amongst them willingly.

Manolo stared.

Perro lay down at his feet and was silent.

The angel's face was turned towards heaven. Amongst the leaves, she had the look of someone who has gone alone into a great cathedral and while seated there is bathed in the light of stained-glass windows. Manolo had seen this once in Avila, when he was taken there as a child in the hopes that a miracle might occur that would cure him of his palsy. There had been no miracle—but Manolo had been inspired to believe the figures in the windows breathed and had life. They were on fire with light, and shimmered in such a way as to convince him he had seen them move.

Now, there was an angel.

Manolo did not speak. It would be improper.

At last, the angel turned and saw him.

"Have you come here to pray?" she asked him.

"No, ma'am. I came thee to see."

"Is this your tree?"

"No, ma'am. The tree its own."

"I see."

The angel took a firmer grasp of the branches where she was seated.

"Do you think you could help me get down?" she said.

"Thee cannot fly?" Manolo asked.

"No."

"Then how thou in the tree?"

"I can't explain. It happens—but I can't explain it."

"Happens?"

"I rise. As you can see, I rise sometimes as far as this—other times, not so far. But it is not my doing. It simply happens."

"Does it hurt thee?"

"No. It makes me dizzy. Then I laugh."

"Perro is afraid of thee."

"Who is Perro?"

"My dog. He thought thou were a bird so big thou would fly away with him to eat."

"I do not eat dogs—and I cannot fly away. I have no wings."

Hearing his name and the tone of the angel's voice, Perro looked up and began to wag his tail.

Then the angel said: "the trouble with rising is that one must come down. Have you a ladder, by any chance?"

"I do not know *ladder*."

"Steps. Stairs. As in houses."

"I do not know houses."

"Well—I shall try to climb down the branches."

So saying, the angel began her descent. First, she had to disentangle her dress from the branches around her—especially her "wings," her billowing white sleeves.

Manolo stood back so as not to be in her way and Perro rose and moved behind him. The angel was clumsy and twice she nearly fell, but at last she stood on the earth and shook out her skirts.

She stared at Manolo frankly and without embarrassment. "You are naked," she said.

Manolo said: "I am often naked. There is no one ever here." The angel smiled. "My name is Teresa de Cepeda y Ahumada," she said. "I have come to *La Sierra de Gredos* to stay with my uncle Don Pedro, who is my father's brother."

Manolo hobbled to one side and attempted to hide behind a tree. "I should like to return to the water," he said.

"The water. Yes. I could see it from the tree. Las Aguas. My uncle told me of it."

Teresa led the way.

"Mind thee the sheep," Manolo said as they started their descent through the woods. "It is their siesta before they go to graze again."

Perro ran ahead, loping between the trees, expertly navigating his way amongst the slumbering sheep and lambs so that none was disturbed.

As they broke into the open, Teresa stopped in her tracks and, gazing at the man-made lake before her, spread her arms as if she wanted to embrace it. "Oh," she said, "I have never seen anywhere so beautiful."

On the far side of the water, a flight of pelicans was resting on the surface amongst the reeds, their feathers stained with yellow dust.

"They come for siesta, too," said Manolo. "And every day ducks, the sheep and Perro and me—we sleep to the song of the cicada. You hear them now?"

They moved out onto the embankment, where Manolo had earlier scattered his clothes. There was wine there, too—in a skin—and the remnants of bread and cheese, tied in a kerchief. Perro walked into the lake to drink.

Then Manolo said: "close thou thine eyes. I am afraid for thee to see me when I walk."

Teresa covered her face with her hands and said to him: "I am blind."

Manolo went to the water's edge with his sticks where, dropping them, he staggered into the lake and paddled far enough away so that he could stand and yet be covered.

"Now thou may look thee."

But Teresa had already looked. Moving her fingers just enough to provide her with a view of Manolo's falling stride as he passed, she had seen his back, noting a birthmark there in the shape of a butterfly. She had also seen quite plainly that without the sticks he was all but helpless.

Dropping her hands, she sat down beside his clothes and asked him how old he was.

"I be eighteen," he said. "By count. I can count to one hundred."

"May you live so long!"

A kingfisher flew down from the trees on the opposite shore and skimmed the waters. Blue. Green. Brilliant.

"That was a messenger from God," said Teresa. "Did you know that? Pelicans, herons and kingfishers—all are messengers in the name of our Lord, Jesus Christ. Jesus was also a fisherman of men and a shepherd of sheep. Shepherd of God, King Fisher, Lord."

Manolo slowly waved his arms in the water. "I am not of God," he said dreamily, smoothing the surface. "I am a shepherd only of sheep."

"But the sheep are of God," said Teresa. "We are all of God."

"Not I," he said. "So broken. God was not present at my birth. And when Don Pedro—your uncle—took me to Avila to receive the Virgin's blessing in the Cathedral there, I came away as I had entered—on my sticks."

Teresa threw a stone into the water. "God is everywhere," she said.

Manolo looked away.

"He is with that stone as it sinks," Teresa went on. "And with every bird as it rises." She sat down and spread her skirts. She was dressed in what appeared to be the habit of a Carmelite nun. The difference was that her hair, which had a reddish tinge, fell freely to her shoulders and beyond. On her feet, there were sandals and at her waist a rosary hung from a twisted silken cord.

"I believe in God the Father. And I believe God the Father believes in me ..." she said. And smiled. "And I know that God the Father believes in you. He believes in all of us. One day, you will know this. He is everywhere—in everyone."

Teresa's mother, Doña Beatriz, had died five years earlier, when Teresa had been thirteen. They had shared a love of romance and of romantic notions concerning everything from literature to music to what one wore and how one presented oneself in a world where, one day, a husband must be won. That was then. Teresa de Cepeda had grown up feasting on chivalry, martyrdom and all noble causes. At the age of six, she had set out with her brother Rodrigo, who was ten, to seek martyrdom amongst the Moors of North Africa. Don Pedro had spied the lost children by chance on the road to Salamanca and had returned them to their parents.

This was the pattern of Teresa's beliefs. To find the Holy Grail, to sail with the great explorers to America and the Orient, to climb through the sky to find the Almighty or to dig through the earth and drag the Devil into the light of day. She read poetry. She read novels. She dressed as Queen Isabella. She affected the robes of the Carmelites. She experimented with theatrical, even whorish cosmetics—and had once dyed her hair with henna. But the discovery of self had not so much to do with one's destination as with one's capacity to achieve it. Clearly, for Teresa de Cepeda, God was at the far end of all these dreamings—but could one reach Him?

She also suffered the dizzying heights of levitation. And worse, she suffered the fiery visions of epilepsy. She was prone to fainting; she endlessly fasted; she retired to her bed; she prayed on her knees for hours on end and then abruptly turned her back on her own sanctuary and went out riding with her brothers into the high Sierra, where she would gallop out of sight and not come home till nightfall.

She was a gross of contradictions, but equally, she never did anything with less than total dedication. Nothing was frivolous. Fun and games were serious occupations. And her love of God was so great, her devotion to prayer so rigid that her father Don Alonso feared he would lose his only daughter to a convent.

In the months prior to her arrival in *la tierra dorada*, she had been extremely ill and a cause for great concern. She had been a paying guest in Avila's Convent of Our Lady of Grace. The nuns there were of the Augustinian order and renowned as teachers. Teresa's acceptance of their teachings was polite and scholarly—but guarded. She took and privatized what was agreeable and quietly discarded the rest. And then, all at once, she fell ill and was so gravely sick, the nuns feared for her life.

Don Alonso and his sons came to the convent and took Teresa home, where slowly she began to recover. There were, however, relapses and she was greatly weakened. It was then that her father brought her to Don Pedro, in order that she might convalesce in the sun and the air and the golden light of *la tierra dorada*.

Now, as Teresa sat on the shore of Las Aguas with Perro at her feet and Manolo standing Baptist-like in the water, a braying sound was heard.

"Oh, dear Heaven!" Teresa exclaimed and jumped to her feet. "My poor Picaro! I forgot all about him."

But she need not have worried. Burros are not adventurous and he would not have wandered off. He had, in fact, found his way down through the trees and safely past the sheep to where his mistress sat on the grass in the sun.

"Picaro," she cried and threw her arms around his neck. "I am so sorry, my Picaro." She turned to Manolo, laughed and said:

"he is my rascal, and I love him." She kissed the burro between his ears. "He carries me everywhere—and I left him all alone up there. Oh, I am so very, very sorry."

"Bring him here and let him drink."

Teresa led Picaro forward and watched him wade out towards Manolo, where he threw his head back and brayed with the sheer joy of the cool water all about him. At the sound of his voice, the cicadas stopped singing and the pelicans almost took flight, but decided he was harmless and resettled.

Looking around her at the hills, the lake, the sky, the woods, the sheep, the dog, the burro, the birds and the naked man, Teresa said to Manolo: "here is God Himself. This place and all of us together, we are God."

From the trees on the opposite shore, a flight of ring-necked doves rose up into the air with a dusty clap of wings, circled three times above the lake and flew away into the hills.

"It is true," Teresa said. "What I tell you is true. God Himself just said so."

5

T.

Carved into the bark of a tree.

T.

Jung sat back.

It was Emma who had made the connection. As her pregnancy had proceeded, she had become increasingly engrossed in reading Pilgrim's journals—most of which still languished locked in their drawer in Jung's study. Carl Gustav had finally given her the key and asked her to read more of them for him, since time had filled up with other aspects of his inquiry into Pilgrim's life and his involvement with other patients. So long as the journals were not removed from his study and were always returned to their place after reading, he agreed she could have access to them. To this, Emma had been faithful.

Perhaps, however, there was also an element of intimidation in Jung's confrontation with the journals. This, at least, was Emma's interpretation. She had watched him withdraw from them over the past few days and had concluded that they were too "personal" for him—too insistent on a single storyline told from one man's point of view, leaving no room for the kind of exploration Carl Gustav found in personal confrontation. Speaking of another patient, he had once told Emma that "the man, not the work, is my purview." He was speaking of an artist—a painter—and had concluded that "some men hide in what they create in a deliberate attempt to remain unknown." Emma's reaction to this had been: "well? Does it matter? Art is not about the artist. Art is about itself."

Jung had merely shrugged.

Three days after he and Archie Menken had discovered the

carved *T*, Emma had led Carl Gustav to the journals and showed him some of the passages she had been reading, pointing out the references to trees, kingfishers and Teresa.

Teresa.

Clearly, this was a figure Jung recognized. But one he mistrusted. She had been a mystic—*an improbable mystic at that, and more than likely the perpetrator of hoaxes.* Levitation, for instance. *Hokum,* he had snorted—a word he had learned from Archie.

Emma insisted it was simply part of who Teresa was. People had seen it happening while she was at prayer.

"A person could pay to have such witnesses," Jung said that night as they lay in their bed with the covers thrown back. "I'm merely postulating," he added. "Merely speculating."

"Would you speculate and postulate on the subject of Haeckel's findings?"

"Once, yes. But not any more."

"Because you now believe."

"Because I now believe."

"And where is your proof?"

"Proof?"

"Proof. You insist that Teresa prove she was the *victim* of levitation ..."

"Stop saying victim!"

"Very well. You insist that Teresa prove that when she prayed, she rose towards God. But couldn't it just be allegorical? This was Teresa's whole desire: to rise into God's presence—His absolute, literal presence. She called God *His Majesty* and to rise to that place where He exists—where He is, was all that mattered—isn't that the perfect representation of levitation? Isn't it? I cannot for the life of me understand why you have a problem with this."

"She was a charlatan."

"She was a Catholic—that's what you mean. She was a Catholic and she believed. And you are a lapsed Protestant—

because of your God-forsaken father's God-forsaken ministry—and you believe nothing. Your basic problem, my dear one, is that you hate and distrust anyone—*anyone*—who believes in God. And maybe even anyone who believes in anything."

"Why are you angry?"

"I'm not angry. I'm just asking. Pay attention to the line you're following. You don't want to admit you know who this woman is because you don't want to admit Mister Pilgrim has the jump on you."

"The *jump* on me? What the hell does that mean? The *jump* on me! *Please!*"

Emma shifted to one side, placing her back before him.

"You don't like anyone to challenge you, my dear one," she said, "my darling. You don't want Mister Pilgrim to know beyond doubt what you don't know at all—that he knew and understood a saint—something you may never do. May I put it this way? In Mister Pilgrim's case, you may be the student and he might be the teacher."

She settled her shoulders and shifted one hand towards her belly, letting it rest without inquisitory intent on the child enfolded there.

"Imagine yourself without questions," she said. "Put yourself in her place—Teresa's. She had no questions. She merely— *only*—waited. This was her wonder: not to predetermine—not to say *it will be thus and so*—not to *know*. She did not demand to know, Carl Gustav. *And you demand to know.* This way, you are a monster."

Jung bellied over towards her.

Monster?

"I love you," he said—not knowing he would say it.

"I'll think about it," said Emma. And smiled.

Jung fitted his hand to her left and uppermost buttock. He began to scrabble at her nightdress.

"You have never been taken from behind," he said, amazed by

his own voice—by its sudden, previously undisclosed lasciviousness. Pure, unadulterated lasciviousness. No disguises. No *I'm your husband.* No *let's pretend.*

He undid the ties of his pyjama trousers and slid them away towards his thighs.

I'm going to rape you, he thought. *I'm going to take you every way a man can take a woman. You will be busy here for hours.*

"Carl Gustav?"

"Yes?"

She had spoken. How dare she?

"Take your hand off my buttock."

Jung deferred. His hand moved. He hardly seemed to be its master. It simply left its place. He hung back, tumescent and confused.

"God *is,*" said Emma, nearing sleep. "You do know that, don't you."

Did he? Maybe. Though he hated the idea of saying so, he knew that Someone was there—or Something. If there was no one there, his own yearnings for articulation would be meaningless.

"Yes," he said. Whispered.

"What is certainty?" Emma asked.

"Knowing nothing," said Jung.

"Good," Emma sighed. "You're learning." She moved farther off. "Do you want me to speculate on an orgasm with my hand? Or is it a certainty without my participation?"

Jung grunted. *Oh, why won't she suck it for me,* he thought.

He began to reach for sleep. It was there like a fish at the end of his line. *Any moment I will net it and be gone.*

What a thoroughly pleasant image. To be standing in his waders down at the far end of the lake on a bright September morning. Sunrise and sunfish. Cool air, cool waters.

Kingfisher.

What is certainty? Emma had asked him. *Knowing nothing,* he had answered.

The fish are there—but will one find them?

The sunlight sparkled on the water. Just for a moment, it blinded him.

And God?

He drifted.

God is in the blinding.

True. True. Possibly true.

There was a nibble on his hook.

Doubt less, believe more, the Grand Inquisitor said. *A few moments ago, Carl Gustav, you considered achieving levitation.*

Never.

Almost sleeping.

Never? Then what is your definition of an orgasm? What else can it be but a rising to another level of existence? You should think about that.

Maybe.

Maybe? Be less doubting, fisherman. The truth is, you have souls to catch—forgive the pun. I have a dreadful sense of humour. Perhaps I should have said you have spirits to catch. But this is true. Emma's little fish. Pilgrim's lost centre. Blavinskeya's Moon. Your own lost faith ...

True. Maybe true.

Good night, Carl Gustav.

Yes. Good night. You old bastard.

He smiled.

Good night—just the right words. A good night in spite of the fact that Emma had refused him.

Would he ever force himself on her? Force himself in the merciless sense? He thought not. Not because of what she might think of him—never that—but of what he would think of himself. He did not really care what she thought of him, so long as she did not lose her respect for him as ...

An artist?

Where had that word come from?

He had meant *scientist*. As long as she did not lose her respect for him as a scientist.

One day the whole world would acknowledge his greatness. His scientific pioneering, his discoveries and his staking of new territories.

There was comfort in this.

No. He would never force himself on Emma. He need not even ask her. She would come back begging for more. In the meantime, there would be others while he fastened his hold on the ultimate goal—the rightness of his genius.

This way, he found sleep.

In the morning, when Emma woke, Carl Gustav had left. She had heard nothing—sensed nothing of his departure. And yet, when she made her own way to the bathroom, the evidence of his presence having preceded hers was everywhere. The laundry hamper was overflowing with damp towels. The smells of soap and of the lemon-lime cologne with which her husband freshened his handkerchiefs were fresh as if he had left the room only seconds before her entrance. The mirror still bore traces of steam.

Low down in the right-hand corner of the glass, the letter *T* had been drawn by Jung's finger. Rather large. Very important. *T. Teresa. Tree.*

Emma wondered how she could bring him to tolerate this difficult woman. This saint. Bring him to her and instruct him in the meaning of her unique genius.

No. Never instruct. He refused instruction unless he had requested it.

Pilgrim's journals were filled with revelations. Leonardo, the *Mona Lisa*. Dogs called Perro and Agamemnon. Rapes and seductions. Findings and losses. Spanish sheep and sheep in dreams. Mister Bleat and Henry James. Shepherds, saints and golden landscapes. Kingfishers, pelicans, doves and eagles ... And at the centre of it all, this tall lonely man who never wrote of loving or of being loved unless it was to tell another's story, not his own.

Or were they his own, these stories, Emma wondered. Had he imagined them—created them or did he honestly believe he had experienced them? And if so, how? In dreams? Daydreams? Were they fictions or were they facts?

But the care with which he had set them down went far beyond mere dreams and daydreams. Carl Gustav said that Mister Pilgrim sometimes spoke in his sleep—sometimes enunciating with perfect clarity, even to the point of giving dictation. This in itself was of very great interest, given the nature of dreams.

Carl Gustav had a theory that what was experienced in dreams was tantamount to reality—that the terror of night-mares could equal the terror of true events. That a man who dreamt of being buried alive might just as well have truly been buried alive because the effect on him was the same. Survival of either the nightmare or the reality left the same psychic scars. This way, many patients had to be sedated with chloral hydrate or comforted with ether until they were convinced their doctors, nurses and orderlies were not intent on returning them to the grave.

And yet, Mister Pilgrim himself had a longing for the grave he could not achieve. How sad he was—this great tall man. Emma had seen him from a distance, walking in the snow with Lady Quartermaine. His hair was now turning white, Carl Gustav had told her, and his loneliness increasing. Long hours were spent in the Music Room listening to recordings of Mozart, Beethoven, Verdi and Puccini—or seated at the piano stumbling through the music of Schumann and Schubert. And always he would rise and stomp out if someone came to disturb his privacy. Much repressed anger—many sudden storms in this great, tall man.

Emma returned to the bedroom and put on her wrapper. She would spend the morning in Carl Gustav's study, unlock the magic drawer (for so it seemed to her, now) and finish the story set in the sun of *la tierra dorada*. Even as she descended the stairs, with one hand on the bannister and the other on her child, she imagined that she could hear the distant barking of a dog and the dusty wings of a flight of pelicans.

6

Horsemen rode out along *la Mujer* every three days to leave supplies for the shepherds and cowherds who were in charge of Don Pedro's sheep and cattle. Bread, wine, onions, cheese and olives were the staples of the diet thus achieved, to which the herders then added dried beans of various kinds and game—when birds and rabbits had been killed—or on very rare occasions, a wild boar. The cowherds ate in groups—the shepherds, for the most part, alone.

Campfires were built. Men slept on the ground using rough blankets and pillows made up of saddles, boots or a rolled garment. Each shepherd had his dog—or two. The cowherds had dogs, a few horses and burros amongst the cattle because the burros' presence warded off marauding wolves. On occasion—perhaps every five to six weeks—the men and dogs were replaced by others, affording a holiday of two to three days.

These were good conditions. Other less wealthy or more stinting landowners might leave their people in the hills for as long as four to five months.

Three days after their first encounter, Teresa de Cepeda rode Picaro out with the horsemen to visit Manolo and to see Las Aguas. She had fallen in love with the landscape, and for all his nearly speechless awkwardness, she missed Manolo's *charming innocence*. That was her phrase for it, written in her notebook, which otherwise was filled with prayers, pressed flowers and injunctions against her personal sins—amongst them, levitation. Anything sensational was clearly a sin—unless it had been commanded by His Majesty. To be the centre of a sensational event was to curry favour in other people's eyes. She had begun to pray in barns and earth closets.

The horsemen, once they heard of Teresa's destination, gave her Manolo's personal supplies and sent her off with them. She was popular with these men, who treated her as a *daughter of the house*—one of their own.

Don Pedro's residence was known as *El Cortijo Imponente—the Grand Farmhouse*. It was home to five children besides Teresa, and had already sent five others out into the world by means of marriages, seminaries and the army. Two, many years before, had died as infants.

In all, Doña Aña de Cepeda y Caridad had given birth to twelve children. She was now, as was Don Pedro her husband, in the late forties of her life and, unlike him, was prone to extended periods of melancholy during which she would sit with her rosary in hand, not praying but merely staring off across the *meseta* at the horizon. She believed, in her deepest states of depression, that the world at large had retreated beyond this place and that, in the end, she would be abandoned by all those she loved and had given birth to and left to die without ever having knelt in the great cathedrals of Madrid or walked in the flowery cloisters of the Alhambra. These were her dreams, and like a child, she often fancied that she would run away to fulfil them.

Teresa, who loved her aunt well enough, was nonetheless happy to escape her company for a day. It was difficult to watch so many hours being wasted on daydreams—hours that might at least have been spent in contemplative prayer. Doña Aña was too much like Teresa's own mother in this—too much brooding, not enough doing.

It was still relatively early when she came to the wood above the lake where she had first encountered Manolo. The eighth hour—perhaps the ninth. This is where she had knelt to pray and had risen into the trees.

Had that been God's doing?

Why should it be?

Why should His Majesty take any more interest in her than

in anyone else? While she believed this was logically so, she nonetheless intended to bring herself to His attention. Though she was well aware His Majesty had greater problems, she was prepared to lecture Him on the subject of Manolo's limbs. If His eye was on the sparrow, why not on the least of men?

Teresa, standing now amongst the trees, wondered if a person dared to pray yet again in such a place?

Had it been the tree—the ground—the wood itself or the sky above that had caused her to rise in Heaven's direction?

Levitation—and well she knew it—was the property of saints. And she was not a saint. This she also knew.

Perhaps it was a trick of diet.

If one was abstemious—as she often was with much effort— perhaps one was simply overcome by a lack of poundage—or whatever it was that kept one tied to the earth. If one *let go*, one rose. This made her laugh. *I am a kite*, she thought, *and the wind may have me whenever it chooses.*

Yet she had never seen levitation in her witness of prayer where other people were concerned.

Picaro was anxious for the waters—but she held him back and got down to wait.

The cicadas sang.

The earth tilted. She could feel this.

There was no cloud—no shade where she stood—no advisory voice saying do this or do that.

She was alone, but for the burro.

"Is anyone here?" she said. "Is anyone—someone—here?"

Bird wings.

A clatter.

Teresa looked upward.

A dove.

And then a second.

Baa.

Sheep voices.

Sheep sounds—shufflings, wallowings, shakings, rustlings below her in the woods.

Baa. Baa.

The voice of God.

Pray. But she was afraid.

And yet, every impetus within her—physical, mental and spiritual—pushed her away from the ground. The sinews behind her knees extended, contracted, convulsed. Her legs quavered. Her brain emptied. She lost consciousness.

When she woke, a bird was singing an exquisite song—one of those curving, long-lined songs that thrushes sing. But the bird itself was not visible. And besides, Teresa's vision was clouded. She had both risen and fallen, and where she had fallen there were leaves, pine needles and the detritus of last year's undergrowth.

I could lie here forever, she thought, *with my cheek against this earth. I could lie here forever and simply become a part of it—a fusion—a mix—a blending, like all dead things ... I am corruptible and one day will be corrupted by this soil.*

She smiled and gave a sigh. Picaro stepped forward and nudged her shoulder with his muzzle.

"All is well," she told him. "I'm alive."

His muzzle was soft as velvet. His breath was sweet as the grass he had eaten. His eyes were full of concern.

Below her amongst the trees, the sheep were mumbling, their lambs kicking dust. Teresa tucked her legs beneath her and knelt.

It had been thought on more than one occasion when she had fainted that she had died. She had lain so still that whether she breathed or not could not be told. As for herself, there was no sense of time or of place during these trances. She was *nowhere.* That was her word for it: *nowhere.* Somewhere in between life and death, where there is no sensation and no awareness.

I am alive, she said to God. *I thank Your Majesty for life.*

She crossed herself and stood up. "Come," she said to Picaro. " Let us go to the water."

Manolo's supplies—and her own bread and wine—were in saddlebags straddling the blanket on Picaro's back. This is where Teresa sat when she rode him. A saddle was not appropriate for a burro. No one used one. Most people rode them bareback, but Teresa liked to think that Picaro might appreciate the blanket. Besides, it was colourful, with its scarlet field and its yellow stripes. It was not unlike having a banner or a flag.

There was no need to lead the burro once Teresa had turned his head towards the bottom of the hill.

It was cool beneath the trees and the sheep were dispersed in such a way that one could make a path between those who rested and those who browsed. They seemed entirely imperturbable. A person could come and go, almost as God could come and go, unremarked but absolutely present.

"Picaro, Picaro, shoo-shoo-shoo," Teresa whispered. The burro's hooves might have been made of cloth. The only sound was the sound of his weight on the earth and the wavering kiss of leaves along his flanks as the branches parted, made way and fluttered, newly dusted, back into their tangled order. If the sheep looked up, it was only to see the gathered skirts of one intruder and the switching tail of the other. The light was all of gold and green and the smell of leaf mould, animal breath and trampled dung.

At the bottom of the descent, where the trees stepped back towards the hill, there was a water-cooled breeze and the scent of yesterday's campfire.

"Manolo?"

There was no sign of him. Nor of Perro. This was clearly unacceptable, since it meant the sheep were unattended, something she assumed Manolo would not allow.

"Manolo? Manolo?" Teresa called somewhat louder.

Pulling the saddlebags and the blanket from Picaro's back, she slapped him gently on the rump and he descended farther towards the water.

A covey of ducks lay basking in the shade on the opposite shore. The cicadas were silent and would remain so until the sun had reached its zenith in three hours' time. A beast, perhaps a weasel or a stoat, brought her young to drink beside the weir, at first sliding down alone to the water's edge like the shadow of a disembodied hand. She looked up briefly at the woman on the other shore and the burro in the shallows and whistled that all was well. Her children—three of them—slid forward to join her. Having drunk, she sat up, gleaming in the sunlight, while her brood bent in towards the water. There was not a sound.

Teresa dared not move until they had finished. But where could Manolo be? All these sheep and no shepherd. If he had been a dog, she could have whistled for him—the way that beast had done to summon her young. She would not have had to call his name. He would simply have come.

Would he be naked again this day? Against her will, she conjured him standing stilled below her, the way she had seen him first from her place in the tree. *Men are not meant to be beautiful, but are*, she thought. The nuns preached otherwise. *Thou shalt not dwell upon the image of man lest the image tempt you with its form.*

The very word *tempt* was meant to invoke the Devil. Darkness. Evil. *But Sister*, Teresa had queried, *is not man made in the image of God?*

This question had produced much blushing and stammering. "Yes, yes, yes." And: "no, no, no. You do not understand. Man is carnal. God is not. God is Spirit. It is man's *spirit* that is created in the image of God, not his body."

Ah. Yes. And *well* ... Smile.

Why are we taught to lie? Teresa wondered. *God does not want us to look away. God wants us to see.*

"Manolo?"

Still no answer.

Teresa, noting that the beast at the weir had departed with her children, went to where Manolo had built his fire the night before in a circle of rocks. A pit had been dug and even now, there was a residue of warm ash.

"Manolo!" This time, she called across the water.

Picaro climbed to the embankment and shook himself.

"Manolo?"

No response. Teresa listened.

There was someone coming. From where? Someone walking on dead leaves.

"Manolo?"

Teresa turned back towards the trees. The sound must be coming from there—behind her. But she was deceived. It came from across the river.

Picaro snorted. Something or someone fell or was pushed into the water. Teresa turned again.

On the far shore, a horseman rode away beneath the trees. She had no time to see his face. Nor even the colour of his clothes.

Manolo lay, apparently unconscious, on the other side, the lower half of his body submerged, the upper half lying back.

Teresa did not know how to swim. She was afraid of water. Hitching her skirts, she ran to the weir.

Manolo appeared to have been hit on the head. Also, the backs of his hands were bleeding. There was blood on his shirt and on his trousers and his sticks lay broken beside him. There was no sign of Perro. Nor any sound of him.

Teresa did not know what to do.

Suddenly, she began to run—retracing her steps across the weir to the far side, where she gathered Picaro's halter in her hand and led him back to where Manolo lay half in, half out of the water. He was breathing. Still alive. But how to get him onto Picaro's back? If one could only make him rise ...

Pray.

Pray?

Teresa manœuvred Picaro into a position roughly parallel to Manolo's and knelt in the dust beside him. "Your Majesty ..." No. *Say nothing.* Prayer is not words.

Teresa fell silent. Her eyes were open. She rarely prayed with them closed. If His Majesty should appear, one must see Him.

The shepherd did not rise. But Teresa did. Reaching down, she caught Manolo by the collar of his already torn shirt and began to lift him to his feet. He seemed to be lighter than air itself. She laid him face down along Picaro's back, his legs and arms hanging on either side.

When she recovered herself, Teresa was barely aware of having risen from her knees, and was standing at Picaro's head. Her hand was on his halter.

"Come," she said. "We shall go."

Together, they walked out over the weir and for the briefest moment stopped at its centre. Teresa looked along the lake to its nether end. There were the pelicans, yellow and dusted, placid in the shallows. There were also three deer—a doe and two fawns—who had come to drink.

A kingfisher hurried forward—dove—and failed to make a catch.

A distant *halloo* informed Teresa that others were in the valley—the retiring horsemen, more than likely, with whom she had journeyed out that morning from *El Cortijo Imponente*. Also, at some farther distance, the barking of a dog.

Perro?

The heat was oppressive—wet. Whatever one wore stuck first to one's skin and then to itself. To move was to walk through a waterfall.

A fish jumped. Lucky fish. At least she would be cool in her depths.

Teresa pulled at Picaro's halter and they moved along farther to the sheltered embankment and into the shade of the trees.

It was relatively easy to achieve Manolo's descent. His limp body offered no resistance. It simply fell. As he lay on the ground, Teresa examined his wounds. He had been struck on the head, perhaps by someone using his own sticks to beat him—and his hands had the look of having been stepped upon by someone wearing boots.

"Manolo?"

He did not stir.

Teresa tore off the hem of her gown and went to the water, where she wrung it out several times to rid it of its golden dust. She then washed Manolo's head and hands and made a lap for him.

In twenty minutes or so he began to recover his senses. "Thee," he said, but nothing more.

Picaro moved away until he stood entirely beneath the trees.

Manolo's arms and legs regained their lives in a series of spasms that flung them in all directions, one hand striking Teresa in the face. When he had quietened, he lay in a position reminiscent of a soldier standing at attention while lying on his back.

"What has happened?" Teresa asked him. "And where is Perro?"

At first, Manolo was almost speechless, but finally his jumble of words began to have meaning. A number of horsemen—three?—three hundred?—had ridden out of the opposite wood, crossed the river and stolen two sheep and five lambs. (Manolo used his fingers to count them off.) Of course, he and Perro had attempted to prevent the thefts, but there were too many adversaries and these, being on horses, were all too easily able to overwhelm him.

One of the horsemen had dismounted and driven Manolo to the ground, where he kicked him and beat him with the handle of a sword.

And Perro?

He too had been kicked and then the horsemen had repeatedly attempted to trample him, but each time, their mounts had instinctively managed to manœuvre their hooves around the frantic animal beneath them. The last that Manolo knew was that Perro had run into the lake, trying without success to pursue the marauders. Manolo himself had caught hold of one of the horse's tails and had been dragged partway through the woods opposite. He could not remember what had happened next.

As Teresa had witnessed, one of the marauders had pulled him back to the shores of Las Aguas and left him there before rejoining his fellows.

Manolo was devastated. He would lose his job. He would never work again. He would die. Above all, he wanted Perro to be returned to him.

Teresa attempted to console him. The dog, the sheep and the lambs were gone. It was not in the order of things that they should be returned.

"I want my dog!" Manolo cried. "I want my dog!"

It was noon. Teresa spread Picaro's blanket like a tent above them, using a forked stick to support its farther end. Then she sat, with Manolo's head in her lap.

The remaining sheep retreated deeper into the woods. Picaro stood with his back against a tree. The birds fell silent. The cicadas sang.

Teresa prayed. *Only concentration. No words. Remember this.*

She fanned Manolo's face with her notebook. Time passed. An hour. Another hour. The cicadas began to sing again. The flies came.

Teresa went on fanning.

Picaro stamped his impatience, switching his tail, and then went to the other side of his tree where perhaps the breeze might drive the flies away. But there was no breeze. There was only the merciless sun and stillness.

All at once, there was the sound of a splash. Teresa glanced towards the opposite shore. The water shimmered, blinding. She squinted, but had no hand to wipe the sweat from her eyes. One hand held the fanning notebook, the other the stick that supported her canopy.

Something was out there in the heat haze. A mirage—a figure

seemingly floating above the water, melting above the reeds ...

"Manolo."

Manolo opened his eyes. Teresa dropped the notebook and pushed at his shoulders until he sat.

"Look," she whispered, "someone is coming."

A golden head could be seen. A streaming in the sunlight. A lifting of something alive. Of eyes.

Of Perro.

When the dog came ashore and had shaken himself, he loped—tail wagging—straight into Manolo's flailing arms. In spite of his wetness, there was matted blood on his ribs—but he seemed otherwise unharmed. He lavished kisses of such extravagant generosity on Manolo's cheeks that Teresa burst out laughing.

"Such a celebration!" she cried. "One should come home more often!"

Some moments later, Manolo looked up at her and said: "thou hast done this, *Doña hermosa—beautiful lady*. Thou hast done this—thee and thy God."

Looking into his face in that moment, Teresa was alarmed. What she saw there was a reflection of her own desire to see His Majesty—and she knew that in Manolo's eyes, she was that self-same figure incarnate, as though she had been transfigured. The thought, *he thinks I am God*, raised itself and left her breathless.

"There are no miracles," she said quietly, "only God's will."

She looked at Perro—a dog. At Manolo—a man. At the departing deer, the drifting pelicans, the languid trees. At nature.

She looked at her own hand, where it rested open by Manolo's shoulder. Flesh. Bone. Nerve ends. Fingernails. She looked at Las Aguas. At water.

These are the true miracles, she thought. *What other miracles are needed?*

7

Emma pushed the chair away from the desk where she had been reading. Pilgrim's journal lay open before her. Closing it, she faced the windows and rested her hands on her belly.

Good morning, child, she said—though not aloud. She had been truthful when she had told Carl Gustav there were unique modes of speech between mother and child. The child pressed upward with an elbow perhaps, or a foot. It was not a kick, merely a signal. Emma loved to think of the rose-coloured light in which it swam—its whole world a liquified Petra. Many years before, her father had taken her there—to Petra. The very air was pink, she remembered, and beyond the ruin itself a world of desolate rock and desert was spread on every side.

There is no desert here, she told the child. *We live in a garden.*

Teresa was right. It was all a miracle, every inch and minute of it.

The clock struck.

Eleven-thirty.

Good heavens! Lunch in half an hour and she was not even dressed.

She returned the journal to its hiding place—closed and locked the drawer.

Perhaps Carl Gustav would not come home to eat. He had failed to do so increasingly of late, claiming the journey was interruptive and the lunch hour too long. He would dine instead in the commissary at the Clinic. This way he could be back at work in less than an hour.

"But I miss you," Emma had said to him.

Jung had not replied.

Half an hour later, Emma was back downstairs, in a pleasant, pale blue morning dress and standing in the kitchen with Frau Emmenthal.

"What will you give us today?" Emma asked.

Frau Emmenthal was hovering at the stove, stirring with a wooden spoon something that smelled delicious in a large iron pot. In her other hand she wielded an antique Viennese fan given to her by her grandmother, who once had been a kitchen maid to royalty. When she spoke, she enunciated every word, as if she were reciting a menu in a restaurant.

"Potato and leek soup. Baked salmon and green salad. A platter of peeled tomatoes garnished with onions, and I also have some freshly baked Parker House rolls."

"What are Parker House rolls?" Emma asked.

"American. I read about them in a magazine, all about different kinds of bread. There's a famous hotel in Boston called the Parker House, and they serve them there. Will you want some wine, or the usual?"

The usual was buttermilk.

"The usual," said Emma, and sighed. "I'd love the wine, but I'd better not. Still, if the Doctor comes, he will want it."

"I've got some chilled Riesling."

"That would be fine. Where's the girl?"

"Lotte? Setting the table."

"Heavens! That will take her an hour, at least!"

Lotte was a vacant dreamer, in Emma's opinion, and her mouth was always open. She had been attempting to cure Lotte of this. It was too embarrassing when guests came. And unfortunately, the children teased the poor girl to such a degree that at times Lotte burst into tears and ran from the room.

Thank heaven, for everyone's sake, the children were away with Emma's parents in Schaffhausen, where the house was big enough to accommodate an army of children in a single wing. Their grandmother adored them and always introduced them to a host of new experiences and people. She would expose them to a world of folklore and of fairy tales, of secret gardens and

medieval castles. She would show them the Rheinfell, where the
river dropped more than seventy feet in a sequence of spectacular cascades—which, even in memory, still thrilled Emma to the
bone. Grandmama Rauschenbach would also take them boating
on the river so they could get out and stand on the great rocks
at the base of the falls. These had been the joys of Emma's own
childhood and she was glad they were all still available to her
own children. Most of all, she was happy to be rid of *The Brood*,
as she called them, in that particular moment of her pregnancy.
The Brood had reached the "difficult" age.

Ah, yes—but then, when wasn't being a child difficult? *From
the moment we break the cawl and give our first cry, we are all at odds
with wherever we are and whoever is in our company.*

Frau Emmenthal said: "I can serve the soup cold this evening
if you would prefer ..."

Emma said: "perhaps that would be best. It is noon already,
and it seems Herr Doktor Jung will not be coming."

As she left the kitchen, Emma saw Lotte returning from the
dining-room with an empty tray in her hand. As soon as the girl
saw Emma, she closed her mouth.

Well, there's one good thing, Emma thought. *She's learning.*

At the stove, Frau Emmenthal pulled the large iron pot to one
side, and fanning herself at a furious rate, she sat at the kitchen
table and said to Lotte: "Riesling, please. In a very large glass.
And be quick." Then she added: "you may also have a little. We
are a family in some sort of trouble, it seems—since Herr
Doktor is so little at home—and we must prepare ourselves to
face the worst."

8

During the salmon course and before the salads, Emma read what turned out to be the final chapter in the lives of Teresa and Manolo. It would change her view of life, though of course she did not realize this until later. In what Mister Pilgrim had written, she was to learn something about herself and the subject of faith—and about her husband and the lack of it. *We have both rejected Jesus*, she would afterwards write to her mother, *but only I have invested my faith in someone other than myself.*

An old man who had long ago been retired was sometimes hired to replace Manolo when Manolo and Perro were brought to El Cortijo Imponente for their *vacaciones*. His name was Orlando and he had two dogs called *Negro* and *Blanco* for obvious reasons—except that Blanco was black and Negro was white. Orlando had thought this was a convenient way of keeping the other dog in mind when one of them went missing. Looking at Negro, he would think *Blanco*. And vice versa. Not that they ran away, but they could go off to round up sheep and be gone for as long as half a day.

Some years before the time of the shepherd whom Manolo had replaced, Orlando had been in charge of the flock at Las Aguas and he claimed to have known Manolo's father, who had since departed for another part of *the kingdom—el raino*, as Orlando referred to Don Pedro's domain. "He was not a good man," Orlando would say, always referring to the absent in the past tense. "He was not a good man, a good husband or a good father. He was entirely full of self. I did not like him. My dogs did not like him. The sheep did not like him. He had a careless spirit. People and sheep might sicken and die—but Manolo's father was always looking the other way, with a smile on his face and wine in his throat."

Not that Manolo was unaware of these faults, but it was good to have them confirmed whenever he found himself wishing that his father would return. As for his mother, Manolo searched in vain. "A woman somewhere, not here," Orlando would tell him with a sigh. "She died young, that is all we know." This was at least a fitting conclusion to the life of a person Manolo would otherwise have anguished over, forever wondering where and how he might meet her. That she was dead meant he had no obligation to her. He could even pray to her without reciting her given name. *Madre*, he would say, *por favor*. He never prayed to his father.

And so it was that Teresa rode out to Las Aguas, bringing with her a second burro and returning to El Cortijo Imponente with Manolo and Perro on the 13th of July, 1533—a Monday.

She had asked that Manolo be treated as an equal, not as an employee, and had this way secured a cot for him in a storeroom beyond the kitchens. The only problem with this was that Manolo did not feel comfortable in a bed, having slept without one since the age of nine. Also, he could not bring himself to use the earth closet, fearing that he would fall in. He therefore slept in the stables and used the animal gutters as his toilet. One of Teresa's cousins, a girl of seven, saw him urinating in the kitchen garden and instantly announced that men were different from women. *They can hold it in their hand*, she told her sisters. Don Pedro was not amused and told Manolo that he must use the stables for all his personal needs.

Otherwise, Manolo gloried in the attention that was showered on him. His clothing was mended and washed—two new pairs of trousers and two new shirts were added to his wardrobe and a new pair of sandals. Also a blanket. Also a bath with soap and warmed water in which Perro joined him. The result of this was a great deal of laughter—more than Manolo could remember in his whole life.

Don Pedro himself supervised the creation of new sticks for Manolo's use. A very old man whose name was Ferdinand cut the crutches from scrub oak and bound the rests with oil-soaked linen which hardened into *linseed pillows* and gave off a pleasant odour whenever Manolo leaned on them. His palsy had left him exhausted until the sticks were completed, because the shaking drained him of so much energy.

Like many people with such a condition, Manolo depended on concentration to overcome the violence of his limbs—defecating, urinating, playing with Perro and eating were activities remarkably free of agitation. For the rest—while walking or while conversing—he was still a prisoner.

Teresa was unnerved by his presence. She had not thought to be so. He was a shepherd. She had met him by chance. He was lame. Disabled. If she was honest, for all his beauty he was grotesque. But she liked him—had been drawn to him immediately. It was not the nakedness.

She repeated this several times. *It was not the nakedness.*

He was not Adam. She was not Eve. The Sierra was not the Garden of Eden. It was the hinterland. The other place. The wilderness. *La tierra ferez.* She was on her way to God—to His Majesty. Men must not—could not—would not stand in her way.

On the Tuesday, Manolo moved his quarters to the stable. On the Wednesday, his new crutches were completed. That night, Manolo had a dream in which—miracle of miracles—he was able to walk with ease and grace and completely without help of any kind.

The rest of the dream was jumbled—and completely beyond Manolo's comprehension.

He was in a strange place, wearing cumbersome clothing, and all about him was a milling crowd of people—none of whom he recognized. Some were dressed as soldiers—but not like any soldiers Manolo had ever seen. Others were more familiar—priests of some kind, their voices raised in holy song. Many in the crowd carried crosses, while others had filled their arms with gifts—paintings in gold frames, rich clothing—even furniture, some of the pieces so heavily decorated that Manolo wondered how they were meant to be used.

At one moment in the dream, he found himself staring at four angels—all dressed in white with enormous wings and carrying the figure of an infant on their shoulders. It must have been the Saviour, Jesus Christ Himself, in swaddling clothes.

Suddenly, a silence fell. And a stillness—one that was soon broken by the crackle of flames. Manolo turned and stared with disbelief. A mountain of fire towered above him, its blistering heat forcing everyone to move back. He twisted away from it only to be confronted by a man's eyes, fixed and menacing, staring at him from beneath the wide brim of a dark hat. This was not a man he had ever seen before.

Manolo began to run—an experience so entirely foreign to him, he might as well have been flying. He ran through streets that had no identification—past buildings that had no names and through a seemingly endless series of gates that all stood open, until he found himself above a precipice—and woke.

He sat bolt upright in the straw of his stable-bed. His skin and shirt drenched with sweat, and his limbs trembled in the cold night air.

All he could think was: *there was fire and I ran and walked and had no sticks ...*

The next morning—Thursday, the 16th of July—Teresa awoke to find Manolo in her bedroom. It did not occur at once that something untoward might be about to happen. She had no fear of him.

"Teresa ..."

His tongue was thick with sleep and with his disability. Her name came out as Manolo might have said *tierra—earth*.

"Yes?"

"I need thee," he said.

He was crouching on the floor in a spill of light from the window.

Teresa sat up, holding the edge of the sheet against her shoulder. "I am here," she said. "What is it?"

Manolo's new sticks rested in the crook of his left elbow. His right hand wavered near his face, as if he would touch himself but could not. There was nowhere, it seemed, he could make contact with himself. His nose eluded him—his mouth, his chin, his eyes were so far distant they might have been joined to a body other than his own. His ears were the closest he could come, and he held them—one and then the other—fiercely between his fingers. The impression given was that Manolo had caught a free-floating head in the air and brought it to a standstill.

Teresa had been schooled in the "needs" of men. It was a word she profoundly distrusted, knowing that man's "needs" had more than likely killed her mother and been instrumental in bringing Tia Aña to her present disorientation. Nonetheless, as most women did of her class and kind, Teresa had no hatred of men, merely disdain. And pity. They were helpless creatures, caught in a circle of desire that began and ended with themselves—*me, my and mine*. Women knew only *thee* and *thine*. They were mothers, servants, cooks and nurses. One day, someone's death—their own or another's—would free them. That was the whole of a woman's life. Waiting for one's own or someone else's death. And all the while, attending the living.

Now, this abused and damaged man crouched near her window. She had befriended and loved him. He might have been her child. A foundling. An orphan in need of shelter—nothing more. But nothing less. He was dear to her. Beloved.

Manolo said: "thou hast created miracles, Teresa. Thou hast saved my life and brought my dog to me." His words—perhaps because of his desperate need to speak them—found their right order.

"Perro. Yes," said Teresa.

"Last night I dreamt another miracle and I believe thou canst make it also come true. Thou canst make me well," Manolo said. And smiled. "I speak already well because of thee. Thou hast caused my sticks to be reborn. Thou hast fed and clothed and sheltered me."

Teresa nodded. "Yes," she said. "And with love, Manolo."

"Take thou my curse," he said. "Destroy it. Thee and thy God. Make me as I was in my dream."

Teresa closed her eyes. *Oh, please,* she thought. *Do not do this. There can be no miracles.*

Manolo moved forward. On his knees—a supplicant.

"I cannot," said Teresa. "You must not expect it. It is wrong."

"To be upright is wrong?"

"Oh, no! No, no, no. Oh, no. To be upright is to be given ..." She was going to say *dignity*, but decided not to. "I cannot," she said. "You must understand. I cannot."

"But thee found me and saved me."

"No, Manolo. You were delivered to me by the horseman who had harmed you. I was merely there."

"Thee brought Perro."

"No, again. Perro came. It was his own doing."

"But thee and thy God. Thee spoke with Him."

"Perhaps. But I am incapable of more than prayer."

I am not a saint.

Teresa knew that a saint does not think in terms of miracles, only of the needs of others. It is the supplicant who seeks to bridge the gap between earth and heaven in order to survive some human disaster—the loss of one's sight, the death of one's child, the prevention of slaughter. The saint's only means of intercession is to indicate the path to salvation. The rest is up to God.

All this, Teresa knew. She also did not wish to be a saint. She wanted only to know His Majesty and to do His work—whatever that work might be.

She had already suffered so many times from the collapse of

her nervous system that she stood in awe of her own resilience. She could not resist the question as to why she had survived. Her interpretation of this was simple: *something must be wanted of me. Not expected—but wanted.*

Was that something—or part of that something—the gift of Manolo's ability to walk and to use his arms like any other human being? She doubted it.

Not that Manolo's needs were insignificant or that he was in any way unworthy. No one is insignificant when it comes to the indignity of pain. And no one is unworthy. Teresa knew and believed all this. But ...

Was she to be the medium? Was this to be her destiny? A destiny even Jesus Christ Himself had rejected. Every one of His miracles had been couched in His own reluctance to effect it. *The miracle is not in me but in the supplicant's belief that God makes all things possible.*

She looked at Manolo.

There he crouched in the early sunlight, his hair newly washed and gleaming, his fingers knotted against their escape into meaningless gestures, his prized white shirt—a gift from Doña Aña—stained already with the perspiration of his earnestness and his eyes like embers about to burst into flame. It was unbearable to think of his anguish and to witness its effect on him.

All at once, he drew himself on his knees to her bedside. He looked like a child who knelt at prayer.

"Bless thou me," he said, "for I would walk as other men. As I walked in the night as I dreamt."

But only the anointed may bless. And women are never anointed. Except, of course, the Blessed Virgin—and today, Teresa all at once remembered, was the saint's day of Our Lady of Mount Carmel. *She* could have performed the laying on of hands—but not Teresa.

"I cannot," she said to Manolo, "for I have not the grace."

"Then why did thou come to me from nowhere? I found thee praying in a tree."

"I cannot say. I do not know."

Teresa was frightened. She was being cast in a role she had never sought to play and had never understood except in the most rudimentary way. She knew that she could nurture, clothe and to some degree protect Manolo, but she could not make him whole.

"Dost thou not love me?" he asked.

And how does one answer that?

"Yes," she said. "You are my friend in the wilderness."

"What is wilderness?" Manolo asked.

"It is nowhere—I suppose—and everywhere," Teresa answered.

"Thee do not know?"

"It is everywhere," she said decisively.

Manolo looked at her with a mixture of disappointment and chagrin. "In my dream, there were priests and crosses, the Christ Child and angels. It was a sign. But thou wilt not bring thy God to me. Thou wilt not bring me to thy God," he said. "I hate thee."

Teresa sat frozen, wrapped in her nightgown and sheets. She looked away from Manolo. She felt endangered. Something was going to happen.

"I do not feel well," she said—but she spoke so quietly Manolo did not hear her.

"Do you think you could find my aunt," she said aloud, "and bring her to me?"

A fire had begun to burn at the base of her skull. There was noise in her brain.

"Please," she said.

"I cannot bring thy aunt," Manolo told her. "I cannot walk."

He turned and began to crawl away to the other side of the room.

"You must. I am ill," Teresa pleaded.

"*Thou must, I am ill!* Did I not say these words to thee?"

"Yes. Yes. Yes. But there was nothing I could do. There is nothing I can do for you. I am unable!"

She burst into tears. The noise in her brain grew harsher. It was a shrieking noise as of someone sawing wood, the wood like a living person screeching in terror.

"Don't! Don't! Don't!" she shouted. "*DON'T!*"

Manolo sat down beside his crutches.

"I can do nothing," he said. "I cannot walk. Thou hast left me so."

It started. The bed began to shake. Teresa drew a corner of the sheet into her mouth and fell back.

People came running. A maidservant. A cousin. A stableboy who had heard the shouting from beyond the window—and, at last, Doña Aña.

She moved to the bed. The others were afraid, being unfamiliar with Teresa's seizures. Doña Aña went to the servant-girl and slapped her in the face.

"Come! At once!"

The girl crept over to the far side of the bed and did as she was told.

"We must hold her arms," Doña Aña said. "We must keep her from harming herself."

This was done.

"Gently, gently," Doña Aña cautioned. "Gently, gently ..."

Slowly, the thrashing in the bed wound down towards stillness, and as Manolo watched from his place in the corner, he recognized the mirror image of his own incompetence.

When it was truly over and Teresa lay against the pillows with her aunt holding her hand, Manolo thought: *her God comes to still her, but I am left forever as I am.*

And yet, he loved her still—though he would never say so again.

In the months remaining of summer and the early days of autumn, Teresa still rode out to La Sierra de Gredos and sat beside Las Aguas while Picaro stood in the shade of the stunted oak and cork trees behind her. The yellowed pelicans, the ducks and the weasels still appeared, but the doe with her fawns, the heron and the kingfisher came no more. Nor did Manolo. He had led his flock to the farthest reaches of *la tierra dorada* and the golden land with its crippled shepherd was soon to be consigned entirely to memory.

Teresa would never see them again. In her dreams, however, a naked man on crutches would stand beneath the branches where she prayed and he would ask her if she knew the way to God.

Beside him, a dusty golden dog looked up and slowly wagged its tail. It had a merry look in its eye, and a look, somehow, of knowing. *People do not sit in trees, but angels do and creatures from another place than this.*

As for the way to God, Teresa wrote in her book one day: *God can happen only when you give up being God.*

Manolo had taught her that, all unknowing and to his sorrow. But it was true. There can be no miracles until the gift of simplicity has been acknowledged and become a way of life.

As always, the doves made their circles in the sky. As always, the cicadas sang. As always, Teresa waited for God to happen— but it seemed that He was waiting, too.

Two years later, at the age of twenty, a young woman appeared at the gates of the Convent of Carmelite nuns in Avila and offered herself as a postulant. This was in 1535. In her lifetime, she would change the face of her religion. And just one hundred years after her birth, Teresa de Cepeda y Ahumada would be sanctified as the medium of miracles.

9

Emma fed the book back into the drawer and turned the key.

A moving and disturbing episode had ended in Pilgrim's chronicles and she could not yet bring herself to digest more. Perhaps this would be a good day to take some air and get some exercise. Doctor Walter, her physician would be pleased. He had recently criticized her for not being more active.

"It encourages circulation," he had told her. "It strengthens the constitution. Too much sitting is bad for the back, and when the time comes, you will be glad if you have taken these precautions."

Emma knew all this and was somewhat dismayed that Doctor Walter had thought he needed to bring such things to her attention. It was not as if she had never given birth before.

She pocketed the key and went to the kitchen, where she told Frau Emmenthal that she was going to go for a stroll and might be some time.

She put on a light spring coat and a hat, and taking a walking stick, she strode down the garden path towards the lake, where she intended to walk on the beach.

I will look for round stones, she thought, *and think about Teresa of Avila.*

Ten minutes later, having found a large round stone that perfectly fitted into the palm of her hand, she stood and stared across the water to the other side.

I should like to be out there, she thought. *I should like to be riding on the lake.*

She looked to one side towards the town. There was the ferry dock and far beyond it, the ferry itself, returning from Zürich.

Emma fished her watch from the pocket where it rested and

saw that, if she hurried, she could be on time to board the ferry before it made its three o'clock departure for the city.

Once on deck and standing near the railing, she began to feel thoroughly rejuvenated. There was a forest-scented breeze and several noisy gulls were floating above the wake of the ferry in the hopes that passengers would throw them bits of bread and rolls from the café-bar on board. Children often did this, but Emma was not inclined. She wanted just to stand and watch the water, dreaming of Manolo and what might have become of him if a miracle had occurred and he had gained the proper use of his limbs. The phrase, *he was only a shepherd*, kept returning in her mind and she wondered why. Did it matter that he was only a shepherd? *Of course not.* And yet …

She would ask Carl Gustav about this reaction—and whether or not it necessarily meant her sense of compassion was qualified. She hoped not—but it worried her. She had once heard her father say a most unfortunate thing to her mother when they were out for a walk on a Sunday afternoon in Schaffhausen. It was in the spring of the year in which Emma turned ten. 1892. How long ago that seemed.

An elderly man with a long white beard had fallen in the street and no one had helped him up. Emma's mother had made a gesture as though she would go to his aid, but Emma's father had pulled her back and said: *pay no attention. It is only an old Jew.*

Emma, the child, had heard of the Jews, but had very little knowledge of them. She knew that the Jews had killed Jesus Christ, but that was more or less the extent of her awareness. Little was said of them at home or at school unless it was in some way or another a reinforcement of this single piece of information. Emma never questioned it. She was never told differently. You were not allowed to know the Jews, or play with them or even to speak to them. You could not ask a Jew the way or the time of day or purchase from them or sell to them and certainly never do them favours.

On that long ago Sunday, Emma had turned to look back at the old man with the white beard, who by then had risen to his knees and looked as if he was praying. Indeed, he might have been, for it was very difficult—almost impossible—for him to rise to his feet. But she saw that he did at last manage this and her final sight of him was the moment in which he retrieved his hat, dusted its brim against his leg and placed it on his head. He did this with the same precision he might have used to place a period at the end of a sentence.

Only an old Jew.

Only a shepherd.

Emma realized she had been taught to think like this and she had blindly continued to do so, never once pausing to assess the consequences. *What, for instance, if people thought of me that way? Well!*

She laughed out loud.

Of course, she thought, *they already do! I'm only a woman!*

Only a Jew. Only a shepherd. Only a woman.

On the other hand, she also knew that if she were to fall in the street, people would come to her assistance. Partly because she was a woman—and *women are weak and totally helpless. They must be coddled* and *women must be protected.* She also realized with a twinge of conscience that people would come to her assistance because she was *Frau Doktor Jung*—and the prestige of coming to her aid would be prized.

As for Manolo, if her mother and father had passed him in the street and seen him fall, would they have helped him up and handed him his sticks? Would she herself have done this? No. Emma knew the answer was *no*, because Manolo was only a shepherd and unworthy of her attention. Then—but not now. Now, she knew better. Now, she knew more of the world and its casual cruelty. Now, she was a grown woman with a mind of her own. And a will.

The ferry was approaching Zürich and Emma could see the first of the bridges over the Limmat, the Grossmünster with its twin spires and the gardens dotted amongst the Quays. All of it was so familiar now, and all of it so dear, though once upon a time she had dreaded this city, with its foreboding dedication to religious revolution—and perfection. It was here that the great reformist Zwingli had brought the Catholic church to its knees in the sixteenth century and it was here that her husband, Carl Gustav Jung, would bring the world of psychiatry to its knees in the twentieth century.

My beloved husband—the father of my children and the father of my mind ...

She would take a cab. This way she could both race to Carl Gustav's side and avoid the impossible strain of climbing the final hill on foot.

When Emma arrived at the Burghölzli, she had to constrain old Konstantine, the concierge, from announcing her presence.

"I want to surprise the good doctor," she told him. "Is he in his office?"

"Yes, Frau Doktor—but I beg of you, let me precede you."

"No, I wouldn't dream of it!" Emma laughed. "What is the fun of a surprise if the whole world knows I'm coming?"

"But, please ..."

"No. I insist. And don't you dare pick up that telephone. I don't want any warning given."

She strode off down the corridor, while Konstantine returned to his station, removed his white cotton gloves and exchanged them for another pair.

"Dear, dear, oh, dear," he muttered. "Dear, dear, oh, dear."

Emma gave her customary rapid three knocks on the door and, preparing herself to speak, pushed it open.

The sight that greeted her eyes could not have been real. Nothing about it could be rationalized. It was cut from images seen exclusively in Emma's worst dreams.

Jung was spread-eagled in his chair, his waistcoat and shirt unbuttoned, his trousers opened and halfway down his thighs. His knees were parted and a woman knelt in the space between them, her back to Emma.

The curtains had been closed—the lights had been dimmed and the air smelled of perfume, smoke and old books.

Emma blinked—and when she opened her eyes again, the woman—or the image of the woman—had completely disappeared. It was as though she had not been there.

Jung had risen, turned his back on his wife and was busy adjusting his clothing.

Emma leaned against the door, afraid she was going to collapse, but could see no way to a chair.

Jung said: "why are you here?"

Emma could not speak.

I wanted to surprise you, she thought.

"Do you realize I could have had a patient with me? How dare you burst in like that! How dare you do this!" Jung, with his back still towards her, was shaking.

At last he drew on his white smock, smoothed his hair and turned.

"It was such a lovely day," Emma said. "I ..."

"How did you get here?" Jung demanded. His voice was like a knife that had just finished cutting ice.

"I came on the ferry," Emma said. "I want to sit down."

"Came on the ferry? By public transport? Showing yourself to everyone? You must be mad."

"I don't know what you mean, Carl Gustav. Please—could there be some light? I must sit down."

Jung switched on the desk lamp with the green shade. With the normal pattern of shadows reversed and thrown upward, he looked demonic.

Emma, using the bookcase, the wall and her walking stick as supports, found her way to a chair at last and sat. All she could think was: *I must not faint.*

Jung was staring at her, saying nothing—seemingly calculating what to say. Then he gave an expansive shrug, sighed and said: "how can you have done this? You, of all people. How can you possibly have done this?"

He was leaning into the light.

"Done what, Carl Gustav?" Emma could barely hear her own voice. "Done what?"

"COME ALL THE WAY FROM KÜSNACHT ON THE FERRY! IN FULL VIEW OF EVERYONE—AND IN THAT CONDITION!"

The desk shook.

Emma was so disoriented she could not understand him. Looking down, she touched her lovely new spring coat and whispered to it: "what—what—what condition?"

"You are *pregnant!*" he said. It was as though he had said: *you are black and blue and crimson.*

Emma said: "I know that. I know that, Carl Gustav. But it was such a lovely day ..."

"I will never hear the end of it, you realize," Jung said—ignoring her words entirely. "There will be no end to this. *There she was—right on the ferry—flaunting herself—the wife of Herr Doktor Jung—and seven months pregnant!*" He mimicked a high-pitched, feminine voice. "*Out in the open—for all the world to see!*"

Emma looked away and said: "you have done up the buttons of your waistcoat in the wrong order, Carl Gustav." She wanted to cry, but refused the temptation. Instead, she said: "some attitudes are changing, you know. It's no crime to appear in public when one is pregnant."

"You may think so, but I know nothing of the kind. And I want you out of this building immediately. Konstantine will telephone for a cab and you will be driven straight back to Küsnacht—I don't care what it costs. Dear Jesus God—what if someone had seen you ...?"

"But ... I came to see you, my darling ..."

"Do not call me your *darling.*" Jung was attempting to right the miscalculated buttons—and failing. "You have done me irreparable damage and it will be some time before I forgive you—if, in fact, I ever do forgive you. Come along."

At last, he stepped away from his desk, and grasping her elbow in a vicelike grip, he turned her and marched her like a prisoner out of his office and down the corridor to the reception area.

Don't let me fall, Emma thought. *Don't let me trip and fall.*

As though he were handing over a perverted murder suspect, Jung requested that Konstantine telephone for a cab, turned and departed without another word, his heels pounding like hammer blows on the marble until, at last, the sound of his office door being slammed brought the episode to an end.

All the way home, Emma fought off the tears. The cab was a two-wheeled hansom and she concentrated her gaze on the horse's swinging gait.

Was Carl Gustav mad? Had he gone mad, somehow, without her knowing it until this moment?

His charges against her were insane, of course. No one had paid the slightest attention to her "condition" on the ferry. Granted, it was more or less accepted as a general custom that women—especially women of Emma's class and station—did not appear in public while noticeably pregnant. But it wasn't a *rule*. There could be exigencies. There could be moments when it was necessary. Moments when it could even be proper—a dinner party—a reception ...

Emma was trying not to think of the woman kneeling between her husband's knees.

I didn't see her. She wasn't there. A person cannot simply disappear. It's impossible.

But she had seen her.

She had.

And she knew it.

Sitting in the chair, dazed by Carl Gustav's attack, she had seen the shape of the woman crouching under the desk, attempting and failing to hide.

She had seen her hair in the modicum of light that fell through the open door to the corridor.

She had seen what they had been doing.

She had seen her husband desperately attempting to adjust his clothing and getting it wrong.

She had seen the woman's hand where it supported her crouching form beneath the desk.

She had seen her fingernails.

She had smelled her perfume and noted the presence of a woman's hat beyond a pile of books on her husband's desk.

Dear God, my life is over, Emma thought.

I am dying. I am dead.

It did not matter who the woman was. How could it matter if she had a name? She *was*, that was the point. And for how long?

All the luncheons eaten alone across the table from her husband's empty place. All the nights when she had already gone to bed before he returned. And all the mornings he was gone before she rose. Weeks? Months? How could she remember how long it had been? How could she tell?

It was over. Everything was over.

That evening—it was Friday, the 31st of May—Jung received a telephone call from Küsnacht. It was Doctor Richard Walter, Emma's physician.

"You should know, Carl Gustav, that Emma has had an accident. My advice would be to return as quickly as you can."

She had fallen down the stairs, having dressed for dinner, and the fall had brought on a miscarriage. The child was dead and Emma was comatose.

Jung did not return for another two hours. The woman had to be informed and dealt with and, for a while, dismissed. The incident in his office would never again be mentioned.

In 1910, at the time of his affair with Sabine Spielrein, Jung had written to Freud about Emma: *she has been staging jealous scenes, groundlessly. She does not understand that the prerequisite for*

a good marriage—or so it seems to me—is a licence to be unfaithful.
Then he had added: *I in my turn have learned a great deal.*

Clearly, what he had learned was how to control his wife—
but not how to control the mother of his children.

10

Emma lay so still that Jung for a moment wondered if she was dead.

He reached for her hand and held it in his own.

Doctor Walter stood to one side.

"Can she have another?" Jung asked.

"One day, perhaps. I suspect, however, she may not choose to."

"I dare say. I dare say." Jung gave Emma's hand a squeeze and laid it back on the coverlet. "Could you tell what sex it was?"

"Yes. You would have had a second son."

"Oh, God."

Jung turned away from the bed.

A nurse had been hired to stay for as long as needed. A week at least, perhaps longer, Doctor Walter said. Her name was Berthe. Schwester Berthe. She was tall and calm and silent. She read books and would content herself with reading *Death in Venice* during the long hours of Emma's silence. As Doctor Jung and Doctor Walter left the room, she set a chair in place at the foot of the bed where she could keep an eye on her patient, and opened the slim volume—breaking its back in three places and lifting it to her nose so that she could drink in its smell. Ink. Paper, binding glue—Venice. Nothing more was required.

Once downstairs and the requisite brandy poured, Jung said to Doctor Walter: "what is done with the remains in such a case?"

Walter, who had attended Emma ever since her marriage and residence in Zürich and Küsnacht, said: "with your permission, the simplest means of disposal is fire."

"I see. May I see it?"

"I wouldn't advise it, Carl Gustav. It is too sad."

"Was it healthy and well formed?"

"Yes."

"And a son, you say?"

"Yes."

"Be honest with me, Richard," Jung said. "Do you think what happened was truly an accident?"

"I have no way of knowing."

"Who found her?"

"Frau Emmenthal."

"And?"

"She heard the sound of the fall and came at once. Your wife was unconscious. I was summoned. The miscarriage took place in my presence—perhaps not quite an hour later. I feared it and was prepared. Emma felt nothing."

"Where is the child now?"

"I have it wrapped in a towel in the kitchen, where it can be disposed of in the stove. Frau Emmenthal is with it—and the girl."

"Disposed of." Jung shivered. "Disposed of."

"The child was too young for survival, Carl Gustav. You mustn't think about it now."

"May we do it together, then? I want to know it has been done."

"Of course. If that is what you wish."

In the kitchen, Frau Emmenthal sat with the bundled towel in her lap and a glass of Riesling at her elbow. There was perfect silence. Lotte, having wept, was seated in the shadows. Both rose and curtsied as the two men entered.

"Oh, Doctor Jung, I am so sorry," Frau Emmenthal said.

"I thank you," said Jung. "I thank you. You may sit."

"No. We will stand," Frau Emmenthal insisted. "It is only fitting."

Jung turned to Doctor Walter and said: "may I do this? I want to hold it just for one moment."

"Of course."

Doctor Walter then asked Frau Emmenthal if the fire in the stove had been properly stoked. It had.

Jung took the silent bundle from the cook's hands and held it against his breast.

I have no one to pray to, he thought. *No one to pray to—and for once I wish I had.*

"Dear little child," he whispered, "please forgive us for failing you. You will never be forgotten."

He stood there, impossibly torn, knowing that he must let it go.

High on the wall a clock ticked. Otherwise, nothing.

Jung turned and went to the stove.

"Very well," he said. "We are ready."

Doctor Walter lifted the lid above the fire box. There was an upward rush of sparks and the sound of crackling flames.

Jung leaned down and kissed the towel-wrapped fœtus three times. Then he held it briefly above the fire, closed his eyes and let it fall.

It made no sound at all.

Doctor Walter replaced the lid and said to Frau Emmenthal: "I will return in half an hour."

"Yes, sir."

The two men then left and Frau Emmenthal poured herself another glass of wine.

Lotte took her place at the table and they waited then without a word for the Doctor's return, neither of them looking at the stove.

11

Under the eaves at the Hôtel Baur au Lac, Forster lived out his days inventing ways of achieving contact with Mister Pilgrim.

He could disguise himself, since they knew him too well, and attempt to visit as a friend from London, innocent of Mister Pilgrim's condition. He could portray himself as a messenger who had been forbidden to give his message unless he was presented to Mister Pilgrim face to face. He could bring a gift— he could dress as a woman and become *Mister Pilgrim's sister*— he could ... he could ... No. There was nothing he could do. They were too clever by half at the Clinic—too wary, too observant and would have nothing of tricks and disguises.

He purchased binoculars and scanned the Burghölzli's façade. How fortunate it was that the windows in his room faced that building four-square. *If I had asked for such windows, I could not have done better*, Forster concluded, *so I will use them accordingly*.

On the morning of June 1, 1912—a Saturday—Pilgrim stepped onto his balcony to feed his birds.

At once, Forster located him.

"I should have known," he said aloud. Doves and pigeons had come and gone on that balcony for two days. "Who else would have so many at his beck and call?"

Pilgrim wore his blue silk robe and white pyjamas. Watching him, Forster felt a twinge of regret for old times—for the smells of toast and Earl Grey tea in Mrs Matheson's cheery kitchen— for the perilous presence of the lapdog Agamemnon, always beneath his feet—for all the breakfast trays, newspapers and letters delivered to Mister Pilgrim in his rooms at number 18 Cheyne Walk. For all the scurrying of little Agamemnon's hurtling, passionate greetings as the door was opened and the day was begun. For all the comfort of these sacred routines and the knowledge that one more night had passed without an attempted ...

Forster refused even to think the word *suicide*.

"Good morning and good day," he said—also aloud, as though Mister Pilgrim was standing close at hand.

There he was, and if one put out one's hand ...

Forster counted the balconies on either side of where Pilgrim stood. *He is there,* he calculated: *precisely there. Now I can watch him every day—and will. Somehow, we will bring this to an end.*

Bring what to an end?

Our separation.

Forster let the binoculars fall on their strap to his breast.

Lady Quartermaine was dead. Forster was now Mister Pilgrim's only contact with the outside world. He alone stood waiting to receive him.

And so, he would watch and he would wait. And he would be ready.

12

Pilgrim had eaten, but not well. Offered fish—which had been his lunch the day before—he pushed it to one side, almost all the way to the floor.

The girl who had served him stood nervously to one side. She did not speak English and Pilgrim refused to speak German. His somewhat childish excuse was: *I don't speak* Swiss. *Go away!*

The fish—it was sole—remained uneaten.

When a dessert of rice pudding was brought, Pilgrim quite deliberately dropped a spoonful of it on the floor, crumpled his napkin and stood up.

"I am living in a dietary nightmare," he said, and left his table. Nearing the dining-room doorway, he turned back and said to the unfortunate girl: "when you have *real* food, I shall return. In the meantime—good day to you. And to all your cowlike kind."

With that, he departed.

The girl, of course, knew only that she had been insulted and turned towards the kitchen in tears. In the meantime, Pilgrim made his way to the elevator where, rising, he looked at the operator's ever-expressionless face and thought: *I live in a world of cattle—a whole, wide world of brainless, cud-chewing cattle!*

Once in his room, Pilgrim opened the doors to the balconies, removed his jacket and shoes, loosened his tie and lay down on his bed.

It was warm, if not hot, and he had to rise again to draw the shutters partway closed in order to shut out an excess of light.

Ten minutes later, he rose yet again, went to the bathroom where he urinated, drank a glass of tap water and refused to see himself in the mirror.

He removed his tie entirely, and his waistcoat—dropped his suspenders, opened his flies and lay back down.

Some pigeons landed on the balcony beyond the shutters, and spoke.

"Go away," Pilgrim whispered. "Go away," he said. "Go AWAY!" he shouted.

Fifteen minutes later, he was asleep.

Drowning in mud. Don't know where I am.

Dark, but not night. Morning light in the sky and am aware of some horizon.

Everything is brown, grey, wet. The smell of earth—the stench overwhelming. Repulsive, yet welcoming. Death, yes—but peace at heart. Green—green. And brown.

Don't know where my feet are. Am wearing boots. These and cloth-ing drag me down. Nothing solid anywhere under me. Try to swim, but effort to keep head above surface is all I can manage. Mud thick as porridge. Bursts of sporadic light, though distant. Not nearby.

See the shapes of other men. All dressed as I am. Our soggy, sagging clothing confirms we are soldiers. Yes—but when? And where?

A clock strikes. I cannot count. I try to cry out, but have no voice.

Sound of gates being opened—the word portals echoes in my mind. P-p-p-portals—the letter like gunfire. A draught has been admitted. There is a rush of windblown rain. P-p-p-p-p-portals.

My hands reach out for someone else's hand—a human, clean-fingered hand—but it disappears.

Wonder why I am here, but have no answer. Here is nowhere. Nothing.

All at once, there is a noise I cannot at first identify—a rushing, monotonic sound not unlike the stutter of a motor-car engine without its being enclosed. No hood. An open, beating sound in the air above my head.

There follow several small explosions I cannot identify. And then another sound—of shouting, yet again overhead—and a moving shadow falls upon me, like the shadow of a giant bird—after which I see there is an aeroplane—one aeroplane and then another.

I have never seen an aeroplane except in photographs, but there must be ten of them—twelve of them—even more, passing overhead—firing guns and dropping shells that tear the earth open wider.

All around me, the stooping shapes of the other men hurry forward, passing me by, not seeing me because they do not look. Everyone is afraid.

Someone says: I am not allowed to see you. *These are the only words I have heard.*

I close my mouth. Another dozen aeroplanes pass.

I begin to sink.

My nostrils fill with mud. I am drowning—then I wake.

Pilgrim, soaking wet, sat on his bed.

Drowning—then I wake.

Aeroplanes.

What he had just experienced could not have been a dream of the past—but a dream of the future.

Of the future—dearest God. Oh, dearest God!

Four o'clock.

Pilgrim put his hands against his face and lowered his head.

The light in the room had a golden hue, and was filtered through the shutters in slanted, shifting patterns reminiscent of Leonardo's *sfumato*, playing through layers of dust and Pilgrim's fingered blindness.

"Oh, God," he said out loud. "Not more. Not more. Not more."

He stood up.

"THERE MUST BE NO MORE!"

13

The following incident occurred at 4:15 that afternoon. It is recorded in Jung's personal journal, in his file on Pilgrim and in both Kessler's and Schwester Dora's daily reports. These can be consulted in the archives.

There were six witnesses—four patients and two staff, the latter being Kessler and Schwester Dora. The patients were the Countess Blavinskeya, the schizophrenic with Robert Schumann's recalcitrant hands, the man who wrote with an imaginary pen and a man who had completely given up communicating through speech. These were all gathered together—except for Kessler—in the Music Room.

On the gramophone, a recording of Saint-Saëns's *Carnival of the Animals* was playing. Blavinskeya was dancing Pavlova's *Dying Swan*.

There was sunlight. The windows were open. The man who wrote with an imaginary pen felt constrained to express himself and had risen to write his message on the wall by the door. Schwester Dora was knitting a shawl for her beloved patient. The others sat watching and listening, lost in their own private worlds.

All at once, there was a sound in the corridor. Someone was being pursued and a voice could be heard crying: "stop! Stop! Stop!"

In seconds, the door burst open and Pilgrim entered in his bathrobe and slippers. It had been Kessler's intention to take him down to the baths in order to calm him after his dream, but Pilgrim had started running towards the Music Room, banging on all the doors as he ran.

When Pilgrim stormed into the room, it so happened that Blavinskeya was coming to the conclusion of her solo. She had descended to the floor, and crouching there with her left leg extended before her, she had begun the famous denouement with its fluttering arms, its lowered head and its arching back.

Pilgrim was barely recognizable. He had lost control entirely of his expression. His face was a mask of rage—his eyes wide and staring, his mouth split in two by what appeared to be a maelstrom of froth and spittle. He crossed the yards of sunlit space with the alarming speed of a cheetah about to bring down its prey, and tearing the needle-arm of the gramophone from its place, he threw it against the nearest open window. Shattered glass exploded into the air.

Blavinskeya looked up fully expecting a tornado to have struck the Clinic. The woman with Schumann's hands screamed and ran into a corner, where she sank onto her heels. The man with the imaginary pen stopped writing, but was unable to turn around. He stood against the wall with his right arm raised and his forehead inches from the plaster.

Schwester Dora rose and set her knitting aside, prepared to go to Blavinskeya's side, but she was prevented by the violence of Pilgrim's next moves.

He lifted the gramophone from its place and crashed it to the floor. Its lid split in two and its disembowelled mechanical innards spilled out. He then systematically took whole albums of recordings from their shelves and heaved them one by one at all four walls, smashing their contents. Whether by chance or by crazed calculation, the album of Schumann's *Scenes of Childhood* struck the pianist crouching in her corner and caused a wound that later would require stitches.

Meanwhile, Kessler was attempting to catch his patient, but at every turn Pilgrim evaded him. His energy was manic. He might have been a juvenile athlete—a wrestler—a runner—a gymnast. Pulling the 'cello from its place he began to kick its prostrate body, crying out: "damn all music! Damn all art! Damn all beauty! Kill! Kill! Kill!"

He next smashed the violin and began to use its remains to

beat against the glassed-in cabinets that contained the librettos and scores of which the Music Librarian had been so proud.

At last, Kessler was able to trip him just as he was about to use Schwester Dora's knitting needles—with wool appended—to stab himself in the face.

As Kessler dragged his patient to the floor and pulled his arms into a locked position behind his back, the Countess Blavinskeya called out: "DON'T!" and Pilgrim subsided.

Schwester Dora went for assistance while Kessler sat on Pilgrim's thighs and twisted his arms every time there was an attempt to escape.

Five minutes later, a quartet of interns arrived and struggled Pilgrim into a straitjacket. His final gesture was to spit in Kessler's face, after which he gave an animal cry and fainted.

Later, when Jung was told of this incident and Pilgrim had been dealt with, Kessler was asked what he imagined might have triggered the outburst.

"He had taken his afternoon nap," Kessler said. "And must have dreamt. When I found him, he was shouting—I don't know what—but shouting. I got his clothes off and put him in his robe to take him down to the baths, where I thought the water might calm him. He kept crying: *it will never end—it will never end!* But what he meant would never end was never made clear. The only thing he said I've never heard him say before was *aeroplane*."

"Aeroplane?"

"Aeroplane. And he said it again and again. *Aeroplane. Aeroplane.* And then he escaped from me and went and broke up all those things."

Jung shook his head. "Well," he said. "Aeroplane. That's a new one."

"Yes, sir. I've never seen one myself," said Kessler.

"Neither have I," said Jung. And then, without knowing he would say it, he added in a whisper: "but I suspect we shall."

"Yes, sir. I suspect we shall."

BOOK FIVE

1

Pilgrim was placed in a padded cell where he could do himself no harm. He now had two new orderlies, or "keepers." This is what they were called on the violent wards. Kessler was told he was free to go home for a week, which he agreed to do only with the proviso that if Mister Pilgrim should call for him, he would return.

One of the keepers was a blond and seemingly harmless giant whose name was Wolf. He had been hired exclusively for his strength. Nothing in him indicated the presence of any particular attitude to his patients other than his willingness to subdue them if, as and when he must. The otherwise harmless aspect of his character was enhanced by his benign expression. Wide-eyed and gently smiling, he might have been an innocent child who thought that every day was Christmas.

The other keeper, Schwarzkopf, was in all ways the antithesis of Wolf—distinctly and all too clearly sadistic. He would stare at Pilgrim and crack his knuckles as if he imagined every patient was an opponent in a wrestling match. When he did this, he squinted at his victim, with his tongue between his teeth. He too was large—not tall, but round and solid.

For the first two days after Pilgrim's rampage, he was completely sedated and had to be tended as a child. He wet the bed and messed his pyjamas and had to be force-fed liquids so that he would not dehydrate.

On the third day, he awoke.

He said only two things: *where are my doves and pigeons?* And: *why is everything white?*

He seemed benign enough and on the fourth day, on Doctor Jung's orders, his restraints were removed.

Schwarzkopf said: "he is tall—his legs will be dangerous."

Wolf was assigned the task of undoing the straps by which Pilgrim's arms had been fastened to the bed. Schwarzkopf sat on Pilgrim's feet and placed his hands on Pilgrim's knees.

The room had a relatively low ceiling and no window. Air was circulated by means of a vent in the wall that went through a series of metal screens to the outside. Schwarzkopf did not wash. He smelled. It was one of his weapons of intimidation. Pilgrim watched him through half-closed eyes.

The straps were difficult. The undoing took some time. Wolf, in his gentle way, was attempting to avoid any injury to Pilgrim's wrists and ankles.

At last it was done and Pilgrim began to feel the return of blood flow.

He said nothing. He did nothing.

He did not move his limbs or close his eyes.

Schwarzkopf stood up.

"You was rise now," he said in his imperfect English.

Pilgrim's eyes slid to Wolf.

Wolf leaned down and supported Pilgrim's shoulders, pulling him to a sitting position.

"Legs," Pilgrim said.

Schwarzkopf lifted Pilgrim's calves and threw his feet towards the floor, where they landed with a jarring of bones and the sound, in Pilgrim's mind, of a slamming door.

Wolf stood to one side.

Watching, Schwarzkopf touched his own chin with his thumb, stroking his skin as if he wished to stimulate an absent beard. Then he stepped backwards and said to Pilgrim: "speak."

Pilgrim said: "I want my doves and my pigeons."

Schwarzkopf smiled and said: "you like doves and pigeons?"

"Yes."

Schwarzkopf then said: "I will find and bring tomorrow."

Pilgrim nodded. "I would like some soup," he said.

*   *   *

In the morning, Wolf was attending to Pilgrim's toilet needs when Schwarzkopf arrived with something wrapped in a towel. Though his tongue was between his teeth, he smiled.

"You were wanting," he said, and set the towel on the foot of the bed.

"I want nothing, now," Pilgrim replied.

"No," Schwarzkopf said. "You were wanting and I have brought."

With which he unrolled the towel, displaying the bodies of one pink dove and one green pigeon.

"They can be breakfast," he said, "if so you wish."

For another week, Pilgrim had again to be forcibly restrained. Kessler returned and at Jung's command, Schwarzkopf was dismissed.

There was no more talk of doves and pigeons. Kessler took it upon himself to bury the dead birds beneath a tree in the garden. Laying them in the earth, he smoothed their wings and whispered a single word. *Forgive.* The ruby eyes were closed and the earth, as it fell on them, smelled of pine cones, mushrooms and rain.

2

On Saturday, the 8th of June, Emma rose from her bed for the first time since the miscarriage—and on the same day Wolf removed the restraints from Pilgrim's wrists and ankles for the last time.

Emma went to sit in the window, where Lotte brought her breakfast tray together with the morning paper. Emma had asked for the latter, thinking: *the world is still happening out there and I'd best rejoin it.*

Pilgrim sat on the edge of his bed, where Kessler fed him a cut orange, toast and marmalade and tea. The birds were not mentioned. Wolf had retired to the staff kitchen, where he drank coffee and stared at the stoves and ovens as if he expected them to speak. He himself remained silent.

Emma unfolded the paper. *Die Neue Zürcher Zeitung*, known fondly as *die N.Z.Z.* The Italian-Ottoman war continued—the Italians seeming the most likely victors. The Balkans were in their usual turmoil—bombs, assassinations, riots and anarchy. Greece was threatening to join in the melee ... On and on and on it went.

Serbs, Macedonians, Bulgars, Turks, Italians, Greeks—who gives a damn? Emma thought and let the paper fall to the floor. Five hundred years of invading armies and shifting borders and nothing had been resolved. All the way back to Alexander the Great. All the way back to Troy—and nothing, nothing, nothing had changed. For centuries, whole lives, from infant cradle to ancient grave, had been lived without a moment's peace, without a second's existence beyond the reach of fear. Just as well not to be born. Just as well to perish.

At eleven o'clock that morning, Jung appeared in the violent ward, checked on the condition of a few others and, at eleven thirty-five, was admitted to Pilgrim's cell.

Wolf by this time had been sitting in the corridor, allowing Kessler to deal with Pilgrim's private needs. Fresh pyjamas and a newly laundered robe had been provided, and for the first time in almost two weeks, Pilgrim had been shaved and allowed to brush his teeth.

Jung told Kessler he could retire and return perhaps in half an hour.

When Kessler had left the room, taking with him last week's soiled pyjamas and the breakfast tray, Jung took the only chair in the room and placed it with its back to the door.

Sitting, he drew a sheet of paper from the music bag and faced his patient. He had not slept, his conscience still suffering the facts of his child's death and of his wife's discovery of the other woman.

As for the first of these troubling episodes, he felt both remorse and guilt. His suspicion that Emma had quite deliberately thrown herself down the stairs had all but been confirmed. *I did not trip*, she told him. *I fell.* As for *the other woman*, he felt no remorse at all—only regret that her presence in his life had to be terminated for the time being. He would miss not only the sexual release she had provided, but also her intellectual company. Her name was Antonia Wolff and she had some time ago—like Sabine Spielrein—been a patient at the Bürgholzli. On her recovery, she consequently became a qualified intern of astonishing talent and insight.

This was the young woman Jung had seen in the corridor some weeks before in the company of Furtwängler. It had helped—and not helped—that physically, she was an almost perfect match for Emma, but that her hair fell forward, whereas Emma's was pulled back away from her face. She had the voluptuous look of a woman whose body was practised in delight and she ... Antonia ... Toni ... she was ...

Forget all this. You are here in pursuit of Pilgrim.

"Good morning," Jung said. "What a bright, sunny, lovely day," he lied. It was, in fact, pouring rain and his child was dead.

Pilgrim said nothing and looked away.

"Is there something you would like to say?" Jung asked.

"Only that you have confined me in the dark with maniacs."

"Which maniacs do you have in mind?"

"Schwarzkopf killed two of my birds."

"You have birds?"

"Doves. Pigeons. I feed them. You know this."

"You own birds? I was not aware. It is my impression that birds belong to themselves."

"Very clever, Doctor Jung. Of course ..." Pilgrim lifted a hand and let it fall again to his knee "... you are right. Nonetheless, I have cared for them."

Jung said: "Mister Schwarzkopf has been let go. You have other complaints?"

"Kessler is mad."

"Oh?"

"He believes in angels."

"And you do not?"

"Of course not. What good are angels?"

"They appear to have been rather useful to Kessler. Do you know that he was once a patient here himself?"

"No. And who cares. It merely proves my point. You call me mad and set me in the care of madmen. Perhaps there is something amiss in your own mind."

"This is possible." Jung smiled. "This is entirely possible."

There was a pause.

"How do you feel today, Mister Pilgrim? Rested? Relieved?"

"Released."

Jung laughed.

"Indeed," he said. "And high time." He waited a moment before he said: "would you have killed Mister Schwarzkopf, as you appeared to want to?"

"I desired it, but I relented. I cannot kill—which is more than can be said for Schwarzkopf. I have seen him eating flies."

"Do flies matter?"

"Everything matters. Wouldn't you agree? Or does it not matter there might be none left over for you?"

Jung sat back.

"Well," he said, "clearly we have a problem here. You do not like me—is this correct?"

"For the moment, yes."

"Just remember, I am your doctor. Doctors cannot always be likeable."

"I'm perfectly aware of that." Pilgrim fixed his gaze on Jung. "What do you want of me, Doctor Jung? Is there something I can do for you?"

"Yes. You can answer some questions for me."

"I get the questions, you get the answers. This is not just."

"Would you rather we reversed our roles?"

"I was not aware we were playing roles."

"Mister Pilgrim, obfuscation gets us nowhere—neither you nor me."

"For someone to whom English is a foreign language, you speak it very well. *Obfuscation.* Remarkable. Your vocabulary is exemplary and wide ranging. In fact, I should say you are—as in other matters—something of a flamboyant expert."

"I'm not sure I understand you."

"Yes you do. Please do not hide behind false modesty. You have no modesty, false or otherwise. In other words, Doctor Jung, you are visible."

"I see."

"No, *I* see. You are, in schoolboy vernacular, what is known as a useless prick."

Jung set aside his list of questions. He would no longer need them. The encounter with Pilgrim had taken a turn in its own direction and, though not the turn he had hoped for, a turn nonetheless that might prove productive.

"*Prick?*" he said. "A needle in the thumb?"

"No, sir. Prick is an English schoolboy pejorative meaning *penis*. A nasty, smelly, incompetent penis, useless for anything other than widdling."

"Widdling?"

"Pissing."

"I see."

"Do you."

"I think so."

"I doubt it. You see, the schoolboy spends his nights rubbing himself in the hopes that one day soon he will gain the full-blown pleasure of ejaculation and consequent orgasm. He has heard of these pleasures, and perhaps even witnessed them in his older fellows. But his own penis remains dormant because his testicles have not yet dropped. For all the erections he may achieve, nothing of gratification is forthcoming other than a vaguely pleasing distant relative called a *blush*. He is worse than a virgin. He is barren. And thus, a *useless prick*."

"So I am an unfulfilled orgasm."

"Yes, sir. Note that I call you *sir*, as a schoolboy should."

"You are not a schoolboy, Mister Pilgrim."

"Are you not my master?"

Silence.

"I hate this room. This cell. Must I stay here forever?"

"No."

"Is it you who carries the key?"

"One of them, yes."

"And the others?"

"Kessler. Wolf. The doctor in charge of this ward. His name is Raddi."

"Ernst Raddi. Yes. I've met him. Or should I say, he has met me? In his presence I was always chained. Another prick."

"There were no chains, Mister Pilgrim. Never."

"Whatever they were, they felt like chains."

"I'm sure."

"How kind of you."

"I'd like to know why you think of me as a prick."

"The description bothers you?"

"To know could be beneficial. If I am to help you, I must know who you think I am."

"Why do you think I need help?"

Jung almost laughed, but contained himself.

"The key is in my pocket, Mister Pilgrim. Only I can set you free."

"You said there were other keys in other pockets."

"Yes—but only mine can set you free. Besides which, it is all too clear you are troubled. You yourself know this. And so ... your answer?"

"Why do I think of you as a prick? Because you are too pleased with who you are and the few minor achievements you have made in your field ..."

Jung closed his eyes, but said nothing.

"And because you are an arrogant, opinionated wielder of unlimited powers. And because you have no notion of your own ignorance and the damage this ignorance inflicts. And because you are unrepentant. And because you abuse the intellects of others in order to protect the reputation of your own. And because you are Swiss!"

Jung stood up—turned away—removed his glasses and dabbed at his eyes with his handkerchief.

"That's quite a list," he said.

"It's just a beginning," said Pilgrim.

Jung shifted his weight and thought of turning again, but did not.

"Would you like another doctor to take you on?" he asked.

"Take me on? Am I a wrestler? A rugby team? An army of insurgents?"

"MISTER PILGRIM!" Jung now did turn and, blazing with visible fury, confronted his patient. "Enough is enough!"

"What a pity. I was enjoying myself."

"No doubt. But you are in trouble, sir. Not with me—but with yourself. I have a job to do here, and I intend to do it. I am not alone in my arrogance and I am not alone in my ignorance and I am not alone in my opinionated wielding of power ..."

"*Unlimited* power!"

"You, sir, are a past master in all these fields, and if I may say so, you are something of a prick yourself!"

Pilgrim blinked. He was genuinely surprised. He turned towards the wall and said: "I want a window."

"You cannot have a window! There will be no windows until I have my answers."

Pilgrim sat down.

"Is that understood?" said Jung.

"Yes."

"Now ..." Jung himself sat down. "We have cleared the air. Let us proceed."

Pilgrim gazed at his knees. The white of his pyjamas seemed to mesmerize him. "Where are we going?" he said, all but whispering.

"We are going to discover who we are," said Jung. "Both you and I. We have no maps, but we must find our way. And we will."

3

Not quite a week later, on Thursday the 13th of June, a man in a bowler hat and a tailored grey coat was seen on the terraces of the Lindenhof, which rise above the Limmat on its west bank. At the top of this wooded park, there was a magnificent esplanade with benches, tables, a café, a fountain and a view of Zürich that was unmatched in its splendour.

To the right, the Grossmünster—to the left, the Prediger-Kirche—and beyond it the University of Zürich, dominated by the Burghölzli Clinic riding on its hillside and rising up from its skirt of protective trees.

Trees. They were everywhere. The linden trees that gave the park its name and the oak, the chestnut, the ash and the aspen crowded amongst the shops and houses across the river, making a froth of green lace on which the roofs and steeples seemed to float.

The man in the bowler hat wore a pair of binoculars which hung from a leather strap around his neck. In his hand, he carried a small leather-bound notebook. From another leather strap, this one hanging from his shoulder, there was a Kodak camera in a cloth case which he pressed against his side with his elbow. The perfect—or seemingly perfect—tourist.

He moved along the balconade entirely engrossed in the view before him. Occasionally he would stop, raise the binoculars, stare at something and afterwards make an annotation in his book. He had been doing this now for more than an hour, while unbeknownst to him, he was himself being observed by a woman seated beneath the trees on one of the benches behind him.

The woman appeared to be in her late twenties—perhaps her early thirties. She was trim and neat and dressed in navy blue, wearing a light spring coat with tortoiseshell buttons and a blue straw hat with a wide mauve ribbon. Its shape was not unlike the bowler worn by the man, although it lacked a turned-up brim.

Her focus was entirely on this curious man with the curious binoculars and curious notebook. He was as trim and neat and small as herself and he seemed almost as lonely, in spite of his attentions to whatever it was he was spying on. Whatever—whomever.

She wondered.

He could be a confidential agent, she speculated. *Or a private investigator. Or perhaps a jealous husband, whose wife is in a dalliance with some romantic, dashing young man. An officer in the Hussars. A naval personage. An artist or a doomed poet. What exciting lives some people lived.*

Some people, yes. Others, no.

All at once, the man turned and looked directly at her.

She closed her eyes and smiled. The thought occurred to her: *I have been chosen.*

When she opened her eyes, she saw that the man was older than expected. Given his almost military bearing, his squared shoulders, his trim waist, his erect posture, she had thought he might be in his mid-to-late twenties, but clearly, he was over forty.

Over forty! A worldly man. A practised man. A challenge.

His eyes, at a distance, appeared to be smoky grey. His nose was handsome, rising straight as an ivory bone to a pair of wing-like eyebrows whose arching shapes mimicked flight. His mouth was a wide, thin line, his lower lip moist and full, his upper lip masked by a full and elegant moustache whose corners he had twisted into the shape of dimples.

O, mercy, mercy! What is going to happen?

His approach was so deliberate, there could be no mistaking his destination.

Even though the young woman was seated in the shade of the

linden trees, she raised her hand to protect her eyes from the light through which he walked towards her.

"Madam," he said when he had stopped within four feet of her, "may one ask if you are alone?"

"One may," she replied, barely audible. She had fully intended to be heard, but something in her throat prevented her voice from rising much beyond a whisper. "Though I may appear to be alone, I am waiting for a friend," she lied. There was no friend. There never had been since childhood. The very word was foreign to her. Nevertheless, it was a useful word when a gentleman called. "She may well attend me at any moment." The word *she*, the woman thought, was a masterstroke. It did not prevent her from being a continued object of desire, but placed her in a protective embrace.

The gentleman had removed his hat. "So much the better," he said. "There is no need to ask but a moment of your time, if you would be so kind."

She was bitterly disappointed by this. A mere moment of her time was hardly likely to lead to a romance.

"May one inquire if madam is of Scots descent? I detect an accent quite familiar to my ears."

"Why, yes. I have come here from Aberdeen. Perhaps you would be kind enough to tell me your name. I am not accustomed to having conversations with people to whom I have not been introduced."

"With pleasure. My name is Henry Forster and I come from London Town." He said the latter almost as one might have sung it—rather gaily, with a lilt.

"London Town?"

"Yes. From Chelsea on the River Thames. Cheyne Walk, to be exact. If madam has never had the pleasure, I would suggest she acquaint herself with this most delightful purview. A landscape of complete enchantment."

Was this an invitation?

The young woman blushed.

"I am called," she said, "Miss Leslie Meikle."

"Most unusual. And pleasing. Meikle—a Celtic name."

"Leslie is my mother's family name. My parents had hoped to have a son, but I arrived instead and they gave the honour to me."

"How do you do."

"How do you do, and how might I be of assistance?"

"I shall be brief, Miss Meikle," said Forster. "I am on a mission and I require some photographs. Two. Perhaps three. If you would be so kind."

He pulled the Kodak from his shoulder and removed it from its cloth case.

"You depress the lever just so," he told her, opening the accordion folds and demonstrating. "I should like one of each profile and one of me facing the lens."

Leslie Meikle rose and, accepting the camera, stepped into the light.

She would be, Forster thought, *a perfect beauty if one had found her in a pastoral setting.* The blue eyes, the apple cheeks, the cherry lips. But her visage was somehow disconcerting in an urban landscape. The appearance of so much good health was upsetting to someone whose life of late had been spent in the depths of a hotel room and beneath the shade of a bowler hat while he grew a moustache to disguise his true appearance.

Forster placed himself in the sunlight and Leslie Meikle stood five paces away and aimed the camera at his left profile. The hat was now on his head.

"May a person ask if these photographs are for a loved one, Mister Forster?"

Snap!

"They are for a colleague who has been incarcerated."

Leslie Meikle let the camera fall to her waist.

"*Incarcerated?* Do you mean imprisoned?"

"Not precisely, no. Nonetheless, he is prevented from free-dom. He is restrained."

Leslie Meikle repositioned herself.

Right profile.

How romantic, she thought. *To have a colleague prevented from freedom. Surely this is intrigue worthy of an Elinor Glyn novel, or one perhaps by Mrs Henry Wood.*

Snap!

Full face next and last.

"I am intrigued, Mister Forster. May I ask what you intend to do—if anything—about your colleague's unfortunate circumstances?"

"You may, but I shall not answer. I only want him to have these photographs to remind him that someone attends to his needs on the outside."

Snap!

On the outside. How utterly dramatic!

In her mind's eye, Leslie Meikle conjured the image of the Incarcerated Colleague clinging to his bars, his gaze on the distant mountains.

"Here is your camera, sir," she said, handing the Kodak over to Forster.

"Perhaps," Forster said with as much diffidence as he could muster, "Miss Meikle would allow me to take a photograph for the sake of having a memento of our encounter." Why pass up a pretty face when it was there for the asking?

"I would be delighted."

Leslie Meikle, Forster would write in his notebook—not quite certain of the spelling but certain enough of the spell. In time, as he gazed at her smiling image on the Lindenhof Terrace, he would regret that his duty to Pilgrim had prevented him from pressing for more of her acquaintance.

As for Leslie Meikle herself, she would never forget Henry Forster, with his bowler hat, his smoky eyes, his ivory bone of a nose and his winglike eyebrows. Nor his shoulders neatly squared, nor his waist as trim as her own. Nor his unkissed lips and their promise of moist embraces.

That shall be Tomorrow
Not tonight:
I must bury sorrow
Out of sight.

Why does one inevitably remember such lines? Leslie Meikle wondered.

She would go home. She would not marry. She would care for her elders and perish. It would take forty years. Not that she would spend those forty years entirely in the shadow of what she would always claim were Forster's advances, but he would be there forever in the company of each year's ungarnered others—her collection of shadows, as she came to think of them—her regiment of *gentlemen-who-might-have-pressed-for-more-but-had-not.*

Divide the human race by two, Pilgrim would write of another unfulfilled encounter, *and there you have them: the millions who never connect.*

As for the photograph of Leslie Meikle, Forster would tuck it into his notebook and remove it from time to time to gaze at the poignant edge of longing in her eyes and the thwarted smile that had all but failed to reach her lips. *What if?* she seemed to be saying. *What if we had met some other time and place? And what if...?* But nothing comes of that and in her eyes she knew it.

4

Lady Quartermaine had been kind enough to secure Forster's accommodation until the end of July. While she herself had been certain of her impending death, she in no way communicated this to Forster. Her excuse for prepaying his expenses was expressed only as a desire to acknowledge his independence of her. She assured him—as he well knew himself—that Mister Pilgrim would repay her on his return to London, once his treatments had proved successful. That Doctor Jung could help him, she said, was undoubted. It was merely a matter of time.

Until the day of the avalanche, which now seemed remote as something from another age, Lady Quartermaine had maintained her liaison with Pilgrim through her meetings with and letters to and from Doctor Jung. Early on, in the wake of their arrival in Zürich, she had also been allowed to visit him twice—perhaps three times. Forster had seen his employer only on the occasion of Lady Quartermaine's remains being removed to England. They had not spoken that day and Pilgrim had been so distracted that it was entirely possible he had not even recognized his valet. There had also been that *other person*—the blond and swaggering Swiss who had taken on Forster's duties, and who looked so entirely unsuitable for the position. The man had not even known how to clothe himself appropriately.

Consequently, Forster had presented himself on five different occasions, requesting that he be allowed to visit with Mister Pilgrim, only to be told each time that *Mister Pilgrim is otherwise engaged. He is receiving treatment ... he is under heavy sedation ... he is in the baths.* Whenever Forster telephoned, he was told the same. The excuses were legion. And clearly, none of his messages was being transmitted. When he tried to leave a note, he was told: *you may, but you should be aware that all written communications to or from patients are monitored—for the sake of the patient's mental stability.*

Mental stability. Psychiatric modes and methods were a complete mystery to Forster. He thought of them as mumbo-jumbo and therefore that his employer had somehow been kidnapped into a system of seance, hypnotism and the darker aspects of voodoo. All this to say nothing of the dreadful possibility that Pilgrim had managed at long last to kill himself, and the clinicians, fearing for their reputations, were plotting to disguise his success as being the result of some disease. All of this had placed Forster on the point of despair. He felt a growing certainty that at some moment soon he would be forced to take matters into his own hands.

Though not a devoted reader as such, Forster was devoted to the tales of Sherlock Holmes. Otherwise, books were not by any means Forster's constant companions. Holmes was a different story. Reading of his exploits was pure heaven. Part of Forster's fascination with the great detective lay in his ingenious use of disguise. It was every child's dream to be someone else and Forster had never lost his fascination for it.

A person can be anyone he wants to be, he came to understand from his reading of Sherlock Holmes, *so long as he believes.*

This was Holmes's great secret. Disguise means nothing if it is purely physical. This way, Forster understood that merely to grow a moustache and dye one's hair was bootless unless the man beneath the disguise was a *red-headed braggart* or a *suave survivor of the Indian campaigns* or a *slumming member of the upper classes who has strayed down the social ladder in search of cocaine and opium.* He had attempted to play all three and, to his disappointment, had discovered there was a fourth incarnation which suited him best—namely, *the bank clerk on holiday abroad.* Only this incarnation was acceptable, so he had found in encounters such as that with Leslie Meikle—though from time to time, he daydreamed of being a bank clerk who had embezzled a million pounds.

And so it was as the bank clerk that Forster had been roaming the town, casually gathering information about the Burghölzli while trying to devise a way of communicating with his employer without revealing his true identity.

Using his binoculars and the several vantage points available to him, Forster had also been keeping a record of Pilgrim's comings and goings for almost three weeks.

Then Pilgrim had disappeared from his windows and balcony—on Saturday, June 1st—and when his absence from view had gone on for three days, Forster at last became alarmed to the degree that he had begun to plot a means of rescue.

He must somehow gain entry to the Clinic, playing the role of the bank clerk. He had gleaned the names of a half-dozen other English patients in residence, by keeping his ears open in the dining-room, bar and lounges of the hotel. He would claim to be a brother or a cousin to any one of these.

And then—as if by his usual arrangement with death—Pilgrim had risen from the grave and shown himself at his windows on Monday last—the 10th of June.

It was on the following Thursday that Forster had met Leslie Meikle. The photographs she had taken would be used to inform Pilgrim of the changes he should expect to see in his valet's appearance, when they next met—whenever that might be.

By then, Forster had already begun plotting how to achieve that meeting. Now that Pilgrim had reappeared, the next step was practical but difficult to achieve. *Communication.*

The only other books Forster had read besides Arthur Conan Doyle's were books on the subject of pigeonry. In London, at Cheyne Walk, Forster had asked for and received permission to build a dovecote, where he raised and nurtured a variety of pigeons. The birds were receiving, at this moment of his absence, the ministrations of Mrs Matheson, the house-keeper/cook, and of her nephew, a young lad of fourteen whose name was Alfred.

Alfred also worked in the garden and slept in the cubby-hole beneath the back stairs. He was dark-haired and seemingly dour, but he loved the birds in his care and had a natural affinity with their needs and desires. He knew precisely when—and when not—to attend them, when they required their moments of freedom and when the shutters must be closed to protect them against the night and early morning visitations of pigeon hawks, owls, rooks and even the occasional ferret.

Forster had a deep affection for this sullen, silent boy, whose demeanour reminded him of his own at an early age—the tragedy of loss, when all that he had known and trusted was swept away in a fire that took, besides his home, his parents and his siblings. In Alfred's case, the reflection of this tragedy was in the vengeful destruction of his mother, his brother and the roof above his head by his drunken, abusive and molesting father. Whatever atrocities of sexual perversion Alfred had suffered had never been revealed in so many words—but they could be told in his eyes and in his sad refusal of male friendship, which Forster had attempted to offer him. And yet, the boy had stayed. He loved his aunt, Eulalie Matheson—he loved "his" gardens and he loved, above all, "his" pigeons.

On the roof of the Hôtel Baur au Lac there was a dovecote of some size. It housed more than thirty birds. And it provided Forster with an idea. *Whose can it be?* he had asked, only to be told it belonged to the sous-chef in the hotel's kitchens—a man called Dominic Fréjus.

For a time, Forster was too perturbed to inquire further. Were the birds supper? This would be unacceptable. Forster was one of those carnivorous creatures who could bear every-thing about the consumption of meat but the killing that provided it. To *know* one's prey was akin to murder. To *choose* one's prey was worst of all. And so he watched and listened and kept a tally.

When, after two weeks of this, it was clear the pigeons in the dovecote were not declining in number, he at last approached

Dominic Fréjus and asked if he might observe the birds at close quarters.

The sous-chef had no problem with this and ultimately allowed Forster to take on one of the feedings.

On the 14th of June—the day after Forster's encounter with Leslie Meikle—he spoke at length with Fréjus in the early morning hours concerning the various types of pigeons collected in the rooftop dovecote. Rock doves; ringed doves; homers and racers. And the doomed passengers, a pair of which Dominic Fréjus had imported from North America in the hopes that he could breed them.

"Alas," he told Forster, "they will not breed in captivity. It is, for me—as for them—a great tragedy. In North America, they are all but exterminated."

Forster had bowed his head and allowed a moment's silence as if *in memoriam*. Not that he felt no sorrow—in fact, he felt it profoundly. But he was on a quest—and he needed an ally. To this end, if Dominic Fréjus was sympathetic, he had found the perfect co-conspirator.

"I need," Forster said, "six homing pigeons."

"I have but four," Fréjus told him. "Why do you need them?"

"To correspond with a friend who is receiving treatment in the Burghölzli Clinic."

"Ah, yes." Fréjus smiled. "A victim of the yellow wagon."

"What is the yellow wagon?"

"It is the wagon used to collect the Clinic's specimens."

"I see."

"You have not observed it?"

"No."

"You will, in time. It passes almost every day through the streets. Mostly, its clients are the families of crazy people, but on occasion it carries people off from the parks and from the steps of the Cathedral. Religious fanatics, you know—or the incapacitated who have drunk themselves into a corner. And so—you want my homers?"

"Only to borrow, if I may. They will, of course, return to you—but I am hoping they will do so bearing messages for me. My friend is devoted to birds, and at home in England we often correspond by this method. I thought it might cheer him up." Forster considered this an inoffensive lie and felt no compunction in telling it.

Dominic Fréjus leaned forward where he sat on the parapet of the hotel roof and looked at the *bank clerk*, slowly nodding his head.

"It would be a good thing," he said, "to brighten the days of one who is ill." He smiled. "Of course, you will need a cage," he added.

"Indeed."

"But you need not worry. I have such a cage in which I transport them on our excursions into the countryside. I release them perhaps a mile, two miles away and they find their own way home. The exercise is good for them. I trust they will be fed by your friend?"

"Of course. I shall send some mixed grain along with them."

"In that case, you may have the use of my homing pigeons, if I may have the use of fifty francs."

"Done," said Forster—and they shook hands.

On Monday the 10th of June, Pilgrim had been discharged from the violent ward and returned to his rooms on the third floor.

He wore white, having requested that Kessler bring the white suit, white shoes and even a white straw hat. His tie on this occasion was green—a colour that, for Pilgrim, denoted freedom. He also carried his walking stick.

"We look," Kessler told him, "as if we were about to depart for Venice."

"Perhaps we are," said Pilgrim. "Destination: San Michele, Isle of the Dead."

"Yes, sir."

Kessler, bearing the last of Pilgrim's toiletries, his pyjamas, bathrobe and slippers plus shaving utensils in a canvas bag, followed his ward along the darkened corridors where all the doors were closed until, at last, they came to a corridor where all the doors stood open.

Pilgrim reached up and pulled the brim of his hat down over his eyes. He had waited so long for the sun that when he saw it he was dazzled.

On arrival at number 306, he allowed Kessler to precede him, and to fling open the succession of doors until it seemed there could be no more room for sunlight but only the sun itself.

Pilgrim went immediately to the windows and opened them one by one, stepping back to let the air and a soft breeze enter.

There were the pigeons—there were the doves.

"Bread," said Pilgrim, laying aside his walking stick.

Kessler went to the bureau and produced a brown paper bag full of crumbled toast and croissants, raisin loaf and rolls.

Pilgrim said: "soo-soo-soo. There, there," and began to scatter bounty.

From his windows at the Baur au Lac, Forster had watched this scene through his binoculars. Pilgrim in white and the cretin Kessler standing in the background, folding clothes.

Another twinge of nostalgic regret pulled at Forster's memory—the thought of all the mornings he had laid out Pilgrim's suits and jackets, shirts and ties and shoes and all the nights he had pulled down the covers of the bed and set out pyjamas, robe and slippers. And Agamemnon, the regrettable but charming little tyke, whose favourite trick was to crawl beneath the covers and lie in wait for his master. Such a long while ago, it seemed. Such a long, long while ago.

Pilgrim removed his hat and slowly began to fan his face with it—back and forth, back and forth in the manner of a lady watching her flock of daughters from the sidelines at a ball.

He turned away. Apparently there had been a knock at the

door. Kessler was laying down the folded clothing. The figure of Doctor Jung made its entrance.

Forster swung his gaze to the right until he had managed to bring the sitting-room into view. Jung appeared to be agitated.

It was both fascinating and maddening not to be able to hear what was being said.

Had Pilgrim done something wrong? Why was Jung so clearly angry?

After a moment, the anger—so it seemed—began to melt and a kind of resigned fatalism took its place—a throwing up of hands—a sequence of shrugs—a wiping of the brow and then dejection, Jung's head bowed, his body stilled.

Pilgrim said something.

Jung replied.

Then Jung spoke to Kessler and Kessler bowed in that beastly, cringing Germanic way that Forster could not abide— the resigned subservience of the soldier to his commandant, the burgher to his mayor, the slave to his master. *Stand up and square yourself!* Forster wanted to shout. In fact, he actually spoke the words aloud. "All you have to do is say: *yes!* You don't have to kiss his boots!"

Jung departed.

Forster waited for the sound of a closing door, but of course it never came.

Then Pilgrim returned to the bedroom, threw his hat on the bed and pulled a chair up closer to the windows open to the balcony.

He looked towards the mountains.

His face was a mask of anguish.

Forster lowered the binoculars. *What can have happened?*

What could it be? Had someone else died? Or was it, as too often, that someone had not?

5

Jung had returned, though not contritely, to the fold. He was there to stabilize and solidify his relationship with Emma, not to forget or to forego his affair with Antonia Wolff. The latter was now an undebatable fact and Emma would have to live with it or leave.

She had chosen to stay.

I can make my own life, she had said. And she would, though it would not be the life she had craved and had once thought was in her grasp. She was to have been the undisputed centrepiece of Carl Gustav's domestic life—his wife, his companion, his intellectual equal. And the mother of his children.

She had delighted in their academic arguments, in providing him with research and in entertaining his friends and colleagues at what everyone had called the most stimulating and rewarding dinner parties in the psychiatric community. Freud had sat at their table—Adler, Jones and James. The poet Ezra Pound and the young Thomas Mann, who had only just published *Death in Venice*—and Gustav Mahler, in 1910, who had come to Zürich to conduct his stupendous *Symphony of a Thousand*, with its tribute to Goethe's *Faust*. Carl Gustav, of course, had particularly gloried in this latter visit because of his claimed, if distant relationship to the great German poet, whose words had provided the choral finale of the work.

Even thinking of it now, Emma was elated by the memory of sitting in the grand concert hall wearing her elegant rose-red gown and her seven long strands of pearls. And the tiny figure of Mahler, caught in her opera glasses, stirring up the souls of both the living and the dead—sweeping the whole of existence towards the heavens ...

Oh, what wonderful times Carl Gustav and I have seen and shared and treasured, she thought. *And now ...?* Who could tell. She must share him with Antonia Wolff, which she would—though never without vigilance and sorrow. All to say nothing of the fact that, as always, she must share Carl Gustav with his work.

On the night of Pilgrim's release from the violent ward, Jung had returned to Küsnacht in a state of great agitation. Something had happened which at first he would not discuss. This failure to communicate was now the norm.

Ever since the sinking of the *Titanic* in April, Jung had developed an irritating habit which Emma could hardly bear to watch. Wetting the index finger of his right hand, he would use it to pick up every last crumb of food from his plate, having stated at the outset that *all survivors must be offered rescue.* The cruel white surface of his dinner plate was now the cruel white surface of the North Atlantic—ice floes and all. Little mounds of mashed or riced potato would be all that remained of his meal by the time he was through playing Lifeboat. He never finished off these latter, perhaps because he feared they would freeze his tongue.

Emma was resigned to sitting out this rescue operation. Once, back in April, she had rung the silver bell for Lotte before the de-crumbing had been completed. As Lotte had reached for Jung's plate, he had locked it to the tabletop in an iron grip.

"Leave it," Emma had said. "I will ring again when the Doctor has finished."

Now, she was worried. Not only had Carl Gustav wandered in the dallying sense, he was wandering increasingly in other ways. Lifeboat was not his only game. There were building games with pencil fortresses erected on his library table—virtually hundreds of pencils piled in interlocked squares and towers—great green and yellow *castle keeps* and *outposts in the wilderness*. There was the pebble game—modelled, so Carl Gustav claimed, on the Japanese game of Go—played not with single stones, but miniature piles of them. There was the dungeon game by the garden shed and a graveyard game in the flowerbeds. The minuscule graves were all left open, as if the dead had risen; and the *dungeon* was a three-sided tent made of sticks in which he had placed a footstool, where he would sit for whole Sunday mornings or Saturday afternoons. He called it his *wigwam*, but it was not. It was his dungeon in the dark, with its back to the shed and its sides overhung with the branches of a rowanberry tree.

These games were never discussed, merely developed and practised. It was Emma who had named them.

On the night of June the 10th, dinner consisted entirely of vegetables—cauliflower, mushrooms, stuffed tomatoes and creamed spinach. The tomatoes were an innovation which Emma herself had concocted: *scoop out the centres, replacing them with raisins, wild rice and a sprinkling of crushed peanuts*. Frau Emmenthal had broiled them on a bed of early basil leaves. They were delicious.

Carl Gustav was not impressed. He pushed his food around his plate, feeding from its corners only, staring at it vacantly, looking away to consult some figure in space—or seemingly so—and locating his focus by means of closing his eyes, tilting his head, reopening his eyes and gazing into whatever distance was consequently offered

Suddenly he said: "there will be no Moon tonight."

It was a complete non sequitur.

Emma laid her knife and fork aside and raised her napkin.

"What makes you say so, my darling? The calendar tells us ..."

"I don't care what the calendar tells us. There will be no Moon."

"Yes, dear."

"The Moon is dead. Furtwängler has killed it."

"I see."

Emma was becoming practised in this form of response—the non-committal reply that left all the doors standing open. She knew that Carl Gustav would explain whatever he was proposing and she knew that it would either be madness, pure and simple, or it would lead to some psychological dilemma he had encountered amongst his patients. There had recently been instances when his opening sentence had caused her heart to stop: *no more dogs—they have all departed*; and: *if you could dance with the Devil, which rhythm would you choose?* And: *did you know that Robert Schumann mutilated his own hands in order to improve his extension?*

Two of these openers had proven to be simple introductions to problems either solved or unsolved in the lives of his patients. The line about dancing with the Devil had never been explained. It lay there between them, begging an answer Emma dared not give. *The tango*, she would have said, but Carl Gustav left the table to shut himself up in his study before she could reply.

Tonight, the Moon had died.

Emma waited.

"I went in this morning expecting to spend the day with Mister Pilgrim," Jung began.

"Yes. You said so as you left."

"When I got there, he was not immediately available. And so I went to check on some of the others—Miss Schumann-hands, the Penless Writer, et cetera. And—oh, dear God ..."

All at once Carl Gustav pushed his chair away from the table and sobbed.

Emma stood up.

Wait.

She waited.

Carl Gustav removed his glasses, fumbled for his handkerchief, found it and pressed it to his eyes.

"I'm sorry. I'm sorry," he said. "I can't—I just cannot bear it."

"Oh, my darling ..." Emma went to the far end of the table, pulled out a side chair and sat down facing him on an angle. She took his left arm in her hand and gently held it. "What—what has happened?"

"Blavinskeya ... the Countess ..."

"No. Please don't tell me. Not that lovely, wondrous woman ..."

"Yes."

Jung could not stop crying.

"I'm sorry. I'm sorry," he said again. "I'm sorry. I'm sorry. I'm sorry."

"But my darling—you did everything you could. Everything. It was that maniac Furtwängler. He simply refused to let her go. Oh, God—how very sad. How wrong. How sad."

They sat for a moment in silence.

Lotte entered.

Emma waved her away.

"Yes, ma'am."

Jung had begun to fold his handkerchief—squaring it—squaring it and squaring it again. Emma, at last, removed it from his hands and handed him her own.

Jung then fell to his knees and laid his head in her lap, embracing her waist—the smell of her own cologne rising from his fingers.

"She was my prize," he said. "She was my undeniable proof that all of us cannot conform to all the rules of normalcy. We dragged her here and held her here against her wishes and—yes—I was a part of that—yes, I was part of it, until I understood she did not belong amongst us. Wasn't it—isn't it—wasn't it wonderful! All these other lives that people live and need to live—and yet, we call them *crazy*."

"Some of them—most of them are, Carl Gustav."

"I know that. I know—but she was crazy all the way to sanity. She lived up there in the sky, alive—*alive*—until we anchored her. Dragged her down to *this*—this dreadful place where everyone is mad and nothing works and the world ends every day. I should never have let her go. I should have insisted. She was mine, but Furtwängler claimed her. And the moment I was distracted by Pilgrim—I lost her."

"You must not blame him. Not Mister Pilgrim."

"I don't. I'm only saying—if I hadn't been distracted, this would not have happened."

Yes, Carl Gustav. If only you had not been distracted.

Emma placed one hand on the back of his head.

"Tell me what happened," she said.

"In the night—last night," he told her.

"Yes?"

"In the night, last night, she went onto the upper balcony—you remember—four storeys up—above the portico ..."

"Yes."

"Somehow, Schwester Dora had lost control of her. I don't really know exactly how. It might have been that she went to get a cup of cocoa, something as simple as that. Whatever it was, however long she was gone, it was long enough for the Countess to escape. God knows how she knew her way to the balcony. God knows why or how there was access. The building has been designed to prevent such things, but somebody failed her—left a door open—a window unlocked. God knows."

Jung sat back, but remained on the floor at Emma's feet.

"Go on."

"In her report this morning, Schwester Dora—for whom I feel so sorry—oh, how she loved the Countess! In her report, she told us that Blavinskeya had been restrained by Doctor Furtwängler—drugged and restrained and abused."

"Abused. Good heavens!"

"Not in any physical way, but she was yelled at, according to Schwester Dora—yelled at repeatedly and, in other sessions, submitted to Furtwängler's *whispering campaign*. His god-damned whispering campaign. I've told you about it before—his insidious whispers in the patient's ear while the patient is drugged and asleep: *you do not live on the Moon—you have never lived on the Moon—the Moon does not exist—come down—come down and join the human race ...!* Come down, come down and join the human race. And so ..."

"She jumped."

"She jumped."

Emma reached out and emptied her husband's wine glass.

"How do we know she wasn't reaching for the Moon?" she said. "I watched it myself, last night—and wished I could have reached it." Then she stood up and said: "you must not blame yourself for this, Carl Gustav. It is right for us to grieve, but she herself would not have blamed you. It is the ignorance of incompetents—of men like Josef Furtwängler, who do not belong in psychiatry—who believe only in mediocrity—in commonality and normalcy and God help those who don't or can't conform to it."

She went to the middle of the table, retrieved the carafe and poured them each a full glass of wine.

"Let us drink to the Countess Blavinskeya," she said.

Jung stood up with some effort. His legs had partially gone to sleep.

Watching her husband, Emma thought: *all survivors must be offered rescue.*

She raised her glass.

"To the Moon," she said, "and to its latest resident."

They drank.

They sat.

The Moon rose, resplendent, ivory white and smiling.

In the morning, before he took the ferry to Zürich, Jung retired to the garden and stayed there for some time. Emma watched him from the window, and after his departure, she went to inspect the flower beds in which he had seemed so interested.

One of his graves had been closed and covered with earth. Digging on her knees, Emma discovered the body of a single rose. She kissed it and laid it back in place, after which she scrabbled the soil so Carl Gustav would not be able to tell she had pulled it aside. The rose was pure white and had been named for Anna Pavlova.

6

Since his time in the violent ward, Pilgrim had been forced to take his exercise in the walled garden at the rear of the Clinic, where he walked in the company of other "dangerous" prisoners and their keepers. He always wore his white suit and carried his walking stick—unless it was raining, in which case he carried his umbrella. The great wet heat of the alpine summer had descended and the consequent discomfort caused everybody to move as though walking on sand through water.

"My legs hurt," he complained to Kessler. "Are you sure this is necessary?"

"Yes, sir. It's a rule. Every patient—unless confined—must take an hour's exercise every day. It keeps you regular and it helps the circulation."

"The circulation of what?" Pilgrim asked facetiously. "My spleen?"

They walked in circles—some in circles of eight, others of six and four—most, like Pilgrim with Kessler, alone with their keepers. The walls were made of whitewashed stone and were twelve feet high. Along their tops, broken glass had been sunk in cement so that its jagged edges would dissuade the inmates from thoughts of escape.

"Convicts," Pilgrim told Kessler. "That's what we are, out here in this yard. It might as well be a prison."

Pilgrim thought of Wilde at Reading Gaol and of the notorious circle of prisoners, some in ankle-irons, in whose company Wilde had been forced to walk every day. Embezzlers, rapists, murderers and a multitude of men whose crimes were as petty as theft of clothing from wash lines, loitering with intent to keep warm or to feed themselves from the refuse left at the rear of restaurants and hotels. *Even,* Oscar had mused, *from my own unfinished plate at the Café Royale.*

As for those who populated the yard at the Burghölzli, there was a common theme of violence—but little else that might have put them there. Some were incurable addicts who, suffering the panic and pain of withdrawal, had struck their nurses and keepers. Some were suicidal—one ate glass, another ate stones. Others were guilty of multiple attempts to escape—men and women who variously disguised themselves as corpses or hid themselves in laundry hampers or dressed themselves as doctors or nurses. There was a woman who had forced herself on a male patient, becoming pregnant in the process and now attempting by various means to abort her child.

Just a normal, everyday selection of human foibles and failures, Pilgrim had remarked. *Just another roll-call of waste.*

On the afternoon of Saturday, June 15th, the sun was so appallingly evident that Pilgrim took his umbrella with him into the exercise yard and used it as a parasol.

White suit—black shade, he said to Kessler.

Some of the patients had managed to dissuade their keepers from keeping this rendezvous with good health. Pilgrim had not succeeded. Kessler was adamant.

Pilgrim noted a patient he had not previously seen.

"What is her *crime?*" he asked.

"She has only just arrived," Kessler told him. "Yesterday, from your own London. It is my understanding she kept a brothel."

"She looks it," Pilgrim said tersely.

The woman was over made-up, with violent red hair and kohl-lidded eyes. Her lips were purple, and though she wore a simple enough dress, she kept pulling it down to reveal her breasts. She would burst all at once into song: "*she was poor but she was honest—victim of a rich man's game. First he loved her, then he left her, and she lost her maiden name!*"

At last, her keeper had to remove her from the yard and lead her back inside the building.

"*It's the same the whole world over!*" she bellowed as she went. "*It's the poor wot gets the blame! It's the rich wot gets the gravy—ain't it all a bleedin' shame!*"

Pilgrim was tempted to give the woman a round of applause, but he refrained. She had troubles enough without being accused of soliciting sympathy amongst her fellows in the yard.

The prison yard.

Pilgrim stared bleakly at the towering stone walls.

He thought about the singing madwoman and her brash and blowsy manner. She could not have really kept a brothel. If she had, they would not have admitted her to the Burghölzli. Perhaps an actress. Perhaps a society matron—perhaps even, a great and titled lady. Stranger things had happened.

We are all locked into other people's perceptions of who we are, he thought. *We are none of us free to live our lives unseen.*

He recalled a poem of Wilde's that described a brothel seen from a street in London.

The dead are dancing with the dead, Wilde had written. *The dust is whirling with the dust ...*

Pilgrim said to Kessler: "may we sit down?"

"Of course."

They did so in a corner.

High above them, a peregrine falcon circled in the sky.

Peregrine, the wanderer.

Pilgrim thought of a similar word. *Pèlerin.*

Pilgrim.

Me.

7

Grief and failure have ways of prompting generosity—or what Jung thought of as generosity, though it was more like magnanimity. *I will give Mister Pilgrim Lady Quartermaine's letter*, he had decided as a result of the Countess Blavinskeya's death.

He refused even to think the word *suicide,* because to grant that the woman had died of her own despair would mean admitting that Jung himself was partly responsible for her death. He now saw that he should have fought harder to allow the Countess her Moon fantasies, rather than giving her over to Furtwängler and what Jung perceived as his colleague's *bungling care.*

By this somewhat convoluted route, he reached his decision to allow Pilgrim to view the letter that had been intended for him in the first place. If nothing else was working, Pilgrim might be shocked into revealing the source of his own fantasies and their role in his impulse to end his life. *But I was protecting him*, Jung added in haste. *I was saving him the pain of having to witness his friend's last words. At the time, that was perfectly legitimate.*

Of course it was. Almost as legitimate as your having invited a certain young woman into your life in a moment of what you insisted was personal need *that otherwise threatened to jeopardize all your work because—how was it you put it at the time? You couldn't concentrate? That was it. You couldn't concentrate unless there was sex.*

Oh, be quiet.

I'm only reminding you. The word legitimate *was used. I was only clarifying. Justifying ...*

Vilifying!

Well, if you put it that way, I won't mention it again.

Please don't.

I'm just trying to keep you honest, Carl Gustav. At least with yourself, if not with others. Emma, for instance ...

I refuse to listen. You will drive me mad.

Perhaps that's my intention.

Stop it.

Played any new games lately? There's a new one I think might interest you ...

Leave me alone.

It's called Tombs at Twilight and in it, you find a suitable graveyard, of which there are dozens in Zürich and environs. And there, just at sundown, you go and sit in a mausoleum with the dead. Very stimulating—very invigorating for the mind ...

For God's sake, stop!

Provides all kinds of fascinating imagery and endless food for thought. As well as food for worms, of course, your being in the company of corpses. Think of words such as decay *and* failure. *The possibilities are infinite. Decay. Failure. Loss. I could go on for hours.*

Don't.

Decay. Failure. Loss. Cowardice. Mendacity ... Tombs at Twilight, Carl Gustav. Think about it. I will leave you now. Goodbye.

Jung was seated on the open deck of the ferry when this interior conversation took place. On his lap, the music bag sat unbuckled. Inside, he carried his notebooks, extra pens and the letter from Sybil Quartermaine to Pilgrim, which he now drew out as much as a distraction as for any other reason. Anything—anything to rid himself of the damned Inquisitor and his dark insinuations.

You will drive me mad ... *perhaps that is my intention.*

He withdrew the letter from its envelope and glanced at its pages one by one. What could Lady Quartermaine have meant when she wrote that *what mortals call "death" was not, for us, even a remote possibility?* And who were *the Envoys—the Messagers,* who seemed to presage her death? And also, what and where was *the Grove* in which she had presumably expected there would be some sort of *meeting?* It was all so completely mysterious and yet it appeared that she had believed Pilgrim would understand all such references. To Jung, however, her declarations signified the twinning of Lady Quartermaine's possible madness with that of Pilgrim.

At the Clinic, having put on his white smock, he went at once to the third floor, fully intending to go straight to Pilgrim. On passing Suite 309, however, he noted that the doors stood open and, curious, he went inside.

There, he found Schwester Dora folding and packing all of the Countess Blavinskeya's ballet costumes—wrapping each of the items carefully in tissue paper before depositing it in a cardboard box, many of which were laid out on various tables and chairs and the bed.

"Good morning, Schwester."

"Good morning, Herr Doktor."

Dora, her hands full of tulle, bobbed in his direction. He could see that she had been crying.

"This is all so sad," said Jung, surveying the rooms with their bright windows shining on a whole world of what now were only the mementos of a dead woman who, while alive, had invested each and every one of them with magic.

There was one whole box devoted exclusively to pointe shoes, each pair tied with its own ribbons—white shoes, blue shoes, red shoes, pink shoes.

"I am keeping the pair she died in for myself," Schwester Dora told Jung—and showed him where she had laid them to one side, together with Blavinskeya's cashmere shawl. They were blood-stained. "I am also taking the photograph of Madame as the Queen of the Wilis. It is in a silver frame, embossed with her husband's crest—a two-headed eagle—but I think no one will mind. There is no one left to mind, except her cruel father and her dreadful brother. They can have the costumes—or perhaps her mother, if we could only find her.

She disappeared, as you know, into some other life so as to escape poor Madame's fate."

"Yes. I will see what can be done. It seems a pity to otherwise waste all this beauty."

"The father and the brother were monsters, Herr Doktor. *Are* monsters. You must be aware they have never paid for their crimes."

"Yes—unfortunately, yes, I am aware," said Jung.

"Madame was raped by her brother—repeatedly—when she was only a girl. Did you know that?"

"Yes. Of course I knew it, though I wish I didn't."

"Repeatedly. And then ... after all that, her sad, sad husband was killed by her father and nothing was done. Nothing. The Tsar protected them. They are too high and mighty to be prosecuted. This is not European. This is not Swiss. It is not just. And it drove her mad. It drove her mad—my lovely lady. It drove her mad."

Schwester Dora sat on the bed amidst the boxes and wept. "Oh, what shall I do without her? What shall I do?" she said, and dragged a handkerchief from her pocket. "She had become my whole life."

"We must learn not to become so attached to our patients, Schwester," Jung said. "We will lose them all, one way or another, over time—either when they get well and leave us, or when they die. It is the way of our profession."

"I loved her," Dora said quietly. "I loved her plain and simple."

"Yes," said Jung. "I know you did. And she loved you. She was devoted. She told me this many times."

"Really?"

"Yes. Many, many times," he lied. "Without you, she would have had no happiness at all." This much was true.

"Thank you for telling me that, Herr Doktor. I will have that now to live with."

Jung, not quite knowing what to say next, merely shrugged and made a careless gesture with his hand.

"Why did the father kill Madame's husband? Why? She loved him so much."

"Apparently the husband was unfaithful," Jung said. It had never been an image he particularly relished whenever the subject arose in his sessions with the Countess. The Avenging Father was something of a nightmare figure—not unlike the image of the evil magician in fairy tales, who rose from the dark and always took his victims by surprise.

"I must leave you, Schwester Dora," Jung told her all at once. "Mister Pilgrim is expecting me."

"Yes, sir. Thank you for stopping to speak. I am grateful."

"You are more than welcome. I extend my sympathy for your loss."

"Thank you."

Schwester Dora rose and bobbed once again, and the last Jung saw of her as he turned in the doorway was the reach of her hand as she extended it to the shoes she had claimed for herself. She raised them to her cheek and caressed them the way one might have caressed the hand of a dead child. She sat then in sunlight, surrounded by all that was left of a woman who had perished reaching for the Moon—the dresses she had worn in her now forgotten hours of triumph. And the shoes. And the shoes. And the shoes.

8

On Tuesday, the 18th of June, the homing pigeons were delivered to the Clinic by a man who gave his name as Fowler. There were four of them in a cage and there was also a sack of grain tied with a red ribbon. They were to be taken to Mister Pilgrim, the patient in Suite number 306.

Old Konstantine required Mister Fowler to sign his name in a ledger in which the concierge kept track of all deliveries.

"Pigeons," he remarked. "Most unusual. We've never had pigeons delivered before. Not in my time. Are they to be eaten? Has Mister Pilgrim dietary needs we are unaware of?"

"No, sir," Fowler replied. "They are to be his pets."

"Well, then," said Old Konstantine, "that's a relief for them, no doubt. Dogs we have, cats we have and a cage of finches, but never pigeons."

"They are Mister Pilgrim's favourites."

"Have I seen you before, Mister Fowler? The voice is somehow familiar."

"Perhaps all Englishmen sound alike," said Fowler.

"Still, I am sure I should have remembered such a magnificent moustache. It is probably just the voice that has tricked me."

Fowler gave Old Konstantine a two-franc piece, tipped his hat and departed.

The concierge lifted the cover of the birdcage and was met with pigeon stares. "There, there, there," he said. "We'll get you up there just as fast as we can."

He then rang his bell, which brought a young assistant.

"These are for number 306—Mister Pilgrim."

"Yes, sir."

"Mind you don't drop them," Old Konstantine said. "In spite of their reputation, birdcages cannot fly." It was his little joke.

9

And so my dearest friend, I address you for the last time ... Pilgrim had gone back to the beginning of Sybil Quartermaine's letter and was starting to read it again when he suddenly stood up, went to the desk in the sitting-room and took out paper, pen and envelope.

Sybil, Marchioness of Quartermaine, he wrote.

Goodbye.

He tore this up and started again.

On the balcony, the dance was over and only a few birds remained in the sun—a pair of doves, a trio of pigeons.

Pilgrim sat at the desk and wrote.

18th June, 1912

Dear Sybil,

I am in a kind of purgatory. As I was certain, I am permitted neither to live nor to die. I am caught in this—I think they call it a "madhouse"—and would be anywhere but here. Now they have me walking in a walled-in yard. I don't know why, though I suspect I must have misbehaved in some way. I broke some wax recordings, as I recall. I also broke some instruments. Musical instruments—a 'cello—perhaps a violin. Is this a bad thing, given that music solves nothing—saves no sanity—prevents no violence on its own? Looking back, I am sorry I was ever the advocate of any form of art— but music is the worst of them—roiling and boiling—overly emotionalized on the one hand, overly intellectualized on the other. Bach and Mozart indeed! Bach inevitably makes me think of fish in a barrel! Round and round and round they go and nothing ever happens. Nothing! Tum-de-dum-dum. Tum-de-dum-dum and that's all! Tum-de-dum-de-bloody-dum-dum! As for Mozart, his emotions did not mature beyond the age of twelve. He never even achieved adolescence, let alone puberty. His music merely combines a popular talent for slapstick and a commercial talent for tears. No—not tears. For sobs. Beethoven—pompous; Chopin—sickly sweet and given to tantrums—tum-de-dum-dum-bang! And Wagner—a self-centred bore. And this young Turk Stravinsky— the name says it all: discordant, rude and blows his music through his nose!

There.

Shall I go on?

Literature. Will it put an end to war? War and Peace *itself is nothing better than enticement to create new battlefields. The Russians are all such blundering fools, their only ally in defeating Napoleon was winter. Will someone attempt to repeat the exercise? Of course they will—the dreadful book is an open invitation. Tolstoy himself was a soldier at Sevastopol and gloried in it—then he pretends to hate it—after which he ends his life as a mad proponent of world peace, for God's sake, while he drives his wife away from his death bed. And I am crazy? Me?*

Yes. So they tell me.

Someone knocked at the door.

Pilgrim set aside his pen.

Kessler came out from the bedroom, where he had been cleaning Pilgrim's boots, and opened the way to the vestibule. Pilgrim could barely hear the voice that greeted him. *Cage ... pigeons ... grain ... Fowler ...*

When the orderly returned, he carried the birds. The young assistant, who was Italian-Swiss, followed with the beribboned sack of grain.

"Just here?"

"Just there. And thank you."

"Is money required?" Pilgrim asked.

"No, sir. The young man works for wages."

The Italian lad retreated. A door closed—then another.

Pilgrim had risen to inspect the sack of grain.

"I don't understand," he said. "Am I to feed on this?"

"I think not, sir. I suspect it is for the birds in this cage."

"Birds?" said Pilgrim.

"Birds," said Kessler. "As if we needed *birds*." Having said this, he retreated to the bedroom and his boot-blacking.

Pilgrim undid the ribbon and rummaged in the sack to see what sort of grain it was. Corn, millet, rye and oats. And a note.

Pilgrim tore it open and read:

To a fellow fancier:
Sir:
These are homing pigeons and can be the bearers of messages. You will see my present likeness in the enclosed photographs. I trust you will approve.

It has been some time since we met and it has occurred to me you might wish to abandon your current quarters. If this is true, some instruction would be useful. I know nothing of your surroundings. A diagram would be helpful—a map or some such description.

A motor car is available.

I am nearby at the Hôtel Baur au Lac.

I shall await communication.

I am watching.

Every day, I can see you.

Faithfully yours,
H. Fowler

Besides the photographs there was a small velvet pouch which contained several metal capsules with clips, appropriate for attaching to the pigeons' legs.

Pilgrim placed the letter, the velvet pouch and the photographs in his pocket and drew the cover from the cage.

It seemed as if the pigeons knew him. They began at once to

croon and to display their feathers. Greys—bricks—purples—whites—the combinations of colours on every bird were perfectly balanced and entrancing.

"Bring them into the light," Pilgrim said to Kessler. "Take them into the light."

Kessler, boot in hand, came and carried the cage into the bedroom. Pilgrim lingered long enough in the sitting-room to fold his letter and place it in the desk, where he turned and pocketed the key.

He then drew the photographs from their envelope and glanced at them one by one. Right side—left side—full face. Moustache—bowler hat—neat, trim figure, standing somewhere in the sunlight.

H. Fowler.

Undoubtedly, someone he knew.

But equally, someone he did not—or had forgotten.

H.

That could be Howard, Henry, Herbert or Harry.

A fowler is one who hunts birds, sells birds, keeps birds ...

An image rose in Pilgrim's mind of a dovecote.

We used to keep birds—someone and I together—in a garden somewhere ...

Cheyne Walk.

Pilgrim placed his fingers over the moustache in the full-faced view of Fowler.

What were their names—those people at Cheyne Walk?

There was a woman—Mrs Something—and a boy named Fred. Not Fred—no. Alfred. *Alfred.*

Pilgrim looked out the window towards the mountains.

Mountains.

Perhaps the woman's name was Matterhorn.

No. Not Matterhorn. Matter-something-else.

Matheson.

Mrs Matheson. Alfred. And a dog named Aggie. Agga. Agamemnon!

Yes. Yes. Yes. And a man called Fowler.

Pilgrim stood up and went to the window to achieve more light.

Howard Harry Henry Herbert Fowler.

"Henry?" he said aloud.

He gazed again at the photograph, masking the man's moustache.

He squinted.

"Forster," he said.

Everything fell into place. Somewhere out there, a man was waiting to help him. Henry Forster, who would come and rescue him. There would be an end to prison.

No more prisons—ever.

He placed the photographs in his pocket.

10

At seven-thirty on the morning of Wednesday, June 19, Emma came and stood in the bedroom doorway.

"Carl Gustav?"

He turned to her out of sleep.

She came and hovered beside his bed.

"Let go of your pillows," she said—and reached for his hands. "You have already ruined your pyjamas. You have torn away your buttons. Here—you must allow me ..."

She reached for his fingers and forced them open. "This is not the *Titanic*," she told him. "You are not drowning. Wake up."

Not only were his hands, arms and shoulders rigid, but also his legs and toes.

"I can't breathe," he said.

"You are breathing. All is well."

"What happened?"

"How am I to know? I am no longer your comrade. You must have dreamt. You cried aloud."

Jung sat up. He looked at his wife.

"Are you going to leave me?" he said all at once, not knowing it was there to be said.

"Never, Carl Gustav," said Emma. "I am bound to you for life. But you, I have now discovered, live only for your own life and in no way for mine."

She sat at the foot of the bed and drew her robe about her. She had been sleeping in the guest room—pleasant enough, but usually reserved for her mother's visits. Frau Rauschenbach was overly fond of flowers and the wallpaper, drapes and bedspread were like indoor gardens, ablaze with roses, irises and peonies. This could be tiring on the eyes, but Emma kept a minimum of lamps alight and the effect was not so overwhelming.

"I have prayed for your death," she told Jung in a grey voice. "I thought you should know. I have prayed for your death and dreamt of a life you will never know: the life of a loving parent and a caring companion. I simply thought you should know. I see that you are in trouble. I watch and listen to you. I want to help, but you won't let me. So be it. I only thought you should know. I love you still, but I no longer like you. Do what you will, I shall watch over you—but come what may, there will be no more love. Take your illness to your patients. Apply it there. Let it spread. I no longer care. You have lost your dancer. Blavinskeya is dead. Your doing, Carl Gustav. Yours. I retract what I said before. I have been thinking—and now I realize that she was abandoned by Carl Gustav Jung precisely as I was abandoned—and his children—because he had interests elsewhere."

"Emma ..."

"No, Carl Gustav. No. Go your own way. The rest of us will survive without you."

Emma rose and left the room.

Jung fell back against the pillows.

Seven forty-five. Birdsong. Blowing curtains.

A new day. A new life. But was it a life he wanted?

Jung arrived at Suite 306 at 10 a.m. as promised.

"Well, and how are we this morning?" he asked.

"Please," Pilgrim said, "do not call me *we*."

"It's only a figure of speech." Jung smiled.

"It may well be," Pilgrim said testily, "but *I* am not a figure of speech. My name is Pilgrim."

"I beg your pardon."

"It's bad enough that Kessler refers to *we* and to *us* with sickening regularity, but you of all people should know better. Kessler at least has the excuse of stupidity. You do not."

"I am sorry."

"I will believe you when you address me by name."

"Mister Pilgrim," Jung said, and gave a curt bow.

They were both standing.

"Will you sit down?" Pilgrim said, and seated himself. He was wearing a dark suit, neither black nor blue but a woven combination of the two. His cravat was yellow. There was also a matching yellow handkerchief in his breast pocket, looking somewhat like a mangled flower. Pilgrim delighted in such things—in flaunting his distaste of good taste while managing never to be less than impeccable. *The art of presenting oneself*, he had once told Sybil, *lies in creating an immediate shock which is countered by a slow retreat into custom. People never quite recover from my cravats, but they will never find the equal of my tailor. To be memorable is all, when it comes to dress.*

Jung, in his tweeds and white smock, seemed perversely sombre by contrast. And the fact that he had slept so badly had left him looking grey and worn. Nonetheless, he attempted to raise some energy and give the appearance at least of being up to the session that lay before them.

"Kessler tells me you have received a gift of pigeons."

"That is correct."

"May I ask from whom?"

"From a fowler."

"I'm afraid you have struck a word I do not know. A *fowler?*"

"A fowler hunts, sells or keeps birds."

"I see. So this would be an anonymous fellow?"

"Yes. Anonymous. Just a fowler."

"Can you explain why he might have sent them?"

"No. Perhaps he had heard of my predicament."

"Which is?"

"My imprisonment. After all, even when caged, birds are a symbol of freedom."

"And how do you suppose this anonymous fowler person might have heard of your predicament, Mister Pilgrim?"

"It is obvious. I am no longer in the world."

Jung said: "you do not consider this the world?"

"Do you?"

"Of course. It is where I spend more than half my life."

"And the other half? Where?"

"At home."

"I think what you mean is *at large*, Doctor. If this is where you spend more than half your life, please remember it is where I spend the whole of mine."

"And you resent that, of course."

"I won't even comment."

"Why do you speak of imprisonment?"

"Am I free to go?"

"When you are well, yes. Of course."

"And when will I be well? When *I* say so—or when *you* say so?"

"When I say so—which is as it should be. I am a better judge of your mental health than you are at this moment."

"What on earth is *mental health?* It sounds like a disease."

Jung laughed. "I suppose, in the case of some people, it is," he said.

"Who, for instance?"

"People whose lives are excessively dull because they have no imagination."

"And?"

"And what?" Jung asked.

"And when you speak of my *mental health*, whose mental health will you match it with? These people who lead excessively dull lives? I trust not."

"I will match it with your own potential to be fulfilled."

"I have no potential to be fulfilled—and could not care less. Except in one instance. I would be happy if I could die."

"In that case, you are not well."

Pilgrim looked away.

"Are you never weary, Doctor?" he said. "Are you never tired?"

"I have my moments. Of course."

"I have no *moments*. It is constant. I have tried to indicate to you by every means at my disposal that I have lived forever—and you don't—you will not believe me. That in itself is over-whelmingly weary-making ..."

Jung stood up and went to look from the windows.

"Why," he said, "when you have such talents and such potential for greatness, do you not want to live?"

"I have no potential for any such thing."

"You do, you know."

"Once, maybe. Not now. Not any longer. And I do not care for it. My only ambition is death."

"And you say you have lived forever."

"I have."

"But how can you possibly believe such a thing?"

"It is not a question of believing. It is a question of knowing."

Jung sighed. "Then tell me this," he said, and turned back to Pilgrim. "If your immortality has taken the form of living many different lives—which is what you have said on previous occasions—why do you think that ending *this* life will end the whole parade of other lives? Will you not simply reappear as someone else? Or is it that you wish only to end *this* life?"

Pilgrim's gaze was fixed on his hands. At first, he said nothing. Then: "for some time, all I have been able to do is to hope. To hope and to pray that one death might be the final death. The absolute. The end. Now, I have more than hope. I have reason to believe that a true ending may be possible."

"What reason?"

Pilgrim looked up at Jung. "I am sure you would not have given me Sybil's letter if you, yourself, had not read it. And if you have read it, you will know that she has been recalled."

"Recalled?"

"Summoned. Called back. The Envoys came to deliver the message. Her mission is over."

"I don't understand."

"Her mission was to be my witness. My protector. My link

with the Others. And if there is no longer a need for any of these roles, then the obvious conclusion is that I, too, may soon be recalled."

Jung decided to take another tack.

"Were you in love with Lady Quartermaine?"

"In a way, yes. Though it wasn't physical. She was my equal in so many ways, our relationship was inevitable."

"Can you explain what you mean by that?"

"I doubt it."

"Will you try?"

"I shall do my best."

Pilgrim adjusted his position in the chair.

"In a sense," he said, "she was my sister. She was the first human being I knew—in fact, the first human being I met in this incarnation, though I disapprove of the word *incarnation*. Some are reborn. Others, such as myself, merely exchange one life for another. We basically remain the same person and our lives go on forever. It is—it has always been a continuous process. One wakes—one sleeps—one wakes again. One day, one wakes as a blind old man, the next as a Spanish shepherd, the next as an English schoolboy. Which is why one wishes to die and put an end to it all. *Our birth is but a sleep*, Doctor Jung, *a sleep and a forgetting: the soul that rises with us, our life's star, hath had elsewhere its setting; and cometh from afar* ... I say this kindness of Mister Wordsworth, who had it right. He also said: *the world is too much with us; late and soon*—and again he had it right. The world has been too much with me. And I have been too much with the world."

Jung had by no means failed to take note of the reference to *a Spanish shepherd*. And yet, Manolo had never been mentioned between them, Jung having maintained his silence about the journals.

"You speak of a Spanish shepherd and an old blind man. Can you tell me who these people are—or were?"

"The old blind man you will know. His name—my name—

was Tiresias. The shepherd? I barely remember him, but I do remember his name. Manolo."

Jung's mind contracted with numbing apprehension. He was forced to turn away.

"You have a problem, Doctor Jung?" Pilgrim said, after a moment.

Jung closed his eyes. Tiresias had been sentenced by the gods to live forever. And, like Cassandra, he had been a seer—but blind.

A seer—but blind.

As if reading Jung's mind, Pilgrim said: "the priestesses at Delphi were blinded by smoke. It was deliberate. They sat on pans above the fire below and offered up the voices of the gods, most especially, Apollo. Cassandra, on the other hand, was sighted, and as a consequence, no one trusted her pronouncements. She was condemned never to be believed, even though time and time again, she was proved to be right. I know that. She was my friend."

No, Jung thought. *This cannot be. It's a story. An intricate, bedeviled, clever story.* Dementia.

"And you," he said, "were you condemned never to be believed?"

Pilgrim's answer was both casual and earnest—as if they were engaged in a perfectly ordinary conversation. "I was condemned several times. It is all too easy to displease the Others. To be summoned into their presence. They condemned me to live forever because in trying not to offend one by telling the truth, I offended another. Consequently, I have had to suffer an eternity of disbelief. The same disbelief you now so evidently feel about my history—the disbelief that has always met my pronouncements. I was equally condemned to experience women's lives as well as men's—simply because—as a young man of eighteen—by chance I happened to witness the mating of the Sacred Serpents in the Sacred Grove—and this was against all the rules set down for mortals by the gods. It was a form of sacrilege."

Jung wondered if he should be taking notes. *The Sacred Grove.*
Was that what Lady Quartermaine had meant in her letter, in
referring to *the Grove*? Both of them, quite mad ...

Pilgrim seemed lost in time. "The war," he said. "The first of
all the wars I have seen. It is with me, still." He smiled as he
closed his eyes. "Throughout the Greek siege of Troy, we
Trojans had a reputation for decadence. While parties of aristo-
crats gathered on the battlements to watch the killing, tea would
be served by slaves in white jackets. Tea, and buttered biscuits
filled with raisins and honey. Tea and what we now call cock-
tails—distilled liquors and many kinds of wine—poured from
silvered pitchers into Venetian goblets and Chinese porcelain
cups."

Jung stared at him, wordless—then looked away.

Pilgrim continued: "and though we never gathered at the
height of battle, we met on the ramparts beneath our parasols
when amusing skirmishes were taking place and always when
two heroes were to meet in combat, man to man—or, as some
would have it, god to god. This is how I saw the death of
Hector. It rained, you know, when he died. A torrent. Achilles
tied him by his heels to the rear of a chariot and drove away with
Hector's arms flung back and his long black hair spread out
behind him in the mud ... And we never saw him again. I
remember that as if it had been yesterday."

Jung then regarded Pilgrim briefly, Pilgrim now with his head
turned towards the sunlit bedroom and the cage of birds.

Dark suit. Yellow tie. Impeccable. Beautiful long-fingered
hands—buffed nails, well manicured. Square knees, thin ankles,
spare but shapely thighs. Wide shoulders (*the better for supporting wings*, Kessler would have said), a long neck, a strong chin, a
gaunt, chiselled face with prominent nose and cheekbones, wide
forehead and brooding eyes. His hair, still falling like a snow-
drift across his brow, was whiter now than it had been in April
when he had arrived. Understandable. Entirely.

"I once had black teeth," Pilgrim said reflectively, still

watching the birdcage. "Stained glass, you know. The lead. Poisons a person. Everything turns black—your teeth, your nails, your skin—and then you die."

"But you cannot die," Jung said, his voice barely more than a whisper.

"I cannot—but others did."

"What have you to do with stained glass?"

"Chartres. You have been there?"

"No. My wife has seen it, but I have not."

"Your wife is fortunate. You are a fool. It is the greatest wonder of the western world." Pilgrim gave a smile. They were still not looking at one another. "I was a shaper there. I took the glass that others had cut and folded it in lead. Many of us worked together. It was amongst the more exhilarating things I did—over time."

"And when might this have been?"

"In what you call the eleventh century."

"I'm not sure I know what you mean by *what I call the eleventh century.*"

"I predate the Christian calendar, Doctor Jung. In both its foolish forms."

"Foolish?"

"Was the birth of Jesus Christ the be-all and end-all of time?"

"Some would say so."

"Some are madmen," Pilgrim said, turning to Jung with a fixed stare. "And some are not."

"You are extremely adamant today, Mister Pilgrim."

"I have good reason. I shall be leaving you soon."

"I think not."

"We shall see."

"Go back to stained glass. What proof have you that you were there at Chartres and took part in its creation?" Jung prepared to write in his notebook.

"I cut my initials into one of the panes. It was blue, in the window now known as *Notre Dame de la Belle Verrière.*"

"Our Lady of the Beautiful Glass."

"The Virgin. And the Christ Child in her lap."

"Yes. Of course."

"*Yes. Of course,*" Pilgrim mimicked Jung's accented delivery. "*Yes. Of course,* Herr Doktor Dimwit. Who else could it be? I'm sure you pray to her every day. Or do you have some other patron saint?"

"I have no saints."

"One is tempted to say that you did have, once, but they deserted you. In time, the gods desert us all. They depart—and the skies are empty."

Jung sat down on the windowsill.

"What might your initials have been, Mister Pilgrim, at that time?" His pen was poised.

"*S.l.J.* Simon le Jeune. I was twenty-two. My father was one of the greatest glass-cutters in France. And a magician with colour. Nobody—to this day—*nobody* knows how he achieved the blue in that window. It is matchless."

Doubtless, the names were true. Simon—and his son, his namesake. Jung was thinking: *he's an art historian. Of course he knows these things. His whole life has been devoted to scholarship—everything he says and knows has been impeccably researched—impeccably imagined.*

Then he thought: *he doesn't seem to realize I've had access to his journals—in spite of that unfortunate accident with La Gioconda's letter. Strange that he has never even mentioned her. I wonder ...*

Aloud, Jung asked: "All these lives, Mister Pilgrim. By what means do you—in one lifetime—come to know about your past lifetimes?"

"The memories come in exactly the same way as the prophecies—in dreams. Dreams that begin around the age of eighteen, with each new personage. And gradually, the dreams become memories ..."

"Surely, you can't remember everything about every life. Or can you?"

"Of course not—no more than you can remember everything about your own life. But I remember who I've been just as you or anyone else remembers who you've known over time. And gradually, the memories of past lives begin to cloud the early years of the present life. As it happens, I remember very little about the boy I was—by which I mean the boy, Pilgrim."

Jung decided to take yet another tack.

"This quest for immortality," he said. "What prompted you to begin it?"

Pilgrim stared at Jung, incredulous.

"Nothing *prompted* me," he said. "DO YOU NEVER LISTEN!"

Pilgrim stood up, and stared around the room, as if in search of something.

"No wonder we are all mad here," he said. "No wonder we are all insane. Our doctors refuse to hear us!"

Jung said nothing.

Pilgrim went into the bathroom and returned with a glass of water. He raised it to his lips, tilted his head back and drained the glass dry, after which he flung it to the floor.

Jung did not move.

Pilgrim said: "you *saw* me drink that water. You saw me. But the glass which contained it is shattered. YES? The truth—my story—is the water. It is in me. The broken glass is your reaction to it. *Also sprach Zarathustra!*"

Pilgrim sat back down in his chair and wiped his lips with the yellow handkerchief, folding it into a ball in his hand.

Finally, Jung said: "tell me who Lady Quartermaine was."

It was such an absolute non sequitur, Pilgrim paused. Then he said: "all you have to do is think of her name."

"Sybil?"

"Sybil."

"A Sybil, Herr Doktor Blockhead, is an oracle—as at Delphi. She was appointed by Apollo to speak in his voice. Some called them *priestesses*—others, *sayers*. In modern times, we call them *mediums*."

"I know all this," Jung said. "I merely wanted to know it was not a coincidental choice of name."

"Not a coincidental choice. Never. It was given her by the gods. The same gods, doubtless, who called her home."

"I see."

Quite mad.

They sat then, silent—Jung on the windowsill, Pilgrim in his chair, his yellow handkerchief still clutched in his hand.

"She is dead, Mister Pilgrim. She was human and she died."

"So you say."

"So I say." And then: "like you, had she lived forever?" Jung's voice was almost without intonation. He spoke as a priest might have spoken to a penitent—matter-of-factly and without emotion.

Pilgrim picked at the wicker arm of his chair.

"Not for so long," he said.

"And her death? You see meaning in the fact that she has died?"

Pilgrim leaned forward.

"I pray," he said, "that it means my days are finally numbered. Perhaps it is true that, at long last, the gods are deserting us and their final gift is death."

Jung blinked. He looked away.

The man's pain was real enough. In fact, it was unbearable.

Jung found himself thinking: *to have waited so long ...*

Then he frowned, and closed his notebook.

He stood up.

"Are you leaving?" Pilgrim asked.

"Yes."

"I cannot say I'm sorry."

Jung walked to the door, pausing to collect the music bag and place his notebook inside it.

"Mister Pilgrim," he said, "I must tell you that I wish with all my heart I could help you. But—at the moment—I cannot."

Pilgrim said nothing.

With his hand on the doorknob, Jung turned back and looked at the figure sitting in the sunlight.

"I had a dream last night," he said. "Not a dream—a nightmare. I dreamt the whole world was on fire and that no one could prevent the flames from spreading ..."

Pilgrim stared at the hand that held his handkerchief. *And if you understood the prophetic nature of your dream,* he thought, *nobody would believe you, either ...*

Jung said: "it was more horrifying than I can say, and I thought it would never end. It was the inferno itself. But I did find a way to make it stop."

"Oh?" said Pilgrim, placing the handkerchief in his pocket. "And how was that?"

"I woke up," said Jung. "Which is what I am hoping you will do."

When Jung had gone, Pilgrim sat motionless.

I am an animal, he thought. *I am an animal without hunters. I have no predators. If only someone would come with a gun. If only some beast not yet named would emerge from the forest and devour me. If only the gods who continue to protect me would turn away and focus on someone—anyone—else. If only the rivers would rise to drown me or the mountains fall to bury me. If only life were not so tenacious. If only life would let go.*

11

Early in the evening of the 19th of June, Pilgrim sent his second message to Forster.

His first message had read: HAVE RECEIVED NEWS YOU ARE PREPARING EVACUATION OF PRESENT SITE. GET MAPS: SWITZ., FRANCE. ALSO £500 TO ZÜR. BANK. P.

His second message read: DAILY EXERCISE WALLED GARDEN REAR CLINIC. BEWARE GLASS. SUGGEST ROPE LADDER WITH PADDING. WILL ADVISE DATE, HOUR NEXT TWO DAYS. EXTRA FUEL FOR M'CAR. LONG JOURNEY. P.

There were two pigeons left in the cage.

The following day, Thursday, the 20th of June, Pilgrim—wearing his white suit and carrying his black shade—it was extremely hot—descended by elevator to the ground level and allowed himself to be escorted to the "prison yard."

Kessler was prattling on about angels.

"Have you heard of the nine levels of celestial hierarchy, Mister Pilgrim? Most intriguing. There are seraphim, cherubim, thrones, dominations, principalities, powers, virtues, archangels and angels. It is my belief that you have the power to be of the ninth order. I saw your wings when you arrived."

"You did, did you."

"Yes, sir."

"And where might my wings be now?"

"I cannot answer that. In my mind, I suppose. I know they weren't real—but the thing is, they seemed real, and I wanted them to be real. Haven't you ever wanted something to be real that wasn't—even when you knew it couldn't be made real? Like beautiful places in dreams—or angels ..."

"Yes. I have wanted much that is not real to be real. Much."

"There you are, then. That's what I say."

Pilgrim smiled. Kessler's simplicity was charming.

In the yard there were many others, some of whom Pilgrim recognized, many of whom he did not. The man who thought he was a dog was there and the man who claimed he had eaten his children. Also, the woman who had tried to kill her keeper and was now so heavily sedated she would barely move. And the woman who looked as if she had run an English brothel.

There were two others who caught Pilgrim's attention—neither of whom he had seen before. One was a man who was collecting a pile of sand on a tabletop and was busily counting the number of grains. "*Neun-tausend-zwei-und-fünfzig,*" he muttered, "*neun-tausend-drei-und-fünfzig ...*" The pile seemed barely diminished.

The other stranger was a woman who had the appearance of a child actress. She was perhaps not quite five feet tall, with loosely brushed hair tied with a large pink bow. She wore a dress that might have been suitable for a twelve-year-old girl, white stockings and a pair of bright red slippers. She was in the charge of Schwester Dora, who was still very much in mourning for the Countess Blavinskeya. Pilgrim noted the black ribbon pinned to the breast of her uniform. They made, these two, a rather despondent pair as they walked arm in arm beneath the shade of a Japanese paper parasol.

What a curious collection we are, Pilgrim thought as he took up his place in the parade. *Dogs, infanticides, would-be murderers, sand obsessives, brothel owners and child-pretenders. All to say nothing of angels, if Kessler had his way.*

Wings would certainly be welcome, he thought. *I could play Icarus and, knowing better, not fly too close to the sun. At least it would get me out of here.*

Freedom.

Whatever that meant. The other side of the wall—a wilderness of unknown possibilities.

This was at two o'clock in the afternoon.

At two-thirty, Doctors Bleuler, Furtwängler, Menken, Raddi and Jung came and stood in an open window overlooking the yard.

This visit was prior to one of their regular meetings in the Director's office, where Bleuler received the others' reports on their progress with patients and assessed them.

Seeing the figures at the window, Pilgrim was made nervous. Pray God none of them—nor anyone—should come to a window during his escape attempt. The wall was all too visible from such a vantage point—possibly even its other side.

Bleuler said: "we have so many in the yard. Are we falling behind?"

Jung looked away. He thought, *the last thing any of us needs is a disparaging remark like that. Not now. Not ever. How can a man of such stature be so insensitive? WE'RE TRYING!* he wanted to yell.

Furtwängler, ever ready to explain, told Doctor Bleuler that he thought the reason there were so many patients in the *yard of confinement*, as he called it, was that too many doctors were interfering in one another's work. He mentioned no names.

"A patient is a patient," Furtwängler said, "and each patient has his own doctor—one and one only. But of late, there has been *interference* ..." giving the word a curious twist— "... and as a result, we have not only more patients in the yard of confinement, but a dead patient, also."

"I presume you mean the Countess Blavinskeya," said Bleuler.

"I do," said Furtwängler. "Unless, of course, we have recently lost another and I am unaware of it."

No one spoke.

Then Jung said: "I am quite prepared to withdraw if Doctor Furtwängler persists in his charges ..."

Furtwängler said: "no names were mentioned, Carl Gustav. Not one name."

Toady, Jung thought. *Courtier. Arse-kisser.*

Aloud, he said: "it was I who failed the Countess Blavinskeya. I failed her because I failed to rescue her in time from Josef Furtwängler's machinations." He turned to Furtwängler, who had himself turned pale, and said directly: "you killed her. You killed her spirit and her will to live. You destroyed her capacity for survival. *And*," he was now blazing to such a degree that some of the patients in the yard halted their parade and turned to look up at the window, "*and—four of those people down there are yours!*"

There was a brief silence and then Bleuler said: "is this true?"

"Yes, sir," said Raddi, who was in charge of the violent ward. "Unfortunately, it is so."

"Which patients might they be?" Bleuler asked coolly.

Doctor Raddi named "the infanticide," "the would-be murderer," "the brothel owner" and the "sandman."

Bleuler nodded and then said: "and the rest?"

"The man-who-has-lived-forever is mine," Jung confessed.

And Archie Menken said: "the woman-who-thinks-she's-a-child is mine."

Bleuler said: "and why have you failed them—these last two? How have you failed them?"

Archie looked at Jung and said: "I think we have a common problem. Neither of these patients seems to have any concept of the real world. It is not a place they avoid, as is true with the others, but a place they do not acknowledge."

"Would you agree with that, Doctor Jung?" Bleuler asked.

"Yes, sir."

"And you, Doctor Furtwängler?" Bleuler continued. "The infanticide, the would-be killer, the brothel owner and the sandman—have they any concept of reality?"

Furtwängler gave one of his charming smiles.

"But of course," he said. "They live in it."

Bleuler looked down again into the yard.

The parade was in progress. Faces were more or less obscured by the steep angle.

If there was a treadmill, Jung was thinking, *they could be drawing water from a well or turning millet into flour ...*

"Let us go in," Bleuler said.

And they went.

The "child actress" stumbled and fell. She screamed.

Her knees were grazed and her stockings were torn.

Schwester Dora lifted her up and carried her to a chair where no sooner was the woman seated than the brothel owner came to comfort her.

"Ooh!" she said. "What a pretty child! And can you sing?"

The child actress, sobbing, nonetheless managed—in that way that children have of weeping while dry-eyed—to choke out an answer.

"I can sing *Mary Had a Little Lamb.*"

"Then *let's,*" said the brothel owner, and began. *"Mary had a little lamb ...* Come on, luv, you sing, too! *Its fleece was white as snow ..."*

The child finally began to sing.

"That's it! Keep going .... *And everywhere that Mary went, the lamb was sure to go ..."*

The others paused to listen. The brothel owner's voice was almost a baritone, but the child's voice was sweet and delicate. They finished Mary and moved on to Bo-peep.

"Little Bo-peep has lost her sheep, And doesn't know where to find them ..."

Pilgrim, feeling *in extremis,* searched the walls.

One must get out of here. One must ...

But if he could promote the sort of diversion offered by the singing, he could be gone in seconds and no one the wiser.

12

That evening, Jung invited Emma to dine with him at the Hôtel Baur au Lac.

"One does not *invite* one's wife," she told him. "One *takes* one's wife."

"In that case, I shall take you."

Jung wore a red bowtie. Emma wore a blue dress. *Blue*, she reminded herself, *is the colour of hope.*

She could not avoid speculating about why Carl Gustav might have chosen this particular evening to eat away from home. And with her. Was it the anniversary of some event—their meeting? Their marriage? The death of a parent? Of course not. She knew all these by heart. They had been married now for more than nine years and already the talisman dates were burned into memory. *How romantic we once were*, she thought, with a rueful smile. *We were married on Saint Valentine's Day in 1903 and I carried paper hearts in my bouquet ...*

Carl Gustav must have something to say he did not wish to say in front of Lotte, or with Frau Emmenthal listening at the kitchen door. Or perhaps there was a surprise—something exciting—a journey or a visit—perhaps a proposal that they try again for another child—or the news that his affair with Antonia Wolff had come to an end. *She is moving to America ... Oh! Wouldn't that be splendid!* China, of course, would be better—but America would do. As long as there could be an ocean or a continent between them.

But none of these things was the answer. It was, as Emma would later realize, simply one more step towards the disaster of Carl Gustav's breakdown.

They drove to Zürich in the motor car. There was a moon.

Halfway there, Jung brought the Fiat to a stop and insisted that they get out and stand by the grass at the side of the road. Then he went to the boot of the car and returned with two glasses and a bottle of chilled champagne.

When the champagne was opened and poured, Jung placed the bottle on the ground, secured between his feet. Emma was calm, but wondered what on earth was happening. She wore an evening wrap and carefully adjusted it before Carl Gustav handed her a filled glass. She felt cold, though in fact the evening was still and warm. Crickets chirped and frogs called out their locations. *I am here!* they sang. *I am here! Where are you?*

"We have come to celebrate the ascent of a goddess," Jung said—and raised his glass to the moon. "To the Countess Tatiana Sergeyevna Blavinskeya," he said. "May the trumpets have sounded and the violins have sustained her flight."

They drank.

Before they returned to the car, Jung withdrew a previously written label from his inner pocket and hung it around the neck of the champagne bottle, which had been recorked. Setting the bottle carefully on the verge of the road where it would be certain to be seen, he told Emma that he had written: *for those who stop here this night, it is requested that you pause and toast the Moon.*

When they returned at midnight, the bottle was empty.

In the restaurant, they sat at the very same table where Jung had sat on two occasions with Lady Quartermaine. Their conversation was seemingly desultory. Nothing of apparent importance was discussed. They talked of patients past and present. They spoke of sandcastles, graves and caves. Emma spoke of Pilgrim's journals—of having discovered passages regarding the great cathedral at Chartres, of an episode at Jerusalem in the fourth century B.C. and of Prussian intrigues in the court of Frederick the Great.

Jung was clearly distracted.

He kept thinking of Lady Quartermaine, of Blavinskeya, of Pilgrim—of anyone but the woman he was with. *She sat there, I sat here; he said this and I said that ...*

A man with an elaborate moustache was watching them from a corner table.

They ate a dinner of beef, roast potatoes and artichokes. Emma was radiant. Jung was not. He faded—red tie and all.

At eleven-thirty, they rose to leave.

The man with the elaborate moustache raised his glass at their backs.

"Your loss," he said aloud.

Stepping into the night air, Emma pulled her wrap about her. *We are not in the world,* she was thinking. *We are not really here. This is nowhere. I am lost. And Carl Gustav? He is somewhere in the fog, leading us on.*

13

On Friday morning, June 21st, Forster received the third pigeon with the following message: TOMORROW. 2 P.M. SONGS. WAIT FOR "NOW!" THEN ROPE LADDER OVER THE WALL. P.

On Saturday, at 1:30 p.m., Pilgrim and Kessler appeared in the "prison yard"—Pilgrim seemingly more bulky than on previous days. The truth was, he was wearing his pyjamas under his suit. In his pockets, he carried his identification, cheque book, diary and the bulk of his favoured handkerchiefs. Each of the latter had been flavoured with *Blenheim Bouquet* cologne, whose bottle he knew he would have to leave behind. He had also removed the photograph of Sybil Quartermaine from its silver frame and placed it in his vest pocket between the folds of one of the scented handkerchiefs. The suit he wore was the dark one, woven of black and blue threads. *After all*, he thought, *I am making for the night.*

There was not a cloud in the sky. Pilgrim carried the black umbrella furled, as if at any moment he might raise it against the sun. But he did not. Unobserved, he threw it over the wall, where Forster reclaimed it and placed it in the back seat of a small Renault. This was a daring move on Pilgrim's part, but he had chosen it deliberately to see how much attention it might attract. The answer: *none.*

At 2:15, the child actress came into the yard with Schwester Dora. She looked particularly appealing. Perhaps she was playing *Little Nell*. There were flowers in her hand, ribbons in her hair and tears in her eyes. Pilgrim spoke to her.

"Yesterday, you sang," he said.

"Yes. I like to sing."

"My favourite songs," Pilgrim said, "are counting songs. Do you know any of these?"

"I can sing *Three*," said Little Nell.

"What is *Three?*" Pilgrim asked, not having heard of it.

"*One and one and one is three,*" the woman sang. "*Four less one and two plus one are three. One into three is only three and me myself and I is three.*"

"That's very clever," said Pilgrim.

The child-woman smiled. "I have ten fingers," she said. "Ten toes, two arms, two legs, two lips, two ears and one head. The rest of me is a muddle."

"I see."

"Can you count?" the woman asked.

"Oh, yes. It is one of my favourite occupations."

"Do you know *Green Grow the Rushes, O?*"

"I think so. It's been a long time since I sang it."

The woman, whose eyes were bright and large and rather alarming because they had no focus, reached out and gathered Schwester Dora by the hand.

"Let us make a circle," she said, "and we can dance it."

Pilgrim was somewhat perturbed by this. Having hoped to get the others singing, he had not expected to take part.

"I will conduct," he said.

The woman was delighted. She tucked her small bouquet of flowers into her belt and put out both her hands. The brothel owner, the infanticide and the man-who-thought-he-was-a-dog immediately joined in. Also Schwester Dora and other keepers and interns—including Kessler.

"Begin!" the woman cried.

Pilgrim began.

"*I will sing you twelve, O!*
Green grow the rushes, O."

Everyone else repeated this.

"*I will sing you twelve, O!*
Green grow the rushes, O."

Pilgrim sang: "*what is your twelve, O?*"

Everyone shouted. Some shouted gibberish, not understanding. Others shouted: "*twelve for the twelve apostles!*" They had started to tighten their circle, closing in on Pilgrim, who stood in the middle.

"Eleven?" Pilgrim asked.

"*Eleven for the eleven who went to heaven!*"

"Ten?"

"*Ten for the ten commandments!*"

Pilgrim turned and scanned the wall.

"Nine?" he shouted.

"*Nine for the nine bright shiners!*
Green grow the rushes, O!"

"Eight?"

Pilgrim ducked under the linked arms and began to back away.

"*Eight for the eight bold rangers!*"

"Seven?"

"*Seven for seven stars in the sky!*
Six for six proud walkers!"

"Five?"

"*Five for the symbol at your door!*
Four for the gospel makers!"

"Three?"

Pilgrim had reached the centre of the wall's length. The singers and dancers were watching the ground at their feet as they shifted one way and then the other.

"*Three for the rivals!*" they sang.

"*Green grow the rushes, O!*"

Pilgrim shouted: "Now!" over the wall and then he shouted back into the yard: "two!"

"*Two—two, the lily-white boys*
Clothed all in green, O!"

The rope ladder touched the ground.

Pilgrim began to climb.

"One!" he called over his shoulder. "One!"

"One is one and all alone
And ever more shall be so!"

Pilgrim paused for one second. In spite of the padding used to augment the ladder, his palms were bleeding.

No matter.

He looked back.

Done with and over.

He stepped down carefully onto Forster's waiting shoulders and jumped to the ground. Forster pulled the ladder free of the wall.

"*One is one*," the singers sang. "*And all alone—and ever more shall be so!*"

Pilgrim ran with Forster guiding him. The ladder was thrown into the back of the motor car. Nothing was said.

Pilgrim retrieved a pair of handkerchiefs and wrapped each hand. The wounds were shallow.

"Drive," he said.

It was a mere whisper.

He was free—and that was all that mattered.

That morning, at dawn, he had released the fourth pigeon. Its message was addressed to *Herr Doktor C.G. Jung, Burghölzli Clinic, Universität Zürich.*

What it said was: *goodbye.*

BOOK SIX

1

By dusk, Pilgrim and Forster had reached Basel. The Renault was small, compact and neat. It was black. Forster had taken a short course in mechanics from an employee at the dealers, who had shown him the rudimentary needs of the car. These were relatively few and simple—how to change a tire—where to put oil and water—how to use the crank and what to do when the cylinders wouldn't fire. Forster had also taken lessons in how to drive and had become rather demonic in the role of chauffeur. He had purchased a tweed peaked cap such as he had seen in newspaper articles regarding the appropriate dress for riding in automobiles, which he now wore back to front in a dashing manner, reminiscent of photographs he had seen of *daring young men driving at sixty m.p.h.!* The cap was augmented by tinted goggles. He also wore leather gauntlets, having been told that oil can ruin one's sleeves if it happens to spit at one during application.

The image of spitting oil cans was amusing, Forster thought.

Not only was one's clothing at risk from oil cans, but one could be scalded when dealing with the radiator, because the radiator was not content with spitting. It belched and hissed and blew steam in your face. Another good reason for wearing gauntlets, goggles and a staunch overcoat. For the latter, Forster had chosen something called a storm wiper. It made him look like the hero of a boys' adventure story.

Throughout the journey, Pilgrim and Forster were mostly silent. Pilgrim, whose memory had been enervated by the prospect of what had seemed to be endless imprisonment, was becoming more aware of the recent past. His valet had slowly emerged from the fog of vague remembrance and was now a fully recognizable figure whose place in Pilgrim's life was both familiar and comforting. It seemed almost as if there was nothing to say, they knew each other so well. Besides which, they had never shared a talkative companionship with one another. It had not been necessary. Their shared passion for pigeons was a silent one. How one felt on any given day could be dealt with in a few discreet sentences and how one intended to allot one's hours and therefore what was required of one's dress was equally a matter of few words.

Dinner parties had been given when necessary—Pilgrim hated playing the role of host—but when they were required, Forster never failed to produce a glittering success which guests would comment on for weeks afterward. He had read Mrs Beeton from cover to cover twenty times and kept a copy of each of her books on a shelf in his pantry. If, as and when he disagreed with her, he simply ignored her advice and took his own counsel. For the most part, however, he was obedient to her superior taste. He loved the running of a house—the quietness of it and the dignity inherent in serving a gentleman whose needs were few but absolute. When a guest arrived, the delivery precisely fifteen minutes later of the sherry decanter and glasses on a silver tray— the dog-walks twice a day—the running of baths and the setting out of clothes. All to say nothing of serving meals.

Forster's co-management of the kitchen with Mrs Matheson was cordial and infrequently argumentative. They would discuss menus and on very rare occasions disagree about which merchant should be patronized. But on the whole, it was a well-ordered household which Forster oversaw and the final inclusion of the boy Alfred had given both him and Mrs Matheson a welcome focus on the future. As for the management of Pilgrim's ultra-personal needs, this was another matter altogether.

One's house is not one's life, Forster knew. It is merely where one functions. Pilgrim's sense of privacy was extreme. He required many hours alone, while he wrote. Equally, when he studied. Knowing how to interrupt had paramount importance and this had been Forster's triumph.

As they drove through the mountains and valleys, he smiled at the memory of one particular lesson in how to interrupt. At a dinner party one evening, Forster had overheard—discreetly, of course—the historian F.R. French discussing protocol at the court of Louis XIV, the Sun King. Professor French, appropriately enough, was one of England's greatest French scholars and looked not unlike Voltaire, with a poke-chinned face and an enormous nose. He spoke of the disgusting habits of the courtiers at Versailles, the palace which Louis had commissioned and in which he spent the latter part of his life.

There was no one at table but the Professor and Mister Pilgrim. They had dined on lamb (never mutton!) and the air was redolent with the smell of mint which Mrs Matheson had crushed and made into a sauce with vinegar and sugar. Forster was offering the freshly shelled green peas as Professor French offered the news that: because there was a strict protocol concerning the order in which various members of the aristocracy were admitted into the presence of the King, they were loath to give up their places in the famous hall of mirrors which led to the Royal Chambers. But persons—even of noble rank— have human needs and chamber pots were secreted amongst the potted orange trees, producing—as Professor French put it— *une odeur infecte!* Not only that, the men relieved their urinary needs behind the curtains without even stepping outside. Because of the aesthetic visual qualities of the scene, the actors in it remain entirely misunderstood, according to Professor French. It was a court dressed in brocade and silk, with the manners of bedlam.

Forster had then brought forth the parsleyed and buttered potatoes.

Professor French went on: in the days when he was still a child, the future king was sent to say goodbye to his aging father, Louis XIII, who lay on his death bed. The protocol regarding entrance to a Royal Chamber was rich in symbolic gesture. While one never knocked, neither did one simply open the door and walk through. One scratched one's way in.

Scratched? Mister Pilgrim had said. *Scratched?*

Yes. With the fingernail of one's index finger, one scratched on the door and waited for the entrée. Many courtiers, in fact, grew this fingernail longer than the rest on their hand in order to leave their mark. At any rate—Forster by now had been serving stewed tomatoes—at any rate, as Louis XIII lay dying, the child who would succeed him went to the bedchamber door and gave the customary scratch. He was a devil child, as we know, and mischievous in spirit. *Who is out there disturbing my dying moments?* asked Louis Treize. *Louis Quatorze*, said the future King of France.

Mister Pilgrim had laughed so hard and long at this that Forster had then and there decided finger scratching would be his future notification that he required entrance, a gesture duly noted and appreciated by Pilgrim, who briefly went through a period where he always answered Forster's scratches by saying: *come in, Louis, come in!*

Now, Forster had become not only valet, butler and chauffeur to Pilgrim, they were about to enter a life of crime together for which their past in one another's company had not prepared them. Gone were all the trappings of charm and leisure; gone too, the days of solitary scholarship and dutiful attentions. If once there had been suicide attempts and deep depression to survive, now there would be a destructive path towards death that had no precedent in Pilgrim's descent into the dark. Previously, Forster had never once questioned his employer's sanity, despite his deepest moments of despair and his seeming inability to vote for life. Pilgrim had always, then, come back up into the light.

But now there was a difference, and Forster—seated opposite Pilgrim at dinner that night in the restaurant of the Hotel du Rhein in Basel—saw all too clearly that something had gone awry. Mister Pilgrim, once the arbiter of taste, was in significant disarray. His cravat was askew. His hair, at the crown, stood up like the hair of a boy athlete returning from the field, and his hands were still bound in what appeared to be mittens created from his handkerchiefs. Perhaps Pilgrim's hold on his reason was gone, and the lack of it showed in his eyes. They were the eyes of an anarchist who has seen that he and he alone can save the world.

2

By Friday evening, Jung had been advised that Pilgrim was missing. A distraught Kessler was sent out with the crew of the yellow wagon to scour the parks and other public places in the hopes that someone might have sighted his former patient and could say where he might have gone.

Since nothing at that point was known or suspected of an accomplice in the escape, no one thought to consider the use of a motor car or of distance. Clearly, under these circumstances, Pilgrim must be somewhere in Zürich.

By the time Jung had returned home to Küsnacht, there had still been no word. At dinner, he sat in his place, breaking the house rules—smoking a cheroot at table.

"Eat," said Emma.

"No," said Jung. And finally, "later."

"It is chicken, Carl Gustav. A favourite. Frau Emmenthal has excelled herself—the best we have been offered in years."

It smelled delicious. There was a tarragon-based sauce with chanterelles in cream; there was a British stuffing, with bread and onions, sage and walnuts; there were *haricots verts* and tiny beets the size of thumbnails. In Jung's case, all this effort had been spent for nothing.

"How can we have lost him?" he said, waving his hand in the air. "How can this have happened?"

"Looking the other way, my darling. It is the very same as happened with the Countess. You were not sufficiently attentive. You were seated in your office receiving favours from that woman."

As Jung looked down the table towards his wife, he realized that from her point of view, he was not there. Emma no longer referred to him physically. Her gaze was elsewhere. When she spoke, she was looking out the windows at the sun in the early stages of its evening decline. She was still enough, but he could perceive in her posture the gentle nodding of someone reciting an interior mantra for survival:

You were
Not there.
You were
Somewhere
Unavailable.
We were
All here
Waiting.
You were absent.
Will you
Never
Understand?

That was the gist of it, he reckoned. And sadly, she was justified—given her grieving. Her own loss—the dead child—the marriage seemingly shipwrecked, the death of Blavinskeya and now the disappearance of Pilgrim.

All his fault.

Nothing in his character would allow Jung to admit this was true—aloud. Never, to Emma. It would give her powers he could not afford to lose. But reluctantly, he did admit it to himself. In the dark, he knew all this was true. Therefore, that evening at table he said nothing in response to Emma's silent recitation.

What he did say was: "is it possible he has somehow managed to kill himself? I have people searching the building—others searching the grounds. We know only that he was last seen in the exercise yard. One minute there—the next, not. Apparently the other patients were singing a song in English, of all things. Then he disappeared."

"Half the patients—*more* than half the patients at the

Burghölzli are English, Carl Gustav. Why should they not sing English songs?"

"I didn't say they shouldn't. I merely said it was what they were doing."

Emma drank from her wine glass, set it aside and went on eating.

"How could he kill himself when he'd already tried so many ways and failed?" she said. "No. He has found some way back into the world. We shall find him here amongst us. Have you sent someone to the Col d'Albis where Lady Quartermaine perished? He might have gone there."

"No. I never thought of that."

"You must stop thinking of Mister Pilgrim's escape as your loss, Carl Gustav, and begin to think of it as his gain. If you were him, knowing what you know, where do you think he would go?"

"To the ends of the earth," Jung said—and smiled at last.

"I don't think so," said Emma. "I think he'd go to Paris."

"Paris?"

"Oscar Wilde. Rodin. The *Mona Lisa*. After all, for Mister Pilgrim, Paris is almost his spiritual home."

In the morning, the messenger in green arrived from the Hôtel Baur au Lac and presented Jung with an envelope on which was written: *from Dominic Fréjus*, plus the address. Inside was Pilgrim's final message: *goodbye*—delivered by pigeon post.

Emma said: "*finito*. Are you satisfied?"

Jung said nothing. He was thinking: *my prize patient is gone—and my wife is sharpening her knives. I will go into the garden and fill another grave.*

3

In Paris, on Friday the 28th of June, Pilgrim and Forster registered at the Hôtel Paul de Vere, rue Berger, on the right bank of the Seine, about six blocks from the Louvre.

The hotel had been selected from a guidebook and offered all the amenities at a modest price. By choosing a middle-class residence rather than one at either end of the social scale, Pilgrim reasoned it would be the last place anyone would expect him to lodge in Paris—if indeed anyone had guessed his destination.

The journey had taken them seven days in all, their route having been determined by the availability of suitable roads. Most of the roads they travelled had once been cattle paths and sheep tracks, elevated to public highways in the days of eighteenth- and nineteenth-century coaching. The towns and villages they passed through or used as stopping places were amply populated with cafés, restaurants, inns and hotels. From Basel, they had journeyed through Alsace to Belfort and from Belfort through Langres and Chaumont to Troyes.

At Troyes, they had the car serviced at a livery stable where the blacksmith had taken up a study of automobiles and was extremely knowledgeable on the subject of internal combustion engines.

While Forster and the blacksmith chatted and the blacksmith cleaned the spark plugs and oiled the crank shaft, Pilgrim went into the stables and revelled in the smell of hay and horses. It was a happy moment in this otherwise anguished episode—a moment to savour and to relish. *Hay and horses*, he thought, *horses and hay. It seems I have loved the smell of them forever.*

His mind slowly formed a previously forgotten picture of himself as a stableboy on a great estate. The word Waterford occurred to him, but all it conjured was glass. And Ireland. *If I was Irish once, I wouldn't mind at all.*

He saw himself elevated to the rank of exercise-boy—of *walker*, as they said—when he would go out on misted mornings with the dew like ice against his naked ankles. And he would walk the horses one by one with another lad or two, and once the view from the stables and the manor house was obscured by a shroud of fog, the boys would mount their charges and ride out into the morning, full tilt.

Oh, the feel of them and the smell of them, and me lying out along their necks ... the black steeds, the roan steeds, the greys and the rare, rare whites. If I could have it back, it was the best of my lives—the simplest of all I ever had, though I don't know when it was, or where, precisely ...

Later, he went and leaned against a stone wall in the livery yard and looked off over the farmland fields towards the city of Troyes itself—its fires and its smoke, its roofs and its trees and towers. He narrowed his eyes and conjured another city in another place and time where the sunlit woods of the landscape had been entirely different than this—less lush, more arid—less serene, more troubled. *The Royal City of Troy* rose up in its majesty from the Truvian steppes descending to the sea and to the Hellespont.

He played with this image the way a child will play with imagined fairy-tale locales. It was his Camelot and his Atlantis. It was his Emerald City of Oz.

It had been walled, its walls of enormous height and thickness, and beyond it rose the slopes of foothills leading off through a dusty haze of heat to distant Mount Ida and her sisters. The trees on the surrounding hillsides were plane trees and oaks and in places had been decimated for the building of supplemental battlements and battle-towers and battle-cars and battle-rams, battle-bridges and battleships. *Battle—battle—battle—battle ...*

Pilgrim closed his eyes.

He could smell the charcoal burning in the forge behind him. He could hear the sound of hammers.

Nothing changes, he thought. All our ingenuity and genius have been turned to the making and devising of war machines. We have followed Leonardo into the darkest reaches of his imagination, forgetting that he also promulgated light.

Pilgrim opened his eyes and looked again at the city in the immediate distance. Troyes. Already it had sprouted factories and industrial warehouses. Buildings of gigantic size and monumental ugliness scarred the approaches to the town. Trains belching smoke and cinders rolled through the meadows, scattering sheep and cows and stampeding horses. A low grey cloud of dusty vapour hung above the rooftops. And it was all ...

The same.

No wonder the gods are departing, he thought. We have driven them away. Once, every tree out there was holy—every tree and every strand of grass and clod of earth. The very stones were holy and everything that lived, no matter how small or large ... every elephant and every ant—every man and every woman. All were holy. Everything— the sea—the sky—the sun—the moon—the wind—the rain—the fairest and the worst of days ... All of it gone and only one deaf God, who cannot see, remains—claiming all of creation as His own. If people would invest one hundredth of their devotion to this God in the living brothers and sisters amongst whom they stand, we might have a chance of surviving one another. As it is ...

Pilgrim closed his eyes again and the vista before him vanished. He turned once more to the livery stable and spoke to Forster.

"We shall make next for Fontainebleu," he said—a name that had the scent of forests to it and the ring of water falling into water.

The Renault was ready, and having thanked and paid the blacksmith and waved goodbye to the horses, they continued their journey.

At Fontainebleu, they had taken a picnic basket organized by

Forster into the woods, where they sat amidst ferns and wild-flowers, eating breast of chicken sandwiches, pears, Boursault and assorted petits fours while consuming also two bottles of Montrachet.

Pilgrim had lain back at the end of their meal and let the leafy tent above him lull him into sleep. Forster also rested, but remained awake. Only one sleeper from now on, he decided. We are on our way to danger.

On waking, Pilgrim had made notes in a book which Forster had secured for him. He wrote down the words: *from here to the end, only earth, air, fire and water. Nothing else.*

He had looked at Forster then and said: *thank you for being with me, now.*

It was the only semblance of an endearment passed between them, but it meant the world to Forster, who would long remember it.

The Hôtel Paul de Vere was not very large. It had twenty *chambres* and did not serve meals. It did offer connecting rooms with a bath and W.C., and a choice of tea, coffee or chocolate with a brioche in the mornings.

On the first evening, they took their dinner in a nearby restaurant on the rue Berger. The height of summer had produced a good many tourists and the voices around them, besides French, were speaking English, German, Italian, Spanish and the now ubiquitous American.

"Can you believe it, Calvin?" said one woman. "We're sittin' here in a French bee-stro! I never felt so sophisticated in my whole life!"

The sophisticates were everywhere, and they were by no means all American. Englishmen complained to their male companions that it was incomprehensible that no one on the Continent seemed to understand the source of Britain's greatness.

"It's our stamina," one insisted.

"It's our industry," said another.

"It's our dedication to bringing civilization to the poor benighted niggers of the world," said a third.

It is our bloody-mindedness, Pilgrim muttered to himself.

When the coffee and cognac arrived, Forster ventured: "may one know, sir, why we have chosen Paris?"

Pilgrim laid his left hand on the white tablecloth, spreading his fingers as wide as they would go. With his other hand, he made a circular motion around the rim of his glass, wetting one finger in his mouth to facilitate the gesture.

"We are here to abduct a certain lady," he said.

To Forster, this was pure Sherlockese. A thrill passed through him. He was, indeed, to play the role of Doctor Watson.

As if in tribute to the character he was about to assume, he fingered his moustache.

"And what lady might that be, sir?" he asked.

"Madonna Elisabetta del Giocondo," said Pilgrim. "La Gioconda."

The *Mona Lisa*.

Forster paled.

"But we can't, sir. They won't allow it."

Pilgrim smiled.

"Of course they won't allow it," he said. "Why would they? She is the greatest treasure in the whole of France. And one day soon, she will be ours."

Forster stared and then forced himself to look away. Say nothing, he told himself. Say not a word.

Pilgrim drank from his glass and said: "a most pleasant evening, Forster. Thoroughly enjoyable."

Forster said: "yes, sir. Indeed."

4

On the morning of Saturday, June 29th, Pilgrim and Forster arrived at the Louvre, where Pilgrim soon recognized a distinct difference in the presentation of the paintings from his last encounter with them three years earlier. Many of the greatest amongst them had been put behind glass. This had been done at the request of the Louvre's curators, and had been decreed by the Director of National Museums, a man whose name was Théophile Homolle. This unprecedented glazing of works in oil had been generated by an increase over the past few years of vandalism and accidental damage. A Rubens had been daubed with excrement (no permanent effect); a Botticelli had been slashed with a knife (repairable); and a Giotto had been found partially cut from its frame in an obviously thwarted attempt to steal it (no noticeable harm).

In spite of the fact that each of these works was salvaged, there were growing fears that a successful attempt at theft or an even more disastrous attempt at outright destruction would result in irreparable losses. Glass, it seemed, was the only answer. Strangely, no one instigated an increase in security staff.

When the newly glazed paintings had been rehung, there was something of a public outcry. *How can one view the pictures if all one can see is oneself!* And: *the Louvre has a new hall of mirrors that rivals Versailles!*

Shame on Homolle and his lackeys! read one headline, and in the item that followed, the Minister and his curators were accused of glazing the *Mona Lisa* in order to mask the fact that the original had been stolen or damaged and had been replaced by a fake. Homolle's response to this was to issue a statement to the effect that *you might as well pretend one could steal the towers of*

Notre Dame de Paris! In a few days' time, he would regret these words.

Because of the influx of tourists from abroad, the Louvre was inundated with visitors. By ten o'clock in the morning, Pilgrim and Forster could barely move when they entered the over-crowded Salon Carré, where the *Mona Lisa* was hung between Correggio's *Mystical Marriage of Saint Catherine* and Titian's *Allegory of Alfonso d'Avalos.*

As it turned out, though it had been primarily the *Mona Lisa* that drew such large numbers of people, there was another spec-tacle taking place in the Salon which kept them there for an uncharacteristically long time. A man was shaving.

Forster ascertained that the man's name was Roland Dorgelés. M. Dorgelés was a Parisian novelist of some repute. He and his valet had arrived with the appropriate paraphernalia at about 9:45 a.m. There was a camp stool, a bowl, a jug of hot water, a razor, brush and shaving soap and a large white towel in which the writer had draped himself.

His "mirror" was a glazed self-portrait by Rembrandt. The scene was both amusing and outrageous—and was intended by Dorgelés as his protest against the glass-covered paintings. It certainly caught the attention of the press, where the novelist would be depicted at his toilette in several cartoons.

Pilgrim, shadowed by Forster, moved through the room at an enforced leisurely pace because of the crowds. He was deter-mined to be seen, and to have Forster seen, by as many of the security guards as possible. He had also announced himself by name as he entered the museum and had presented his card, requesting that it be delivered to the chief curator, whose name was Emile Moncrieff. Moncrieff would recognize the name instantly—which was Pilgrim's intention.

He barely glanced at the *Mona Lisa*, noting at once that the portrait was now behind glass. This worried him. One could not simply smash the glass and pull away the painting. One would have to work from the rear of the frame.

It had been his initial intention to destroy her on the spot. But this presented the problem of a quick arrest and, if nothing else, a forced return to Zürich. This would not do. There were other works of art to destroy. There was a whole world of chaos he wanted to achieve. He must at all costs remain at large.

He had told Forster at breakfast that one essential result of their Saturday-morning visit—besides the impressing of their presence on the staff—was the memorization of distances between the entrance to the Salon Carré, its exit and what lay beyond that exit—the various escape routes. He was physically aware of his age and knew that he would not be able to manage running for any great period of time, especially if stairs were to be involved.

It had occurred to him that, while Forster escaped with the painting, he himself might saunter away from the event and still achieve the streets before the theft was discovered. It was at this juncture that he intended to take advantage of his knowing that the Louvre was always closed on Mondays.

Before leaving, he approached one of the uniformed staff and inquired if Monsieur Moncrieff were available. The answer being yes, Pilgrim and Forster were ushered into the executive quarters and told to wait. Within minutes, Moncrieff appeared—an overly effusive, scented and coiffed man in his forties, who greeted Pilgrim like a long-lost friend. They had, of course, never met—except by reputation. The chief curator on Pilgrim's earlier journeys to the Louvre had since died and Moncrieff, it appeared, had been his protégé.

Speaking French, Pilgrim wondered politely if Monsieur Moncrieff would be averse to allowing a private visit on Monday, when—because of the closing—there would be no crowds to stand in the way of Pilgrim's close scrutiny of one or two paintings about which he intended to write.

But certainly not. And did M. Pilgrim wish to be attended by M. Moncrieff or one of the other curators in his quest for information?

On any other occasion, most certainly but for the present, a private viewing would be sufficient.

Moncrieff invited Pilgrim and Forster into the sanctum of his office, where he wrote and signed a waiver which could be presented on Monday morning at the main entrance.

Pilgrim was extremely grateful and would never forget Monsieur's kindness.

Much hand-shaking and bowing and an offer to summon a cab if one was required.

Pilgrim said no—that he had his own transportation. His feet.

Moncrieff escorted them from the executive offices and walked with them to the great courtyard beyond—La Place du Carrousel. In doing so, he said that regrettably, they would not be entirely alone on the Monday morning. Some security staff would of course be in place and—because it was an off day— there were one or two house painters and artisans who came in on such occasions to make repairs and touch up damaged or aging plaster.

This would be no problem, Pilgrim told the chief curator, but he was grateful for the information.

At noon, Pilgrim and Forster passed through the portals and out onto the Quai du Louvre, where Pilgrim said: "we shall take our luncheon on the other side. What a splendid day! What a splendid, informative, brilliant day! If only it was the season for oysters, I would eat a dozen!"

5

Jung had already driven off to Zürich in the Fiat by the time Emma descended for her breakfast on the morning of Wednesday, July 3rd.

It was a sultry, midsummer day and at nine o'clock, already windless and humid. Windows had been opened in the hopes that a cool breeze might blow in from the lake, but it was not to be. The air was totally without movement. A thousand candles could have been lighted and not one of them would have been extinguished.

Lotte had been to the garden and, having asked Frau Emmenthal for permission, had cut a bouquet of one dozen roses—pink and white and red and yellow—which greeted Emma on the breakfast table. Emma, thinking Carl Gustav had placed them there, burst into tears.

When Lotte appeared with the coffee pot, Emma said: "look what my husband has left me. Aren't they beautiful. I'm the luckiest woman alive. Someone loves me."

Lotte bobbed and said nothing. When she returned to the kitchen and sat at the table, she was disconsolate.

"She will thank Doctor Jung and I will be in trouble."

"No you won't," said Frau Emmenthal and patted the girl's hand. "You've made a lovely gesture and it will raise her spirits. I can protect you from Doctor Jung. He will understand. In the end, he will thank you."

In the dining-room, Emma lighted an uncharacteristic cigarette and drank her coffee.

I want to see the smoke, she was thinking, *rising about the roses—mellowing the view. And the gardens—and the sound of songbirds singing in our trees ...*

*And way, way off above the lake, the gulls adrift on stillness itself
and the mountains in their mists that define all this, the stillness I
have made of smoke and silence.*

Smoke and silence.

All would be well.

Surely, if there are roses, all will be well.

We shall one day have another child, she thought—and,
thinking, reached out to touch the nearest petals of the bouquet.
If only ...

*Do not say that. Do not think that ever again. Never. If only is a
deadly phrase. It means you have given up. And you have not given
up. You merely wanted to. Damn you! Damn you. Damn me. I will
never give up.*

She stubbed the cigarette.

There was orange juice. There was a brioche. There was apricot preserve. There was muesli, which she ignored. And there
was the paper—*die Neue Zürcher Zeitung.*

Emma drank the orange juice, broke the brioche into quarters, ate two of them with butter, one of them with the apricot
preserve and set the last aside for the birds, as Carl Gustav had
told her Mister Pilgrim used to do with his morning toast.

When all of this had been done, she poured another cup of
coffee and lighted a second cigarette. (*How wicked I am today!*)
She then sat back and opened *die N.Z.Z.*

Emma sputtered.

Coffee drops fell to the napkin in her lap.

There was a headline three inches deep.

MONA LISA *STOLEN!*

She let the paper fall to the tabletop.

I don't want to know this, she thought—already knowing,
before she read another word, what had happened and who had
perpetrated the crime.

At last she raised the paper again and confronted it—reading
details only, skipping all the theories, all the accumulated speculations and most eye-witness accounts.

It had happened the day before yesterday, Monday, the day on which by tradition the Louvre was closed every week to the public. "Someone"—possibly with one or more accomplices—had entered the Salon Carré, where the *Mona Lisa* was hung, and absconded with the painting, possibly during a fifteen-minute interlude during which the only guard on duty in the Salon—a substitute for the regular guard—was taking his leisure in the W.C., where he smoked a cigarette.

Emma lighted her own cigarette, smiled and took a deep pull of smoke. *It's what we all do under stress ...*

When the discovery of the painting's absence was first made, it was some hours later. The assumption had been that *La Gioconda* was away in the Photography Annex being photographed. This often happened. On the Tuesday, a witness—who happened to be a painter by the name of Louis Béroud—remarked that *when women are not with their lovers they are apt to be with their photographers.*

Emma skipped ahead, turning pages furiously, until she came to the next salient details.

By noon on the Tuesday, all the necessary inquiries had been made regarding the Photography Annex and the laboratory where paintings were taken to be cleaned. The *Mona Lisa* was nowhere to be found. Plainly, she was gone.

At this juncture, the sûreté and the gendarmerie had been notified and the Louvre immediately filled with more than a hundred policemen.

The painting, which had been secured to the wall by means of four iron pegs, had clearly been removed by an expert who had brought the appropriate implement with which to loose it from its place. And not only this, the culprit had also brought whatever was required to release the canvas itself from its frame. The frame and its glass were discovered in one of the stairwells leading to an emergency exit.

Pilgrim.

It could only be Mister Pilgrim. Emma had "known" he was

going to Paris. Now, she "knew" why. How, it barely mattered. She had read him in both senses: his journals, and his personal angst as Carl Gustav had related it.

What would the outcome be? If Pilgrim were truly mad, he might destroy the painting. Yet this was unthinkable—not from Pilgrim's point of view, Emma realized, but from the point of view of western civilization at large. The *Mona Lisa* was seminal. She was the centrepiece of all painted thought. She was the goddess of perfection and the patron saint of attitude. A woman's integrity depended on her protection. Men so deeply feared her, it could not be told what magic powers she possessed. No man, Emma thought, has ever understood her—but every woman has.

No man but Pilgrim.

She was the very air he breathed.

Oh, do not—do not—do not do this, Emma prayed.

And yet, Pilgrim wanted so desperately to die. Would the destruction of a painting—of this painting—this one painting release him? He believed with such vehemence that he himself had been La Gioconda that he might well think that, like Dorian Gray, if he plunged a knife through the portrait's heart, it would bring about his own longed for death. What if Wilde had also known? What if Wilde had been privy to Pilgrim's dilemma, and had fashioned his novel on the basis of what he knew? After all, they had been friends—they had confided in one another, and Pilgrim had mourned for Wilde as one mourns only for those one trusts. The words *Dorian Lisa* presented themselves. And *Mona Gray*.

She lighted a final cigarette. The smoke rose. The roses, having been cut, and warmed by the interior air, leaned forward in their bowl and opened wider. Their scent was overwhelming—wondrous and rich and provocative—but Emma watched them with dismay. We cut and kill everything, she thought. We cut and kill everything that stands in our way. Just as Carl Gustav cut and killed me. Just as I cut and killed my child. Just as Mister Pilgrim will cut and kill *La Gioconda*. Because she stands between himself and eternity.

At the Clinic, Jung—not knowing of the theft—went to the third floor and let himself into Suite 306.

The useless pigeon cage was still there—its doors standing open, the very symbol of Pilgrim's escape—a symbol so blatant and indiscreet that Jung had to smile.

He looked about the rooms. Some drawers had not been closed—nor the doors of the armoire—nor one of the windows, where a few doves and pigeons had gathered expectantly.

Jung inspected the bureau and found a brown paper bag of stale crumbs, with which he fed the birds.

In another drawer, he found the photograph Pilgrim had removed from the silver frame that now was emptied, lying face down, where he had placed the photograph of Sybil Quartermaine.

The photograph in Jung's hand showed the head and shoulders of a sad but beautiful woman—the person Pilgrim had described as *the woman who claimed to be my mother*.

She would have been perhaps forty-five years old when the picture was taken late in the nineteenth century. Oddly, she faced the camera in precisely the same position as Elisabetta Gherardini Giocondo had faced the gaze of Leonardo da Vinci. Perhaps this was merely a trick—or perhaps, from the artist's point of view, it offered the perfect view of the sitter's face. Leonardo himself had written: *always require your subject to sit so the head is at an angle to the torso*.

There she was: *the woman who claimed to be my mother*.

There was no smile. There was no guile. There was only sadness.

Pilgrim had seemingly hated her—dismissing her as a poseur, since in his own view he had no parents but merely was. This was, indeed, a unique form of madness—not to have been born, yet to be.

Jung placed the photograph in his pocket. He looked about

the bedroom and the sitting-room and decided, before he left, that Kessler must pack all of Pilgrim's possessions—his clothing, jewellery, books and toiletries—against the time when the escapee would be returned to them. In the meantime, he would see to it that no one else would occupy these rooms. In the strangest way, they were sacrosanct. Jung wanted them to remain, whether empty or not, as a part of his purview.

To that end, he returned every morning to feed the birds.

6

Two days earlier, on Monday, July 1st, Pilgrim and Forster had risen early, packed their bags and locked them in the boot of the Renault. They checked out of the Hôtel Paul de Vere and drove to a service station where they had the car prepared for its next journey. The petrol tank was filled and extra petrol was set on the floor of the back seat. Pilgrim had insisted on two containers, in spite of Forster's protestations that one was ample and more was possibly dangerous.

"I have my reasons," Pilgrim said—and that was that.

There was also a checklist in Pilgrim's inner pocket.

Soft cotton gloves for both.

Walking shoes.

Light overcoats.

An artist's portfolio with twelve sheets of drawing paper.

Conté crayons and pencils.

Canvas camp stool.

Pliers.

Razor knife.

Money.

Picnic hamper—pâté—bread—fruit—chocolate—wine.

All of this had duly been assembled and put in place.

Forster parked the Renault on the rue du Pont Neuf, just around the corner from their hotel and only a block or two from the morning's destination.

At ten o'clock on the dot, they arrived at the Louvre and presented M. Moncrieff's waiver to the guard at the door. Pilgrim was then saluted as if he might have been visiting royalty.

The great halls were empty. The echoes of far distant footsteps were the only presences besides the silent statuary and the mirrored images of Pilgrim and Forster as they passed on their way to the Salon Carré. Then, at a greater distance still, someone unseen began to whistle and a door slammed.

"*Merde*," a man said.

The whistling continued.

The light, though diffused, was ample and bright enough to reveal every detail as they went along—the carved lintels above the doorways—the marble figures ensconced in their niches—the glorious tapestries and the gilded mirrors.

Stairways curved away hither and yon and one of these had an arrowed sign that pointed to *La Mona Lisa*. Forster carried the camp stool, the portfolio and the box of artist's supplies in which the pliers and the razor knife were secreted. Pilgrim carried the picnic basket. He looked as if he were bound for the Tuileries.

There was a guard at the entrance to the Salon Carré, to whom Pilgrim showed the chief curator's waiver. More saluting, more nodding, and they continued on their way.

At the far end of the Salon Carré, an artisan in a white smock was standing on a ladder attending to some painting that was needed on the exit door frame. Apparently, earlier in the morning, the man had repaired the plaster there and was now disguising the joins where the new work met the old.

Pilgrim and Forster walked about the room as if they had all the time in the world—though on each pass before the *Mona Lisa* they lingered longer and longer until at last they stopped.

Forster set aside the portfolio and opened the camp stool, placing it about five feet away from the painting.

Pilgrim removed his topcoat and hat and laid them on one of the benches provided for viewers. He did not, however, remove his gloves. Sitting, he opened the portfolio and spread it on his lap. Forster handed him his box of drawing materials and stood back gazing at the portrait.

"See what you can find out about that fellow at the far end of the room," Pilgrim said, *sotto voce*. "We may need to do something about him."

"Yes, sir."

As Pilgrim sketched what he already knew was his own portrait, he was amused by the juxtaposition of his present image over that of the painted lady. The glass that covered her reflected only the roughest contours of his face—its basic shape, its bones and its shining highlights. The rest was a melding of artifice and reality. A portrait of time.

The artisan's name turned out to be Vincenzo Peruggia. He was a northern Italian from the town of Domena in the Lake Como district. His true profession was house-painting, but he had extended his talents to plastering and repair. This much Forster learned in the course of a preliminary conversation, standing at the foot of the ladder as the moustachioed Italian worked above him.

They also discussed the care and growing of moustaches, Forster confessing that growing his own had been a relatively new adventure.

Peruggia was not very large—being even shorter than Forster, who stood at five-foot-nine. He had a dark, overly serious face, though not unattractive. His body was spare and compact, his posture exemplary. Oddly—or so it seemed to Forster—he had extremely small hands. But his work was delicate and fine and exquisitely executed. Forster was fascinated by the process of how the paints were mixed to mask the lines between the old and new plaster.

Their conversation in itself was a charming, almost comical mix of English and Italian sprinkled with French.

At the same time, the guard on duty—whose name was Verronet—came and stood behind Pilgrim and his sketching.

It was clear almost at once that Verronet was an amateur—a substitute guardian with no real interest in what he did. The *Mona Lisa* meant nothing to him. *It is just another painting and I am here to watch the paintings*—as if his job was to be a voyeur.

"Do you like her?" Pilgrim asked in French.

"She's all right. I could do with larger breasts."

Pilgrim smiled, thinking he could remember the weight of them.

"She was not a large woman, you know."

"Well, she's sitting down—how is a man to tell? I think I would not have made love to her."

"Oh? And why is that?"

"I do not like superior women. A woman should stay in her place."

"You think she is superior?"

"In attitude, yes. But I wouldn't call her beauty superior. I think she is too aloof. I feel no humanity."

"Are you a student?"

"No."

"You talk like a student. You know nothing—yet you have opinions."

This was a mistake.

"I am not a fool," Verronet said indignantly. "And, if I may say so, judging by your scribbles, you are not an artist. May a man not have opinions?"

"Of course," said Pilgrim. "I apologize. I meant only that I think you are wrong about her lack of humanity. I think she is supremely human."

"Each man to his own taste. If I were to have a woman of that station, I should want her to seem less above me."

"I see."

There was an awkward pause. Pilgrim withheld his sketching hand. Verronet gave a cough. "I will leave you now," he said. "I am going to the W.C. for a cigarette. And while I am gone, if I may say so, I should keep an eye on the Italian at the other end of the room. Anyone can be a thief, you know—and Italians are notorious for it. Like gypsies and all other dark-skinned people."

"Very well," said Pilgrim—and resumed his sketching.

At noon hour, Forster returned from his conversation and suggested that now would be an appropriate time to take their lunch.

"And the man on the ladder?"

"I think we need not fear him."

"But can we use him?"

"It is possible. Though how, I do not know."

"Why not invite him to dine with us?" Pilgrim smiled, like a conniving child. Then he said: "after all, generosity breeds compliance."

They ate in the Place du Carrousel.

Peruggia had brought his own bread, cheese and wine, but accepted pears, more wine and some chocolate from the hamper.

The sun was shining. It was all very pleasant. Pilgrim had sufficient Italian to be able to manage something of a conversation with the house-painter. In the course of this, he discovered that Peruggia was single, thirty-two years of age and had come to Paris in order to escape the intransigent reign of poverty in Italy, where there had been so little employment he had been in danger of starving.

The man was barely literate. He could write his name and garner the gist of a headline in the Italian papers, but he had never read a book nor had one read to him. He had never gone to school and he could calculate figures only by counting on his fingers. And yet, he was a craftsman of great skill and had worked many times at the Louvre.

As they ate and drank, Pilgrim worked his way further into Peruggia's passions—having sensed that, as with most uneducated people, his passions were many and profound. The inability to read and write was a source of deep frustration—not to be able to communicate made the need to do so overwhelmingly urgent.

Peruggia's greatest passion was his patriotism. *Italy is the mother of all the living world.* It was that simple and that straightforward. *La Donna Italia!* he called her, raising his glass. And he said that in all his many working hours at the Louvre, it had not been lost on him that the greatest works of art were every single one of them Italian! *Titian! Tintoretto! Caravaggio! Botticelli! Leonardo!*

He sang these names as if they had been set to music by Verdi.

"And the greatest of the treasures in the Louvre is *La Gioconda! La Gioconda* is *La Donna Italia* herself! The mother of us all!"

Pilgrim smiled and nodded, but said nothing.

Vincenzo Peruggia went on: "if it had not been for Napoleon, *La Gioconda* and all these other wonders would have remained in Italy, where they were born."

"Napoleon?" Pilgrim tried not to sound too incredulous.

"Of course," said Peruggia. "He came into our country and raped it of all its great works of art. This is what, everywhere, the French have done. Invade, make war, slaughter, burn and walk away with the spoils. It is all Napoleon's fault. My greatest wish would be to return every one of the Italian paintings in the Louvre to Florence, Rome and Venice—to wherever they were born—and to keep them there forever."

"An admirable idea," Pilgrim said. "But quite impossible."

"No, no," Peruggia countered. "Not impossible at all. For instance, I have studied how one may free the *Mona Lisa* from her pinnings."

Pilgrim said nothing.

He was thinking: *to return her to where she belongs. Yes. To want the light to return. To want the light instead of darkness. This is my whole intention.*

He remembered his rampage in the Music Room at the Burghölzli. He remembered throwing the wax recordings and smashing the violin. He remembered his rage and the overwhelming sense that art—all art—was impotent. And he remembered the figure of the Countess Blavinskeya crouching on the floor, looking up at Kessler and shouting: *DON'T!*

To want the light back. To want the light instead of darkness. How could one make them understand? More must be wanted than the mere presence of art—something must be lifted in the spirit of the viewer, the reader, the listener. Something must be lifted out of the gutters of violence and degradation into which the human race had sunk so willingly. Could the answer lie in such simple men as this, as Peruggia, with his illiterate, uneducated notion that to restore a painting to its birthplace would be to shed light on a failed and failing people?

"My problem is," Peruggia said, "I have not sufficient courage. Many times I have been alone in her company, but I do not possess the bravery to take her down and run."

Pilgrim said: "but if someone else were to take her down and hand her to you, would you then at least be able to run with her?"

Peruggia sat silent.

Then he said: "what is Monsieur suggesting?"

"That I agree with you," said Pilgrim. "I agree that her place is in Italy. In Florence. I like what you say about art being born. It is absolutely true. All great art is born—its mother is its country, its culture; its father is its painter, its sculptor, its composer or its writer."

Peruggia smiled. "I could not have said it like that," he said, "but I do believe it."

And that is how it happened.

At 2:00 p.m., the guard, Verronet, went again to the W.C. to smoke another cigarette.

Peruggia cut the painting from the wall.

Pilgrim withdrew it from its frame.

Peruggia was handed the canvas, wrapped in the portfolio.

Each man left the Salon Carré by a different route, Forster leaving the frame and glass in the stairwell and all emerging from the Louvre at 2:20 in the afternoon.

Pilgrim handed Peruggia five hundred francs and said: "journey well."

On parting, none looked back. Pilgrim and Forster walked to the Renault—deposited the picnic hamper, the pencil-box and the camp stool in the rear seat above the petrol. Pilgrim—exuberant and beaming—threw his topcoat onto the hamper and said: "we shall leave Paris at four. But first, we shall celebrate. To *Le Jardin des Lilas* for champagne!"

As they drove out onto the Quai du Louvre, Pilgrim watched the tiny figure of Vincenzo Peruggia making his way across the Pont Neuf—overwhelmed, so it seemed, by the size of the artist's portfolio clutched beneath his arm with its precious cargo.

She is free, Pilgrim thought. *I am free. We are free*.

It was done.

There was now the next target. Chartres.

The American novelist and historian Henry Adams had read Pilgrim's book on Leonardo, *Sfumato—The Veil of Smoke*, in 1910 and had taken the liberty of sending the Englishman a copy of his own privately printed *Mont Saint Michel and Chartres*, which had been published in 1904. Consequently, Adams and Pilgrim had corresponded, but never met. (Seven of Pilgrim's letters are preserved in the Adams archive with the Massachusetts Historical Society.)

The coincidence of Adams's passion for Chartres and Pilgrim's disjointed "memories" of it was a source, from the beginning, of fascination for Pilgrim, though he never felt compelled to write more than scholarly praise for the book to his new American friend. Adams, on the other hand, did feel a special bond with *the man across the waters*, as he called Pilgrim. He was fascinated by the Englishman's informed response to his own exploration of what he called *the last great age of understanding before reason intervened*. What Pilgrim had to say confirmed, for Adams, the connection between his own singular reading of the past and the past itself. He never questioned the source of Pilgrim's knowledge regarding that past, simply accepting his given standing as a knowledgeable art historian.

Mister Pilgrim's voice, Adams noted in his journals, *is unique and one in which I rejoice, because like myself, he casts aside all the clever academic veils of reason that have clouded scholars' ability to see the past as it was, and not as they would have preferred it to be.*

At the same time Pilgrim made entries about Adams's treatise on the twelfth century which read like a checklist of hits and misses. The negatives were never mentioned between them. *For the most part*, Pilgrim concluded: *he got it right.*

But scholasticism was no longer what Pilgrim's life was about. He had now veered towards what he called, in the notebook Forster had provided for him, *rejectionism. Let us turn our back on humanity's failed ambitions and confront the lower order we have become.*

The success of the "Gioconda escapade" had buoyed him to the degree that Pilgrim actually sang out loud in the car as he and Forster headed southwest along the newly gravelled road between Paris and Chartres.

> *Beautiful dreamer, wake unto me,*
> *Starlight and dewdrops are waiting for thee ...*

Perhaps, Forster ventured to think, *the champagne Mister Pilgrim spent the last hour consuming will allow him to sleep tonight.*

Perhaps. But not in the car.

"Look at the ship of the sun go sinking down," Pilgrim enthused, sitting up rigid beside Forster, who drove with his goggles in place. "Look at all the birds a-flying, and all the trees—the trees—the trees ..."

Poetic talk, Forster decided. *He's off on one of his flights of fancy.*

All at once Pilgrim said: "we are for Chartres Cathedral, Forster—the greatest, grandest and the most sacred of Christian houses. It awaits us all unsuspecting. The last great fire at Chartres occurred in 1194. Seven hundred and eighteen years ago. Seven hundred and eighteen years. She knows we are coming. She knows, I tell you. We have been there before. She will smell the soles of my shoes. She will know the touch of my fingers. She will know I have come back. She will remember me."

Forster pulled the collar of his duster higher. The sun was directly in his eyes and he vowed to buy a pair of goggles with a darker tint. *What might we have for our dinner?* he was thinking. *Where might we spend the night?*

"Mister Henry Adams—an American—wrote of Chartres Cathedral that *it has moods.* And he added that *at times, these moods are severe,*" said Pilgrim—laughing afterwards, but lightly.

"I wonder what the grande dame's mood is tonight. Apprehensive, I should think."

There was now an unimpeded view of the descending sun. It was a vivid burnt orange, shimmering beyond the earth's steaming mists and gases. One could almost see its flames.

"Dreadful fires," Pilgrim drawled on. "Three of them, all told. One in my own lifetime ..."

Oh, dear, Forster was thinking. *Now we've gone all the way back to imaginary lives.* Such episodes had happened before—moments in the garden at Cheyne Walk when the mind boiled over—in Mrs Matheson's phrase. Thrusting one's walking stick at the branches of a tree in the belief that the Saracens were coming over the wall—standing in the wheelbarrow being tumbrelled to the guillotine—clutching the dog Agamemnon, saying that Clytemnestra must not find him. Traumatic moments, to be sure—but all had been survived. Now, they were going to destroy Chartres Cathedral.

Well.

They had stolen and given away the *Mona Lisa.* Not bad, for a fantasy. Thinking about it, Forster had to wonder—at least for a moment—if it had really happened. *Did we really do that?*

Yes. Yes, we did. And she is now somewhere in Paris, more than likely hiding under a bed.

And so they drove on to Chartres.

"We shall not be staying," Pilgrim told him. "We shall register, but by four in the morning, we shall be gone."

The chosen venue was L'Auberge du Pèlerin. By the time they arrived, the journey had robbed Pilgrim of his good humour—so much so that he did not even bother to point out to Forster that they were about to stay in The Pilgrim's Inn. There was a tiny dining-room, of which they took advantage, though without pleasure. The food was not good—a ragoût—and the wine was worse. They retired to their room equally bad-tempered, though only Pilgrim was allowed to show it. He threw his boots at the wall.

For twenty minutes, he presented a diatribe against the discomfort of automobiles. After this, he retreated to the W.C. and complained that he was constipated. At 11:00 he retired fully dressed, announcing that at 2:00 a.m. precisely, he must be wakened.

8

On the morning of Tuesday, July 2nd, at 4:00 a.m., Pilgrim and Forster left the lobby of L'Auberge du Pèlerin and made their way, suitcases in hand, to the Renault, which was parked in the stable yard.

Since the advent of the automobile, such yards had become a pleasant olfactory mix of horse manure, oil spills and the fumes of petrol. Added to this were the scent of hay and the grey aroma of dusty cobbles. Pilgrim paused to drink all this in, the few hours of sleep having restored his good spirits.

Pilgrims over time, he thought. *Think of all the pilgrims who have paused here in this place—L'Auberge du Pèlerin—knowing that at the end of their journey, the great cathedral awaited them with its storied spires and windows and its Christian relics. Seven hundred years and more of journeys—seven hundred years of pilgrims. And I, the last pilgrim—who shall raze it to the ground. To know that God is dead, we need proof.* Habeus Corpus. *The ruins of this cathedral dedicated to Jesus Christ will tell us Christ is nowhere and that all his heroic chroniclers were liars. Here is where art first perished.*

He reflected on the building's history. After the last great fire in 1194, it was said that the survival of three icons demonstrated the Virgin Mary's continued love and respect for the faithful of Chartres. These were the skull of Saint Anne, the Virgin's mother; the stained-glass window in which the Virgin is depicted holding the Christ Child—and the mystical Palladium.

The Palladium was said to be the tunic Mary had worn on the night she gave birth to Jesus. It had been donated to the original cathedral—also destroyed by fire—by Charles the Bald, Charlemagne's grandson, in 876.

The surviving window was the one which, so Pilgrim had

informed Jung, contained his initials *when I played the role of Simon le Jeune, lead-man to my father's glass-cutter*. Then, he had been *a chronicler in glass*. Only Heaven knew why this single window had been selected by destiny to survive—but there it was.

The figure of the Virgin was seven feet tall. Above her head, a dove was tilted downward, its wings spread as a forewarning of the Cross. In her lap, the Virgin held the Christ Child, whose right hand was raised in blessing. In His left hand, He held an open book which showed the words—in Latin—EVERY VALLEY SHALL BE EXALTED—a quote from Isaiah.

And every mountain and hill shall be made low, Pilgrim remembered.

Well—this night the whole of Chartres would be made low.

The journey to the great cathedral was brief, though somewhat confused, due to a lack of universal street lamps. Many turnings took them down darkened alleys and past what appeared to be, in the dim light, a disabled cityscape. It had the look of a deserted village—or of a place under siege, with all its citizens barricaded behind locked shutters.

In the dooryard, beggars and lepers slept in separate compounds, both of which were enclosed behind wooden fences. Roofs of thatch and board had been erected to protect them from the rain. Each of these communities of outcasts had its own fires and its own sense of identity. The lepers' fires were low and almost devoid of heat, since it was forbidden that lepers should venture into the larger community in order to gather firewood and coal. They depended entirely on charity. And the blessings of God.

They might have been there for ten thousand years, these people of poverty and disease. Pilgrim went so far as to believe he recognized individuals as their faces loomed up beyond the firelight as he passed.

The only words spoken were whispered: "pilgrim, have you any bread for us?"

No bread, but money—which Pilgrim gave without comment.

As they entered the building, the great door creaked and groaned as though it had not been opened in a century. Inside the cathedral, hundreds of votive candles provided the only light, but it was adequate—spread as it was from chapel to chapel, corner to corner and near the various altars erected to saints, the Virgin and Saint Anne.

The naves of all the great cathedrals of Europe point to the east, in the direction of Jerusalem. Each and every altar is consecrated to that holy place. This means that each cathedral's main port faces west. In the morning, matins—in the evenings, vespers—the prayers lighted by the sun ascendant and the sun descendant. The choir stalls lie mostly along the south wall, though this is not universally so. But at Chartres, it holds true—and it was there, beyond the choir, that Pilgrim's "personal window" rose.

He went at once to the High Altar, where he knelt and crossed himself. With no religion, he nonetheless felt obliged to pay his respects to a monument he was about to destroy.

He had the vaguest, dreamlike memory of having knelt in the same place more than once before—*when I knew my God*. It had always been sacred here, even before the Christians came. In Druid times, the earth above which he now knelt had been dedicated to the pagan "miracle" of a virgin giving birth. *Virgo paritura*, Pilgrim muttered. And then: *Ave Maria, gratia plena, Dominus tecum ... Hail Mary, full of grace, the Lord is with thee ...*

Having had his say, he rose and walked over to the choir stalls on the south wall. Peering through the gloom, he gazed at one of the windows in the upper series above him. *Notre Dame de la Belle Verrière—Our Lady of the Beautiful Glass*. There was not enough light outside to show the incredible blue, ruby and rose of its ancient panels—and it was too far above Pilgrim for him to see the initials he maintained were etched in one of the blue lozenges near the Virgin's feet. But he knew they were there. He knew. *S.l.J.—Simon le Jeune*.

After a moment, he turned back to where Forster waited for him, the containers of petrol resting on the floor beside him.

"We shall begin here." Pilgrim indicated the wooden choir stalls beneath Our Lady.

Taking the petrol, he spread it liberally over the benches with their carved facings and, having done so, he stepped back.

"Well," he said to Forster—as he handed the valet the emptied containers and withdrew a box of matches from his pocket—"say goodbye to it all and we shall leave."

Forster said nothing. He was pale with fright and emptied of hope. In his mind, he would not survive this—nor would Mister Pilgrim. It was an act of dreamlike madness.

"Are you ready?" Pilgrim finally asked.

"Yes, sir. Yes," Forster muttered.

"You precede me. I shall follow."

Forster, not looking back, began his exit. The nave, so it seemed, was suddenly twenty miles long, and as he headed towards the great door at the far end, he felt as though he must wade through an incoming tide.

Pilgrim reached into his pocket and withdrew the three hand-kerchiefs he had placed there before leaving the inn. He tied them together, forming a linen rope which he then placed on the floor, one end of it just touching a puddle of petrol.

Then, with great care, he lighted two matches, held side by side.

He closed his eyes—opened them—and dropped the matches onto the nearest end of the handkerchiefs. He watched the flames begin to creep along towards the petrol, and then turned and rapidly strode down the nave towards the door.

At 5:00 a.m. they were on the road to Tours, while behind them, the windows of the great cathedral at Chartres began to glow with fiery light.

9

Die N.Z.Z.'s lead headline on Thursday, July 4th, had to do with the hundred-and-thirty-sixth anniversary of American Independence. A second headline declared that the Emperor of Japan was sinking towards death—and indeed, he would die some three weeks later.

Jung, being angered by America's recent sabre-rattling in Honduras, paid no attention to the lead article. As for the Emperor of Japan, he had been given to sabre-rattling of his own—most notably with Russia—and his regime had been entirely one of power-mongering. Jung skimmed the piece and turned to what remained on the page.

A mysterious fire in the cathedral at Chartres in France.

Good God.

He skimmed the short article: fortunately, little damage ... authorities baffled ... investigation about to begin ...

Pilgrim. It could only be Pilgrim.

First he had stolen the *Mona Lisa*—it must have been him—and now he had set fire to his beloved cathedral. Did he intend to sack the whole of France of its treasures? Somehow, he must be stopped.

On reaching the Clinic, he asked Fräulein Unger to find out how to get in touch with the French Ambassador at Berne. Jung's reputation would lend credibility to what he had to say—that an escaped patient had "declared war on art" and that, undoubtedly, the incidents at the Louvre and Chartres were his doing. How to find the man would be another matter, but surely at least to know who he was would help.

At Küsnacht, Emma regarded the day's news with equal despair, but for a different reason. If Mister Pilgrim was

captured, what would it do to his passionate quest to reclaim the
past? This was her interpretation of Pilgrim's dilemma: all that
stood between an ominous present and a disastrous future was
recognition of the true meaning of the past. In his writings, she
had found again and again a plea for the innate integrity of art.
PAY ATTENTION! he had shouted in capital letters, over and
over. But no one had listened. Now, in order to draw attention
to that integrity—and its double message of compassion and
reconciliation—he was on a campaign to destroy the very presence of its most articulate voices. *Once the evidence of compassion
and reconciliation is gone*, he had written in one of his journals, *our
memory of it will turn us back to its true meaning*. Now, he had
begun his rampage—and where would it end?

10

As Pilgrim and Forster arrived at Tours in the evening hours of Wednesday, July 3rd, news of the fire at Chartres had already reached the press. FIRST THE MONA LISA, NOW THIS! one headline read. CHARTRES AFLAME! read another.

There were photographs of smoke pouring from the cathedral's doors and of the ruined choir stalls, but the story itself was sadder than that.

It was not until investigators began probing the damaged areas that the remains of a man had been discovered. It seemed that one of the lepers in the churchyard, seeing the flickering light of fire on the stained-glass windows, had crawled inside to fight the flames any way he could, and had perished in the process. Other lepers and beggars had already formed a bucket brigade by the time *les pompiers* arrived and finally brought the fire under control—but no one had managed to save the first man in.

When Pilgrim read of these things, he fell silent and refused to eat. Nonetheless, he and Forster went and sat in the dining-room of L'Hôtel Touraine, shuffled the menus and drank wine.

"I shall take up smoking again," Pilgrim said at last, and sent Forster to buy cigarettes. He had not smoked for some years, having given it up when he noted that Sybil Quartermaine had become addicted to it. *Most unbecoming*, he had told her, *particularly in a woman*. But now he needed the distraction—something to fiddle with—fuss with—concentrate on when the boredom of Forster's pathetic countenance became too much to bear. Forster had started to look not unlike Mole in *The Wind in the Willows*—a little lost, a trifle disoriented—endlessly sad. Like Mole, Forster wanted to go home.

In the night, Pilgrim dreamt of the fingerless, toeless man who had been described in the newspaper accounts, crawling to the flames, unable to subdue them. A life had been lost. The last thing Pilgrim had had in mind—and the only thing he had prayed would not happen. The cathedral stood, largely undamaged, but a man had died. Pilgrim's dream addressed this irony with images so vivid that he called out for them to stop and Forster had to wake him.

In the morning it rained. Too late.

At noon on Thursday, the 4th of July, Pilgrim and Forster got into the Renault, having eaten a light breakfast. They headed south.

"May we know where in Spain?" Forster asked, attempting to sound casual, as if the question was of no real interest.

"Avila," Pilgrim told him. And that was all.

Forster had never heard of Avila. It meant nothing to him.

At two o'clock, they stopped on the outskirts of a small village by the name of Le Virage, which meant *the bend*, referring to an elbow in the river—the river being the Loire.

There was an inn at the crossroads. The next stop was to have been Poitiers, but Forster was doubtful they could achieve it by nightfall.

Having had only café au lait and a shared croissant, they decided to pause at the inn, named for the family who had owned and run it since before the Revolution—L'Auberge Chandoraise.

Pilgrim, discontented and restless, sent Forster in to see if a meal could be arranged.

"Get us a decent table," he said, "and order a bottle of claret. Tell them we are ravenous, and to kill the fatted calf."

Forster did not even smile. Standing beside the motor car, he nodded, pushed back his cap and made for the entrance.

I shall go and look at the river, Pilgrim thought, watching his valet go his way. *I have always been partial to rivers, and the Loire is amongst the most beautiful.*

Sliding into Forster's seat behind the wheel, Pilgrim threw the still-vibrating engine into gear.

As Forster entered L'Auberge Chandoraise, he imagined that he heard the Renault drive away, but knowing this was impossible—since Mister Pilgrim had never driven—he proceeded to find the *propriétaire*.

Pilgrim was approaching the river on a cart track when he had a moment of blind panic, suddenly realizing he did not know how to stop the motor car.

He had watched Forster do so at least twenty times, but all he could think of was the gesture that had accompanied the end of each journey. *Handle. Handle.* He had pulled a handle. But where, where?

Left hand. Left hand. It had to be with the left hand. Frantically, his eyes still on the cart track, Pilgrim grasped at the air between his left leg and the door.

Brake! Brake! For God's sake!

At the very last minute, he found it and gave a mighty pull. The Renault shuddered to a stop, throwing Pilgrim against the steering wheel so violently that he thought it might have pierced his diaphragm. The breath was knocked completely out of him and he had to struggle to regain it.

The river was no more than five feet from the front wheels— five feet of tall grass and willow wands and five feet of incline— downwards.

Pilgrim got out and leaned for a moment against the hood of the Renault. From a bridge nearby, he heard the sound of children at play. A dog barked. The proximity of the river was pleasing to him. He had always enjoyed the sight and sound of water. And its smell.

Here the Loire was wide and somewhat treacherous. Its undercurrent was swift and powerful, though its surface seemed languid enough, moving at a seemingly leisurely pace. But, standing at the edge and looking down, Pilgrim could see the turmoil in the depths, where a profusion of dangerous weeds could drag a man under in seconds.

The image of Sybil rose in his mind—he could not tell why. Possibly it had to do with his near disaster with the motor car and the fact that she had been swept away by an avalanche just as he had so nearly been swept away by the river.

He gazed across the water at the opposite bank. There were cows over there in a field. And a dog. A cowherd's dog. A black dog. A dog at the river's edge, who eyed him with an almost merry look and wagged its tail.

The river, he thought. *The Styx, Loire, the Thames, Las Aguas, the Arno, the Scamander at Troy ... There has always been a river near at hand.*

Once, he had attempted to drown himself in the Serpentine. To no avail.

But who was to say that water could not become his ally and his accomplice, now that Sybil was dead and the gods were departing?

In the wilderness, I found an altar with this inscription: TO THE UNKNOWN GOD *... And I have made my sacrifice accordingly.*

Here was wilderness enough. Fields where vistas had no visible conclusion—a sky as wide as Creation—trees and the chatter of unseen children—a river whose depths he could barely fathom. Pilgrim did not even know where he was, except that he knew it was somewhere south of Chartres en route to Spain and Avila.

He glanced over his shoulder at the Renault, where it sat amidst the tall grass looking like an intruder from another planet.

Almost all the way, he thought.

And then: *why not?*

He tried to conjure *the Unknown God*—the one remaining god of whom he had no experience.

Pray.

There may be answers. There may even be forgiveness for the death of that man I killed at Chartres. Mea culpa. Mea culpa. Mea maxima culpa ...

Pilgrim lightly beat his breast, and as if the dog were not enough, he swept the sky in search of a further sign.

It was there, as always. The ever-present wings of an eagle.

Pilgrim walked back to the motor car.

Think nothing. Do.

He opened the door and climbed inside.

The incline was such that he need not even start the engine. Releasing the brake would be enough.

He smiled.

There is a willow grows aslant the brook ... he remembered. And there it was before him—Ophelia's willow tree—standing to one side as if making way for his passage, just as it made way for hers.

Slowly, he reached down and released the brake.

May it finally be over, he murmured—and closed his eyes.

Someone presently came running into the courtyard of the Auberge Chandoraise. A boy who had been fishing from the nearby bridge with an older friend.

An automobile had been driven into the river, he claimed, and his friend was diving to see if the occupant could be saved. *Come at once!*

That was all.

Everyone ran.

The boy who had remained behind was pulled from the water, exhausted. Men stripped off their clothes and took his place.

"I saw him! I saw him!" the boy kept repeating. "He was in there! I saw him! But when I went down to find him, there was no one ..."

The motor car was empty, except for its baggage.

Forster waited. He begged to be allowed to join the divers but they would not allow him. These men knew the river. He did not. He was unaware of its dangerous currents and its weeds.

One life was enough to lose. Two would be pure waste.

Police, villagers and passing travellers all collected on the riverbank. For a death site, it was a scene of extraordinary vibrancy, what with its naked divers, its women, its children and the resplendent figures of overdressed tourists, some of whom retrieved picnic hampers from their motor cars and told their chauffeurs to spread blankets on the grass.

The search lasted for four hours—and then the local prefect called it off. "We shall find the deceased," he announced, "at some future time down-river. Clearly, he has been swept away."

Forster stayed until it was dark. Had Mister Pilgrim succeeded at last in committing suicide, or had he survived some accident that had befallen him? Forster would never know—but he could guess. On the far side of the river, a black dog raised its head towards the moon and bayed.

11

One week later—on Thursday, July 11th—Jung received an envelope at the Clinic. It had no return address, but had been mailed from Dieppe, in Normandy.

It was from *H. Forster, Esq.*—and Jung had to smile at the mild pretension of the signature, clearly long contemplated but never before used. *Mister Forster is now a gentleman*, he thought. *Well—as the English say*, bully for him!

On the other hand, it was not a welcome letter, containing as it did the news of Pilgrim's presumed demise.

Oddly, neither Forster in his communiqué nor Jung in his reaction to it could bring himself to use the word death. It was as though, in reference to Pilgrim, the word was forbidden.

Forster did not write of the events at the Louvre, nor did he write of what had taken place at Chartres. He did admit to having played a role in Pilgrim's escape and he described their flight in the Renault and what he called Mister Pilgrim's desire to pay his final respects to certain temples of art.

And how were these respects known to be final?

The enclosed letter from Mister Pilgrim would explain.

Forster had written with a kind of simple respect for another man's integrity that was rare and touching. There was not an ounce of condescension to Pilgrim's illness or mental distress. The man was simply who he was, and that was that. He had beliefs and passions that were both unique and disturbing, moving and unsettling. His love of art and of nature—especially of birds—and of his dog Agamemnon had been unyielding.

He had a most original sense of dress, Forster wrote, *and it was a privilege to lay out his clothes.*

His foibles, if I may call them that, were endearing. His rejection of certain foods—his insistence on having his bath be of a certain temperature—his bad-tempered letters to The Times—*his unfailing loyalty to friends, et cetera, et cetera. His discipline was exemplary and he wrote every day. He could be wonderfully rude to people of whom he despaired and equally patient and polite with people, however boring, who felt they had something of importance to say to him. He never required me to shut the door in anyone's face—a form of rudeness he deplored—but he did instruct me on some occasions, having ascertained who had rung the bell by looking down from above, not to open the door.* That will save you from slamming it, he would say.

As to Mister Pilgrim's demise, I can only say this: that I was absent in the Auberge for no longer than ten minutes, during which time I arranged our luncheon as instructed. When I emerged to inform Mister Pilgrim of this, he was nowhere to be seen.

A young person came and told us someone had driven an automobile into the Loire. I knew at once that it was him. Mister Pilgrim.

Everything was done that could be done to recover him, but he was gone. Now we are without him. I will grieve until I die. Though he was, of course, my employer, I believe he was also my friend.

You and I did not meet, but I got what I know of you from Lady Quartermaine, who had the utmost faith in your care of Mister Pilgrim. As it turned out, she was mistaken; and while I do not intend that as an insult, the truth remains—we all lost him.

In a few days, or many, we shall no doubt hear of the discovery of Mister Pilgrim's body, in which case, I shall return to France to reclaim it. It will then be my sad duty to see him properly dealt with—cremated, as he wished, and scattered in the garden at Cheyne Walk, where he was happy.

In the meantime, I wish to say that I discovered the enclosed letter in Mister Pilgrim's luggage. It is addressed to yourself and so I must assume that he meant you to read it—which, of course, I have not done. I have kept his fountain pen as a memento. It is blue—his favourite colour.

I remain,
Sincerely yours,
H. Forster, Esq.

Pilgrim was never found. Forster never returned to France. A lifetime had ended. Or one of them.

12

Jung set Forster's letter aside and sat for a moment mourning the loss of Pilgrim and also, as he sat there, mourning his increasing awareness of what had been lost to him forever in Pilgrim's imagined recreation of the past.

He flirted with the phrase *creative recreation of the past*—also, *a decisive recreation of the past*—and even *a definitive recreation of the past*. But he could not settle on any one of these. What was it that Pilgrim had achieved with such supreme confidence?

Madness is always confident of its own resources, Jung decided. *Madness always knows its own boundaries and never wavers. It speaks more truly from its own heart than I am able to speak from mine ...*

He smiled.

Madness knows itself through and through, he went on, *and we who are not mad know nothing through and through. We guess—we stumble towards truths—we disguise our uncertainty with apologies and silences, claiming politely that we "know" nothing, while giving the appearance of knowing everything. Mister Pilgrim never once stepped back from being himself. He lived entirely on the brink of everyone's acceptance, while suffering the endless deprivation of anyone's belief. He was never allowed to cross the line ...*

Who had ever said to him: I believe you.

Only Lady Quartermaine, so far as Jung could tell—and even with her, there was a wariness. She wanted to believe. At least that much was true.

Jung took the second letter and unfolded it.

It was no longer than three and a half pages. Its salutation said: *My dear Herr Doktor Blockhead ...*

Jung smiled yet again. Here was Mister Pilgrim, intransigent to the end—ever pressing forward with his attack on reason.

"You don't have to believe this, but you should," Jung whispered—echoing Pilgrim's voice.

My dear Herr Doktor Blockhead,

As I near the end of my journey, I remind you that you once said to me that if you were to believe me, I must imagine myself in Galileo's shoes, or the shoes of Joan of Arc or of Louis Pasteur. You made the point that each of these visionaries had faced tribunals entirely made up of sceptics but that none had retreated from the need to be believed. Each had pressed forward, even after death, until in time they were proven right. The earth does revolve around the sun, God does seek to be heard through His saints and inoculation does prevent disease. An eclectic trio of believers, to say the least.

But I am wary, now, of tribunals. Wary and weary. You have pondered the question of whether there might be what you called in my presence once: the collective unconscious of humanity, *a phrase I believe you coined. Clearly, Herr Doktor Dunce, the answer is yes—for I am living proof of it. I have been present at every turning of humanity's fortunes and, as I have attempted to impress upon you, the burden of the* collective unconscious *has been, for me, doubly unbearable—since in all my time the human race has steadfastly turned away from the gravity of its own warnings, the integrity of its own enlightenment and the beauty of its own worth.*

The evidence is overwhelming. At every given opportunity, we have rejected the truth of our collective memory and marched back into the flames as if fire were our only possible salvation.

I have been much and often aware over the past few years of yet another conflagration standing in our immediate path. I cannot tell what form it will take, but it is there and it awaits us. Sooner rather than later, we shall be impelled to embrace it. All because we have refused yet again to pay attention to the educated voices inside of us that have called out universally: STOP!

And of course, neither you nor anyone else believes that what I have foreseen will actually come to pass. Not to be believed is part of my eternal punishment—my life sentence, that extends through so many lives and so much time.

The point I am making is this: your collective unconscious *is already proven worthless. You, Herr Doktor Bumble, turned your own back on it when you confronted me and refused to believe. But is it not true in science that a theory is nothing until it is proved? When you interrogated me, you stumbled and fell because you refused to accept me as proof of your own theory. You have failed because you cannot differentiate between the consequences of being right and the consequences of being wrong. You forget that in between these two, there are the consequences of being neither—but merely lost.*

You are lost, Herr Doktor. You have yet many miles to go and I have few. I have prayed for this moment all my life. In the years that confront you, bear such prayers in mind.

Perhaps I will become a part of the mythology you are attempting to create. It seems likely. You may call me The Old Man. *For after all, the image of the old man who has seen enough is eternally true.*

As I say goodbye, I think it is important that you know why I never speak of my existence, but always of my life. Passing through it all was the spirit of one human being—one spirit shared by many. Soon, I trust, that spirit will achieve its due rest—a universal privilege too long denied me.

The so-called Mysteries have been with us forever. There is not a society on the face of the earth nor of time that does not and did not have its own version of what these Mysteries reveal of the Great Spirit, God, the gods and their relationship to our lives—and our lives to theirs. Sun-dancing, circumcision, birth itself, animal and human sacrifice, virginity, Ra, Raven, Tarot, Voodoo, I Ching, Zen, totems personal and tribal, the cult of Mary and the cult of Satan—the list is endless. In modern times, we call such Mysteries art. *Our greatest shamans of the moment are Rodin, Stravinsky (much as I hate his music) and Mann. And what else are they telling us but:* go back and look again. *In time, these shamans will be replaced by others—but all speaking in a single voice. It was ever thus. But no one listens.*

What life requires of one is that one live beyond the endurance of

it. It asks of us that we accept both its limitations and its possibili-
ties, while at the same time demanding that we push beyond its own
frontiers in search of eternity. I want no eternity. I never did. I
don't believe in eternity. I believe in now.

If I am the embodiment of anything, I am the embodiment of
enduring truths—and of the blindness of my fellow human beings.
And yet, I trust in your intuition to this degree: I can say to you
without qualm—be brave; press on. If you do so, you stand a chance
of closing the circle of your understanding.

P.

13

Jung stood up, gathered Forster's and Pilgrim's letters and put them into the music bag. Then he added his illicit brandy in its bottle and his notebook and his pen. He stripped off his smock, put on his jacket and patted his pockets to make sure his cheroots and matches were in place. Then he opened the shutters, turned out his desk lamp, stubbed the last cheroot he had smoked and went out into the hallway.

Walk or ride?

Ride.

He climbed into the elevator, muttered *up* and stood back.

The implacable operator, as always, said nothing. His placid, seemingly immobilized expression could not be read. And yet, his passengers were exclusively the mad and those who cared for them, and his daily lot was to ferry them between one hell and another; nonetheless, he appeared to remain entirely unconscious of either.

The gate opened—the gate closed. Inside his cage, he lived in limbo.

In the third-floor corridor, Jung stood for a moment utterly still.

So many memories. Expectations. Defeats.

The penless writer. The silent pianist. The bear pit. The Moon. At number 306, he knocked and entered.

Doors.

Doors.

Doors.

Nothing.

The wicker furniture smelled of dust.

He coughed.

Then he went briefly and stood looking into the bedroom, where the bathroom door stood ajar.

He opened windows.

He fed the birds.

The doves crooned. The pigeons danced and Jung remained with them for more than an hour—lost, as the elevator man was lost, in an emptied world.

EPILOGUE

For a year after Pilgrim's demise, Jung continued to be hounded by his own failures. In his private view, these were many. His relations with Bleuler and Furtwängler deteriorated almost daily. The schism with Freud deepened and widened. Freud had renounced and even denounced him. At the heart of the schism lay Freud's insistence that theory and method could be codified and offered as dogma. Jung deplored dogma, believing it would destroy the essential value of analysis. *All the doors must be left standing open.* In 1913, Jung published *Psychology of the Unconscious*, in which he argued the difference between Freud's psychoanalysis and his own analytical psychology. He might as well have declared war.

In the psychiatric community, Jung was now branded a mere "mystic." He became isolated from his former colleagues, who once had championed his rising star. Even Archie Menken backed away, in spite of the fact that their companionship had always fed on creative argument. For Archie, the argument had finally soured and was no longer worth continuing.

There was no more joy in Jung, no more effervescence, no more daring. He had turned a corner and, in many people's eyes—including Emma's—gone off into the dark.

It felt this way to Jung himself. His affair with Antonia Wolff had brought him nothing but anguish—the double anguish of being unable to give her up while he clung like a drowning man to his marriage. He insisted, with increasing vehemence, that it was his right—not his privilege—to live under one roof with two women who would never be reconciled to one another, in spite of their awkward public avowals that "reconciliation" had long been concluded. Toni's visits to Küsnacht during this time not only multiplied—they lengthened from days to weeks.

The children returned and were sent away again. While living at home, they regarded their mother with increasing disdain—that she should be so seemingly compliant—and their father with increasing bafflement. Why did he play, as they had once done, with stone cities on the beach and with empty graves in the garden? Why did he hand them pebbles, saying as he did so: *pay attention?* And who was this too often silent, overly serious lady they were required to call *Aunt Toni?*

The atmosphere at Küsnacht was tense and wearing. Meals were silent. Comings and goings were abrupt and unexplained. It was a house of closed doors.

In the summer of 1913, while the children and their nurse, Albertine, were away yet again at Schaffhausen, Jung had a series of dreams that would prove to be the nadir of his depression and withdrawal.

In the first, he dreamt that Emma's bed—they no longer slept in the same room—was a deep pit with stone walls. It was a grave, and somehow had a suggestion of antiquity about it. *Then,* he wrote in his journal, *I heard a deep sigh, as if someone were giving up the ghost. A figure that resembled my wife sat up in the pit and floated upward. It wore a white gown into which curious black symbols had been woven.*

Jung awoke and went to wake Emma. He asked her to be his witness by verifying the time. It was three o'clock in the morning.

Jung went back to bed convinced that a warning of some kind had been delivered by means of his dream.

At seven o'clock, the telephone rang to inform them that a beloved cousin of Emma's had died at 3:00 a.m.

Prescience.

It was one of the most contentious concepts in the world of psychiatry. Freud had always fought against it, claiming there was too much flummery in the notion of mediums and others claiming to predict the future. But Jung believed—though his belief was cautious. He had so far never managed to speak his belief aloud with conviction.

This was not the first nor the last time prescience was to play a role in Jung's darkened life that year. Other deaths and accidents had been foreshadowed, either in dreams or in "waking visions." A drowned boatman had washed ashore after a storm that had occurred only in Jung's mind as he sat at the foot of the garden. The body of a dog had appeared in a dream the night before the animal itself was killed on the road nearby. Expected visitors had called to say they would not arrive. Moments before, as Jung had stood contemplating their pre-set chairs at table, he had suddenly acted on impulse and gathered up the silverware from their places and returned it to the sideboard, without knowing why.

After the publication of his book in the autumn of 1913, Jung received two visions which were to haunt and trouble him for the rest of his life.

In the first he was on a journey and, as happens to anyone riding on a train, his mind wandered away from the scenery beyond the windows to other mountains, other valleys, plains and rivers; other landscapes altogether than the real one at hand. All at once, these pleasant reveries were disturbed by a distant sound—a series of sounds—that Jung found so real he peered from the windows on either side of the carriage in which he rode in order to verify them.

But he could not. Nothing he could see offered any explanation. Something gigantic was cracking apart at the seams. A wall of unimaginable dimensions and height was collapsing somewhere to the north. The sky darkened and the noise increased until it was unbearable, made up as it was of animal and human cries and of falling buildings, surging waters and torrential rains.

In his journal, Jung wrote: *I saw a monstrous flood covering all the low-lying lands between the North Sea and the Alps. When it came up to Switzerland I saw that the mountains grew higher and higher to protect our country. I realized that a frightful catastrophe was in progress. I saw the mighty yellow waves, the floating rubble of civilization and the drowned bodies of uncounted thousands. Then the whole sea turned to blood. This vision lasted about one hour ...*

Two weeks later, when Jung had returned from his journey, the vision was repeated—*more vividly*, as he wrote. *The blood was more emphasized.* On this occasion, he heard an inner voice which told him to *look at this with care, it is wholly real and it will be so.*

These visions receded, but they presented themselves as full-blown dreams one year later, in the spring and summer of 1914.

An Arctic cold wave descended and froze the land to ice, Jung wrote. *All green things were killed by frost. I saw the whole of Lorraine and its canals frozen and the entire region deserted by human beings ...*

Waking, on this occasion, Jung put on his robe and walked out into the garden in a mood of absolute despair.

And it will be so, he thought. *It will be so.*

It was then he remembered his final encounter with Pilgrim, and the words that had left him so shaken.

And though we never gathered at the height of battle, we met on the ramparts beneath our parasols and fans when amusing skirmishes were taking place and always when two heroes were to meet in combat, man to man—or, as some would have it, god to god.

Before Jung's inner eye, the figures wavered on the Trojan ramparts, standing in their smoke and rain above the battlefield below them.

And he thought: *if this were true, it had happened so long ago that even archaeologists could make no true accounting of their presence there.*

To which he reluctantly added: *it will be so.*

It was a clear moonlit night as beautiful as one could imagine. Frogs and crickets called and sang to one another. An owl of gigantic size sat up at the top of the chimney and surveyed his kingdom. Far, far away, a dog barked. The nightingales were singing in the woods, and out over the lake, the nightjars were plunging through the moonlight in search of insects. Jung almost wept at the perfection of it all.

And yet ...

"And yet," he said aloud. "And yet, we are all imperilled. How and by what means I do not know—but it is true. We are."

It was in his dreams and visions—the cracking walls, the tidal waves of blood, the floating corpses, the debris of civilization and the frozen landscape.

Prescience.

Yes.

It was coming.

Something.

He stood there and wavered for a moment, watched by the owl. For the first time in his whole life, he considered killing himself. The weight of his depression was unbearable—yet what other answer was there but this terrible certainty? It was all too clear; *the world is going to end. Why wait?*

In his bedside table, he kept a loaded revolver against the possibility of intruders in the night. He so rarely remembered it, the thought of it now surprised him.

It would be cold in his hand.

Out on this lawn, with my feet wet with dew ...

He turned towards the house.

The owl spoke.

Jung looked up.

It might have been *The Old Man*—Pilgrim himself—grey in the moonlight, watching.

Don't, he seemed to say.

Wait, Jung thought. *There is always time for death.*

He went down then to the shore, where he sat on the bench there, smoking a cheroot and holding a small stone in his left hand.

Let us see what happens, he said to himself. *Let us wait and see what happens.*

This all occurred on the night of Wednesday, July 31st, 1914.

On August 1st, the whole of Europe woke to the sound of gunfire.

The war that battered its way into everyone's daily life by way of headlines, proclamations, hysterical emergencies and the presence of refugees was everywhere in evidence. Switzerland, though neutral, was not neutralized. The horror came like a fog and settled over every life. A person could not escape it.

The number of patients at the Burghölzli proliferated. Cases of dementia tripled—quadrupled—and then got entirely out of hand. The mad, it seemed, were everywhere.

Men with eyes that seemed never to have looked on anything human sat catatonic before Jung—voiceless—yet begging for his assistance.

Assistance that Jung no longer felt capable of giving.

He no longer had confidence in his theories—or in their application. As well, he had developed a fear of the blank page. Apart from the casebook notes he was obliged to keep, he stopped writing altogether. Even his journals were abandoned.

Added to all this, in 1914, Emma gave birth.

A new life—perhaps the result of Toni Wolff's increasing presence and Emma's increasing panic that she was losing her husband not only to his mistress but to his "madness."

Well.

The child was a girl. Emma named her Emma. *Mine*. Jung called her *nuisance*. She stood in his way.

Jung might himself have been a battlefield. Inside him, all the guns went off. There was not a soul—with the possible exception of Toni Wolff and, pray God, his wife—who was not an enemy. He could have been divided like the map of Europe—every day he woke to wade through Belgian rain and mud and every night lay down in what he called *Germanic darkness*—a *Götterdämmerung* of sound and fury.

This lasted all through the spring of 1915.

And then, one night ...

For the first time since the outbreak of war, Jung picked up his pen and began to write.

Are these not wonderful words? he asked, in his journal. *And then, one night ...*

And then, one night I had a dream. And in this dream I saw my old friend, Pilgrim, my Old Man—*standing over against a wall that lay in ruins all around him. And he said to me:* will you not join me where I stand? *Seeing the ruins, I of course hung back in the dark. Yet surely he was standing in sunlight or moonlight—I could not tell which. It seemed not to matter until I came to understand that all around us both there was the darkness in which I stood, myself—and so it must have been by moonlight that I saw him there.*

This, *he said,* is where everything begins. Please, *he said,* come and see what I have to offer you.

I stood quite still. Afraid. After all, I knew that he was dead. Did he mean that everything begins with death? I could not—and did not want to believe that.

And then he said: there is this and I would give it to you.

I hardly dared look. But I did—and in his hand I saw that he held a stone—something red and squared. I could not quite tell what it was.

The wind blew.

The Old Man wore a long, pale robe—a seeming prophet—Job himself—Elijah, Isaiah—how could one know?

And he said: all things are forever. Nothing shall be that has not been.

I stood forward—still afraid. I did not speak.

The world, *he said,* ends every day—and begins the next. But not for you unless you accept this gift.

I went towards him. The air was frigid. There was, it seemed, ice over everything.

Please, *he said.*

I was astounded. He was asking me to forgive him his endless intransigence—his endless refusal to live.

I put out my hand. And into it, he placed a building stone. Squared and fired and red with life.

It is only one, *he said.* You will need more.

It seemed to burn in my palm. Yet it had no weight.

It was just a stone.

And I wondered: after so many beginnings—can there be another?

And then I woke and it was now.

Now. *And now is all we have.* Now—*and now again and nothing more.*

AUTHOR'S NOTE

It has been suggested that readers might like to know which of the characters and events in this novel have an historical basis. Here are some of the realities in the fiction you have just read.

LONDON AND PARIS

Oscar Wilde (Irish playwright and poet. Proudly, but with some trepidation, I have had my photograph taken sitting on Wilde's bed in the Paris hotel where he died.)

Gilbert (his newest young man, a French marine)

Robert Ross (Wilde's Canadian friend and one-time lover, whose loyalty to Wilde is legendary. I am often asked if the character of Robert Ross in my novel *The Wars* is a reflection of this man. He is not—being entirely fictional.)

Auguste Rodin (French sculptor, whose studio Wilde did visit)

Gertrude Stein (American writer)

Alice B. Toklas (her companion. Each time I'm in Paris, I pay homage to them at the atelier they once occupied in the rue de Fleurus.)

Pierre Janet (French psychiatrist at Saltpêtrière Hospital—along with Gertrude Stein and Alice Toklas, one of the only real characters mentioned in the wholly fictional story of Robert Daniel Parsons)

Théophile Homolle (Director of Museums, Paris, 1912)

Roland Dorgelés (French novelist who protested against the glassed paintings in the Louvre)

Vincenzo Peruggia (Louvre artisan who stole the *Mona Lisa*. I have changed the date of the theft, which actually occurred in August, 1911, and have provided fictional accomplices. His motives were, as in the novel, to return the painting to Florence—where it was ultimately recovered when Peruggia tried to sell it to an art dealer there, after having kept it for more than a year beneath his bed in Paris.)

James McNeill Whistler (American portraitist who was contemptuous of Wilde)

Henry James (American novelist whose practice of listing possible names for his characters did include the name "Bleat")

BURGHÖLZLI CLINIC, ZÜRICH AND KÜSNACHT

Carl Gustav Jung (Swiss psychiatrist/physician; originator of the theory of the collective unconscious. By 1912, Jung had actually shifted his clinic from the Burghölzli to his home in Küsnacht, down the Zürichsee from Zürich. Otherwise, most of the major facts of his life and the beliefs attributed to him in this novel can be documented—including his war nightmares in the years before 1914.)

Emma Rauschenbach Jung (his wife and researcher)

Agathe, Anna, Marianne, Emma (their daughters; Emma Sr.'s miscarriage is fictional.)

Karl Franz (their son)

Grandmama Rauschenbach (Emma Sr.'s mother)

Ernst Haeckel (German biologist who originated the theory of recapitulation: ontogeny repeats phylogeny)

Gustav Mahler (Austrian composer who died in 1911)

Eugen Bleuler (psychiatrist and Director of the Burghölzli Clinic)

Auguste Forel (his predecessor)

Sabine Spielrein (Jung's ex-patient/lover)

Antonia Wolff (another ex-patient who became a psychiatric intern and was Jung's lover until her death in 1953. Jung's letters to Freud outline his conviction that marriage must make room for such polygamous affairs.)

Sigmund Freud (Austrian psychiatrist and Jung's early mentor)

William James (American psychiatrist who originated the notion of "the stream of consciousness")

OXFORD
Walter Pater (English critic and Oxford don who published *Studies in the History of the Renaissance* in 1873, containing his famous description of the *Mona Lisa*, which is paraphrased on page 238 of this novel ["All the thoughts ... mother of Mary."])

FLORENCE
Elisabetta Gherardini (Madonna Elisabetta del Giocondo—the *Mona Lisa, La Gioconda*)
Signor Antonio de Noldo Gherardini (her father)
Signora Alicia Gherardini (her mother)
Leonardo da Vinci (artist/tyrant, who did refuse to paint the face of Christ in *The Last Supper*, and who did keep the *Mona Lisa* by his bedside until his death in France in 1519)
Gerolamo Savonarola (Dominican priest and zealot)

SPAIN
Teresa de Cepeda y Ahumada (Saint Teresa of Avila)
Alonso de Cepeda (her father)
Doña Beatriz de Cepeda y Ahumada (her mother)
Rodrigo de Cepeda (Teresa's brother)
Pedro de Cepeda (Alonso's brother)

CHARTRES
Henry Adams (American author/critic, whose vivid descriptions of the building of Chartres Cathedral include the many destructive fires in its history [except the fictional one presented here]. Adams also describes the stained-glass window known as *Notre Dame de la Belle Verrière*, the only window to survive the 1194 fire.)

Aside from the books already mentioned, the following have been invaluable sources of information: *Memories, Dreams and Reflections*, by C.G. Jung; *The Freud/Jung Letters*, edited by William McGuire; *Carl Gustav Jung* by Frank McLynn; Mona Lisa: *The Picture and the Myth*, by Roy McMullen; *The Greek Myths* by Robert Graves; *The Biography of Oscar Wilde*, by Richard Ellman; *Teresa of Avila* by Kate O'Brien and *The Eagle and the Dove* by Vita Sackville-West.

My thanks also to Beverley Roberts for her exhaustive research; Mary Adachi for her matchless copy editing; Nicole Langlois, Karen Hanson and Sabine Roth for their sharp-eyed spotting of inconsistencies; David Staines for his helpful reading of an early draft; and to Iris Tupholme, Larry Ashmead and Doris Janhsen for their editorial wisdom. Thanks also to my agent, Bruce Westwood, for his unflagging energy, enthusiasm and support. Lastly, I thank William Whitehead, who suffered endless emendations in the transformation of virtually thousands of unreadable handwritten pages into legible typing—and for his equally endless encouragement.